HOWARD ELMAN'S FAREWELL

ERNEST HEBERT

HOWARD ELMAN'S FAREWELL

UNIVERSITY PRESS OF NEW ENGLAND

HANOVER AND LONDON

University Press of New England

www.upne.com

© 2014 Ernest Hebert

Manufactured in the United States of America

Designed by Eric M. Brooks

Typeset in Whitman by Passumpsic Publishing

For permission to reproduce any of the material in this book,
contact Permissions, University Press of New England, One Court
Street, Suite 250, Lebanon NH 03766; or visit www.upne.com

Library of Congress Cataloging-in-Publication Data

Hebert, Ernest.

Howard Elman's farewell / Ernest Hebert.

pages   cm

ISBN 978-1-61168-541-1 (pbk.: alk. paper) —

ISBN 978-1-61168-590-9 (ebook)

1. Men — New Hampshire — Fiction.

2. City and town life — Fiction. I. Title.

PS3558.E277H59   2014

813'.54—dc23   2014003075

5 4 3 2 1

CONTENTS

HOWARD ELMAN'S
FAREWELL

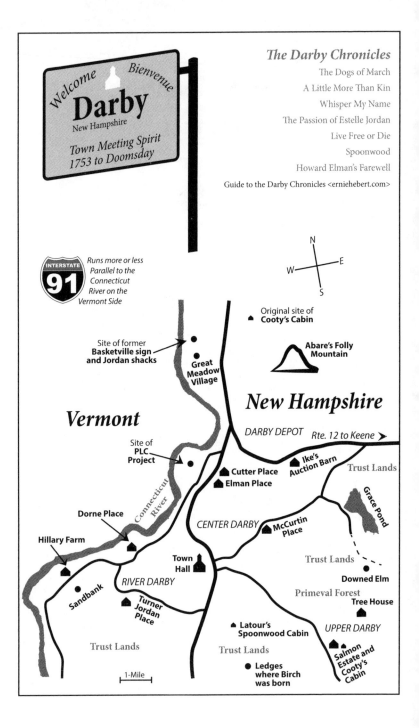

Welcome · **Bienvenue**

Darby
New Hampshire

Town Meeting Spirit
1753 to Doomsday

The Darby Chronicles
The Dogs of March
A Little More Than Kin
Whisper My Name
The Passion of Estelle Jordan
Live Free or Die
Spoonwood
Howard Elman's Farewell
Guide to the Darby Chronicles <erniehebert.com>

INTERSTATE **91** *Runs more or less Parallel to the Connecticut River on the Vermont Side*

N · E · W · S

Original site of **Cooty's Cabin**

Site of former **Basketville sign and Jordan shacks**

Abare's Folly Mountain

Great Meadow Village

Vermont

New Hampshire

DARBY DEPOT Rte. 12 to Keene ➤

Site of **PLC Project**

Ike's Auction Barn

Trust Lands

Cutter Place
Elman Place

Grace Pond

Dorne Place

CENTER DARBY **McCurtin Place**

Hillary Farm

Connecticut River

Trust Lands

Downed Elm

Town Hall

RIVER DARBY

Primeval Forest **Tree House**

Sandbank

Turner Jordan Place

▲ **Latour's Spoonwood Cabin**

UPPER DARBY

Salmon Estate and Cooty's Cabin

Trust Lands

Trust Lands

● **Ledges where Birch was born**

⊢ 1-Mile ⊣

THE VOICE

RIGHT TO THE END Howard Elman remembered the first words uttered by the Voice in his head: *Ain't you smaht!*

RE IN CAR NATION

DARBY CONSTABLE HOWARD ELMAN woke with the mocking words of the Voice still in his head.

You are 87 years old and you still have not done that great thing to allow you to pass on into the next realm in peace.

Peace! I never cared diddly-squat for peace. And, hey, maybe I'm not 87, only 85.

It doesn't matter. In your long life you have never accomplished a single great thing and you never will because you are too average.

What about the Re In Car Nation of the property?

That's not a great thing — it's just peculiar. "After his wife died Howard Elman succumbed to peculiarity" is what Dot McCurtin is saying about you, Howie.

Howard sat up and reached with his feet for his slippers on the floor. Ever since Elenore died Howard no longer slept in their marital bed in just his shorts. He slept barefoot but otherwise fully clothed in his forest-green work outfit on the couch in the parlor under a "Darby Old Home Day" quilt Elenore had made. He never liked the idea of "going to bed." It seemed to him more like "going to bedlam," the bedlam of regrets, or maybe the bedlam of egrets, those weird birds that Charlene, his eldest living daughter, talked about in her emails.

Feet in slippers, he stood, put his hands on his hips and bent backwards to loosen his spine.

He used to tell Elenore that he envied her ability to sleep soundly ten hours a night, but actually he didn't; actually, he liked being a light sleeper. Dreamland was an entertainment medium, better than TV.

There's more to it than that, Howie. You figure that the day you fall into a deep sleep that will be The End.

And just what is that end?

He tried to put himself in line with Elenore's hybrid Catholic thinking, that there was a heaven, a hell, a purgatory, and a limbo, which was some kind of waiting room for the souls of dead babies.

Soul? What's a soul?

A flat fish.

No, that's spelled different.

Constable Elman grabbed his cap from the end table and put it on his tender, bald head. The cap, like his matching trousers and shirt, was the same deep green as his grandson Birch Latour's Dartmouth green. On the peak of the cap, in white, were the words *Darby Police*. He owned half a dozen such hats that he had specially made and that he'd paid for himself after he was elected town constable as a joke, the year Darby had voted to turn the town's law enforcement over to the state police. The unpaid constable position was purely honorary, though in theory the constable had real powers. Or so said Birch, his favorite grandson, who this year had moved back to Darby with Missy Mendelson, his best friend from his rather bizarre childhood. Missy had a baby; her husband was another Darby playmate, Bez Woodward, a computer whiz and drone pilot fighting in a far-off war he was not allowed to discuss. Birch and Missy had started a computer business Howard didn't know much about.

Howard stoked the fire in the woodstove, started coffee, put on his black and red wool coat, and, as was his daily habit, stepped outside to admire his property. He would come back in when his slippered feet whined about the cold.

It was a gray November dawn, no bird calls, no lament from wind dying in the tops of the trees. He cranked up his hearing aid to listen to the occasional car that drove Center Darby Road; maybe he'd have luck and hear honking geese flying south, too. He hoped for kindly late fall weather. He and some volunteers were moving Cooty Patterson and his cabin today. "Rain or shine" said the flyer on the bulletin board of Darby's condemned town hall.

Howard carefully negotiated the concrete blocks that served as steps to the front door and walked to the middle of the gravel driveway so he could please his eye with a view of his property.

Quite a sight. I'm proud.

Pride is a sin.

Yeah, maybe for a Catholic. For me it's the branch sticking out of the cliff that I'm holding on to.

After Elenore's long, lingering, exhausting, sole-wrenching—or soul-wrenching—death you brooded for a year, and then you embarked on a project that sucked up your time, energy, and . . . and . . .

I know, I know, sucked up my good sense. So what?

So it's more than peculiar. You rebuilt the property to resemble what it looked like decades ago, before the fire that destroyed your house. But you didn't build it right.

I didn't have the money.

No foundation, no floors, just plywood over a two-by-four frame, windows salvaged from a tear down, the place no more than a stage set. A shell, a mere shell. Like you, old man. Like you!

Hardest part was matching the purple asphalt shingles for the siding on the house that burned.

The fire that you set, Howie, that you set!

I had my reasons.

The Voice left him and he was just thinking now, like any ordinary octogenarian. He had bought derelict cars from Donald Jordan's junkyard and placed them on the property so they would be visible up slope from the prospect of the Cutter house. Howard's poet son Freddy (who had legally changed his name to F. Latour) had dubbed the property "Howard Elman's Re In Car Nation."

Howard knew his son was being sarcastic, and he had retaliated by spitting words in his own sarcastic tone that he knew would rub snow in F. Latour's face, "Ain't you smaht." But after Howard calmed down and thought about it, he decided he liked the lingo. Why not advertise the sarcasm? He had put up a sign in front of the junk cars, "Welcome to Re In Car Nation." It had taken him five years—all through Birch's college education—but he finally got the place to look just about the way he had pictured it in his mind before the fire.

Many townspeople claimed Howard was trying to spite Zoe Cutter, his former neighbor up the hill, but as Mrs. Dorothy McCurtin, Darby's high-tech gossip, pointed out, Zoe Cutter was long dead, and her house, though it was kept up by her estate, was without occupants. So what had been Howard's motive? Mrs. McCurtin opined that Howard was just trying to keep busy after his wife died. "Grief has many faces," Dot would say. Other people doubted that Howard Elman had much capacity for an emotion as sublime as grief.

He's got old timer's disease: that's what people are saying, Howie.

Good. I don't want them to know my real reason.

Your true self died in that fire, didn't it?

Yes.

And you pulled the charred body out of the debris.

Yes.

You stood him up on a stick like a scarecrow.

Yes.

And you built that phony-baloney house to give him a home.

Yes. And yes. And yes. I can spit in the Devil's eye. And for the moment he knew he had quelled the Voice.

As Howard stood in his gravel driveway, he turned from the house to the stone wall boundary line that crawled across the field to the tree line, then angled to define the rear of his property and the woods beyond. In the days before the fire, he owned the field that swept up to the Cutter place and a hundred or so acres behind the wall, a never ending source of firewood, forest creatures, and awe. A man doesn't hunt the deer and the partridge; he hunts the awe. Which was one of Ollie Jordan's sayings. Hard times had forced Howard to sell the woodlot and field to Mrs. Cutter. She wanted all the property just to get rid of the sight of his junked cars.

In the end you made a deal. Your shame, Howie. Worst thing you ever did.

I don't have shame. Shame is for Catholics and the weak-minded.

At the end of the driveway was a gray barn, and beside it an ancient gnarled sugar maple with a swing Howard had put up for the kids. He had pushed all his children on that swing—Sherry Ann (she called herself Shan), Charlene, Pegeen, Freddy, and Heather—until they'd learned to pump for themselves. A sad day. Once a child learns to pump on a swing, the child no longer needs the male parent.

He paused at an overturned wheelbarrow that lay half in the driveway, half on matted, unmowed grass. He'd bought the wheelbarrow at Ike's Auction Barn for a dollar and loose change. The wooden side boards were weathered and rotting and the metal wheel hub was corroded. The device's purpose was no longer to carry the burdens of a homeowner's ambition but to please the eye of a man who found beauty in rusted pipes, flat tires, cockeyed side mirrors, spider lines made by shattered windshields, and overturned wooden wheelbarrows from an era gone by.

Another item he'd bought cheap at the auction barn was a nonfunctioning washing machine, which he had set up in the yard between the maple tree and the junked cars for target practice with his .357 magnum double-action revolver that he had bought from Critter Jordan, who'd told him that it was the murder weapon that had killed his father, the notorious Ike. Howard knew Critter was pulling his chain, but he had bought the gun anyway. The actual murder weapon was somewhere in a plastic bag in a police warehouse. Howard tried to interest his son and grandson in shooting. No luck. And though Missy Mendelson had been an eager student, she never got over the tendency to shoot low. Constable Elman did not carry the gun on his person. He did not even own a holster for it. Nor did Constable Elman wear a uniform. He had never made an arrest, had never investigated a crime. He wore his Darby Police cap at town meeting and was reelected every year, because his budget always read $0.00.

Howard walked to the barn, slid open the door, and went inside. Firewood was neatly stacked against a wall. He had his wood delivered by an out-of-town dealer so local people would not know he was no longer able to cut and split his own wood. When he needed wood, he'd carry some from the barn to the back of his car, drive it a hundred feet to his mobile home house shell, and lug it inside. Some days his bad leg buckled and hurt from the weight of an armload of wood. No doubt the Voice that questioned so much of his judgment and behavior had birthed from the pains of old age. As Ollie Jordan would say, "The Devil enjoys his torments, which most naturally pisses off his creator, which is why the Devil enjoys his torments." The main feature of the barn was the car-repair pit that Howard and his son had dug years ago by hand. Howard had spent more hours in the pit than he had in his house. These days he was too pooped to work in the woods, too pooped to work in the pit.

You're just a housebound old poop, Howie.

I know, leave me alone.

He stopped at the secret compartment he'd built behind a drawer in his workbench. Inside was his police pistol.

You have a use for this weapon?

No.

Sell it back to Critter, then.

I don't want to sell it separate from house and land—it's part of this property.

With that thought, he decided to leave the gun in the secret compartment. He liked to think that its discovery after he had sold the place would leave some fear of him in the hearts of the new owners.

Howard walked by the peg boards where his tools hung. Though he didn't use them anymore, he kept them oiled so they wouldn't rust.

What's this?

Ice tongs that you bought for no good reason at the flea market of Ike's Auction Barn.

As Leo Lavoie used to say, "Come in handy even if you never use 'em."

Look up at the shelf.

He turned and there it was: a reminder, the wood baby Jesus that he had carved for Elenore's Christmas nativity scene decades ago. Howard made a mental note to set up the crèche come December.

Mental note! Are you kidding? Write it down, else you'll never remember!

What's the diff—I don't believe in writing down, I don't believe in Jesus, I don't even believe in Christmas, and I don't believe there's heaven for Elenore or anybody else.

The nativity rig is part of the property, and Elenore's faith is as much a part of this land as your sarcasm and junked cars.

Howard took his FFone from his pocket and punched in a memo, "set up jesus."

Howard spent most of his morning viewing-time on his property gazing at his junked cars. In the old days they served as spare parts to keep his functioning vehicles running—pickup truck, trash collection truck, cars. Howard never brought his vehicles to a mechanic. He had been his own mechanic. But no more. These days the junk cars existed only to be admired. As another man might wander in an art gallery, Howard Elman wandered among Re In Car Nation. He loved the startling shapes, textures brought on by time, paint losing struggle with air, incursions of plant life in the crannies of stressed metal, patterns and play of light made by smashed glass, the fading from something to nothing. It seemed to Howard that an aura of the former owners of the vehicles glowed in a half halo around the cars.

That's just your imagination.

Suppose all a man has left is his imagination, then what?

Then say farewell and let go of the branch!

He walked right by Elenore's garden without a perusal. He had tried tilling the soil, but the work didn't suit his back. Pulling weeds reminded him of his army days, on a detail to pick up cigarette butts and candy wrappers, the sergeant barking, "All I want to see is assholes and elbows." He glanced at the bathtub Mary he'd built for his Catholic wife.

Guess what, Howie, when you die, time itself dies. The universe is no more and no less than your expelled breath.

Who said that? Was it Ollie Jordan?

No, Howie, it was Professor Hadly Blue.

What happened to him anyway?

Remember? He married Persephone Salmon and after she expired he moved south, which is what any sensible widower does. Why are you still here?

He was about to go inside when the wind kicked up and he raised his head to watch the sway in the tops of the trees behind the stone wall. The swing hanging on the great limb of the giant maple trembled. He heard a noise like singing.

Is it the wind?

No it's memory. Can you hear her, Howie, your youngest child, Heather? Look. The music stops, she sits on the swing, sings a sad song that gives voice to the wind. Constable Elman, don't you wish now that you believed in God, somebody who would mete out a just punishment for the terrible sin committed against your daughter Heather.

His feet were getting cold and he was about to go in when his FFone buzzed in his pocket. He whipped on his glasses, glanced at the number of his eldest living daughter, and said, "Hello, Texas, how's the weather down there?"

"I don't know, I just got up, and we're an hour back end to you, and I haven't been outside, but you can bet it's more copacetic than Darby," said Charlene, the sane one among the Elmans, even if she did rattle on.

"It's not that bad here," Howard said. "Thanks to global warming. I've planted palm trees and am eating coconuts for breakfast."

"Daddy, you are such a riot. Are you okay, are you sentient?"

"You've been Facebooking Dot McCurtin again, she's spreading rumors that Howie Elman is not . . . what was that word you used?"

"Sentient, it means . . ."

"I know what it means. I can read."

Just barely, Howie; you can just barely get through the newspaper and the town meeting warrant.

Oh, shut the fuck up.

"Did you say something, Daddy? I thought I heard a mumbled f-bomb."

"No, I'm sentient."

"I was wondering . . . you know, whether you had a buyer for the property yet and when we can expect you to join us in our not so humble abode. With Julia getting married again and Ricky in Vegas, we have plenty of room for you, and it's real nice year-round in Port Mansfield, South Texas, well, a little blistering in the summer, which no doubt is why the people here believe in hellfire, but we have air, everybody has air, and today I believe is the day you move Cooty Patterson to the Salmon mansion, cabin and all, and you won't have to babysit the old gentleman any more, because Birch has taken upon himself that awesome responsibility, bless his heart . . . a hundred years old, imagine that. Well? Well?"

"I was waiting for you to stop talking."

"I like to run on my sentences and I don't apologize for it."

"I always did admire your independent spirit, Charlene. To answer your question, I got an appointment to mull over an offer for the property." He gave her the figure.

"Holy guacamole! They offered your asking price! Grab 'em and hug 'em like family. Who's the buyer?"

Howard could hear a little bit of a Texas accent in Charlene's voice. Maybe when he moved south he could learn to talk like a cowboy. He tried to cheer himself up with the idea. "I don't know who the buyer is. Some company. I'll let you know after I meet with the real estate lovely in Keene."

"Okay, Daddy, we'd love to see you here on the Laguna Madre. Did I tell you we have an orange tree in the yard and that it grows real oranges?"

"Yes, you did, three or four times." He wanted to add, maybe you're not so sentient yourself, but he held back. Instead, he said, "Did I tell you that my beer can tree blossomed this year?"

"What?"

"I said my feet are cold, and I'm going in for a cup of coffee."

In the end, he agreed to ship his personal items to Port Mansfield, and move in with Charlene and her second husband, Number Two. Number Two: that was what she called him. Howard had reminded her that Number Two was slang for going to the bathroom, and she told him he had a dirty mind, which was true, though he wasn't about to admit it to a daughter. She wanted him to fly down and hire some recent retiree to drive his car, but Howard insisted on driving. He tried to entertain himself by imagining he'd swapped his constable cap for a cowboy hat, but the picture didn't look right in his mind.

Half an hour later, after a couple of English muffins slathered with real butter and coffee sweetened with maple syrup, Howard put on his work boots and left the mobile home. Even though a rash of burglaries had infected nearby towns, Howard did not lock his front door. He wondered if they locked their doors in Port Mansfield, South Texas. Probably. To keep out the rattlesnakes. He pictured a rattlesnake ringing a doorbell. Amazing the powers of the mind to abuse reality. Why did reality spit so close to realty? Real tea?

He tried to hut-horp-walk to his car. Leg said, no, I want to limp. He stopped for a quick look at his junked cars.

Was a time when I had as many as half a dozen registered vehicles: a honeywagon to serve the trash collection business, a pickup truck with agricultural plates to lug this and that, a DeSoto for showing off, a Ford wagon for not showing off, and most recently Elenore's PT Cruiser (her idea).

Howie, that's only five.

I can't remember the sixth vehicle.

One fine day they'll take your license away, Howie. That's what they do to golden agers, to encourage them to voluntarily kick the bucket.

Hard to do when you're standing on it.

Never mind balancing on a bucket, you have enough problems just finding the limber to cut your toenails.

Weeding the feet.

He hopped in the car, did a u-eee in his driveway, ripped up another piece of shaggy lawn, and took off toward town on Center Darby Road.

Even at his advanced age Howard Elman drove too fast. He liked motion. He liked power at his fingertips. He liked objects in service to his desires, his robots. A car, a toaster, an electric drill, a penile implant (which Howard was contemplating, if only he could find an accomplice to use it with) were all robots that one instructed to perform a function to please the operator. The older he got and the more his own functions declined, the more faith he put into his robots.

On the drive to Cooty's cabin he started thinking about his grandson, Birch Latour. Birch's mother had died giving birth to him up on the ledges of the Salmon Trust. Birch's father, Howard's son, wrought up with grief and anger, moved himself and Birch into the woods to get away from booze.

One fine afternoon when Birch was about ten, Howard had a little talk with the boy as they strolled in the woodlands of the Salmon Trust. In the old days when Howard had been feuding with the Salmons, he'd call them the Saamins, but now that he had a grandson who was half a Salmon, he'd become more respectful pronouncing the name the way they preferred, Sahl-mohn. As he drove, Howard's lips moved in whispered memory.

☞ ☞ ☞

"Some day you'll be the boss man of this place," Howard says to the boy.

"I already know that," Birch says.

Howard chuckles. Birch is very curious about the world outside his woodsy home. When he learns something new, he checks it off and moves on to the next nugget of knowledge. No repeats, please. Birch has a special gift. He remembers everything. Claims he can remember his birth on the ledges, his mother's last breath.

As they come out from under the canopy of pine trees into the sunlight, Howard points, "There's the apple orchard your father started."

"No, Grandpa, Dad didn't start it. A farmer from olden days started it. When Dad found the orchard, the forest had taken over, and the pines were killing the apple trees. Dad cut them down to let the light in."

"Let the light in — that's admirable."

Howard's son Freddy homeschools Birch and teaches him everything about the woods but very little about the town of Darby, so Howard decides to instruct his grandson on the ways of the Darby world by comparing what Birch knows, trees, with what he doesn't know, people.

"Pine trees are more likable as products than as plants," Howard says. "They make beautiful boards that nail well and age real pretty, and they take paint okay if that's your pleasure. It's too bad they're so ugly and numerous, and they drop their acid-ass needles, pardon my French, so nothing else can grow under them. Your Center Darby commuters are like pine trees. Only instead of dropping pine needles they make acid-ass zoning laws.

"Down along the river you got your farmers, who have been selling out in recent decades. Farmers are like red oak trees, stalwart and respectable; they provide us with food just as the oak mast provides acorns for the deer and the bear to eat. Just like the red oak doesn't scale well in comparison to the white oak and the southern oak you see how your New Hampshire farmer can't compete with your delta and plains farmer. He gets by on guile.

"In Center Darby you have all these new people coming in, and they're flashy, like a grove of white birches. The white birch makes an okay saw log to mill into Scrabble squares, because the wood don't split or check easy, and as your Aunt Charlene might say it's copacetic to burn; the bark makes a really nice smell in the fireplace, though it'll clog your chimney. New people are like white birch, a mixed blessing or a mixed curse, depending. As your Grandma Persephone would say, come see come saw down that doggone tree."

"Grandpa, I'm named after a birch tree."

"Yes, but Birch, you were named after a black birch, which like yellow birch has better wood than a white birch, and a nice minty smell when you cut into the bark. I believe the Indians used the bark to make a tea out of it. Your personality, Birch, is like the minty aroma of a black birch."

"My mom planted lilac bushes just before she had me," Birch said.

"Yes, your mother was partial to lilac, which produces a wonderful wood. When you split lilac, the heartwood is the color of the flower, but the purple vanishes before your eyes, the wood in the end turning a reddish brown. Every time you see a lilac bush, think of your mother."

"I already do that, grandpa."

Howard thinks Birch might cry, which would do him some good, but he does not cry. Indeed, he never cries. Howard wonders, just where in mind and materiality is this boy?

"Grandpa, what kind of tree people are Upper Darby?"

"Your mother's people."

"Yes, Grandma Persephone and Grandpa Raphael."

"The Squire."

"Yes, I love him."

"You never met him—he died before you were born."

"I already know that, but I still love him."

"Upper Darby are like sugar maples, which are our most uppity tree. Very beautiful in all the seasons, but especially when the leaves fall. And in the spring the maple tree's sap runs. Who says money doesn't grow on trees? The bark is very beautiful in old age, except . . . except . . ."

"Except what, Grandpa."

"Except a sugar maple will rot from the inside. It rots and rots and rots until the heartwood support for the trunk is gone, and then it topples over from the weight of its own self-aggrandizement. With all due respect to your grandmother Persephone and the Squire, I think something like that has happened to the Upper Darby folks.

"Now I want to tell you about the poor and uneducated people, because part of you comes from that line. In fact, a little bit of all of America is inside of you. You should be proud. Back in the old days in Darby Depot we had all these shacks, where people like the Jordans would lower the property values by the way they lived. The Darby Depot people are like weed trees—pin cherry and popple and gray birch and sumac, trees nobody wants, people nobody wants, but that keep popping up or maybe poppling up. Still a few shacks out there, but most of the folks in Darby Depot and their ilk these days live in trailers that don't trail and mobile homes that don't motorvate."

"Grandpa, what's an ilk?"

Howard stops and thinks, dangerous activity. Finally, he answers, "Ilk is like family. People you're stuck with."

"Grandpa, what kind of tree are you?"

The question startles Howard. Should I tell him, he wonders. They walk for a while in silence, and then lo and behold there it is: a tall, mature elm tree on the edge of the Trust lands. Howard recognizes the tree from a time when he had taken his daughter Heather on a walk similar to the one he is now taking with Birch. "See that tree."

"It's an American elm," Birch says, and he salutes it just as Howard has taught him. I love this boy, Howard thinks. I love this grandson more than I loved his father.

"You know, of course, that me and your grandmother Elenore were foundlings," Howard says. "We didn't know where we came from. Poor Elenore, she never did find out, but she did track down my people. Didn't I learn that my birth name was Claude de Repentigny Latour, but by that time in my own mind I had become Howard Elman."

Howard pauses, and in that pause, he finds that great big beautiful lie he had told Heather years earlier. "This tree here is the last great elm, the lo and behold elm. You know the story behind the elm trees, don't you?"

"Yes, Grandpa, the elms were killed off by an invasive species."

"That's correct. But every once in a while you find an elm tree that escaped the dreaded disease. When I came across this great tree, I said to myself, 'Self, this is the lo and behold elm, a lone ranger, just like me.' That was it. I knew right then and there that I was the elm man, Howard Elman. I got my name from this tree."

Now, years later, as he drove the roads of Darby, New Hampshire, Howard Elman was thinking that his lie, which he had told his youngest child, the one he loved more than the others, the one he betrayed, this lie that he had passed on to his grandson, who he loved more than anyone since Heather, this lie had changed into something else. It was no longer a lie, but it couldn't possibly be a truth. What was it?

THE CENTENARIAN

DARBY CONSTABLE HOWARD ELMAN (just barely) climbed a low boulder with a flat top, and that action got the attention of the thirty or so townspeople who had gathered at Cooty Patterson's cabin in the hills above Darby Depot. Howard glanced at his left wrist as if it held a watch, and said in as grave tones as he could muster, "It's twelve o'clock (actually it was 11:37 AM) and here we are during this beautiful day (actually it was overcast, raw, gloomy) to celebrate the five hundredth birthday of Cooty Patterson, the man who discovered America."

Everybody but Cooty grinned. The old gentleman raised his stick-cane and drew in the air, doing the math. "I ain't five hundred; I'm only a hundred, Howie," Cooty said in all seriousness, his thin lips vibrating in harmony with various shades of pink and blue, his wispy, wild white hair like spider webs fluttering on zephyrs of angel breath. The scraggly chin whiskers and beard were gone, apparently having been shaved off by his nurses.

Cooty wore high-top sneakers, wrinkled dark pants with the fly unzipped, a heavy, blue smashed-toe colored wool sweater, no buttons, held together with a safety pin, and a blaze-orange hanky tied around his skinny chicken neck. When he leaned on his cane with one hand folded over the other, he reminded Howard of one of those twisty high-country California trees that have been around since the pyramids.

Tess Jordan reached into the pouch she kept on a cord around her neck, lifted her fake cell phone, brought it to her ear, and said, "The old man is so thin that a breeze might pick him up and blow him to smithereen land."

Howard didn't like the way Birch looked at her, with a bashful and appreciative smile that revealed the braces on his teeth. Jordan women were dangerous.

The ladies of the Darby Snowmobile Club had just finished lighting the hundred candles on the giant cake that rested on the tailgate of Bev Boufford's station wagon under a maple tree. They were led by Priscilla Landry, a childhood friend of Howard's youngest daughter.

Remember Heather? The one you lost, the one you and Elenore gave away?

We didn't give her away. She was stolen from us by Mrs. Cutter.

Birch cupped his hands and shouted, "Cooty, blow out the candles."

The centenarian had the idea to blow them out one by one to prolong the pleasure of the experience, but he got help from half a dozen little kids in attendance and the candle fires died very quickly in streamers of white smoke that resembled Cooty's hair.

Out of the corner of his eye Howard watched Tess Jordan. He wondered if she'd made peace with the voices on her imaginary cell phone. Did she control them, or did they control her? She was too pretty, too sharp-eyed for a crazy woman.

Everybody sang "Happy Birthday," everybody ate cake, everybody went to work. The volunteers had gathered in the woods by the old man's cabin to move it and him to the grounds of the Salmon estate in Upper Darby so that Birch Latour, who lived there now, could keep an eye on Cooty in his declining years.

A reporter for *The Keene Sentinel* took the centenarian's picture and asked him the secret to his long life.

"I like well-aged stew," Cooty said, leaning on his cane, blinking in fear and wonder, the way he always did with strangers.

Howard pointed to the blackened pot simmering on a grate over a tiny open fire not ten feet from the front steps of the cabin. "The secret's in the stew pot," Howard said in his usual too loud voice to the reporter, who jotted the information on a notepad.

The reporter turned to Cooty, "How many years have you had the pot?"

"I don't totally recall." Cooty looked at Howard for an answer.

"He bought it at Ike's Auction barn for seventy-five cents back before the fire that burned my house down when Carter was the president," Howard said.

Not strictly true, Howie.

I know, but not a perdition lie either. Why are so many things like that?

Howard continued the story of the stew pot, not sure in his own mind which parts he was embellishing, nor caring. "Cooty used to make his rounds picking up road meat and vegetables from grocery dumpsters Tuesdays and Thursdays in Keene and then hitchhiking back home. The pot simmered around the clock, three-sixty-five a year."

"Did rain put out the fire?" the reporter asked.

"Good question," Howard said, stalling for time to figure what to say next. "Oh, he might of taken in the stew pot during a hail storm or a blizzard."

"And put it on the woodstove," Cooty said.

"And put it on the woodstove," Howard said.

The reporter turned again to Cooty and said, "How do you clean it?"

Confusion came over the centenarian, and he looked to Howard to supply an explanation.

"Cleaning it would ruin the flavor," Howard said. "See, most people serve a stew while it's too green. Takes some time for a stew to find its flavor."

"How much time?" the reporter asked.

"Time? Sometimes I wonder," Cooty said with a shrug.

"It takes a year, maybe two, for a stew to taste just right," Howard said with a straight face; he told the reporter that in recent years the centenarian had weakened and could no longer make his road meat rounds on the highways and byways of the region. To keep the stew going, townspeople brought meat and veggies for the pot and sticks to burn in the fire. Hunters, hikers, joggers, mountain bikers, snow-mobilers, teen lovers, elementary school students and their underpaid teachers, naturalists and unnaturalists, lost souls, the fallen, the felonious, and the merely fucked-up dropped in to taste Cooty Patterson's stew. Which was all true if somewhat overly combobulated in the telling by the Darby constable.

"So, why is Cooty leaving?" the reporter asked the obvious question.

"One fine day, my grandson and I visited Cooty and found the embers cold, the stew room-temperature."

"I suppose I forgot," Cooty said in voice that actually had a bit of cheer in it.

"Do you remember what you said when Birch woke you up?" Howard asked.

Cooty shook his head.

"You whispered, you said, 'I'm tired.'"

"And that's when you knew Cooty had to be moved where he could get some care?" the reporter said.

"Yes, that's correct."

Howard stopped speaking when he saw his fellow townspeople coming out of the cabin carrying Cooty's tiny table. End of an era.

"Did you make that table?" the reporter asked Cooty.

"I think so."

"The barn boards for the table — is there a story behind this table?" the reporter said.

"I don't know." Cooty turned to Howard.

"The boards were salvaged from what used to be horse stalls in my barn," Howard said.

"You're a horse farmer?" the reporter asked.

"Not quite," Howard said.

Birch came over and introduced himself to the reporter. No doubt the reporter was impressed, though he didn't show it. Birch was handsome like his grandfather Raphael Salmon, though not in that regal lion way. More like the shy catamount that was rumored to have crossed the river from Vermont into the Trust lands. Birch smiled with his mouth shut so his braces wouldn't show.

"My grandson, but don't hold that against him," Howard said with pride.

"My father and grandfather have tended to Cooty's needs for as long as I can remember," Birch said. "Now it's my turn. We are moving him and his cabin to be near my home in Upper Darby. He'll continue to live in his cabin, but he will have round-the-clock care. Our goal is to keep Cooty alive forever and a perpetual flame under the stew pot."

"This going in the paper?" asked Howard.

"Yes, and online," the reporter said, and turned to Birch. "Why are you doing this for the old man?"

"Cooty has been and continues to be a spiritual advisor to three generations of my family," Birch said. "My father—who couldn't make it today—used to tell me that a bowl of Cooty's stew could change your luck, but only if your heart, like Cooty's, was empty of desire."

Howard was so impressed by the quality of his grandson's talk and charm-school delivery that he succeeded in forcing himself to remain quiet.

There was an old apple tree near the cabin with a broken branch and the woeful look that came over such trees when taller trees grew over them and stole their sunlight. Cooty pointed to the apple tree, interrupting the interview. "Can I take it with me?" he asked nobody.

"What does he mean?" the reporter asked Howard.

Howard shook his head, Birch smiled—he knew the answer, but he wasn't saying.

"Look," Cooty said.

The men stared at the small, distressed apple tree. One main branch had rotted and fallen off.

"See," Birch pointed, "even though it's November, way after apple-picking time, three apples—still more or less red—are clinging to the tree."

"That's it," Cooty said. "One apple is you, Birch, another is Freddy, and that one about to drop . . ." He stopped talking and smiled.

"Gotta be me," Howard said.

"That's right, Grandpa," Birch said. "I've arranged to have Johnny Matthews move the tree with his heavy equipment to replant it in the new location for the cabin. Johnny's a real artist with his excavator, and he'll move that tree without shaking off the apples."

The centenarian smiled.

While Birch continued his interview with the newsman, Howard busied himself by joining the moving crew.

The original builder of the twelve-by-sixteen-foot cabin had been a lifer-felon who Cooty met in a stint at the mental hospital in Concord. Over the years Cooty, with Howard's help, had remodeled the cabin with recycled barn boards, odds and ends from construction sites, and dump pickings. It had a window on each of the four walls and a door of zigzagging rough-cut pine boards. Three of the windows were ordinary enough, but Cooty (with Howard's help) had installed a new one crooked, "to remind me I see better when I cock my head." Inside was a woodstove, a cot, a shelf, a GI footlocker, Cooty's collection of pretty sticks hanging from nails on pine board walls; there was no toilet. Cooty did his business in the woods. The crane was already in place to lift the structure onto the bed of a truck. Howard could offer nothing to the enterprise.

They don't need you, Howie. Nobody needs you.

He gazed out into the deep forest in wonder at his own isolation, and he thought about that elm tree, the lo and behold elm.

Tess came over to Howard. She had the Jordan look—lean but muscular, dark-complected, black eyes—but while Jordans of old had rotten teeth, pocked faces, and cruel smiles, Tess had white even teeth, a healthy complexion, and a wry smile that suggested she'd figured out the world. How could she be crazy? Maybe she was part catamount. She wore a short skirt over black leggings. Her long black hair lounged over her shoulders in a way that reminded Howard of Estelle Jordan before Estelle's hair went white. He couldn't help thinking about sticking his nose in Tess's hair.

"You and Birch are pretty funny when you walk together," Tess said.

"Right, because we both limp," Howard said.

"I know why he limps—no toes on his bad foot and pain every time he puts pressure on it—but why do you limp?" she asked.

"Because I'm old." Actually, he'd broken his leg some years before, and because he put off going to the doctor's, the break never healed right.

"You ever wear braces like Birch?"

"No, he inherited nature's love of buck teeth from my departed wife." Howard jabbed his finger at the cell phone, and added, "Are you, you? Are you for real?" He thought he saw his question open a window of fear on her face.

"Excuse me, grandpa, I have a call," Tess said, and brought the fake cell phone to her ear. She muffled her voice with her hand and moved away from him.

Howard thought about his son, who was thick in the shoulders and hips like himself, not like Birch, who was more delicately made. Birch didn't resemble his mother either, who was big-boned like Squire Salmon.

He looks like Elenore.

Which is why you love him.

The insight, a surprise to Howard, sent his thoughts to his son.

Freddy and his wife Katharine Ramchand had moved sixty miles north when Katharine landed a tenure-track position in Dartmouth College's Anthropology Department. She was the main breadwinner in the household. Freddy kept busy, though. He took care of the couple's two kids, carved elegant wooden spoons that he sold for outrageous sums at the Sunapee Craft Fair in competition with that master spoon maker, Dan Dustin, published a few poems under the name of F. Latour, and recently was working as a writer with Birch and Missy in the new company that Howard didn't know much about. Frederick, Freddy, now Latour, liked being a househusband and, as Howard was painfully aware, liked being sixty miles away from his horse's ass father.

Among the gathered that Howard took note of were Selectman Lawrence Dracut, who Howard loathed for many reasons, including the fact that he drove a Mini Cooper, which seemed to mock Howard's ancient PT Cruiser; Darby's high-tech gossip, Dot McCurtin; horse loggers Obadiah Handy and Charley Snow, who had recently announced their engagement; and a couple Howard hadn't yet met but had heard about, Cooty's new nurses, Luci Sanz and Willard "Wiqi" Durocher. Howard didn't think they looked like nurses. They were too young and too perfect in a department store manikin kind of way. Luci and Wiqi would do double duty, as employees of Birch and Missy's company and as nurses to tend to Cooty's needs.

Howard was surprised to see Carleton "Critter" Jordan and his youngest child, Billy, make an appearance at the party. While Tess might be otter-lean, Critter was reptile-lean with a beer-drinker's protruding belly that made him look like a snake that had swallowed a woodchuck. He dyed his dark hair Reagan red, which did not match his swarthy skin. Billy was late-high-school age, heavier built and fair-skinned like his mother, with a dirty-blond buzz-cut hairdo. He had a sullen, vengeful look, as if somewhere along the line he had been terribly wronged and sought Biblical justice. Dot McCurtin had spread the word that the boy carried a gun. What bothered Howard was that Dot was rarely wrong.

Billy stayed close to Critter's shit-box Bedford truck that had the steering wheel on the wrong side. Everything in Billy's body language screamed get me outta here.

Critter walked over to Tess and said something to her. She gave him a don't-tread-on-me look, and he walked away to circulate among the townspeople. It was obvious he wanted everyone to know that he had come to celebrate the birthday boy. Cooty was nothing to Critter, and Critter wasn't known to go out of his way unless there was something in it for Critter.

Critter, what kind mischief are you up to?

He won't tell you, Howie; he probably doesn't know himself what he's going to do next.

I can relate.

Critter had recently been divorced by his wife Delphina Rayno, who had left town. It was public knowledge that Critter owed the town back taxes and that the bank was likely to foreclose on a second mortgage he'd taken out on his auction barn properties. Critter's father, Ike Jordan (murdered years ago by a party unknown), had been a burglar who was so good he had never been caught. By all appearances Critter had gone straight after he married Delphina. However, Howard was pretty sure that since the divorce, or maybe before, Critter had returned to the family trade and was behind recent break-ins in surrounding towns. But Howard was not about to tip off the staties unless Critter started hitting Darby properties. Howard had his own history with the Jordan Kinship.

Tess was the daughter of the deaf but not so dumb hunchback Turtle Jordan, who was the son of Ollie Jordan, deceased like his brother Ike. Turtle had long ago moved out of Cheshire County and, according to Dot McCurtin, had made something of himself as a graphic artist. Tess had showed up one day and moved into the auction barn in the apartment that her uncle Critter rented. Dot McCurtin, who was rarely wrong about these things, said that the rumor that Tess had broken up Critter's marriage was not true. Howard thought that Tess had way too much sex appeal not to be involved with somebody in the town. Tess had appeared normal enough until the word went around that the cell phone she constantly talked into was a fake. Tess held conversations with voices in her head.

"Let's get Cooty's stuff out of the cabin, so it don't rattle around," Howard said. He went inside and grabbed the GI footlocker. It didn't weigh all that much. He brought it to his car and put it in the back seat. He felt Cooty, who stood nearby with his nurses, watching him. In bygone years—before Cooty's unsentience had cartwheeled past his eccentricities—Cooty had told Howard that the footlocker held private things. Howard had nodded without comment, and never raised the subject again. Now, on moving day, Howard blurted out what was on his mind.

"I've always wondered just what 'things' you keep in there," Howard said.

"But you never asked."

"Something tells me I don't want to know."

"Because finding out is never as good as wondering," Cooty said in that way he had of saying smart things but sounding stupid, or maybe stupid things that sounded smart. The more Howard knew Cooty, the less he understood him.

"So you won't tell me," Howard said.

"I would if I could, but I can't remember," Cooty said.

"Really? Why don't you open it and find out?"

"I can't, I hid the key and don't know where I put it," Cooty said.

"No doubt we can jimmy it open," Howard said.

Cooty stopped to think for a moment. "When I remember what's in it I'll remember where the key is, and then . . ." He broke off.

"Well?" Howard said.

"Then I'll be a free man, Howie."

Howard turned to Cooty's nurses. "This is how all conversations with Cooty go."

"Go?" said Wiqi to Luci. "In English, does the meaning change when the verb is at the end?"

"Not usually. I'll explain the grammar later," Luci said to Wiqi, then turned to Howard. "Wiqi has a learning disability in areas relating to language."

"Welcome to the club," Howard said to Wiqi. "It pains me to read, but I'm not stupid. Are you stupid?"

Wiqi's eyes rolled. "Difficult to calculate a satisfactory answer that is also accurate. It'll take some hours."

"Just kidding," Howard said.

Wiqi surprised him then by offering his hand.

Howard hated handshakes. It seemed to him that the people who shook your hand picked your pocket with the free one. But this handsome young man was the sincere type. Howard took the hand.

"No crushing," Luci said with some alarm.

"Confirmed," Wiqi said.

Howard was surprised by the grip. It was not a big hand but it was cool, hard, dry. Wiqi didn't squeeze hard, yet Howard could sense the reserve power in the hand.

Cooty's cabin, though in the woods, was just off a town road, so it was no big deal to jack it up, place it on a trailer bed, and haul it behind Teddy Ferguson's truck to Upper Darby onto the Salmon Trust lands. It was more trouble getting the apple tree safely out of the ground, securing the root ball, and loading it with delicacy, but Johnny Matthews got the job done. And when the tree was settled into its new location, it still held the three apples.

Howard led the caravan of townspeople in his PT Cruiser, traveling past his own place, through Center Darby Village, then up the long hill to Upper Darby and the Salmon estate with its mansion, sprawling lawns, and gardens in a wide high valley surrounded by the forested hills of the Salmon Trust lands, the hump of Abare's Folly mountain looming over the foothills.

The cabin was placed on a stone foundation that had been built in the woods behind the Salmon mansion that everyone these days called "the Manse." The stew pot remained on the original old iron grate over a tiny open wood fire. By now it was nightfall. Cooty hung his cane on the hook on the wall beside a window, lay down, and immediately dropped into dreamland. Luci and Wiqi monitored his vital signs on equipment that to Howard looked as if it belonged in a submarine. Cooty in sleep-realm appeared both at peace and excited. Maybe he was communing with God almighty.

God? After all these years of denying the idea of a deity, Howie, are you suddenly amenable?

Not really.

Howard's hearing aid reported the slurpy sounds of Cooty's lips. Howard turned down the hearing aid.

While the centenarian slept, the volunteers gathered in the Manse for a party. Birch provided bottles of wine, hard cider, sweet cider, and munchies. Howard thought Birch acted like a politician looking for votes, but it was Missy, his childhood friend and business sidekick, who was running for the state senate. She caught Howard's eye, pointed her finger at him like a gun, and said, "Bang, bang, you're dead." Howard pretended to duck. It was their private joke, since the days Howard had taught her to shoot.

Around 10 PM, when the older folks were winding down to go home, Howard made an announcement: "Now that I know that Cooty is being taken care of, I'm telling you people that Howie Elman is retiring to South Texas to be near his daughters Charlene and Pegeen and their families. Tomorrow I will submit my resignation as town constable. Let me add that I have an offer on my property." He named the figure. "Anybody want to best it, gimme a call on my cell."

What followed was a puzzled silence, then some questions regarding his health that Howard fumbled with. Finally, he muttered, "It's time."

"He doesn't sound all that enthused about leaving," Tess spoke into her fake cell phone. Howard realized that she was looking at Birch, who returned a mysterious, endearing wired-mouth smile that conveyed not so much amusement as pity for the human condition.

Howie, you don't know what to think about young people these days.

Maybe so, but they don't scare me.

They should.

On the drive home from Upper Darby Howard figured if he got stopped by a statie (not likely), he'd blow just under the drunk-driving limit. As constable, he had access to their machines and had tested himself, so he knew how much he could drink — three and a half beers, maybe four over a couple hours — and still stay legal. He congratulated himself for his cleverness, but his mood quickly deteriorated. He was thinking about Latour, a no-show for the birthday boy. He couldn't really blame Freddy for changing his name. After all his own name, Howard Elman, was a fiction. It had appeared on some paperwork when he was a boy in a foster home, and it had stuck.

He had certified the name long ago on that walk in the woods with Heather. It had been the same kind of day as today, cold, gray, color gone from the fallen leaves and crispy under foot. The kind of day to appreciate an elm tree, the way its branches spread out like Abraham crying out to God, "You want me to do what?"

When he arrived home and parked the PT Cruiser, he realized the sky had cleared. Under moonglow and starlight he stood in the drive-way and contemplated his property.

Wonder how much it will cost to ship my junked cars to South Texas.

Don't be stupid.

I'm not stupid, I'm selfish.

Give some thought to the idea of setting up Elenore's nativity scene. That little rig meant a lot to Elenore.

I will, but not tonight.

Think about Tess Jordan telling her troubles over her fake cell phone to nobody.

The Voice was annoying him now, so he went inside his phony house and had another beer.

The next morning he woke on the couch in that familiar state of mind between dreaming and remembering.

※ ※ ※

He and Elenore are sitting down to Sunday dinner. It's a few days be-fore the doctor will tell Elenore that she has a bad tumor. At the mo-ment, they're talking about selling off the property and moving to South Texas. Elenore, usually suspicious or dour, is giddy over the prospect of living in a warm climate. Elenore reads Howard's mood be-fore he notices it himself.

"It'll be all right, Howie, I'll buy you a pair of those high heel cow-boy boots," Elenore speaks in that sweet voice that makes him want to weep with love.

"You know what I hate about getting old, besides the aches, pains, and the general all over loss of Geritol?" Howard says. He knows she won't respond, because she knows he is going to answer his own question. "It's that I have these urges to cry for no good reason—gets my goat."

"It's your female side coming out, Howie."

"You're welcome to it."

"We're swapping genders—it's the way of old age," Elenore says. "Me, I don't cry much anymore, and I grow hairs on my chinny chin chin."

"I used to have pectoral muscles—now I got a nice tit on me." Howard cups his hands around his old man breasts.

"Don't worry about it, God will take us before the gender switch is complete."

"You sound like you're looking forward to dying," Howard says.

"Well, of course." Elenore raises her eyes to that heaven she believes in.

Now he really is dreaming, seeing Elenore as a young vibrant woman. Beside her stands Birch. They might be brother and sister, beautiful and delicate on the outside, flexible and strong on the inside. Unlike himself and Latour, Birch and Elenore are finely made with features like movie stars or models in magazine ads featuring underwear.

Except for the you know what. Look again, Howie.

Howard peers at the faces in the dream. As in real life, Elenore has buck teeth and Birch wears his braces. Heather suddenly appears in the dream carrying a guitar. She smiles at Birch to display her own braces. The glitter dazzles and accosts the dreamer.

⚜ ⚜ ⚜

The FFone buzzing in his pocket woke Howard.

Howard growled at the FFone, "It's your dime."

(Inaudible)

"What?" Howard said.

"Grandpa, turn on your hearing aid," Birch shouted.

"Oh, yeah," Howard grabbed his hearing aid from the end table and plugged it into his head. "Okay, the icepick's in my brain."

"Listen, Grandpa, I got kinda disturbing news. You know the primeval forest?"

"Yeah, the one that Katharine discovered on the Trust lands and wrote up." The first time Howard had heard that word, primeval, it registered as "prime evil." He knew better these days, but even so the defective translation was still in his head: the prime evil forest.

"Yes, and that American elm tree that you took me to when I was a kid, right on the edge of the primeval forest?"

"Yeah, the last great elm, the Howard Elman American elm, the lo and behold elm," Howard Elman said in portentous tones.

"Grandpa, somebody cut it down."

"Cut it down?"

"That's right. Grandpa, they had professional equipment and they hauled off the logs. There's nothing left but stump and slash. Our primeval forest has been violated."

It was at that moment that Howard remembered his dream and words from the Voice: *Teeth, straight teeth!*

THE LAST GREAT ELM

MINUTES LATER HOWARD drove to the scene of the crime along a
Class VI dirt road that wound through the Trust lands. The road pe-
tered out into a path that ended somewhere up a tree in a knothole
where perhaps the ghost of Lilith Salmon, Birch's mother, resided in
her reincarnated life as a red squirrel. The car would go no farther.
Howard got out and started to walk, dragging his bad leg.

He knew the area well. There was a gorge only a few hundred yards
from here that was the home of one of his shameful acts. Years ago,
when he had started his trash collection business and he was feuding
with the Salmon family, he'd dumped some refuse into the gorge from
the road above. It was Birch who had brought the Elmans and the Salmons together finally, but he was a boy then and that time had gone
by. Good times, bad times — they all leave you driving a bumpy road to
catch up. Howard followed the ruined ground where a tracked vehicle
had pulled the logs out of the woods. Quite a ways. He was huffing and
puffing, and his bad leg ached.

*The prime evil forest has been desecrated all right, and now it's dese-
crating you.*

Sunlight slashed through dark green hemlock shadows that gave
the place an air of mystery and majesty.

Like a church at night lit by candles only.

*How would you know? You avoided churches. You'd wait in the car while
Elenore attended service.*

Truth is, I felt embarrassed in a church.

Like God, if there was one, didn't want you there.

That's right.

The tracked vehicle had steered around huge mossy fallen trees.

Howard was surprised to find that Birch was already at the crime scene. He wore blue jeans and hiking boots, carried a small backpack, and held a hand-carved walking stick. It helped his limp. "How'd you beat me here?" Howard said.

Birch flashed his cell phone. "Grandpa, I called you from here. I've been waiting."

"Every kid growing up wants a walkie-talkie — now everybody's got one," Howard said. "What's left to want, I wonder?"

"How about a sustainable future for the generations to come?" Birch said.

"I guess," Howard said. He wasn't sure what Birch meant by "sustainable." He turned his eyes to the elm stump. It was about three feet in diameter, a mature but modest-sized elm tree.

"The last great elm on the Trust lands," Birch said, his voice sad with a touch of anger. "Look at the saw cuts. They felled it so it wouldn't get hung up in the hemlocks. Whoever did this knew what he was doing."

"Indubitably," Howard said. He respected his grandson's opinions and observations. F. Latour had brought Birch up in the woods, and he knew the Trust and forest lore. Howard knelt with a groan on the forest duff and sniffed the elm stump. "I always wondered why this tree was never infected."

"Because it happened to grow in an area with no other elm trees and so it wasn't exposed," Birch said. "Want to bet they cut the tree down during Cooty's birthday party?"

"No doubt some of our Darby neighbors were in on it," Howard said in those droll tones that infuriated his son but amused his grandson.

"Probably, but I hate to think," Birch said. "Whoever did this knew about this tree, knew about our private road, and knew the hours when we wouldn't be vigilant. What I'm wondering is — why?"

The old constable and the young forest conservancy steward stood silent for a few moments, contemplating the issue of motivation.

"The obvious one is spite," Howard said. "I know spite. Spite beats even religion as a trouble starter. Somebody knew how to hurt us here." Howard thumped his chest.

"Pretty elaborate scheme just to inflict a psychic wound, Grandpa. It might be something more subtle."

"Okay, try this," Howard said. "Some rich bastard, he wants something special, real special, something you can't get in the normal market, let's say, some goddamn piece of furniture he could show off to his friends, like from an elm tree in a virgin forest?"

"It's possible." There was doubt in the grandson's response.

"Think about this," Howard blustered on. "That tree had some value to those curmudgeons who make bowls out of burls. That tree had burls."

"Wood turners?"

"Uh-huh. You know what a big bowl turned from a figured burl can cost?" Howard paused only long enough to shout an answer to his own question. "They cost like the dickens!" As soon as he spoke Howard realized it was a dumb idea thinking that someone would cut a tree down for the burls, and he knew that Birch knew.

"And what is the monetary value of a dicken, Grandpa Howard?" Birch said.

"Oh, about two iotas."

Birch answered with one of his little smoothing-over laughs.

"Birch, you laugh like a girl—it troubles me," Howard said.

And they both laughed. Howard thought that he had never loved anyone—his wife, his children, his own worthless self—the way he loved this young man.

Unless it was Heather.

Oh, please, not now.

"They took the logs," Birch said. "Maybe they're headed for the sawmill."

"Spite and special together add up," Howard said. "Somebody who doesn't like you or me or both of us and wants the wood for his own private reasons. The son of a bee will give himself away, mark my words."

"There's another possible motive," Birch said with just a trace of exasperation, which Howard barely registered. Since he exasperated most people, Howard had concluded that exasperation in conversation was part of the deal so he hardly noticed it. Birch continued, "I said earlier that I thought this tree might have avoided being infected simply because it was isolated, but there's another factor to consider. Elms are susceptible to a number of diseases, not just Dutch elm."

"Really?"

"Really. Elm Leaf Beetle, Verticillium Wilt, Elm Yellows, Elm Leaf Black Spot, Elm Leaf Miner, and Asian Longhorned Beetle."

"Momma manure, but that's a mouthful," Howard said, his thoughts pure but his voice carrying some unintentional sarcasm.

"What I'm getting at," Birch said, "is that this tree never seemed to be infected by anything. Silviculturists the world over have been looking for a strain of elm that is immune to disease."

You do not deserve the name Elman. Unlike Birch you have no depth of understanding of elm trees. Or anything else.

All the old feelings of inferiority at his ignorance and illiteracy that he had thought he had got over with in middle age when he had learned, more or less, to read came flooding back to Howard. He had to will the tears of self-pity from flowing. He compensated for this temporary moment of weakness with his usual horse's assness, and even while he performed the action he loathed himself for it: he climbed on the stump and began to pontificate.

"You know, I've always wanted to live as a tree. Imagine myself standing tall, but not going anywhere."

"Good idea," Birch said. "Stay in one spot and you'll see that so much happens if only you pay attention."

"Mark time, weather, and the random occurrences in the neighborhood: birds shitting on your leaves, squirrels using your limbs for a racetrack, those damn owls thinking you're some kind of launchpad for supper."

"And don't forget the millions of insects and fungi invading your privacy," Birch said. He was used to his grandfather's theatrics. Indeed, he was a bit of a pontificator himself.

Howard's hearing aid didn't quite pick up Birch's frequencies, so that in place of "invading your privacy" his brain substituted "invading your privates," and he thought: how profound this boy is, the word "profound" having been copped from the vocabulary of his son F. Latour.

They followed the wounds on the forest duff to the dirt path that passed for a road and took a long careful walk around the area, looking for clues. Howard found a plastic bag that crumbled when he picked it up and spilled out some beer cans. Howard looked up at the steep walls of the gorge. He could not see the turnoff on the road high up, but he knew it was there.

Do you get it, Howie? You dumped that bag back in your litter bug days. You yourself besmirched the virgin forest. If Elenore's right and there's a judgment day, you are in for it.

"Grandpa, you're talking to yourself again," Birch said.

"I keep good company."

"Hey, what about this?" Birch pointed to a small empty plastic bottle of two-cycle oil for chain saws. He picked it up through the open neck with a stick.

"Good boy," Howard said. "There might be a fingerprint on it. I'll bring it to the staties first thing. And I'll question some suspicious characters."

"Really, who do you have in mind?" Birch asked.

"I'm going to meander over to Critter Jordan's Auction Barn," Howard said, but he wasn't thinking about Critter; he was thinking about Tess, that big hair.

A man your age shouldn't have thoughts like that, they might kill you, Howie.

It's not a bad way to go.

"Didn't I see Critter at Cooty's birthday party?" Birch asked.

"Yeah, I wondered about that. Now it makes sense. In Jordan reasoning that's an alibi. He's got kin galore that would cut that tree for a twelve-pack of beer."

"Really?"

"Really. He's a Jordan. Reason enough to talk to him. Even if he had nothing to do with it, he might know some bad guys around town I have yet to make the acquaintance of."

Birch seemed about to speak, but stopped himself.

They hopped into the PT Cruiser, Howard behind the wheel, Birch on the passenger side in the front.

"I'll get some of my friends to go door to door on Center Darby Road," Birch said. "Somebody must have seen a logging truck. I'll talk to Obadiah and Charley. They'll have a line on possible maverick loggers. Meanwhile, I'll do some Internet research to find out if there was any eccentric scientific reason that anyone would want to steal an elm tree."

Birch had already figured a plan.

Young people today, you have to take your hat off to them even if it reveals your bald head, Howie.

"What do you think?" Birch said.

"All's I know is it wasn't a skidder that pulled the logs out, it was a small bulldozer, like excavators use, not loggers, least not in these parts," Howard said, trying to look meditative by burying his chin in his fingers and furrowing his brow. "The trucker woulda had to make two maybe three trips to haul off the logs, then come back for the dozer."

A few minutes later they arrived at the shingle-style mansion. The structure had devolved into a great big sprawling rooming house and office building after Birch's renovations. It seemed to Howard that since Birch had taken over the Manse, he'd turned it into a kind of fancy bunk house for his friends. Howard wondered if maybe one of Birch's "green warriors" was really a double-crossing essSOBee with his own reasons for cutting down the last great elm.

Just before Howard dropped him off, Birch said, "Grandpa, I can take care of this."

"What do you mean?"

"I mean there's no need for you hang around Darby for this. You're selling your house, headed south — right?"

"I suppose. I did promise your Aunt Charlene I'd clear out soon as possible, yeah yeah yeah." He paused to build some suspense, and then he spilled his thought. "But I want to find the perpetrator who cut down my elm tree."

"I know you do, Grandpa, but you shouldn't let this little . . ." Birch seemed to struggle to find a word. He repeated, "this little . . . episode interfere with your plans."

Howard mumbled an "Uh-huh." He felt a pang. Something was wrong. What was it? That tree — the bastards had taken the last great elm. But it was more than the tree. It was . . . what? He didn't know.

Old age is making you stupid, leaving you without knowledge, a feeling of your tether having been cut. Remember what Ollie Jordan used to say?

Yeah, he said, "That fella who dropped over the cliff when you sawed the branch he was hanging onto was your better half."

So, are you going to respect your grandson's wishes that you butt out?

No.

Birch went into the Manse. Howard got out of the car and walked over to the cabin for a brief visit with Cooty. The stew pot on the grate bubbled over a low fire. Howard didn't bother to knock, just walked in. Cooty lay dozing on his cot, eyes shut, mouth partly open.

"You awake?" Howard said much too loudly, but he got no response. Perhaps Cooty had died. Howard cranked up his hearing aid to the max and held his ear to Cooty's lips. Howard heard what sounded like a soft rain on a pup tent. The centenarian's breath smelled like the wintergreen of black birch sap.

"They cut down my tree, Cooty — what should I do?"

The centenarian's lips trembled, but he did not speak.

Howard brushed his finger tips against Cooty's wild hair and quietly withdrew from the cabin.

DECISION

HOWARD DROPPED THE two-cycle oil container at the state police barracks. ("You really think you'll get a print off this? Har-har-har.") Then he drove directly to Critter Jordan's place on the main highway in Darby Depot. The rambling structure of connected wood-frame buildings was so rundown it appeared about to collapse, but it had two brand new signs. One sign said in capital letters, "IKE'S AUCTION BARN." The other sign said, "Look for Grand Re-Opening." There was no construction activity.

Ike Jordan, Critter's father, had started the flea market and auction barn business as a cover for his burglary forays. After Ike's violent end, Critter had taken over the auction barn and had eked out a living from the flea market business and added a dirty book store with peep show booths. But the easy porn found on the Internet and some kind of Jordan mayhem Howard didn't know much about put an end to the store. After Critter's wife left him, he shut down everything.

Critter's Bedford truck was not in the lot, but Howard knocked on the door to Critter's apartment in the auction barn anyway. No answer, no lights on inside.

Howard walked over to the other apartment up the rotten wood stairs, which swayed as he ascended, to the second-story deck. It was like walking on a rope bridge. Estelle, the Jordan Witch, once had lived in this place.

Tess Jordan opened the door before Howard had a chance to knock. Apparently, she'd watched him approach. She stood, blocking the doorway. Her black hair seemed to avalanche off her head, and she wore something that displayed her tidy cleavage.

"You didn't come to see me. I don't get much company." She didn't talk in a Jordan accent, upcountry New England with a touch of southern hillbilly in it. She talked like a college girl, her voice rising slightly at the end of her utterances as if all human communication had a question in it.

Behind Tess was a cat with a J. Edgar Hoover face on a table with a slanted top, the kind artists used for sketching.

"Copacetic cat," Howard said.

"That's Dali, my Himalayan, very curious about our Western ways."

"Tess, are you going to let me in?"

"I don't think so."

"I'm looking for Critter."

"He took off with Billy."

"I was surprised when I saw Billy at Cooty's birthday party. I thought Delphina took the kids."

"Billy ran away, or maybe she threw him out. They don't tell me anything."

"Well, when they coming back?" Howard asked.

"Or if they're coming back?" It was as if she didn't know the answer but somehow she thought Howard did. He decided to oblige her.

"They'll be back for supper, I imagine," Howard said.

"It's suppertime now, but he's not here, is he?" It was hard to tell whether she was conversing with him or talking to herself.

Howard figured he could play the confusion game, too. "I'll wait, or I'll come back — take your pick," he said.

"Excuse me, that's my phone chime." Howard heard no sound. Tess reached into the pouch she kept on a cord around her neck.

Dali watched Howard as one might watch a freak at a booth at the Cheshire Fair. Howard stuck out his tongue, but Dali did not seem to notice.

Tess held the phone to her ear and listened with studied intensity to the imaginary voice. Then she said to Howard, "It was for you."

Keep playing along.

Okay.

"What's the message?" he asked.

Tess spoke in a different voice now that did not sound like her own but was vaguely familiar to Howard. "Men like you, Howard Elman, are passing from the scene. We have no use for you. Your best intentions can only bring harm to us, to yourself, to your loved ones. Don't inflict the wounds of your century upon my century." Tess snapped off her cell phone, stepped back, and softly shut the door.

"I'll be back tonight," Howard hollered in his Terminator voice at the door, even though he had already decided not to come back, to forget the whole thing. "You tell Critter. Okay? Tess — you tell him."

No answer.

He peeked through the window. Dali had hopped on Tess's lap, and she squinched his ears as she talked on the fake phone. On the wall Howard could see line drawings of what looked like the Darby town hall. He withdrew.

Wait around, see what happens.

No, I'm gone.

He hurried off to the cocoon of the PT Cruiser. He started the engine, but did not engage the transmission. He was remembering where he had heard that voice that Tess had spoken in to put him down, a voice wise but cruel; it was the voice of Estelle, the woman the Jordan Kinship had called the Witch.

Why are you shaking, Howie? You're not going to let a crazy Jordan girl set your pants on fire, are you?

❧ ❧ ❧

Later in the mobile home encased in its phony house shell, Howard Elman sat at the kitchen table and munched on an Ancharsky's Store grinder while he imagined Elenore standing at the sink and gazing out the window at the bird feeder, just as she had done in life. He wanted to tell her how sad he was at the loss of his tree, and that he was further plunged into despair at the prospect of selling his property and losing those connections and conniption fits that had enriched his life: Cooty Patterson's stew pot, Birch's manse, Ancharsky's Store, dead man's corner, a thousand memorized glimpses of Darby trees, stone walls, ledges, old grave stones, fences and horses and cows and chickens and porcupines and deer and skunks and woodchucks and beavers and squirrels, gray and red, and damn raccoons and screeching foxes and screechier fisher cats and once in a while a coyote, couple times a bear, bobcats, sugar on snow, Saturday morning yard sales, old tools, junk cars, rides to the dump, his mechanic's pit, the sky over his property, town meetings, disasters in the son (Freddy, Freddy, why did you change your name?), even black flies, yes, even you, evil ones. Home! Don't you understand, Elenore? We are giving up our home, our town, our region, our weather, our soil, our nighttime star show, our very selves. The worst of it was that his anger, the fire that had kept him stoked all these decades, and that had produced smoke to shield his fear, had died to embers. The figure of Elenore in his imagination faded, and without it his loneliness enveloped him, a kind of suffo-cating protection like a poncho in a foxhole on a rainy night in war. He wondered if Cooty remembered that night they spent in the hole during the only rain in months in North Africa.

Probably.

Probably not. Cooty doesn't conjure over his memories, he feels them.

Later, still on the couch Howard didn't so much sleep as pass out after too much drink, useless cogitating, and running baldacky bareass through the brambles of memory.

⚜ ⚜ ⚜

Next morning he went to Keene, to the real estate office. He had to wait an hour for the "buyer." Connie Joyce, his statuesque and beau-tiful real estate agent, told him that her agency had been paid a fee by the buyer — very unusual — and she left the room. Moments later Howard was surprised to find himself with a woman of color who spoke with a Massachusetts accent, young, hardly out of college, and didn't even know where Darby was. She had arrived only minutes ear-lier in a rental car. She apologized, didn't realize she had this closing until she saw the work order on her queue this morning at her desk in Boston.

"What are they going to do with my land?" Howard asked. He was thinking of the battles he'd fought decades ago to hold on to it.

"I can't say," said the woman.

"Does that mean won't say or don't know?" Howard asked.

"To tell you the truth Mr. Elman . . . is that how you say your name, ell-man? Or does it rush together, ellmun?"

"Close enough either way. You were saying?"

"My company is not the actual buyer, we're a proxy for the buyer," the woman said.

Howard grimaced. Foxy proxy.

"I didn't come here to go away empty handed, Mr. Ell-man," the woman said, all business in her demeanor. "Look at the sales agreement, your asking price, plus the buyer pays the realtor fee instead of you. It's more than generous. Who knows if the offer will be on the table tomorrow?"

Somebody had sent this woman here all the way from Boston just to snatch his property. It was as if Zoe Cutter had come back from the grave. He was going to turn down the offer on general principles when he heard Tess Jordan's words echoing in his head, "You can only bring harm"; he remembered seeing how Birch had looked at Tess.

You can only bring harm, you can only bring harm. The message is clear.
I'm fated to leave Darby.

Fated? We're all fated for some kind of disaster. Everything after birth is a waiting game for that moment.

"Excuse me, I didn't get that," the proxy lady said.

"Sorry, I talk to myself," Howard said. "How much time you going to give me before I have to get out?"

He thought he heard her say, "tweaks," and he gave her a "what the" look.

"Two weeks," she repeated.

As he signed the papers he tried to imagine himself on new soil in Port Mansfield, South Texas, growing a few orange trees, roping steers, humping a pump jack, saying farewell at the Alamo, doing that great thing that had eluded him all these decades.

Howie, you fell with the great American elm that was cut in the prime evil forest of the Salmon Trust Conservancy. Soon you'll be Howard Orange Tree man!

It doesn't sound right in my head.

Howard called Charlene on his FFone, told her the good news, then he went to the bank and deposited the check, keeping five thousand in hundred dollar bills because he always wanted to feel the lump of a lump sum in a bulging wallet against his fanny pocket.

He was in the PT Cruiser on his way back to Darby when his phone vibrated in his non-wallet pocket. He thought it might be Birch, but it was the chairman of the Darby board of selectmen, Lawrence Dracut. When was Howard going to formally resign his position as constable?

"I forgot," Howard said to the FFone.

"I guess your advanced age must be catching up to you?" Dracut said in the sly way of one delivering an insult by pretending to make a friendly remark.

Something of the old anger came back to Howard now, and he was grateful for it.

"I get forgetful. Sometimes I even forget to change my adult diaper. I can tell by the smell. The fumes are rising out of my phone even as we speak."

"We'd appreciate it if you'd come in to take care of this technicality."

"In due time, or maybe in doo-doo time."

"I'm in the town hall for a meeting, and I've got the papers in my hand," Dracut said.

Howard had just crossed the town line into Darby, when memory shot through him.

⚶ ⚶ ⚶

Six years ago at town meeting, upon the retirement of Darby Constable Godfrey Perkins, Darby citizens vote to cut the salary of the town constable to zero, turning over law enforcement to the state police. There was a time — before he learned to read — when Howard avoided town meeting out of shame, but partial literacy has changed his attitude so that he has become a regular. Howard argues that the state police are already stretched too thin to be depended on to police the town.

"Does that mean that we have a venerable citizen volunteering to be constable for no pay?" Dracut says with a snicker.

The comment draws additional snickers from a few townspeople, and the next thing he knows Howard finds himself volunteering for the post.

"What's your platform?" shouts Pitchfork Parkinson, Howard's former employee who has bought Howard's trash collection business.

Howard stands before the townspeople and says, "Avoid police work past my bedtime and march in all the parades."

That gets a big laugh from the entire meeting, and the townspeople, despite the objections from the board of selectmen (or perhaps because of them), vote Howard in. Every year Howard submits a report and it is always the same: salary $0.00, expenses $0.00, arrests zero, parades four. He is reelected by acclamation every year. It is all a big town meeting joke, and Howard is happy to be part of it.

They aren't laughing with you, Howie, they're laughing at you.

So what?

So somebody cut your tree down. They want what's left of your pride, Howie.

It's not the loss of pride the troubles me.

Right, it's the gonzo gonads.

⚓ ⚓ ⚓

"Elman! Elman! You still on the line?" The sound of Dracut's voice brought Howard back to the moment.

"Yeah, what now?" Howard said.

"Come over so we can get this resignation thing out of the way, puh-leahase," Dracut said in the soothing voice polite folks use to address old people, royalty, and idiots. Howard knew what would come next. The man had a talent for mockery. "This whole business, a constable without even a week at the police academy, could get the town into some touchy legal trouble with the state, not to mention it makes us look like a bunch a rubes and you, sir, a buffoon."

Howard was thinking so what's wrong with being a rube and a buffoon—we're entertaining and harmless? But he said, "Okay, I'll be right over." He snapped shut the jaws of the FFone.

He didn't stop at his home but drove to the town offices in the decrepit town hall in Center Darby village. He tried to think about South Texas—warm, dry, flat, and far from Dracut; he tried to use the thought to bring himself some comfort, but the image slipped away replaced by the memory of the elm stump in sunlight surrounded by hemlock trees and their mysterious deep, black-green shadows.

The Darby town hall was in sad shape, the beams full of tunnels, hideouts, and amphitheaters built by carpenter ants. There were days when Howard thought his hearing aid picked up the sounds of their labors.

Why do they call them "carpenter" ants? Carpenter ants don't build, they unbuild.

From their point of view, they're making a home.

But eventually it's going to come down around them. What is built will someday collapse.

You reach a certain age and all you have left are questions you don't really want answers to.

To get to the selectmen's office Howard had to enter through the office of the town's administrative assistant for the planning board, conservation commission, and selectmen. Howard walked right past Bev Boufford's desk. She gave him a dirty look, but he ignored it as he pushed open the door to the selectmen's office without knocking. Miraculously, Howard didn't make any noise, and he stood there for a moment unnoticed.

Sitting behind a table were Dracut and the two other selectmen, Harvey Colebrook, retired farmer and current part-time plumbing contractor, and the widow Frances Peet, who was educated. Harvey and the Widow Peet were both in their late seventies. At age fifty-seven, Dracut represented youth on the board of selectmen. Nobody who held a real job wanted the selectman's position. It didn't pay, there was no glory, and there were a lot of headaches associated with the decisions selectmen had to make. In theory, the selectmen were not partisan politicians but dispassionate money managers representing the town.

The selectmen were watching a PowerPoint presentation by C. Odysseus Prell. Cod Prell, as he was known locally, was from an old Upper Darby family distantly related to Birch on his mother's side. Cod had made a name for himself as an architect in Boston. Now he was back in Darby, "to reinvent myself" as he was fond of saying, and he had been elected chair of the planning board.

"With all due respect, Cod, what's in this master plan for the town?" asked Harvey Colebrook who, like Howard, was a practical-minded man but, unlike Howard, soft-spoken.

"I'm glad you asked, Harvey," said Cod. He was slender but wiry with a dapper mustache, a taste for creased, designer blue jeans that he wore with a blue blazer, black watch Pendelton shirt, brown loafers, and a smile that said I know more than thou. "PLC is working with both political parties to sponsor a town meeting debate by the presidential candidates—whoever they may be—just before the election. That's why we need Darby to look good in a brand new but traditional meetinghouse. We also have to do something about our eyesore trailer park. This town will be in the national spotlight."

"Wow. I guess the problem is the poor people are in the way of progress," said Harvey totally without irony and slightly above a whisper. "Oh, hello, Howard."

"Oopsie-daisy," shouted Howard Elman, "I'm here to see Selectman Dracut."

Cod clicked off the computer slide on the projector screen. No doubt the content of his talk was not ready for public consumption.

Dracut rose to his feet, "Can't it wait—we're in the middle of a private presentation?"

"You did tell me to drop by. You said you had the papers in your hand."

"I was speaking metaphorically. I figured half an hour, not five minutes after our phone call," Dracut said, a man more interested in winning than persuading.

"No problem, I'm just finishing up," Cod Prell said, but nobody was listening to him. They were intent on the drama between Constable Elman and Selectman Dracut.

Something about Dracut's superior tone brought Howard to his senses. He was relaxed, ready to speak from that throat-frog that resided in the gullet above his old man breasts, though he didn't know what he was going to say until the words spewed forth from his mouth, "That's okay, Mr. Selectman, I have changed my mind. You have backtalked me into it. I am not resigning, I remain your town constable." He knew he had done the right thing, which was not to allow Lawrence Dracut a victory. Howard bowed slightly to the Widow Peet, stepped backward through the door, and shut it perhaps a bit too hard, since Bev Boufford, not a woman to be intimidated or upset by untoward behavior, made an uh-sound, as if she were having sex.

THE GEEK CHORUS

BIRCH LATOUR WAS the sole heir of the Salmon estate and steward of the Salmon Trust Conservancy. Howard thought he took his legacy too seriously for his own good. Even before he went to college Birch had committed his life to the guardianship of the Trust, inspired by his own boyhood experiences on the land, his peculiar upbringing, and the spirits who lingered on the land—his mother, Lilith Salmon, who had died giving birth to him on the ledges of the Trust and, his grandmother Persephone Butterworth Salmon, who raised him, and perhaps most important, his other grandfather, the Squire, Raphael Salmon who had created the conservancy that everyone called the Trust and who had also died on the ledges before Birch was born. Birch had a bachelor of arts degree in environmental studies and a master's degree in computer science from Dartmouth College, and upon graduation had moved into the Manse, bringing along his friends to work in the company that he and Missy Mendelson had founded, Geek Chorus Software.

Birch got around on dirt roads of the Trust in a vintage Ford Bronco. His grandfather Raphael had bought it new in 1983. After the Squire died, his widow—a madwoman behind the wheel of any vehicle—kept the Bronco going. After she died, the Bronco sat untouched in a corner of the driveway for a couple years. Katharine Ramchand—Persephone's niece, Birch's stepmother, and the executor of Persephone's will—was about to have the Bronco hauled off to Donald Jordan's junkyard, but Birch, by then a teenager with a brand-new driver's license, got an idea. He took some of his inheritance money and at great expense had the Bronco completely rebuilt. For Birch the vehicle was more than transportation, it was a link to his ancestry and responsibilities as steward of the forest conservancy.

Some of the lands of the Trust had been set aside to be "untouched by human hands in perpetuity," in the words of Raphael Salmon. Other parts, through "wise logging practices," were expected to produce revenue to pay taxes, maintain the Salmon residence, and support the Trust steward and his staff. Most of the land was open to the public for hunting, day hiking, and even snowmobiling. Birch knew that technically he, as lifetime steward, was an agent of the Trust's board of directors, but since he had stacked the board with his friends, relatives, and admirers, Birch Latour, at age twenty-four, ruled over the Trust. Most of the board members lived in and around the Salmon estate in Upper Darby.

The Manse had been built by Raphael Salmon's progenitors back when there was big money in the family. The Salmons, along with the Butterworths and Prells, had bought up the properties in the highlands of the town and established Upper Darby. Birch had remodeled the Manse by wiring it to accommodate computers and by hanging landscape paintings of the Trust lands.

The night Howard showed up at the Manse, Birch was giving a talk to his friends and some visiting investors in Geek Chorus Software. Howard took a seat in the back of the ballroom, turned up his hearing aid, and listened to his grandson. The young steward talked easily, and while his voice carried well, it had a soft quality to it that lulled and comforted his audience.

"In the historical gardens of this estate I see the beauty, complexity, confusion, and isolation of my Salmon forbears. What they seemed to have had in common was an inability to agree among themselves. My great-grandmother established formal Italian gardens. My grandmother Persephone grew flowers in the profligate style of the English garden. Gertrude Jekyll had been her inspiration. My own mother's last act before her death giving birth to me had been to plant lilac bushes from cuttings from the Governor Wentworth estate in New Castle, New Hampshire. The gardens were the first frames we built into our video game, because — with the exception of the lilacs — the gardens no longer exist in reality. Human neglect and the change-machine that is nature has reclaimed the land, but from research in journals and photographs we have reconstructed the gardens in all their glory and then some for our video game." Birch paused for a moment, then made eye contact with his investors. "I tell you all this because I want you to know that your investment in our enterprise runs deep." Birch paused, then repeated, "Runs deep."

He's got 'em in the palm of his hand, Howard thought, and then he stopped listening; he was thinking about family and about this mansion—how he, a common working man, had somehow lucked into Upper Darby society through his son.

You were a lousy father to Freddy.

I must have done something right, because Freddy has been a good father to Birch.

Howard remembered listening while Freddy told Birch that the Salmons and the Elmans, indeed all of America, existed only in interstices of the continent's tectonic plates. What did he mean, Howard wondered. Even after looking up "interstice" and "tectonic" in the dictionary, Howard remained mystified. The son was as much a mystery to the father as the words he used.

🎣 🎣 🎣

Howard wandered into the other great room downstairs, the library. Like the ballroom, the library seemed to want to be a museum space or an art gallery. Both rooms included huge fireplaces that accommodated six-foot logs. Birch liked to sit before the fire to think, to warm his bones, to lose himself in the flame. Just like his father and grandfathers, Howard thought. The love of a wood fire was about the only thing Howard Elman and Raphael Salmon had had in common.

Raphael? Remember when everybody used to call the Squire Reggie?

In death, a man sometimes is promoted by the living.

Only some men. Upon your farewell what will they call you, Howie?

I don't know.

I'll tell you, then. They won't call you anything. You'll be forgotten.

Eventually, everybody is forgotten.

Birch had bought paintings of the Trust lands in varying styles by local artists and put them on the walls in the great rooms downstairs, and he had completely renovated the library with computer stations everywhere, huge computer monitors to display graphics, and desks with a zillion outlets where the geeks of Geek Chorus Software could plug in their laptops.

Birch had kept the opulent Persian rugs and his grandfather Salmon's leather chair. Without Birch having to say anything, everyone knew that this had been the Squire's chair and that no one should sit in it. Birch's taste in books ran from environmentalism, to conservancy law, to local history, to philosophy and religion, but above all to computer science tracts and scripts for video games, many many games.

Go ahead, Howie, sit in the Squire's chair. You can't, can you?

I don't want to.

You mean you don't deserve to.

Howard put his hands behind his back as if handcuffed, and sauntered slowly as he perused the books in the library. That was the word in his mind—perused. Deliberating over the word made him feel a little smarter. Howard believed that if Birch and all the Salmon folk thought well enough of a book to put it in the library it must be worth reading. Not that Howard actually read any of those books. He found reading unpleasant, and he had it in the back of his mind whenever he was reading that he could be doing something more productive with his time. Even so, at this moment he loved the library. Maybe just being in the presence of books is enough to smarten up a person.

If books could kill: Which sarcastic philosopher had said that?

Ollie? Was it Ollie Jordan?

Yes, of course it was. Ollie Jordan educated you about the Jordan clan and their gift for conjuring.

Maybe so, but he couldn't conjure his way out of the woods on a cold night.

"Grandpa, you're talking to yourself again."

Howard was back in the material world looking at his grandson and the minions who had followed him into the library.

"I was thinking about this house, this library, how it makes me feel . . . I don't know . . . small but important in my own way," Howard said.

"I'm having all the books digitized," Birch said, as much to the minions as to his grandfather. "I'm going to put this entire library on my mobile phone, so it's with me all the time."

"Then you won't need the books," Howard said.

"Yes, that's correct. In the future books will be collector items. I'm debating whether to donate them to the town library, except for Grandpa Raphael's journals of course. They'll stay here as long I'm alive, and then they're going to the Rauner Special Collections Library."

"Well, I guess if it's a collector item it ought to go a collector library," Howard bellowed.

Birch started back for the ballroom, gesturing for his grandfather to follow, but Howard shook his head and remained stationary to finish musing over this, the most magnificent house in Darby. He looked up at the high ceiling as if he had x-ray vision.

The second floor of the Manse was broken up into bedroom suites inhabited by the permanent residents: Birch, Missy Mendelson and her baby, Grace. Missy would live in the Manse until Bez returned from the long war. They planned to build a house on Grace Pond. A couple rooms were set aside for guests—consultants, visiting investors, friends, relatives. There were empty rooms on the second floor, yet to be filled. Birch believed he had to marry to produce an heir who one day could take over his position as steward of the Salmon Trust.

Imagine that! Having to fuck for posterity. Must be an awful burden.

Howie, all creatures fuck for posterity.

No they don't—they fuck for pleasure. Posterity is a side effect they are not aware of.

So what's your point?

That if there's a god he's got a wicked sense of humor.

And then there was that room on the second floor that was under lock and key that Birch wouldn't talk about.

The third floor had been cut up into small rooms, originally for servants. The occupants these days include the loggers, Obadiah Handy and his fiancé, Charley Snow, and the geeks of Geek Chorus Software, the engineers who wrote code for the video game: Scotty "Trek" Prell, an Upper Darby product, short but athletic and cocksure of himself, a wise ass; Jane Yu, "Jayu", who was very beautiful and very serious; Solomon Poisson from Haiti, a high on the hog kind of guy, who was teaching Birch to speak French. Trek, Jayu, and Solomon were inseparable. Jayu referred to both Trek and Solomon as "my husband." Howard tried to imagine a three-way love arrangement that included two genders and three races, but the idea was too much for his mind to ponder, so he unpondered it. The three were always arguing and disagreeing, apparently for sport, because they never seemed to be angry with one another.

And then there were the new arrivals, Luci and Wiqi, the nurses Birch had hired to meet Cooty's health needs and who also worked for Geek Chorus Software.

The only other occupant on the third floor was the quiet man who always wore a white suit and tie, and a sneaky smile that suggested he was laughing at everybody else. He was entirely bald and as near as Howard could tell was incapable of even growing facial hair. He rarely spoke, and his real name was unknown to Howard; he went by Origen. He was probably in his fifties, the oldest by a generation of the geeks. Howard didn't know just what Origen did for Geek Chorus Software. Howard had heard Birch introduce him to the investors as "our ethicist." He was the creator of the company's motto: All Can Be Saved.

Howard knew he had seen Origen before, but he couldn't remember where.

⚜ ⚜ ⚜

The evening meals in the Manse went on for hours. Diners helped themselves to food, wine, hard cider, and beer from a long table in the hall between the ballroom and the library. People came and went at their own whims. The conversations often galloped on past midnight and into the dawn. Birch rarely took a side in the arguments; indeed, he spoke sparingly at these gatherings, though it was clear to his guests that they had been brought together to perform for their host. If you weren't invited back, it meant you hadn't met his standards. Volunteers among the geeks kept the place more or less picked up, and once a week a janitorial crew came in from Keene for major cleaning.

The investors mingled over the casual dinner with the employees. Howard nibbled at the food and drank too much. He noticed that, like himself, Birch ate lightly.

He's saving room for Cooty's stew.

That makes two of us.

Birch invited the investors to join "the seminar," which was what he called the evening discussions in the ballroom.

That night the main topic was world population and the impact of carbon emissions on the earth. As usual the discussion strayed far and wide. Geeks and guests gathered around the huge fireplace. Some sat in lounge chairs or on couches, but most half-reclined on pillows on the thick rugs in the floor.

Howard wandered around. He liked the geeks, since they didn't seem to mind his horse's assness, though Cooty's nurses, Luci and Wiqi, gave him pause. They owned no motorized vehicle, but traversed on a mountain bike built for two even in the worst weather. Despite their extraordinary good looks and physiques there was a blandness about them that Howard couldn't figure. They appeared too perfect.

Maybe they're from California, which would account for their peculiarity.

What would account for your peculiarity, Howie?

Birch sat on the floor in front of the fire. Howard could tell that Birch's bad foot was acting up again, as it did almost every night; he was in pain, though he tried not to show it. Howard liked listening to the young people gab. It was like they were on stage.

JAYU: More important for the long-term health of this planet, even more important than new technologies to limit emissions, is population control.

SOLOMON: The most effective way for population control would be the age-old solution from nature, a plague of some kind, like a global pandemic that would reduce the numbers to near zero.

TREK: Seems a little extreme, even for a Malthusian.

JAYU: The way the elm trees have been devastated by the Dutch elm disease.

SOLOMON: Actually, from a Darwinian perspective elm trees are not devastated: they are merely stressed. There are plenty of elm trees. It's just that the trees do not grow old. They die young, but in time to reproduce. The tragedy of the elms is in our minds, not among the species.

JAYU: If you're looking for tragedy look to the Chestnut tree, an entire continent's best forest stock devastated by a blight.

TREK: Maybe in the end, it will be wind-borne spores that our senses cannot account for that will eradicate us.

SOLOMON: We should return to our primary purpose here, discussing the preservation of the Salmon Trust lands.

JAYU: Preservation? I don't think so. The Trust is a collection of organisms each of which changes not just year to year but moment to moment. Weather, climate, and biological processes create a constant state of flux within the Trust, and indeed within every human body. We can't impose a stasis, because organisms by their nature are dynamic.

SOLOMON: We may not be able to stop change or even to control change to any great degree, but what if we incite change? What would be the best change for the Trust and the planet itself as we know it? That's the question we need to answer for ourselves and take action accordingly.

TREK: Yes, by incorporating it into our video game.

Laughter from the minions.

"Yes, into our game." Howard recognized Missy's voice just before he saw her, coming down the grand staircase after putting baby Grace to bed.

Birch, who hadn't said a word so far, looked at Missy and broke into the conversation, "With the baby in your arms you looked like Giovanni da Modena's La Vierge et l'Enfant."

"You think?" said Missy. She could be droll. Howard wondered if she'd learned droll from him.

TREK: Suppose we pose you like the painting for the game?

"Good idea," Missy said.

JAYU: Some observers might see a contradiction between the makers of a video game and the keepers of a land trust.

"Without the revenue source from our game, none of us gets paid and for sure we'll lose the Trust lands," Birch said. He glanced at Missy, and Howard knew she would finish his thought.

"Reggie Salmon shaped the Trust by hook and by crook, often by crook, and he was passionate about it, but a little careless with the legal language," Missy said. "There are too many old ideas, too many different political entities."

Notice she called the Squire Reggie and not Raphael, just like the old days. Only Missy can get away with calling the Squire by his nickname.

SOLOMON: The main enemy of this planet right now is human wealth. The richer the nation, the richer the individual, the deeper and dirtier is his footprint on the planet. The only way the earth can heal itself is with a severe decline in human population and with the remaining population living poor, I mean literally dirt poor, the way primitive peoples always lived, with high childhood mortality, premature death for most of the population, and short life spans. In other words, like the people of my island nation.

TREK: Yo, bro, the Four Horsemen of the Apocalypse in the end will be our saviors: kinda funny and sad, because it's so true.

JAYU: People will not opt for self-imposed poverty.

"We have a role model for this lifestyle right here on our premises," said Missy.

SOLOMON: The hermit, Cooty Patterson, a long-lived human being who does not breed, who lives off the land without screwing it up.

JAYU: Very very few human beings would elect to live like Cooty Patterson.

SOLOMON: What if a Papa Duvalier elite imposed poverty on the masses on a planetary scale?

TREK: Extermination would follow, and the earth would be inhabited by the children of Cain.

SOLOMON: If the human animal survives, it's likely that the planet will degrade in such a way that it will be uninhabitable by human beings whether we're poor or not. The only solution is that a small elite carries on humanity by escaping to the stars.

JAYU: Given the technology of our time period, there is no known habitable star system within range to escape to.

TREK: We're effed.

"What do you think?" Birch spoke, and the minions paused. He looked at Luci and Wiqi.

Luci Sanz said, "Wiqi and I believe there is another solution."

"Yes, we have a possible answer to the dill enema," said Wiqi.

"Dilemma," Luci corrected.

Trek hummed a old tune from the album *Enema of the State.*

Wiqi blushed in embarrassment. "Excuse me."

"Wiqi is a little — or maybe a lot — dyslexic," Luci said.

Up until now Wiqi and Luci had been quiet, which was probably the reason that when they spoke they had the attention of the minions. Birch had a knack for finding people he got along with who also could contribute to the Trust and Geek Chorus Software. Luci and Wiqi were attractive, pleasant, and knowledgeable about many things, but eccentric, which of course made them welcome in the eccentric town of Darby, New Hampshire.

"It's impractical to try to reverse the changes to the earth that already are producing a new and disturbing planetary ecology," Luci said. "Given the political and cultural divisions among humanity, given the differences among individuals, the chances of humans doing the right thing to save the planet and, ultimately, the species are close to zero. The solution is to change the species to adapt to the planet."

She talked with just a hint of a foreign accent. Polish? Hungarian? Howard didn't have a clue.

"We may not have the technology for long haul space travel," Lucy continued, "but we do have, or let's say we are close to, the technology to allow us to replace human biomass with factory-made components."

TREK: Do away with the human body?

"As we know it, yes," Luci said. "Eventually we will be able to transfer human identity, that is, everything in your brain that makes you you, into a computer chip. Human beings could live, for all practical purposes, as immortals. As spirits, let us say."

JAYU: You can't be serious.

"I am serious," Luci said. "We will exist as spirits but with all the human sensual apparatus available virtually, with no biological bodies to degrade."

"It sounds appalling to me," Missy said, but there was nothing in her tone to support her words.

She doesn't mean it, Howie. She wants "appalling."

"Are infirmity and death less appalling?" Luci asked. "Isn't death the one part of the human experience that most people could do without? And isn't the fear of infirmity one of the great burdens of human consciousness?"

Missy frowned at Luci's words. Howard had always liked Missy because she was feisty.

"You're saying," Missy said, "that it's possible that I could transfer my baby's identity, her very being, her self awareness, her memories, her emotions — everything — into a permanent state of consciousness without a body?"

Howard was thinking that Missy, like Tess Jordan, had big hair, but Missy's was messier, frizzy strawberry blond curls.

"Not only possible but likely, given the rapid growth of technology," Luci said. "Even if you — we — don't work toward this end, other factions in the world will. Whoever gets there first will inherit the earth."

At this point Origen, who until now Howard had not even noticed, said in a soft voice, "What's left of it."

JAYU: What about bodies? How can you be human and not have a body?

Luci turned to her partner. "Wiqi?"

"We can make bodies that resemble humans, that have human sensation, feelings and appetites, but with minds that have much more processing power," Wiqi said with a slight tremor in his voice. "We can stimulate, no, I mean simulate all human experiences, from the appreciation of the colors of leaves to the rupture, I mean rapture, of ffffffffffffalling in love."

JAYU: In other words, all that you are can be made in a factory, the parts replaced?

"Yes, when the parts weird out. I mean — Luci, what do I mean?"

"When the human parts wear out, not weird out," Luci said.

"The ability to transfer an identity from a biological state to a computer is already something our writers are working on for our game," Missy smiled now.

Do you get it, Howie? She's been playing dumb; she knew all along what Luci would say.

Why?

This whole scene is an act to impress the investors.

Missy talked on, "Imagine a breakdown in civility and order, in which everyone fights for immortality. It's a great situation for a video game, because it pits the haves against the have nots. But real world? I don't now."

"What is halved knot?" Wiqi asked.

"I'll explain later, Wiqi," Luci said.

SOLOMON: We are talking here about the Singularity.

JAYU: Yes, the theory that eventually humans and computers will merge. In fact, they already have.

TREK: Nobody believes in the Singularity anymore. It's an idea that has run off its rails.

"Though it lives in our game, but . . . ?" That was Birch who spoke, leaving his thought to be completed by his minions.

Wiqi looked at Luci. "Shall I?" he said.

"Now is as good a time as any," Luci said.

Wiqi held his hands up and wiggled his fingers. Then he pressed the inside of the left wrist with his right thumb. There was a clicking sound and a second later the hand was removed.

"It's a prosthesis, and you can't tell it from the real thing," Luci said. "Wiqi lost the hand and parts when he fell out of a hot air balloon when he was ten years old."

Something in Birch changed. His public facial expression of authority and charm disappeared and Howard could see the curiosity in him, an eagerness to know, even a hint of desperation.

Wiqi returned the hand to its position at the left wrist.

Luci seemed to anticipate Birch's question. "Wiqi designs and assembles the hardware," Luci said. "I write the software that the brain uses to operate the prosthesis."

"What's the next step?" Birch asked.

TREK: Let me guess, brain implantation.

"Correct," Wiqi said.

"We're experimenting with Cooty using . . . let us call them 'mono bots,'" Luci said.

Birch made eye contact with the investors, though he spoke to the nurses. "You did get his permission?"

"And in writing?" said Missy, who had a law degree.

"Of course. He's a willing subject," Luci said. "We're working right now not only to improve Cooty Patterson's recall but to replace his brain cells with tiny computer chips."

"Delivered by mono bots," Wiqi said.

Birch nodded in approval. "You've noticed that I walk with a limp," he said.

"Yes, and if I'm scanning you properly, that you live with pain," Luci said. "Is your defect due to genetics?"

"No, frostbite when I was a boy," Birch said. "I had my toes amputated, and my foot has never been right since. I don't get enough circulation, the nerves flare on me, and the skin is discolored."

"I'm hearing a song in my head," Wiqi said. "Why am I so black and blue?"

JAYU: A cultural metaphor, the song sung by Billie Holiday.

"He must have picked it up from Wikipedia," Luci said and turned to Birch. "Wiqi has trouble with words that contain multiple meanings. He's a Wikipedia devotee, which is why his parents started calling him Wiki when he was a little boy, but he didn't like the 'k' so he settled on Wiqi with a q."

"I love u, too," Wiqi said.

"Most of the words in all languages I know of have more than one meaning," Birch said.

"Yes, languages do need to be cleaned up," Luci said. "Wiqi might have linguistic problems, but he's quite good at what he does. Birch, in order for us to outfit you with a functional prosthesis of your bad foot, we will have to take several MRIs of your brain."

Birch turned to Missy and smiled. She seemed to read his thoughts, then speak them. "We'll incorporate this situation in our video game," she said.

That elicited a spontaneous cheer from the geek chorus.

"You can program my artificial foot to coordinate with electrical impulses generated from my brain?" Birch said to Luci.

"Exactly. You get it, you understand. It's why we agreed to conduct our experiments here in Upper Darby," Luci said.

Missy smiled; she did know all along.

But Birch didn't. Or did he? Who's in charge here?

Don't you get it, Howie? For these people, everything is a show for the investors.

No doubt to get dough for their game.

Yes.

"All of us in Geek Chorus Software see the implications, the possibilities," Birch glowed with hope and a kind of love that Howard could imagine but could not experience, love for the particular person he happened to be with at a particular moment but also love for the group, love for all, minion-love.

"All can be saved: we at Geek Chorus Software live and work to manifest that idea," Origen said.

At that moment a dark-complected woman in her sixties entered. She wore a full billowing skirt, a white blouse, a necklace, and matching bracelet of silver fashioned to represent sticks and feathers. Her long straight black hair only held a few white hairs. On the back of her right hand was a small tattoo of a stick.

Birch glanced at the investors and said, "Our surprise guest for the evening. You've all read her work, and you know she will be joining F. Latour and Web Clements as writers for Darby Doomsday; here she is in person. Formerly of Quebec, now a resident of the Butterworth house in Upper Darby, please welcome Josephine Abare."

Josephine worked her way through the investors and the geeks— who Howard now thought looked like raccoons without their masks— and shook Birch's hand. Then she stood with her back to the fireplace and addressed the minions.

"Thank you, Birch. I'm very happy to be under contract with Geek Chorus Software. Writing about Darby is more than a job for me, it's almost like writing a family memoir. As some of you know, our little mountain, Abare's Folly, was named after one of my ancestors, who was a farmer and drover. Local people say the folly was trying to establish a hill farm above the 2,000-foot level, but in family lore the folly was leaving Canada and putting aside the French language in favor of English."

Josephine talked in a musical voice in an accent that seemed a mix-master of Canadian French, New England Yankee, and Native American.

"My main motivation in joining Geek Chorus Software is in helping Birch and the conservancy board preserve the Trust lands forever. I have a personal stake in the land. Shortly before she died, my mother confessed that she was a member of the Connissadawaga Native American tribe. She had rejected her people to marry my father, but the guilt remained with her. On her deathbed she asked me to be more involved with the tribe. It's a very small group with few members left. Our ancestral lands are on what we now call the Trust. I would like to see those lands remain undeveloped, so our interests are the same as Birch Latour's and all of you gathered here.

"The Connissadawaga people have no representation in Washington; we are not recognized as a nation. The few of us remaining hope to change that situation, but it will take time. After much research and after long talks with the few living elders of the tribe, I've come to the conclusion that what we think of as core American values—do your own thing, the individual before the group, some kind of loose-knit democracy, and above all a belief in the idea of individual freedom—is actually derived through cultural osmosis from the native peoples. The values of what it means to be American were already here when the Europeans arrived. I see those values personified in the land itself, which is another reason we support the idea of the Trust."

"Even aboriginal peoples need money in these times," said one of the investors, a woman in scarves who carried a computer tablet.

"Excuse me," Birch interrupted, "would you identify yourself so that my colleagues know who you represent?"

"Of course," the investor said. "I represent H.C. Wentworth, the CEO and president of Paradise Lots Covenant."

"Yes, we understand that we need to raise funds," Josephine Abare said. "Once we gain recognition as a nation, we have a plan to open a riverboat gambling casino in the Connecticut River."

"All can be saved," Origen said.

"The all will end up in our game, Darby Doomsday," said Missy with a faint smile as she looked at Birch.

"I'm afraid so, yes," Birch said.

"Excuse me. Grace will be hollering for sustenance early, so I'm going to bed," Missy said. On her way up the stairs she passed Howard, pointed her finger at him, and said, "Bang, bang you're dead."

Howard ducked.

"It's past my bed time, too," Origen said.

Howard stopped Origen in the hall just before the staircase.

"I remember you now," Howard said.

"And your point is . . . ?" Origen gave Howard that malicious smile.

"You used to be a . . ."

"A punk."

"Yeah, that's it. If I remember correctly you ripped up the country-side in a Trans Am and you had some kind of run-in with the Jordans over the Witch. There were rumors."

"That I was a serial killer. Do I look like a killer?"

"To me you do, yes."

Origen laughed. "I had a misspent youth, Constable — I will admit that much." Origen held out his hands. "If it will make you feel better, put the cuffs on. I actually enjoy restraints."

"Not today, I lost the key," Howard said, taking a step backwards.

"All can be saved, even you, Constable."

That was the end of the encounter, though it left Howard uneasy. He didn't trust Trans Am, or Origen, whatever his name was.

⚜ ⚜ ⚜

Later in the evening after the discussions had quieted down, geeks and guests went off to their rooms, and Howard and Birch sat alone before the dying fire.

"You believe all that stuff?" Howard asked Birch.

"Of course. I am a believer; I believe in all the -isms, and I believe in all the gods; I believe in everything and everybody," Birch said. "No one religion, no one economic system, no one philosophy has all the answers, but they all have an answer or two. The key to a sustainable future is to piece together the good parts of the -isms and religions of the cultural past of our species into something like one of Grandma Elenore's quilts."

"You got those ideas from Origen?"

"Partly, yes."

"And you're serious about them," Howard said.

"I'm afraid I am serious, yes."

"Must weigh you down. I was never serious," Howard said.

"That's your strategy for getting through this sad life, Grandpa, but it's not available to me; I have so many other people to think about." He made a circling motion with the index finger of his right hand to indicate the minions that filled the Manse.

61

"Your company, the whichimcallits?" said Howard.

"Geek Chorus Software."

"You're making a computer game?"

"A video game, yes," Birch said, flashing his mysterious smile. "In Darby Doomsday, the forests all over the world are dying. Plagues are killing off humanity. One answer is to change human beings through 'transfer,' just like Luci said, alter human genetics to accommodate a polluted world."

"You and Missy knew all along what Luci and Wiqi were talking about. I thought so."

"Oh, was it that obvious?" Birch gave a little laugh. "It's always better that our investors believe that they are discovering us through their own devices or through casual interaction than for us to preach to them, which I am afraid I am prone to do."

"You were telling me about the game."

"Yes. An alternate solution to changing human beings through transfer is to find an antidote to the diseases that are killing the forests and people. The game players choose a side to fight on. Or they can join a terrorist organization, which attempts to destabilize both sides. They want to secede from the United States. One of the subplots is to destroy the meetinghouse where a presidential debate is being held. We have the Civil War all over again, and it starts right here in Darby."

"How can you sound so cheerful about it?"

"It's just a game, Grandpa, and I think it will provoke discussion and generate some revenue: that's the smily-face part."

Howard thought something was wrong with all this, but he couldn't find words to voice his reservations. He compromised by giving Birch his best glower, but it only made Birch smile with affection and pity — there there, Grandpa, you can't help it if you can't catch up.

Finally, Birch said, "Big theme we're dealing with: breaking apart the United States of America — from USA to DSA, the Divided States of America. In the real world, who knows? In our game, it all gets played out in Darby in different ways."

"Why Darby?"

"This is my home, Grandpa. It's what I know, what I love. I want to save the Trust lands from the upheaval caused by global climate change, overpopulation, an economic system structured along the lines of a pyramid scheme, retro governments, religious turmoil, not to mention just plain human greed. The game is a way to test real world ideas without harm. Plus, as I mentioned earlier . . ."

"It fills the piggy bank. I'm figuring this game has to be Missy's idea?"

"Not really," Birch said. "Missy and I and Bez are synthesizers, facilitators, coordinators, not creators. Well, Bez is a creator in his own way. Darby Doomsday grew out of an unpublished novel called *I LOVE U* by film scriptwriter Web Clements, who is Wiqi's uncle. In the game different forces fight each other for the soul and the very existence of humanity and the secrets to the Singularity."

"Good guys and bad guys," said Howard.

"No, Grandpa," Birch shook his head. "In a way they're all good guys, and they're all bad guys. The competing forces—the environmental freaks, the transfer visionaries, the misplaced romantic seceders—each group has an idea that may or may not save Darby. It's up to the game players to decide which ideas to use and how to implement them while at the same time fighting competing groups, which have their own ideas. Meanwhile, in the real world we feed the game data from our players into a main frame to produce some meaning that might have value. The overarching idea is that no one or two players can produce a solution to the world's problems, but all the players together can prepare humanity for the future; big data only needs to be stitched together with computing power to do that job."

"Like your Grandma Elenore's quilts."

"That's right, Grandpa. It was Grandma Elenore who gave me the idea to unite the -isms."

"Sounds to me, though, there's going to be no end of war to get the fabric for this quilt," Howard said.

"Well, yeah, it's a video game. You have to spill blood and splash guts, or else you can't get the investors."

"Investors. What do you need them for?"

"For the money, Grandpa. You can't do anything without money— somebody has to pay Trek, Jayu, and Solomon," Birch laughed, sad and rueful. "But it's also because I believe." He thumped his chest with his fist. "I believe in computer simulations that tell us about climate change, demographics, economics, even the stock market; the future of humanity is in a chip and the cookies we leave in the computers of our gamers. Darby Doomsday is a computer simulation of real-world Darby. By creating the game and by exploiting the creativity of the players, I can do a better job as steward of the Trust lands."

"I got a question for you, Birch."

"Sure, Grandpa."

"All those educated people here tonight, they kind of worship you, don't they."

"I think worship is too strong a word."

"Well, you gotta admit you're head honcho around here."

"So I am."

"You know what that means, right? You get to the top of the heap and somebody wants to knock you off."

"Yes, I am aware of that."

Something in Birch's voice told Howard that Birch didn't want to think about the possibility that one or more of his friends, not to mention random enemies, might want to betray him. There were so many parts to this young man. Howard wanted to hug him as if Birch were a small boy again, but of course he didn't.

DRIVING FOR JESUS

LATER THAT NIGHT, Howard and Birch met with Obadiah and Charley in Birch's office, formerly the pool room in the days when men smoked cigars. The room was cluttered with samples of Birch's hall-of-mirrors identity: a crucifix (gift from his grandmother Elenore Elman); pictures of the mother he had never known; an artist rendition of the hippy bus in the woods where his father had raised him; a black and white photograph of his grandmother Persephone Salmon teaching him to drive, and another of his grandfather Raphael dressed for bird hunting standing beside the Bronco when it was new; various wooden spoons, some hand-carved by Birch's dad, some by Birch; storyboard drawings from Darby Doomsday. Howard was cheered by snapshots of himself and his trash collection truck in bygone days with his crew, Cooty Patterson and Pitchfork Parkinson. There were also computer printouts of pictures of Birch with his first best friends and confidants, Missy and Bez, on Grace Pond and in the tree house they built on the Trust when they were kids, and Birch's photographs of deer that he had stalked on the Trust lands with all the guile of a hunter, though he did not kill. There was also a framed and glassed copy on vellum of the Trust's charter beside Birch's degrees from Dartmouth College.

Birch had a great big desk that held a great big computer, but it was a smaller table that caught Howard's attention. The table was three feet wide, five feet long, designed like a three-by-five index card. In place of the white space of the card was the blond sapwood of lilac. In place of the blue lines and of the one red line was the darker heartwood of lilac. Lilac had been Lilith Salmon's favorite flower. Inlaid on the table in dark lilac heartwood, as if typed, along the first line was the phrase "EXT. DARBY — DOOMSDAY."

You don't know what "EXT." means, do you, Howie?

So what?

The table was off to the side under a window that overlooked the lilac bushes Birch's mother had planted on the day he was born. The lilacs were now mature and grand. In May they would burst forth with fragrant purple flowers. Howard occasionally would catch Birch sitting at the chair, reading, or writing on a note card, or gazing out the window, perhaps thinking of his mother. In a corner were a dozen or so walking sticks of various kinds of hardwood one might find on the Trust lands — sugar maple, red maple, white oak, red oak, ash, cherry, apple, elm, locust, beech, shag bark hickory.

You can make songs from the names of trees. Who had said that?

It was Heather. Remember her, the daughter you betrayed?

Another furnishing in the office might confuse the casual visitor, but Howard knew what it was: a shaving horse, a low bench with a foot-operated vice. F. Latour carved his wooden spoons on such a device. He had made this particular shaving horse for his son. On the floor were wood shavings, and on the bench of the shaving horse was a draw knife and a walking stick Birch had shaved out of a maple sapling. Birch had told Howard that working with a draw knife on the shaving horse was his way of relaxing. Howard knew it was more than that. It was Birch's way of staying connected to his father. Howard admired F. Latour tremendously for the way he had brought up Birch; the two were so close.

How to say, Son, you done good with your boy, like I never done with you.

You want me to apologize for being myself?

Yes, and while you're at it, confess love without being sarcastic.

I don't know how to do any of that.

Too bad, old man, too bad.

Birch sat in an arm chair in a circle with Howard and the loggers. He made it a point never to sit behind his huge desk with its wide computer screen when he had guests in his office, because he didn't want to appear in a superior position. He would be a leader among the people, not above them.

"We've found out that a logging truck with a faded blue cab and a crunched right fender was coming down the road from the Trust," Birch said.

"That would be Buzz Dorne's rig," Obadiah said.

"Old Man Dorne's boy," Howard said.

"I don't know him," Birch said.

"Buzz was the youngest Dorne," Obadiah said. "The old man left his place to the oldest boy. The daughters cleared out of Darby."

"Buzz bought that truck and went out on his own," Charley said.

"Time payments, no doubt," Howard said.

"Charley," Obadiah asked, "do you remember who he drives for?"

"He's pretty much a freelancer. He's done some work for us."

"Really?" said Birch. "That means he knows the Trust."

"That's right, but he wouldn't of stole that elm tree. He's an honest man, if I'm any judge of character," Obadiah said.

"Plus he doesn't do logging, he's just a hauler," Charley said. He was looking at Howard.

"Yeah, I know Buzz," Howard said. He was amused by the gurgle of Obadiah's strong local upcountry accent backwashing against Charley's thick urban New Jersey accent.

Quite a pair. Just what do they do when they get together?

I'd rather not think about it.

Yeah, and they probably don't want to think about your connubials either.

🦅 🦅 🦅

After the loggers retired to their room, Howard and Birch went outside to Cooty's cabin to check on the centenarian. The sky was overcast and it was dark, so that the glow from embers of the fire under the stew pot seemed like concentrated starlight that had fallen out of the sky. In the background was the apple tree from the original site of Cooty's cabin. Howard looked to see if any apples still clung to the tree. It was too dark to tell.

As they approached they saw a light go on in the cabin. How did they get electricity into the cabin? Underground? Generator? Howard wasn't sure. Cooty was at the door leaning on his cane before they arrived. He was wearing a hospital johnny gown. Howard worked very hard to avert his eyes from the occasional revelations of the old man's privates, surprisingly outlandish.

"Luci told me you were asleep when she checked an hour ago," Birch said.

"I might have been asleep, I can't remember," Cooty said.

Birch fetched Cooty's smashed-toe colored sweater and put it around the centenarian's shoulders. The three men sat on stools at Cooty's tiny table, on top of which rested today's *Keene Sentinel*. Cooty had cut out a story about a rash of burglaries. He handed the story to Birch.

"Look, they hit every town surrounding Darby but not Darby," Birch said.

"Maybe there's an angel in Darby," Cooty said.

"Protecting us from burglars, like a guardian angel?" Birch posed the question. His faint smile told Howard that Birch was humoring the centenarian.

"Or maybe the angel works for the burglar," Cooty said with a chuckle. Was he humoring Birch?

"Cooty, after all these years I can never figure you out," Howard said.

"Me neither," Cooty said. "You fellas look hungry to me."

Howard and Birch realized they hadn't eaten in quite a while. They went outside and returned with bowls of stew. They quietly ate the stew with wooden spoons.

Cooty fell into a state somewhere between a nap and a trance. Howard and Birch put Cooty to bed, then they shut off the light and headed out, stopping at Howard's PT Cruiser for a brief conversation in the dark. Howard cranked up his hearing aid.

"Birch, you find anything on the Internet about elm trees?" Howard asked.

"Maybe," Birch said. "There's a visiting fellow at Dartmouth, expert on elm trees and the treatment of diseased elms. He helps the college with its few remaining elms. I've made an appointment to talk with him late tomorrow morning. I'll drive up. I want to see what he has to say and spend some time in the library."

"Give you a chance to drop in on your dad while you're at it," Howard said.

"Yes, and my brother and sister."

"Meanwhile, I'll catch Buzz Dorne first thing in the morn before he takes off for work."

※ ※ ※

When Howard got home he had the crazy idea that Elenore was in their bed and fast asleep with Music, the cat they had decades ago when Heather was still with them. The door to the bedroom was closed, and Howard did not open it. He knew his wife was dead — he knew — but he was afraid that somehow he would involuntarily conjure her from the nether world and she would appear in their bed.

He slept in his usual place on the couch. He was up twice during the night to pee, awake at 5:30 for yet another pee. He was bone weary, and he tried to sneak in another hour of shut-eye but his brain said no. He made himself a cup of instant coffee and downed it with an English muffin globbed with peanut butter.

Why did they call them "English" muffins, and why "French" fries? Or "Irish" stew? Or "Danish" pastries?

Who cares, shut up.

He ate his breakfast while he checked his email on the computer that he'd taught himself to use when he had the trash collection route. Howard, who was mechanically inclined, had no problems learning the computer. Elenore had been scared of it at first, but eventually taught herself to work a spreadsheet to do the trash collection bookkeeping, and she loved her mobile phone.

There was a reminder message from Birch that he was going to spend the day at Dartmouth "researching" and stay that night at his dad's place in nearby West Lebanon. The weatherman called for rain in the afternoon.

At 6:45 AM Howard got up the courage to go into the bedroom. He threw open the door and leaped forward, or anyway put on a show of leaping. The bed was made, and he was relieved to find that nobody was in it. He backed out and shut the door.

He pulled on his boots and his black and red, went outside, took a quick look around at his junked cars, slid his fanny into the PT Cruiser and headed for the Buzz Dorne Place, turning down River Road, which ran more or less parallel to the Connecticut River, the boundary line between New Hampshire and Vermont. It was a pretty road, one side wooded hills and deep gorges whose steepness and depth were often invisible because of the thick forest cover, the other side river flats where farmers grew corn and other crops and where black and white cows grazed like twisted out of shape ambulatory checkerboards.

Ambulatory? Where'd you get that word, Howie?

Why, from that EMT guy, Archer Mayor.

Every once in a while there'd be a glimpse of the river, slow moving here, because it was backed up by a dam in Brattleboro, Vermont, ten or so miles downstream. He noticed some truck tracks down by the Town Farm and he could see cars and pickups parked by the former county jail. Some kind of construction project was under way. The Town Farm, which sat on a bluff above the river, had evolved over the decades into a jail, but the county had built a new, modern facility in another town and put up the Town Farm property for sale. Howard made a mental note to check with Bev Boufford, Darby's administrative assistant, to find out what was going on.

Down the road from the Town Farm was an exempt sand bank that had been owned by that big-hipped farmer Avalon Hillary, but Hillary had sold out and moved to parts unknown after his wife passed away. The sand bank was a famous lovers lane for young couples or cheating marrieds going parking.

Beyond the Hillary acreage was Morgan Grayson's housing development that hadn't worked out too well. Only four homes had been put up before Grayson had been arrested for diddling young boys. One of those homes was the Dorne property, a simple ranch-style house, a two-car garage with basketball hoop, a great big lawn, a bird feeder, and a snowmobile with a blue plastic cover. Howard could understand why a family would go into debt to buy a snow machine, but why would these same people spend good money to establish a lawn, which required purchase of a lawn mower?

Why spend money on unnecessary machines? Why make work for yourself? Why a lawn? What is the point of a lawn?

That's just loose thinking, Howie.

It's the only kind of thinking I know.

The driveway was oversized to accommodate Buzz Dorne's weary International logging truck with picker loader mounted behind the cab. All the new ones had the loader in the rear. Howard got out of his PT Cruiser and before knocking at the door took a long look at the logging truck. He hoped to find a branch or maybe some bark from the elm tree but, remarkably, the bed of the truck was spotless. Since when did Buzz Dorne hose down his rig?

The Dorne household was in an uproar.

Howie, you forgot what morning is like when parents are getting ready to go to work and preparing kids for school.

Howard sat embarrassed and mute for fifteen minutes while children and parents vied for the one bathroom in the house and slurped bowls of cereal. Finally, the missus drove away with two of the kids to drop off at the elementary school before she went to her job at the train car fix-up shop in North Walpole, and the other kid, the oldest boy, waited outside for the bus to bring him to the high school in Keene. Howard took note of a fake parchment of the ten commandments held by magnets on the door of the fridge. Thou shalt have no strange gods before me.

What the hell does that mean?

God fears the competition.

Eventually, Howard was left alone with Buzz Dorne.

Buzz was medium height, on the heavy side, with big, thick hands, but he had a cheerful face, part angel maybe, Howard thought, remembering Cooty's words. Buzz's buzz-cut blond hair was getting a little thin. Howard thought Buzz had the body of a pulling guard and the face of a water boy.

"What's up?" Buzz said, sipping his coffee.

"I'm here on police business," Howard said.

"I didn't think you actually did any of that, know what I mean." Buzz's "know what I mean" was more a call for approval than a question.

Howard laughed, "First time for anything."

"Look, Howie, this is not the best time for us log truckers, know what I mean," Buzz said. "It's fall mud season and not much logging going on, but I got a job lined up today, the only one this week. Can't this wait until the morrow?"

"A job? Why I'll tag along and we can talk while you work," Howard said.

Howard admired Buzz's skill in manipulating the big truck out of the driveway without any apparent forethought or nervousness, even though his rear wheels were only inches from the ditch that dropped down four feet.

"I gotta get these logs on the rig before the sky takes a douche," Buzz said. "It's already pretty muddy in that field, and I'm afraid we'd sink to the axles with a full load if it rains, especially on that wicked curve off the bluff onto the flats, know what I mean?"

"Something tells me I don't have to ask a question—you know the question," Howard said. "Were you out and about with your truck in the last couple days?"

"No. I was pruning my apple trees and I burned a little brush. Look, I didn't get the permit, but it was just a small fire. I thought, God will forgive me for this one. My oldest boy he wants to go to divinity school. It's going to cost me, know what I mean."

"Day Cooty Patterson turned one hundred, your rig was seen with a load on. Tell me about that. When I get a load on everybody notices."

"Oh, Lord, forgive me," Buzz said, and Howard knew it was a sincere prayer directed at the all mighty.

Suppose the all mighty is only partly mighty, then what?

Then we got a more familiar world.

"I know you're working your way up to telling me something, Buzz. Take your time."

"Here we are," Buzz said, and he surprised Howard by turning into the drive of the Town Farm only a mile down the road. They drove onto a tractor road in the cornfield. It was muddy and Howard could feel the truck laboring as Buzz shifted gears.

"See, I gotta get the logs out this morning, because by this afternoon what with the rain predicted, know what I mean."

The river looked like a long brown lake from this prospect. Across were cornfields in Great Meadow, Vermont. Howard figured there'd be a family of wild turkeys in the field picking at the leftovers from the cut corn. Here on the New Hampshire side Howard could see logs stacked up and beyond them the start of a construction project.

Buzz anticipated Howard's question and said. "It's going to be a pavilion."

"For what?"

You don't actually know what a pavilion is, do you?

Probably neither does Buzz.

"Nobody knows, except maybe Cod Prell — he's the architect," Buzz said.

"Looks to me like it's going to be a dock, a great big dock. I don't get it."

"That's why they call it a pavilion." As Buzz spoke, he skillfully turned his rig around and backed it to the logging yard, which contained white birch logs and a few pines.

Howard helped Buzz wrap chains around one log at a time, and then he stepped back and watched as Buzz worked the loader to hoist the log in position on the truck. It wasn't much of a job, but it had Howard huffing and puffing.

"I gotta make two stops," Buzz said. "The pines are going to Cersosimo's and the birch down the road to Ouellette's."

On the drive to the mills Howard couldn't shut Buzz up, but he wouldn't divulge any information that the constable was looking for.

"You know it's a shame that there's so few sawmills left in New Hampshire and Vermont," Buzz said as the big truck rumbled down River Road headed for Brattleboro. "Take a look at the logging trucks on the interstate. They all got Quebec plates and they're all headed north with our natural resources, know what I mean. Our towns, they're dying, Howie. Pretty soon Darby will be just another burb of Keene. Already is actually."

"You like to talk when you get nervous, doncha?" Howard said.

"I was always the quiet one in the family growing up, but I was just busting at the seams to speak my piece. Well, I found a good woman and she brought Jesus into my life, and Jesus he said, 'Buzz, you can talk a blue streak, and I'll be with you to listen even if the world puts in the ear plugs.'"

"When Jesus talks do you actually hear him, and what does he sound like, Bing Crosby, or somebody like that?"

"Bing Crosby, the hockey player?"

"No, that's Sidney Crosby. I'm talking about a singer."

"I don't know no Bing Crosby."

"Before your time. The trouble with getting old, Buzz, is you know too many things that don't mean anything anymore. It's like your mind is an overfilled dumpster and the trash collector is on strike."

"I remember growing up, you were the trash collector in town, Howie."

Howard and Buzz talked on. The pine logs were dropped at the Cersosimo mill in Brattleboro, and the birch logs at Ouellette's Birch Mill, where the logs were cut with a band saw and put through machines to make Scrabble squares to be stamped with letters, which would be arranged on game boards to make words that would be scattered by a cat and rearranged into a pattern and questioned on the basis of their authenticity and so on until the human epoch ended with fire or perhaps ice or maybe just a great stillness.

That's your end, Howie. No fire, no ice, just stillness, a long word but only worth a point per letter on Elenore's Scrabble board, which she played alone because you didn't like losing and would not indulge her and, face it, didn't know that many words to spell. Cowreckly? "Howie," Elenore had said, "'correctly' does not have a 'wreck' in it."

"Constable, are you listening to me?" Buzz said, his feelings hurt by Howard's inattention.

"I'm sorry, Buzz, sometimes I turn down my hearing aid so I can hear my own thoughts," Howard said, and he cranked up the gadget. "Now what were you saying?"

"I was saying that the boy's going South to divinity school because there aren't no good ones up here. Darby's got a church, but it's kinda of a godless place, I gotta admit, but don't get me wrong, Darby is home, God's country, even if He's a no show, know what I mean."

"Last time I was in a church I was thinking that the main aisle would make a nice bowling alley."

"I bowled a 294 once."

"You're lying to me, Buzz."

"Okay, 254."

"Thank you."

It was almost noontime, and Buzz was pulling his rig back into the driveway of his nice little ranch house on River Road in (according to Buzz's lights) the doomed town of Darby. It was starting to rain, a cold November rain.

"You were saying?" Howard said, and he gave Buzz his steely eyed look that usually elicited cooperation from weak minds.

"I thought you were leaving," Buzz said.

"Buzz, this is your constable talking," Howard said. "If you don't tell me what I need to know, I'm going to move into your house, stink up your bathroom, drink your beer, steal your dog's loyalty, boss your kids around, and enjoy connubials with your old lady."

"Okay, Howie, I get it." Buzz took a deep breath, puffed his cheeks, blew out the air, sucked in more air. "This fella shows up at my house, and I could tell right away something wasn't right, know what I mean, but I went against my better judgment. He says we want to rent your truck for a small job. Cash on the barrelhead."

"He said 'we.'"

"Yeah, he said we."

"What did he look like?"

"He looked like anybody else, like you or me, like I knew him but I didn't know him."

"What the hell does that mean?"

"I can't say. He looked familiar, but I knew I hadn't seen him before, know what I mean."

Howard wanted pull Buzz's nose, but calmed himself and said, "What did he talk like?"

"Like you or me."

"How old was he?"

"Like you or me."

"Buzz, you're maybe forty. I'm times two plus that."

"To tell you the truth I don't pay much attention to what people look like unless they're of the female persuasion, know what I mean."

"When you say like you or me, you mean he was not like one of the new people, not from down country, nor a big shot?"

"Right, just regular people, like I knew him but I didn't know him."

"Anything unusual — unregular?"

"He was carrying a wad of bills."

Howard was thinking of his own wad of bills, the comfortable feeling of five thousand in your pocket, of the Jordan men who didn't trust banks or anybody and who often carried their life savings in their wallets. "You trusted your rig to a stranger?" Howard said.

"Howie, he gave me a deposit, and well, like I said, my business is slow at this time of year and I'm trying to save a little extra . . ."

"To help your boy in divinity school — and?"

"And wasn't I surprised when he returned the truck all cleaned up, know . . ." Buzz didn't finish, because Howard put his hand over his mouth.

✧ ✧ ✧

Howard headed for home, not thinking about what he had learned and not learned from Buzz Dorne, not even thinking about dinner; he was thinking about how he was going to tell Charlene he was not going to Port Mansfield, South Texas, until he had caught the people who had cut down his tree.

How to say it and make it make sense?

How? Maybe cop talk. I am not going to exit the premises until I catch the perpetrator that absconded with my elm tree.

He ate tuna out of the can along with three slices of toast, and with no Elenore around to check up on him, what the hell, he had a beer and just a teensy shot of Four Roses, but before he poured it he opened the bedroom door just to make sure Elenore had not returned from the dead to snick at him for drinking in the middle of the day. "If you were here, I'd give up the booze altogether," he said aloud to the empty bed. The bed responded, "Liar!" He shut the door. He figured he had about an hour of stimulation before his body yelped for a nap.

He drove off in the PT Cruiser, glancing in the rear view mirror for a flash of his junked cars, objects to admire.

What is it about you, Howie?

I like rust, I like dead end streets, I like a break in a Jack Landry curve ball, I like a crack in the pavement; there's humanity in a mistake; there's entertainment in guesswork; and hope is a four-letter word.

He arrived at the town offices and parked in the space reserved for the Mini Cooper of Selectman Lawrence Dracut.

The only person at this hour in the town hall was Bev Boufford. Bev was only maybe fifty, but she acted seventy-five. She refused to use a computer and typed all the town business on an ancient IBM Selectric typewriter. Howard figured she was sexually titillated by her power to manipulate the ball that struck the platen. Actually, it was Howard who was titillated watching her type. He had to resist the urge to shout "type my balls." Bev was one those women blessed with giant bazzooms. She had a big frame, wide all the way around, grand hips, protruding ass, shoulders like a sidewalk curb. With her squared glasses and drab gray dress she looked like a cement truck driving into the sun. Howard pictured himself with her naked, rasslin' in a giant bowl of Jello, an idea he got from the sight of her dessert on her desk.

"Bev," he said, "you know your way around these file cabinets."

Bev knew he was trying to butter her up, so she ignored him until she finished her typing, then she looked up at him as at a recently discovered stain on a prized blouse. She did not speak, just looked him over with a "well?"

"I'm happy to see you, too," Howard said, and then he explained what he was searching for. Bev might not be the most cheerful woman in Darby, but she was certainly good at her job. She knew right where to look for the files Howard wanted. He learned that some outfit called Paradise Lots Covenant, PLC, had bought the Town Farm property from the strapped-for-cash county government. PLC, where had he heard that name?

It was at the Manse, Howie.

Howard had felt like a real police detective uncovering privileged information until Bev set him straight. "Howie, this is not a secret — it was in the paper last week, because the company's plans are in the hands of the planning board."

"I only read the obituaries." He wondered how in the world the people who made up words could label stories about dead people with a word that sounded like oh-bitch-you-worry.

The company was proposing a "river walk" shopping plaza that would serve the entire region. Up on the bluff overlooking the river would be shops and restaurants; condominium units would be built around a town common dominated by a perfect replica of a functioning meetinghouse. Howard couldn't understand how such a plan could be a good investment until he read further. Below would be a pavilion and the Connissadawaga Native American Riverboat Gambling Casino anchored out in the middle of the river. Parking on the Vermont side would be in what was now a cornfield in the village of Great Meadow. A ferry would transport patrons to the gambling boat docked on the New Hampshire side.

Darby town officials had been working closely with the company on the plan. The current town hall would be razed and the town offices established in the new meetinghouse on the new common. The political parties were considering the new meetinghouse as a site for a debate between the presidential candidates. Darby was going to be on the map. All that remained to be done was the recommendation of the planning board's master plan and the voters' approval of the plan at the town meeting in March. The idea seemed unreal to Howard.

A presidential debate in little Darby, New Hampshire? And what about the Indian gambling casino? Just like in Birch's game. What to make of this combobulation between PLC and a computer game?

You don't know, do you?

Howard returned home pooped. One of the benefits of old age was that you didn't have to put in a day's work to feel as if you'd put in a day's work. He took his shoes off and lay on the couch. It was raining hard now, and the wind was blowing, and with his hearing aid at the max he could hear the rain tapping on the windows, a soothing sound. It wouldn't be a bad farewell to die listening to the rain in Darby, New Hampshire.

He shut his eyes and tried to think his way into a death knell or, more likely, just a nap. No doubt Buzz Dorne's truck had been used to transport the elm tree. It couldn't have gone too far since the truck had been returned all cleaned up not too much later. Howard made a mental note to check with local sawmills.

What about motivation, Howie? You still don't know why anyone would cut down a lone elm in the middle of nowhere.

Why does "nowhere" spell "now here"?

Howard tried to make a connection between PLC's plan for Darby and the cutting of his elm tree. PLC sought to completely transform the town of Darby. Good or bad for the town? Would the planning board endorse PLC? How did the Trust figure in? No answers.

Soon Howard was embroiled in one of those dreams that the dreamer partly controls.

He saw a shape in the window of his mobile home, Elenore trying to get in. She materialized and stood in front of him wearing a house dress and carrying her purse as if she had just returned from shopping.

"So the big C didn't get you after all?" Howard said.

She put the cell phone in her purse and said. "Why are you hanging on in Darby, Howie? It's crazy."

"They cut my tree down," he said in his usual defensive growl that Elenore had long ago learned to ignore.

"Howie, it's not your tree, and what difference does it make?"

"I can't figure," he said, weakly now.

"You know what I think," she paused.

Oh-oh, he thought, here comes the icepick in the eye.

"I think you are just looking for an excuse to stay in Darby."

"That occurred to me — yes. So what?"

"So, you signed the papers to divest yourself of this property. You can't stay here no more," she said.

"I can stay. Might be years before the new owners lay their claim." Funny how in a dream you can't tell a truth from a lie. Just like waking life, except in a dream the humor is more apparent. "I want to be at the town meeting to have my say on the PLC plan."

"And just what is your say, Howie?"

"I don't know. Politics confounds me. They're all trying to sharpen a steak to drive through your heart."

"Howie, it's not s-t-e-a-k, that's meat, it's stake, s-t-a-k-e." Howard saw the letters appear on giant scrabble squares made from white birch wood.

It's not just Wiqi Durocher who can't figure with the alphabet. Suppose Wiqi, not Latour, is my true son?

Then Birch would not be related to you. Might be better that way — for him.

And now the dream joined with memory.

"Howie, you're talking to yourself," Elenore said.

"Keeps me from getting too lonesome."

"Come with me to South Texas," she said.

"But you're dead." As soon as he spoke, he knew he'd said one of those terrible things. He had to find a way to make it up to her. "Okay, I'll go."

"You bum," Elenore said, and kicked a loose shoe across the room, as on occasion she had done in life.

Finally, he was angry, and it felt good to be angry. "Why did you do that?" He stood so he could look down instead of up at her. "I said I'd go didn't I, what the hell else do you want from me?"

"You'll go, but you'll be impossible to live with. You are such a horse's ass, Howie." She managed to be both near tears and in control. Howard marveled. "Here's what we're going to do," she jabbed the air with a finger. "You stay!"

"Don't point that thing at me, it might go off," Howard said to the finger.

Elenore gave him her you-idiot look. "Get this bug out of your system, then come and visit. Me, I'm gone."

She vanished, and Howard woke with a pang, thought he might be having a heart attack, but no, he was just a scared old man alone in a trailer encompassed by a fake house and the burden of time.

FIRST SNOW

THE WEATHER TURNED COLD and the sky threatened snow, though the forecast called for nothing more than a few flurries. Howard hoped for a big storm. He spent the rest of that day and the following steadily drinking beer and working on his vehicle. He changed the oil, put on snow tires, freshened the coolant, and installed winter wipers. What used to be a hour or so job dragged on over two days.

Why is it that the car companies can invent all these computer gizmos to make cars run better, but they can't make a windshield wiper that's worth a sweet patootee? Maybe I'll invent a new wiper system, and sell it to the Toy-oh-oh company for a zillion bucks and buy back my property.

Sure, Howie, and while you're at it turn back the clock so you can get a hard-on.

It used to be he'd be cheered when he saw the PT Cruiser in the driveway, parked a little turvy-topsy, because that meant Elenore was home. It meant a picked up house, food on the table, clean dishes, and the news of the day delivered in a delightful amazing-grace voice. After Elenore died Howard junked his pickup and adopted Elenore's PT Cruiser as his transportation so he could imagine that he was taking her to church.

Day three he decided to stop feeling sorry for himself, and drank coffee instead of beer with his breakfast. Now that he was sober his leg pains flared up. Good. Pain tells you you're alive. He drove to the auction barn. This time he got lucky, catching Critter and his boy as they were coming out the door about to leave.

Critter Jordan looked like an actor who wouldn't quite make the grade auditioning to play Evel Knievel. Billy boy looked at Howard as if Howard was the Devil's agent for the day-of-reckoning plan. Howard gave him a glower, and the boy averted his eyes.

"Critter," Howard barked from the rolled down window of the PT Cruiser, "I'd like to talk to you for a few minutes."

"Can't do it now, Howie, I'm off on a job," Critter said with the false cheer that was his trademark.

"It's official business, Critter. I'm here in my capacity as town constable."

"We didn't do nothing, right Billy?"

Billy appeared unsure what his reaction should be before he returned a bare nod.

Howard was thinking that Critter could just give him the finger and walk away and there would be nothing he could do about it. But Howard also knew how to use his voice to cow a man, and he knew Critter. Sneaky. But not one to call a bluff.

"It's talk to me or talk to Trooper Durling in the interrogation room of the state police barracks," Howard said, and he could see that Critter had already caved but was looking for a way to save face. Howard was fascinated, wondering how Critter would go about this task, and why saving face was so important to him. Then he understood. Critter wanted to look good in front of his boy. He'd have to give Critter an opening.

"Look, Critter, I know you got work to do, you're a busy man, so suppose I give you a hand while we talk?" Howard said.

Critter pretended with great gravity to consider this offer. "You're kind of elderly for moving furniture, aincha, Constable?" Critter said.

"I'll do as much as I can for a seventy-five year old with a bad leg," said Howard, who was eighty-six or eighty-five or maybe eighty-seven.

It took almost an hour to load the Bedford, which Critter and Billy would drive to a dealer downcountry someplace. Howard had to remind the Jordans that he couldn't walk fast. He didn't tell Critter that it hurt like the dickens to carry a load.

How many dickens, Howie?

Three or four.

Howard loved the inside of the auction barn. He had been a regular in the summer flea market Saturday mornings and Sunday afternoons after church, though he rarely bought anything. He liked looking at pictures of old cars, and he was attracted to wooden handmade items, especially furniture. He had little interest in the aesthetics of the objects and zilch knowledge of period pieces. His interest was purely in how furniture was made. He loved the joinery work, the remnant mark of a saw cut, the dovetail joints of desk drawers, the secret notes the craftsmen put on the parts of the wood that didn't show.

Howard's favorite aisle in the flea market was the tool aisle. The look, smell, and feel of old tools, especially tools no longer used, such as ice saws, stirred him. The way some men pictured themselves making money, or out-arguing or out-fighting other men, or creating great works of art, or being applauded for contributions to society, or worshipped for athletic exploits, or leading minions in battle, Howard Elman pictured cheering crowds watching him use those old tools with primo skill for their intended purposes.

Why does "purposes" sound so much like "porpoises"?

Intended porpoises?

He remembered as a boy watching men on Bent's Ice Pond in Keene sawing out blocks of ice. Today he visualized himself as a young single man in South Texas, wearing the dark leather-backed apron of an iceman. He picks up the block of ice with his tongs, those beautiful tongs, and flips it on that dark leather apron on his strong back, and delivers the block to a ranch fridge. Grabs a connubial from the ranch wife. And now he's back in New Hampshire sawing the ice.

Howard Elman, you are your hands.

Who had said that? Was it Ollie Jordan?

No, it was Elenore when she was young and beautiful and full of passion for you.

Howard, as he had labored with Buzz Dorne, now labored with Critter Jordan. No doubt the items he was helping load had been recently burgled. Critter accepting Howard's assistance in return for information was classic Jordan humor. Howard wondered: Who is using who here?

"You heard about the elm tree on the Trust lands that some sniveling coward cut down," Howard said as one making small talk.

"How do you know it was a coward?"

"A coward knows himself before everybody else by the way he over plans."

"Careful planning is just good sense. Nothing to do with a man's intestinal fortitude."

"Fortitude fartitude, what's the diff? Critter, I was in the state police barracks the other day, dropping off some evidence."

"Really?"

"That's right, and I was talking to Trooper Durling about the recent break-ins—the staties investigation." Howard put lot of emphasis on that word "investigation." He could see Critter wince. "Trooper Durling tells me there's some pro outfit working Cheshire County. I says to him I says 'pro,' how can you tell a pro from a couple high school kids breaking into a camp to party? And he says . . ." Howard paused until he sensed that Critter had that kicked in the solar plexus feeling, and he said, "Critter, I bet you can tell me what he said."

"Look, Constable, we both know my father was in the breaking and entering business, even Billy knows—right Billy?—but Billy and me, we're legit."

"I know that, Critter, but what surprised me was that the Trooper he called a bunch of low down, sneaky, snaky, house-breakers 'professionals.' There ain't no such thing as a professional burglar."

"You're wrong, Constable. My father may have been a felon, but remember he was never caught, and he had standards. Billy, tell the Constable about your grandfather Ike's standards."

Billy was obviously surprised and frightened that his father had brought him into the conversation.

"Go ahead, don't be shy, son. The Constable and I are just making conversation. You're pretty hale for a ninety-year-old, Howard. Go on now, Billy, tell him. We're not admitting to anything now. We're talking about standards."

"Grandpa Ike's Rule One," Billy said, speaking very carefully, as if in school, "is never take anything you can't use or sell. Rule Two, do not vandalize property. Only vandals vandalize."

"And what about vandals?" Critter coaxed his son.

"Vandals are the scum of the earth. They give the professional a bad name."

Howard said, "Critter, did Ike have a rule about how the burglar, professional or amateur, sticks his nose in the hamper to sniff the lady's dirty underwear to pleasure himself?"

Billy blushed a deep red, and Critter's smarmy smile vanished from his face. Howard could see the hatred in the man.

"A real professional could burgle you, Constable, and you wouldn't even know it," Critter said, and there was no false cheer in his voice.

Billy still hadn't recovered from his embarrassment; he was breathing in little gasps, choking back tears of rage and humiliation. Critter did not appear to notice.

Howard thought it was time to ease off. "Listen, Critter, I'm not going to worry myself over a bunch of burglaries in the region unless they happen in my town. Understood?"

Critter nodded. "Constable, my father had a bad reputation among certain people, but he was good to me and never stole from a poor family's cupboard."

Howard had to force himself to smile. Critter seemed to have forgotten that at one time he was under Ike's thumb.

"What I want you to know," Critter went on, "is these state police, they wasted a lot of time harassing a true gentleman that didn't do nobody no harm, stole only from the rich—a real Robinhood—but they would not investigate his murder." Critter waited for Howard to speak, but Howard held back, knowing Critter had more to say. "I don't put faith in law enforcement, Constable. Not only didn't you people not find my father's murderer, you didn't try."

"If I remember correctly, Constable Perkins interrogated you for the crime, so he did try," Howard said, droll.

"Yeah, right, it was because I was a Jordan. But you know what?" Critter paused.

"What?" Howard said straining to keep his voice soft. "What is it you're trying to tell me?"

"I know who killed Ike."

"You have evidence or only suspicions or what?" Howard realized as soon as he spoke that his sudden superior cop tone was all wrong for the moment. Oh-oh, Critter is going to clam up. And he did.

"Just kidding," Critter said with a phony ha-ha. "I think Billy and me can get the rest of the stuff on the truck. Thanks for your help."

"One more thing," Howard said, trying to wangle more information out of Critter, "I know you didn't take down that elm in the Trust."

"How could I when I was at Cooty's birthday party?"

That was the mistake Howard was looking for. If Critter didn't have something to do with the downing of his elm, how would he know that the act occurred during Cooty's party? Now what? Confront him?

He'll just shut down. Better play it cagey.

"If you hear anybody bragging I'd appreciate you giving me a call."

"Of course, Constable."

"Say, is Tess around? I'd like to talk to her."

Billy's demeanor suddenly changed. He was no longer embarrassed and enraged, he was righteous. Howard thought: they're in love with her, both of 'em.

"I don't think she wants to talk to you, Howie. She's a little—you know." Critter held an index finger at his temple and made circle motions.

"I see," said Howard.

He left Critter and Billy and went to Tess Jordan's apartment. No lights on. He knocked. No answer. He tried the door. Locked. He knew that Tess didn't own a vehicle. Where would she have taken off to on foot? He never saw her hitchhiking.

Wait a minute—how did she get to Cooty's birthday party? She'd arrived before Critter and Billy. Obviously somebody gave her a lift.

A lift? You mean like an English elevator?

Critter and his boy are behind the rash of burglaries in the county. Critter is teaching his son to be a felon. It's possible that Tess is involved. No doubt Critter also had something to do with the downing of the elm tree. But why? What's going on?

Admit it, you don't know anything, and even if you did . . .

I know, I know, so what?

Constable Elman drove back to his mobile home and couch and took a long nap. It wasn't the verbal and psychological struggle with Critter that wore him down, nor even the useless cogitating with the Voice, it was the manual labor. He woke in the early evening with an appetite. He was too lazy to prepare supper, so he drove over to Birch's place to mooch off Cooty's stew pot.

The cabin still looked rustic, but essentially it had been turned into a hospital sick room that just happened to be heated by a woodstove, though even that was not needed. A gas heater had been installed in case nobody was around to stoke the stove, and Cooty had electric lights and a buzzer to call his nurses from his cot. The centenarian was sleeping when Howard entered. Howard sat down at the tiny table and dug into the stew. He liked eating with a wooden spoon. The action made him feel like a tree, his arm a branch that ended with a twig that was the spoon.

Luci came in to check on Cooty as Howard was finishing up. Luci was dressed in blue jeans, a casual blouse, and track shoes lit up with colors.

How come nurses don't wear whites any more?

Because white means pure and nobody is pure anymore.

"He's been awful quiet—is he failing?" Howard asked.

"Oh, no, he's gaining," Luci said.

"Are you going to wake him up?"

"I never do that. I just like to check on him from time to time." She talked in an excited chirp in the strange accent Howard couldn't place. She struck Howard as a girl too curious ever to be bored, but also very competent. Not the kind of girl you protect, but the kind who protects you.

"I bet nothing throws you," Howard said.

"That's true," Luci said. "Grandpa—you don't mind if I call you Grandpa, do you?"

"No problem."

"We're doing some memory experiments with Cooty. You, Birch, and, when he's around, Latour all talk to Cooty. I've asked Cooty to remember those conversations as accurately as possible and then pass them on to me. Is that all right with you?"

"I suppose, but what's the point?"

"Two points. Measurement of Cooty's faculties and content for our game."

Howard nodded, though he had little idea what he was acceding to.

Luci left and Howard was alone with the old man. He watched Cooty's body fluttering with dreams. The centenarian reminded Howard of one of Elenore's nighties hanging on the clothesline in a light breeze. Even his breath smelled like what sunlight does drying fresh laundry.

"Good-bye old man," Howard said, and blew a kiss on Cooty's wispy hair. Then he walked next door to the Manse. The sky had cleared and the stars were out. Howard let himself in without knocking. Inside, the usual heated dinner discussion among the geeks of Geek Chorus Software was underway, but Birch was not among the minions. Howard found his grandson in his office with Luci and Wiqi, who was dressed pretty much identically to Luci. They looked like models for outdoor magazine ads. Birch sat in his desk chair, his bad foot bare and propped on a stool with a towel as a pad. The foot was swollen and bluish; without toes it didn't even look like a part of human anatomy.

"It's going to be amputated," Birch said with surprising cheer in his voice and a smile that revealed his braces.

"I'm sorry," Howard said.

"I'm not," Birch said. "The ankle doesn't work, and what's left of the foot is a constant pain. I hate it. Luci and Wiqi are going to outfit me with a prosthesis."

"He'll be able to run, hike, jump just like any normal person, and he'll be without pain," Luci said.

"Sometimes it's okie-dokie to be dee-feeted," Wiqi said, and turned to Luci. "Was that an appropriate metaphor?"

"Pretty close," said Luci. "I don't think watching Comedy Central is good for you."

"You people originally from Poland or maybe California?" Howard guessed.

"We're New Hampshire natives from Hanover," Luci said.

"That explains it," Howard said.

Luci and Wiqi left, and Howard updated Birch on his interviews with Buzz Dorne and Critter Jordan and his visit to the town hall. Then he asked Birch what he had learned about elm trees on his visit to Dartmouth College.

Later, that was the part of the conversation that Howard remembered most vividly, repeating the story to Cooty: Birch sitting at his desk, one shoe on, one shoe off, Howard on the guest chair.

"There's been a lot of work done on elm trees, but nothing that suggests a motive for our tree thief," Birch said.

"How's Freddy—excuse me, F. Latour? Still making fancy spoons from mountain laurel crotches?"

"Oh, sure, plus dad is working on his book of poems and taking care of Sephy and Nigel."

"I'm glad to hear he's keeping busy. I'll have to go up and see him sometime."

That's half a lie. You want to visit Freddy and those stuck up grandchildren, but you know that Katharine doesn't approve of you.

It's best for all concerned that I keep my distance.

Come on, Howie, tell the truth to yourself. You're afraid of an argument.

Okay, I'm afraid of an argument.

"What was that, Grandpa?"

"His poetry book has that funny name that I can't say."

"Yes, *Interstices.* Some of the stuff in it will probably find its way into our game."

"What about me, am I in it? Luci said something that rang a bell," Howard asked.

I don't care if I'm in the game.

Of course you care. Care is what is hanging you up.

"Yes, Grandpa, you're in it. Everybody in Darby we know is sort of in it," Birch said.

"What the hell is it, like a movie?"

"No, Grandpa, a movie ends after two hours. Darby Doomsday doesn't have an ending. We will keep adding to it the way Cooty adds to his stew pot. The game goes on and on like real life, and the players get to change the fictional world in ways that even we, the creators, cannot predict. Each player has his own alternative universe. It's interactive. It's sci-fi, fantasy, soap opera, Shakespearian drama, and a reality show all wrapped up in one. Those of us who founded Geek Chorus Software believe that the world of entertainment and the material world are joined like siamese twins. In other words, the virtual world and the real world nudge one another like particles in an unstable molecule and eventually coalesce into a new element, a new reality, and yet remain separate entities. Quantum physics meets pop culture."

"Birch, I have no effing idea what you're talking about."

"Yes, you do, Grandpa. Deep down you do."

Howard figured it was time to return to the important subject matter. "Our tree has been stolen, and there's a new group in town buying properties. I'm wondering if they're connected."

"New group? You mean PLC?"

"Right, what do you know about them?"

"Paradise Lots Covenant is a company with a mission that I admire. They want what the Trust board members want, to save this town; we and they are going about it in complementary ways."

Howard pressed on. "Can you think of a reason PLC would want our elm tree?"

"Not really. What makes you think there might be a connection?"

"The logs were pulled out with a small dozer. The loggers in these parts use skidders or sometimes tractors, not bulldozers."

"And PLC has bulldozers at their construction site."

"Uh-huh. What do you think?"

Birch's next move was not what Howard expected. Birch smiled, but it wasn't his regular smile, nor a smile that displayed the braces. It was a Critter Jordan-type smile.

Birch got up from his chair and, holding his bad leg with a hand, hopped on his good leg to the window that looked out on the starlit Trust lands. "You're lucky, Grandpa, you know who you are, you know what you believe."

"I believe in Darby, town meeting spirit 1753 to doomsday."

"Yes, the town motto."

Birch didn't look at Howard but through the window as if someone was out there he wanted to address. "I'm not a whole person, Grandpa. I'm a collection of puzzle parts: my mother's confused paganism, my father's skeptical agnosticism, Grandma Elenore's hybrid Catholicism, Grandmother Purse's mocking atheism, Grandfather Raphael's uncompromising environmentalism, with a touch of Missy Mendelson's Judaism. Then, too, there's the half-assed Hindu beliefs of my cousin stepmother, Katharine Ramchand. It's only you and Cooty that give me hope that somehow I can put myself together."

"I know the Cooty part, because he does it for me. I can think when I'm with Cooty, even if he can't. I tell him everything, and when I'm done I know what to do—kinda."

"Yes, me too."

"Cooty has done a lot for me, for your dad, and for you, but me I never done much for you, Birch."

Birch paused for moment before he spoke. "You taught me to track deer. When the face fell off the old man in the mountain, I replaced it with yours."

"Well, that's a downgrade for him," Howard said in his best droll, and that drew a sad laugh from Birch, whose attention remained at the window.

Howard took the awkward silence that followed to think. Finally, he said, "You know, Birch, I never saw you cry. When your Grandma Persephone died, you grieved, I could see it, but you didn't cry, and you didn't cry when Grandmother Elenore passed on. Do you ever cry?"

Birch turned away from the window and looked at his grandfather. "I only cried once, Grandpa, and it changed me forever. It was the moment I decided to devote my life to the Trust lands, to this town, to the world—if only I was smart enough, if only I had the courage. It was the lack, the knowledge that I would fail, that made me cry."

"Really, let me guess. You were in the woods, at the ledges where you were born and where your mom died."

"No, it wasn't even in Darby; it was in a classroom at Dartmouth, and it was a single word that moved me."

"Really?"

"Yes, the professor read us a poem by Walt Whitman. It was about the funeral procession of Abraham Lincoln, but I was thinking about my mother. I still remember the words that mattered to me."

"You remember too much."

"It's the way I'm made. I remember everything. I'm an involuntary data collector. It helped through school, and it's totally necessary for the work I'm doing now. But all that data, it weighs on me sometimes."

"Remember that poem for me," Howard said.

Birch shut his eyes, and began to recite.

Coffin that passes through lanes and streets,
Through day and night with the great cloud darkening the land,
With the pomp of the inloop'd flags with the cities draped in
    black,
With the show of the States themselves as of crape-veil'd
    women standing,
With processions long and winding and the flambeaus of the
    night,
With the countless torches lit, with the silent sea of faces and
    the unbared heads,
With the waiting depot, the arriving coffin, and the sombre
    faces,
With dirges through the night, with the thousand voices rising
    strong and solemn,
With all the mournful voices of the dirges pour'd around the
    coffin,
The dim-lit churches and the shuddering organs — where amid
    these you journey,
With the tolling tolling bells' perpetual clang,
Here, coffin that slowly passes,
I give you my sprig of lilac.

Howard said. "Your mother planted lilacs the day she died. She loved lilacs."

"Yes, it was that word in the phrase from the poet, 'sprig of lilac,' that changed my life. At that moment in that classroom I stopped being a boy, and I wept."

In the young man's recitation of the poem by this Walt guy, Howard saw his country, its diminished grandeur but also its hope in youths like Birch Latour, a sprig of lilac. Youth.

What about old age, Howie?

With that realization from the Voice, Howard could feel the sweetness between himself and his grandson fade like the colors of a flag that had seen too much sun.

"I'm in your way, aren't I?" Howard said in a voice completely without droll or sarcasm of any kind, a true self, perhaps.

"No, I wouldn't say that." Those were Birch's words, but something in his voice said get out of town.

"You'd rest easier if your grandpa left Darby, wouldn't you?"

"I'd miss you, Grandpa."

So, telling the story to Cooty, Howard said, "I got the hint."

🦗 🦗 🦗

Later, on his sleeping couch, in the mobile home, encased in the phony house:

Go put your pajamas on.

I don't wear pajamas. I don't even own pajamas.

Yes you do. Elenore gave you a pair for Christmas. Don't you remember? Got tired of looking at you in your boxer shorts.

But I never wore 'em. Pajama—what kind of a word is that? It can't be American.

Come with me to the auction barn, see the old tools, the history of throwaway, come, come with me.

Don't do it, Howie—it's Mr. Death calling you.

Howard jerked to a sitting position fully awake. Neither Elenore nor Mr. Death were with him. He was on the couch—alone and fully clothed. He'd woken for a middle of the night mark-the-territory piss call.

He put on his slippers, snapped on the driveway light, and went outside, surprised to discover that it was beginning to snow. One of those gentle, no-wind snows.

Darby is in for a makeover and Birch, your own flesh and blood, is one of the architects of the disaster. Darby Doomsday, the game. PLC, another game. And all you care about is finding the cutter of a tree. Such is the vanity of an old man.

AUCTION BARN SURPRISE

I'VE ALWAYS FOLLOWED my gut.

But what if your gut has gone stupid? Old age softens the intestines among other body parts.

If I can't trust my gut, maybe I'll try my brain.

Oh-oh. Now we're in for trouble.

It snowed only enough to cover the ground. Charlene called after breakfast while he was finishing his coffee, caught him in a weak moment of musing, and Howard said, "I sold the house, land, everything, as is. They gave me a couple weeks to get out."

"Then there's nothing keeping you. It's 71 degrees here even as I speak, and last night we saw some deer, they are so brazen, not as big as the white tails of Darby, but frequent, though I won't go in the woods, well not woods exactly, more like galoot-sized bushes, there's trails, because of the snakes, which are numerous I have to admit, but birds, too. You'll love it here Daddy, especially the fishing, boats galore, start newbie with us for Thanksgiving, everybody is going to be here, Julia and her clan, but no Ricky, and Pegeen will come with that most recent husband, who unlike the rest of her husbands actually has a job and is respectful. Grab a flight to Dallas and from there McAllen, and Number Two will pick you up at the airport, it's 'bout sixty or maybe eighty miles to our little piece of heaven on earth."

When he was finally able to get a word in edgewise, Howard said, "No airplane flight for Howie Elman. I'll drive. See you in four or five days," and hung up. He couldn't tell whether it was his gut or his brain that had spoken.

After breakfast Howard continued making a plan.

Pack the PT Cruiser.

Pack it with what?

Four days of driving equals one extra pair of socks and a change of underwear.

Why bother with the underwear, you're not going to pull down your pants in public, are you?

Howard hauled a couple of suitcases from his gray barn and packed for his trip, bringing along the ice tongs he'd bought at Ike's Auction Barn three summers ago. He wished he had one of those leather-backed aprons worn by the iceman when he cometh.

Later that morning Howard drove to Keene and on impulse bought and had installed a blue police light and siren for the PT Cruiser. That little errand took him into the afternoon. He told himself that the blue light and siren would be useful if he got behind a slowpoke and needed to pass. He called F. Latour and told him he was moving in with Charlene in South Texas, gone maybe forever. From his son's guarded response Howard didn't think Freddy — excuse me, Latour — believed him, which led him to doubting himself.

If the gut instinct proves unreliable then a strong will is a liability.

On the drive from Keene all the way back to Darby he ran the blue light and siren. It was exhilarating.

Which is why they call the gas pedal the exhilarator.

The right thing to do now is to haul ass to the town hall and submit your resignation as constable.

I can't do it.

As is so often the case in your long life, you can't bring yourself to do the right thing.

The right thing for thee is the wrong thing for me. Who had said that?

It was one of Ollie Jordan's many sayings, which in the end could not save him.

I miss you, Ollie, you pitiful, hopeless fool.

Birch offered to store Howard's tools and valuables in one of the barns on the Trust property, but Howard waved off the idea. He decided to leave everything where it was, in the language of the contract "as is," and let the new owners decide what to bring to the landfill, what to set out for a Saturday yard sale, and what to keep.

He told himself he was driving instead of flying because he didn't want to have to depend on Charlene and Number Two for transportation once he arrived in Texas.

That's one of those partial truths that makes St. Peter scratch his head at the pearly gates, wondering: If "X" has sinned but believes he has not sinned, has he sinned? The real reason is that you are afraid of airplane flight.

It wasn't always so. In World War II when I was only a teenager I found flying thrilling. "Everything is a thrill for you, don't lose that part of yourself."

Who said that—Ollie Jordan?

No, those were the first words Cooty Patterson—while he was still whole—uttered to me.

It was only after middle age that you began to fear placing yourself into the hands of pilots, who you knew to be crazy men. Now, in old age, you just don't want to die in a plane crash.

I want to die with my feet close to the ground, in particular close to hallowed Darby, New Hampshire, ground. Or was it hollowed ground? Haloed ground?

No, it's hallowed.

Well, what the hell does hallowed mean anyway? Hallow, how are you? I'm How-ard, happy hallo-ween.

He drove all day and into the night to the dawn of the next day, and that was when he fell asleep at the wheel, startled to wakefulness in machine gun fury, which in reality was the rattle of his tires running over the safety grooves on the highway edge. He pulled off at the next rest stop, put the seat back, and fell asleep almost immediately.

First day on the road is an up day. You are excited and optimistic. Day two is a down day. You question yourself. All the worries of the regular life hang over you. On day three distance substitutes for memory and the old life fades. All you know is the road. The trip begins.

By the time Howard reached Port Mansfield, Texas, on day four and a half, he was very tired but relaxed, if constipated. It was as if nothing in that old life mattered. What mattered was that he was here, with his loved ones, who had gathered for . . .

What?

The Thanksgiving feast. Howie, you forgot about Thanksgiving!

I'm slipping.

You slipped a long time ago. You're in free fall.

That thought led him to an impulse buy, a used book at yard sale called *Freefall*, by Ariela Anhalt, that he presented to Charlene as a gift, which surprised her.

Charlene was here, Pegeen was here, the husbands (who Howard hardly knew) were here, and the grandchildren, who by now were adults with little people of their own, loved ones whose names Howard could not keep straight, were here. It gave Howard a smug feeling that he and Elenore had somehow generated this hunk of Texas humanity, but was that feeling love? Other loved ones were missing.

Besides Freddy and Birch, there was Shan who had run away from home and turned against both him and Elenore and, as they had learned too late to attempt to save her, had died a degenerate. Unbearable the pain of it. And Heather, the best of the bunch who had vanished into money because he, Howard, had surrendered her, his beloved youngest daughter, to Mrs. Zoe Cutter, who had raised her as her own daughter. Unbearable the pain of it.

Ones you love most hurt you hardest.

Was that an Ollie Jordan saying or an Elenore saying? I can't remember.

And then there was your love for another man.

Cooty Patterson. I watched over him for decades.

He never gave you anything in return.

Yes he did. He gave me access to his stew pot.

Loved ones accumulate over the years until there are too many of them. About when you really really need them, in your old age, they go away or die off or grow feeble, stupid, and useless. If you live long enough, the loved ones, the ones that really matter, remain only in memory.

Gentle Heather, spirited Shan—and Elenore, the dear one.

In the end loved ones by the fact of their remove remind you that you are alone. Howie,—are you crying again?

Howard was surprised to find himself sort of loving Port Mansfield, a small fishing village cut off from other towns by range land.

What do you mean by "sort of loving"? A person can't "sort of love." Either you love or you don't love. There are no meaningful "sorts of love."

I don't know, leave me alone, I don't care.

Of course you care.

Howard liked the isolation, liked the lazy lagoon, liked the fishing boats in their little water cubbies in the man-made harbor, liked his fellow retirees who made a career of waiting to die, liked the red fish served breaded and cooked in boiling oil. With his Social Security check, the small retirement account he and Elenore had, and the dough from the sale of his property he could get a nice mobile home here in the local trailer park and maybe, just maybe, have enough left over to buy a boat. Imagine that — a boat for local ocean travel.

Howard could see himself working part time repairing boat motors. Catching fish. Musing. Eating the local oranges that grew on trees. Imagine that — oranges grow on trees in South Texas. Pick your orange from a tree in your yard. Eat the local cows cooked on mesquite fires. He more or less resigned himself to this new life right into December, weather so nice it was a joy to walk the gravel flats of the Laguna Madre, just watch birds for a while: waiting to die in Port Mansfield, South Texas, not home, expire without a grumble, not home. He almost convinced himself that he was going to stay. The only problem was Elenore. She was not with him to enjoy all this. His loneliness, an ache in Darby, was an agony in Port Mansfield.

He took to walking into the range land and was observing a rattler sunning itself when it occurred to him he had left Elenore's creche in Darby. A sign. A sign of what? The FFone buzzed in his pants pocket.

He thought it might be Birch or Latour or one of the Texas daughters — at any rate a loved one, but he didn't recognize the number. He cranked up the ear gadget, and heard himself shout, "It's your dime."

The snake slithered off.

"Constable? It's Delphina." He recognized the voice.

"Critter's wife?"

"Ex-wife. I heard you were after Critter. Do you know where he is?"

"You heard? I didn't think anybody had that information but my immediate family."

"Dot McCurtin clued me in."

"I might of known. I'm sort of off the case, taking a vacation."

Sort of? Sort of? Sort of? You have lost your manhood, Howie.

Howard heard the strangling sounds of a woman fighting back tears.

"Take a deep breath, Delphina, and tell me what's up."

"It's my boy, Billy. He had some trouble. I thought maybe Critter might have straightened him out. I should of known better."

"What's the problem now?" Howard asked.

"I don't know the problem, that's the problem. See, Billy texts me two, three times a week, and he's always on his Facebook page, sending pictures of snowmobiles—he's crazy about snowmobiles. He was waiting for the first snow. His father promised him a snowmobile soon as the snows fell. So they fell but. . . ."

"Yeah, I remember, week before Thanksgiving, that was the day I absconded from Darby."

"Constable, I haven't heard from Billy. His cell phone is not on and he hasn't posted on his Facebook wall. I couldn't get a hold of Critter either, nor that crazy whore cousin of his."

"Tess."

"Yes, they're all MIA."

"Missing? Did you notify the state police?"

"I'm notifying you—don't call the state police, please."

"Okay, I won't. Tell me why."

"It's Billy. He's sort of wanted."

Sort of? There it is again, another sort of.

"What?"

"Never mind. I talk to myself sometimes. What's the skinny on Billy?"

Skinny? Why does skinny mean story?

Who cares, what's the diff?

Only old people use the word "skinny" today.

"He sort of steals things from stores, useless things. He doesn't do it for profit or spite. Or to show off. It's a psyche thing. I thought maybe his father, since his side of the family has similar problems multiplied ad infinitum, maybe he could help him."

"So that's why you shipped him to Darby."

"Yes, and he seemed to get better. I credit Critter for that. Now I can't raise either of them. Where are they, Constable?"

"I can't say, Delphina—I'm out of town. It's likely, though, that they ran off. Critter had debts, back taxes owed—that auction barn just wasn't paying. I'm guessing he had some money stashed away, and he and Tess and the boy took off for the territory. You know the Jordans— you married one."

"Yes, I was thinking the same thing, but Billy would keep in touch with me and with his friends. Even if he took off he wouldn't abandon his Facebook page. I know my son, Constable."

It was her repeated use of that word "Constable," the way she spoke it, with a capital C, that galvanized Howard into action.

"Listen, Delphina, I'm guessing that you've still got a set of keys to the auction barn and your former apartment."

"Gee, how could you know?"

"Detective reasoning powers. You mail them to my name: Constable Howard Latour Elman, Darby Post Office, general delivery. I'll take a look, okay?"

"Okay. Constable, you gotta promise not to tell the cops—I mean the real cops."

Howard stopped to think for a moment, but he wasn't thinking about Delphina's plea.

Howie, why did you throw the Latour name between the 'Howard' and the 'Elman'?

I don't know, maybe I'm working my way up to owning it.

"What did you say, Constable—I didn't get it?"

"It's nothing—I was just combobulating my thoughts. Listen, Delphina, I don't want to make promises, but I can give you this much. I won't report your information unless it's absolutely mandatory."

Mandatory? Why did you say that?

Cow patties enrich the soil.

"All right, Constable," Delphina said. "Your word is good enough for me."

Howard had some luck on the drive back to New Hampshire. He picked up a hitchhiker outside of Houston headed for Bean Town. With two drivers they were able to sleep and drive in shifts around the clock, all that night and into late morning of the following day. He dropped off the hitchhiker near the Mass Pike, and continued alone North on I-91. It had snowed pretty good, and he had missed it.

He drove by his former place in Darby on Center Darby Road. Mobile home cocooned inside the purple asphalt shingled house shell, gray barn, stone wall, junked vehicles, washing machine riddled with bullet holes, swing on the limb of a maple tree, lay of land — all intact. Except the driveway was not plowed.

Must call plow guy.

Howie, you no longer own this property, remember?

I don't care, I'm going to get the driveway plowed.

He drove to the post office and picked up the keys Delphina had mailed him, then he drove to Upper Darby. There was more snow here, and it was prettier. He parked and he noticed now, with the engine still idling, a sound coming from underneath the car.

Going to need to replace the muffler, Howie.

It's just pin hole. I can hold off another month or so.

Remember you used to replace all those parts yourself.

I wouldn't dare to go down in my mechanics pit today.

Because you might not be able to climb out.

Howard barged into the Manse, as usual not knocking. He found Birch sitting on a recliner in his office, a notebook computer on his lap and his bare bad foot on a pillow at the end of the recliner.

"Holy smoke, you got new toes," Howard said.

"Not just toes, a new foot. They cut the old one off and fitted me with a brand new high tech prosthesis. Go ahead, feel it."

Howard gently squeezed the foot. "It feels real, it's even warm," he said.

"Yes, I can actually experience the touch of your hand," Birch said.

"The wonders of science," Howard said.

"Yeah, and get a load of this." Birch opened his mouth.

"No braces."

"Right. They did their job. I'm a new person, at least on the outside."

"Hey, can I bunk up here?"

"Of course. I got your message on my phone. I have a room set aside for you on the second floor."

"Thanks, Birch, I'm desperate for a nap."

Howard not only had a room, he had a suite all of his own. It included a view overlooking the hills on the Trust lands, Abare's Folly in the distance, and Cooty's cabin on the edge of the woods below just visible now that the leaves were off the trees. Beside the master bedroom was a small parlor, a huge closet, a dumbwaiter where food could be hauled up from the kitchen below, and a bathroom with an old-fashioned claw-foot tub. The suite was destined for a future heir of the Salmon empire, if that was the right term for what Birch was presiding over.

Howard took his shoes and socks off but kept his clothes on and crawled under the covers of the bed. He shut his eyes.

You should feel guilty for mooching off your grandson.

What the hell, everybody else mooches off him — at least I'm family.

Howard slept just enough to wake refreshed. It was part of the miracle of his constitution that no matter how fatigued, pained, or down in the dumps, he could jolt himself with joy just waking up alive. In high spirits he rode the bannister down the grand curved stairway of the Manse, or that's what Cooty Patterson said Howard said when Cooty reported to Luci and Wiqi.

After his visit with Cooty, Howard hopped in the PT Cruiser and headed for the auction barn in Darby Depot. Just for fun he turned on the blue light, though he didn't run the siren.

Everything at Ike's Auction Barn seemed normal enough, though the lettering on the "Look for Grand Re-Opening" sign was already fading. Cheap paint.

The parking lot was plowed, and Critter's Bedford truck was parked in its usual spot. Howard could see a light on in the kitchen of the living quarters. He knocked on the door, no answer. Knocked again. Shouted, "Anybody home?" Tried the door. It was locked. He let himself in with the keys Delphina had mailed him. The heat was on. He looked in all the rooms, even the closets. There was no evidence anybody had moved out. He opened the door to the fridge and smelled the milk. It had gone sour. Howard grabbed a can of Natural Ice.

It'll help me think better.

Yeah, right.

Beer in hand, he went outside, climbed the stairs to the second floor landing, and with one of the keys Delphina sent him let himself into Tess Jordan's apartment. He sucked on the beer as he inspected the place. Everything looked normal. Then it struck him. No Dali the cat, no cat food dish, no litter box. Howard was not sure what happened to Critter and Billy, but he was pretty sure that Tess Jordan had vacated the premises and brought her cat with her. She must have left in a hurry, because her closet was still full. Why did women own so many shoes? Howard remembered that Birch, before he had his operation, had to buy different sized shoes, one size for his good foot, another size for his shorter, wider, swollen bad foot.

Such useless thinking, Howie.

Why is most thinking mostly useless?

Howard went out into the parking lot and opened the hood of Critter's truck and touched the engine. It was cold. The inside of the truck was clean — too clean. It wasn't like Critter to clean his truck — or clean anything. Buzz Dorne's logging truck had been clean, too. Coincidence?

On a hunch Howard decided to give the flea market part of the auction barn a look-see. It was unheated, which was one reason the flea market was open only in the summer. At a glance it all appeared the way it had been when Howard had questioned Critter and Billy a month ago. Howard walked up and down the aisles. Most of the stuff was the worthless crap you couldn't hardly give away at a yard sale, let alone sell for a decent price.

Like the iceman's ice tongs that you bought, Howie?

He came to some neatly folded mover blankets. Folded? Critter wasn't the type to fold anything with care. Howard flung some of the mover blankets on the floor. Almost immediately a hand seemed to reach out palm up as if for a handout. Howard squeezed the hand. It was more than cold — it was frozen solid. After removing more blankets Howard uncovered the naked body of Billy Jordan.

Billy had been propped onto a straight back chair. He had a what-me-worry? grin on his Frosty-the-Snowman face. After inspecting the body Howard concluded that Billy had been shot in the thigh, the bullet no doubt severing an artery. The boy had bled out.

You've seen such deaths before.

Yes, in war.

Where is Critter Jordan, where is Tess Jordan?

How to break the news to Delphina: your son is dead.

Call the state police, Howie, tell them every damn thing.

They'll take the case over, push me out.

He decided to worry about contacting the higher authorities after he informed Delphina. He punched in Delphina's number on his FFone. She answered almost immediately.

"Have you seen Billy?" she asked in a surprisingly cheerful voice.

"Well, sort of," Howard said as he stared at Billy's cold, inert body. Howard remembered seeing Billy now and then at the village store. "He's a quiet boy," Howard said.

Still is. Still — that word with the low Scrabble point total.

"Guess what — I heard from him just half an hour ago," Delphina said.

"You heard from Billy?"

"Yeah, he sent me a picture of himself beside his new snowmobile. And a text message."

A mother's enthusiasm for her children must be what keeps St. Peter from despair at the antics of human beings.

"A text message — what did it say?"

"I'll read it to you. 'Dear Ma, Dad and me are on retreat with our new church. We're not allowed to talk. Just wanted you to know I'm all right. I'll be in touch, but not too often. We're meditating. I love you. Billy.'"

Howard stared at the dead body as he spoke, "That's just a little ray of sunshine for you, Delphina. Did Billy mention a church before?"

"No, I'm surprised. I used to take him to church, but he was like his father, only made fun of it, and to tell you the truth, he tapped the poor box once. You know it's never too late to come to Jesus, to better yourself before heaven and the Son of man."

"I always wondered how come they called Jesus the Son of man and the Son of God, how he could be both," Howard said. It was this kind of reflexive sarcasm that would infuriate Elenore, but Delphina didn't pick up on the tone of his voice.

"I guess it's part of the wonders." Delphina talked on, but Howard had stopped listening.

After he hung up the FFone, Howard thought for a few minutes.

Whoever killed Billy Jordan took his cell phone and is now posing as Billy. They want Delphina to think that Billy is still alive. Suspects?

Had to be Critter and Tess.

Motive?

Who knows—family members do weird things to each other. I don't really know Tess, but she doesn't seem like the type to gun anybody down. Maybe Critter killed Billy and Tess.

Or Tess killed Billy and Critter.

Howard searched the rest of the auction barn, but he did not find a second body, nor anything of interest connected to his investigation.

What the hell was it you read on the Internet about police work?

Motive, opportunity, and . . .

You can't remember the other one.

Tess had the opportunity all right, but what would be her motive? Money? Jealousy? Irrational exuberance?

No, that was something else. Where did you see that? TV?

Maybe irrational exuberance is a motive after all. Bang bang you're dead—yippee! Okay, irrational exuberance is not a likely motive for a murder.

Howie, he was shot in the thigh! That's not exuberance. It's poor marksmanship.

So?

So maybe Tess belongs to the Missy Mendelson shoot-low school.

Howard pondered some more, and after a few moments in which his mind was blissfully blank he began to see pieces in a puzzle: the felling of his elm tree, PLC's plan to hijack Darby, Birch's foot operation and his confused resolve to maintain his grandfather Salmon's Trust lands, the riverboat gambling joint run by phony Indians to dodge the law, the future of the state of New Hampshire, the future of the U.S.

of A., the future of planet earth, the very future of the future—the pieces were all part of the motive behind this murder, no?

Yes.

Well, maybe. Probably it wasn't Tess. Probably it was Critter or both of 'em. Neither?

What do you care, Howie? Call the staties. They'll be able to get the phone company to locate the phone and therefore the killer or killers.

Bottom line: they will ease me out.

Constable Elman, you old poop. Lawrence Dracut will kick up his heels with irrational exuberance.

"No, he won't," Howard said aloud, his words echoing in the cold, coming back to him in mockery.

Howard turned to the body, "Too bad you got killed; you never had a chance, kid, not with a Jordan as a father."

Eventually, you'll have to do the right thing and notify the authorities, if for no better reason than Delphina needs closure and the opportunity to bury her son.

Is Tess still alive, and if she is, does she love Critter? Can anybody who talks to imaginary voices love a flesh and blood human being?

You ought to know—takes one to know one. Is there much difference between an old man muttering to himself and a young woman conversing with voices in her head over a fake mobile phone?

Maybe Billy killed himself. Accidental shooting? It was rumored he carried a gun.

Well, then, why did Critter run away?

Maybe he didn't run away. Maybe he's dead, too, along with Tess. Another Jordan could have killed all three of them, some kind of clan miscombobulation?

You're too old to shovel this bat guano, Howie.

Hey, as long as I get a nap in two or three times a day, I'll be all right.

Howard carefully stacked the mover blankets around the body until it was covered and the auction barn looked more or less the way it did when he had come in. He was thinking that if he could find the no good, rotten essSOBee who cut down the last great elm on the Salmon Trust, the lo and behold elm, he would find . . . he would find . . . what?

Admit it, you don't really know.

"I don't admit any such thing," he spoke, but in a whisper so that the mocking echo lacked authority.

After a few more minutes of thinking Howard concluded that he should act on the supposition that Critter had paid some felons to cut down his elm tree and furthermore that Critter was a . . . what was that silly line real cops used?

Person of interest.

Yes, that's it. Critter Jordan is a person of interest in the death of Billy Jordan.

TRAIL OF THE TREE

BY THE TIME Howard returned to his suite in the Manse he was so weak with fatigue from the excitement of finding the body and the long car ride from South Texas that he didn't even have the energy to crack open a beer and have a bowl of stew. He went right to bed, slept through supper, into the night, until dawn kissed his cheek and whispered, "Go pee." He hurried to the bathroom.

Birch and the other young people of Geek Chorus Software routinely slept later than the average hibernating bear, so in the early morning Howard had the Manse pretty much to himself. He didn't like the experience. The place was too big and historical without the sound of human beings. He made himself a cup of instant coffee and went outside to the stew pot. There was a skim of ice on the liquid of the stew and the embers of the fire were cold. Without Cooty to keep the fire going Howard figured eventually Birch and his minions would lose interest in the stew pot. Just then a young woman in blue jeans, parka, Russian fur hat, and an effervescent demeanor bounded out of the wood shed with an armload of kindling. It was Luci Sanz.

"Too bad Cooty can't keep his stew pot fire going anymore." Howard said.

"He will again when the treatments take hold," she said. "The old man's up and around. Why don't you visit with him? When the pot heats up, I'll bring you both a bowl of stew."

"Thanks, Luci," Howard said, and he went into the cabin, just as he always had—without knocking.

Cooty was sitting at his tiny table whittling a stick. He wasn't carving so much as following the natural contours of a cherry wood branch. He was dressed in his baggy outfit, which had been laundered. Cooty hadn't looked so alert in months.

"Hi, Howie," he said, as if he had expected Howard.

"What are you doing, old man?" Howard said, pulling up a stool.

"Luci, she brings me whittle dee-dees."

Howard watched while Cooty held the stick against his body and worked the knife blade to remove the bark.

"Kinda looks like the curves of a woman," Howard said.

"Yeah, it's Pasha."

"You remember her?"

"Oh, sure. We named our tank after her. She was like a sister to me."

"I thought you forgot all that."

"It's the treatments, Howie. My memories are coming back and I'm feeling chipper," Cooty said. When the assemblage was complete Cooty notched a ring around the stick, wrapped a string in the groove, and hung up the stick with others on the pine board walls.

Cooty stood for a moment before his crooked window, then he bent his neck so that his head was at the same angle as the window.

"You need a bigger place," Howard said.

Cooty pointed to the great beyond behind the glass, and said, "Not really, my cabin goes on into the forever."

Howard wondered what Cooty meant, but he didn't really want to hear what was sure to be a discombobulatory explanation, so he held back his question.

Soon Luci came in with two wooden bowls of stew and wooden spoons. Howard recognized the spoons as handmade by Birch at his shaving horse. Birch's spoons were not as finely made as his father's, but they were more daring and expressive with quirky twists and flutes. You looked at F. Latour's spoons and you thought, this carver knows himself and his craft. You looked at a Birch's spoons and you thought, this carver is seeking. After Luci left the cabin, Howard wanted to tell Cooty about Billy Jordan getting himself shot dead, but he remembered that Cooty would tell Luci who would pass on the knowledge to the game builders, so he said, "Big doings at the auction barn."

Cooty's eyes grew moist. "I know the whole sad story, Howie," Cooty said. The tears flowed down the creases in his ancient face and spread out into a sheen. The face looked like one of those pictures relayed from the Mars mobile unit. "I don't like carrying around all this knowledge. It presses on my bladder."

"Well, relieve yourself and tell me," Howard said, his mind a little turvy-topsy.

Cooty stood and sauntered over to the curtain that concealed his potty.

When he returned he said, "I won't tell, Howie; it would ruin everybody's fun."

"All righty, then, help me with the fun."

"Okay, I'll give you a hint." Cooty tapped the edge of his wooden bowl with his wooden spoon.

"Something to do with wood," Howard said. After some pretend thinking, Howard added, "If I find out who cut down my elm tree, I'll save the world, right, and get enough credits from St. Peter to qualify for heaven?"

"Yes, of course."

Howard laughed. "You and me, we've gone off the deep end."

"Deep end? End of what?" Cooty said, and seemed to ponder the phrase. Then he repeated, "Deep end, end deep. How deep is deep, how far the end, and where do we go from there?" Smacking his lips as if tasting the words, but of course it was only stew.

Just how much does Cooty know, and what will he say to Luci?

Not possible to know. Let it go, Howie.

Okay.

After the meal, Howard pulled out his FFone and scrolled his address book until he found Dorothy McCurtin. Pressed.

"Dot, it's Howard Elman," he said in a formal voice. "I'm calling in my capacity as Darby Constable. I was wondering if I could drop by and ask you a few questions."

"Why of course, and while we're at it I'll ask a few my own," said Darby's high-tech gossip.

"How I dread it."

"I always got a kick out of your wit, Howard," Dot said, and clicked off.

Howard said good-bye to the centenarian and drove off.

Like Howard, Dot McCurtin was widowed. Her children were grown up and had fled Darby. She was seventy or thereabouts; nobody really knew for sure what the number was. Dot took her work seriously. She thought of herself as something of a journalist, acquiring and disseminating information in an objective fashion. Her main technique was to exchange tidbits of knowledge. You told Dot something, and she told you something. She had a way about her that persuaded people to spill out their most intimate secrets. "She unburdens you," Elenore had said.

Upon the death of her husband, Dot sold her ranch style house and bought the Flagg place, an old New England Colonial-style house painted yellow with black shutters that no longer shuttered. She had the house completely remodeled to resemble its original purpose, a tavern in the years before the American revolution.

She welcomed Howard into her home, gave him a cup of coffee, and referred to him by his title, Constable. You'd think that the town gossip would be a nasty, vindictive old thing, perhaps with a wart on her nose, and a mean eye, but Dot McCurtin did not fit the stereotype. She was lighthearted, a woman with a forgiving nature. In her senior years she dressed very stylishly. When she wasn't on the phone or checking her email gathering and filing information, she was scanning the news agencies on the Internet, and she maintained her connection with the local newspaper as a correspondent. Her computer devices were all up to date. Her philosophy was that if everyone knew everything about everybody, massive empathy would prevail and world peace surely would follow.

They chatted sitting around an antique table. Dot sat rather close to him. He was a little flummoxed by her beauty, which seemed to have grown more lush since her husband's death. Howard thought it a miracle that Dot looked younger as she grew older; he was not aware of the wonders of cosmetic surgery. Howard sipped the coffee, which was even better than Dunkin Donut coffee, while he watched her pour herself some tea. Was that a cigarette he smelled on her? He knew what he wanted to ask her, and he was winding up to question her, when she knocked him off his pins.

"Wasn't the anniversary of Elenore's passing just last week?" she said.

"My gosh, but you remembered and I forgot," Howard said. "I guess you know more than I do about me and mine."

"I wish I did," Dot said with a laugh, "but the fact is I can't catch up with my own self, let alone anybody else, but maybe that's a good thing. Trying to catch up, knowing it'll never happen, is what keeps me bopping." It was the rich, rueful almost mannish chortle that got to Howard. Dot McCurtin chortled at the world, but she chortled at herself, too. Perhaps she even chortled at God. It was the kind of laugh that would have made his dick jump in some previous decade. He wished he was sixty.

Like so many people who sat at this kitchen counter, Howard found himself talking about personal matters, what a daring young man he had been during the war, how in recent years he'd been possessed by a great and mysterious fear of leaving Darby and how it came into conflict with Elenore's desire to start a new life in a warm climate in their old age, and how after she passed away he drove himself to bring his property back to the state it had been in when he was at the peak of his glories, not that he actually enjoyed those glory days while they were occurring, and it was at that point in his attempt to explain himself that he realized he had no fucking idea. He didn't use the word "fuck" in front of her, but it was in his head.

Why, Howie? Why is everything all about fuck this and fuck that?

I don't know, I don't fucking know nothing.

He told Dot everything on his mind, with the emphasis on recent events, except the part about finding the body of young Billy Jordan.

Finally, after she'd sucked him dry of info, Dot said, "So, Constable, how can I help you?"

Constable Elman had completely forgotten just what he wanted from her. He rummaged around in his flea market attic of memories and images and useless facts and a few idiot jokes whose punchlines he'd forgotten, like the one about a horse in a bar with a long face, and his droll (perhaps soon to be drool) and his snide remarks that he was so proud of, but that troubled his children.

I'm sorry, Freddy—excuse me, Latour—I'm sorry. Sherry Ann—excuse me, Shan—I'm sorry. Heather, I didn't mean to be a bad father, I just am.

"Excuse me, I didn't get that, Constable," Mrs. McCurtin said.

"Who plows Critter Jordan's driveway?" Howard shouted.

"Charley Kruger."

"Charley Kruger, that old fart is taking in plow jobs?" Howard didn't know whether to be amused or suspicious.

"He cashed in some bonds to buy that monster pickup after he learned about his condition, and he put a plow on it, because he needs some justification for the expenditure, except right now he's at the gun show in Tucson, so he won't be plowing the auction barn for this storm we got coming day after tomorrow, but his son probably will fill in for him."

"I guess I must be slipping, I didn't check the weather this morning."

"Ten to twelve inches," she said in a husky voice that made Howard think she was talking about some guy's dick, certainly not his. "If you're asking about the plow man, does that mean you suspect the Jordans of a crime?"

"That's police business, Dot, I can't talk about that," Howard said. The half-lie left a surprisingly sweet taste in his mouth and that gave him courage to follow up. "I wonder about Tess Jordan. What do you know about her?"

"She was seen in Keene at the St. James thrift shop just yesterday, looked downright normal, so I heard anyway."

"She doesn't have a car, I never see her hitchhiking, how does she get around?"

"Good question," Dot said. "She's a funny duck—quack quack. Sometimes I wonder just how crazy she is, but that's just speculation. Quack quack. What I know about her is she went to college, and that her father turned out a lot better than expected."

"Turtle—Ollie Jordan's oldest son. Ollie was a good friend of mine."

"I know, but you have to admit Ollie wasn't much of a father. Turtle, he had operations to fix his hearing and that crooked back of his, went to school, lives in the Big Apple."

Dot got up, walked to her desk, futzed around in one of the drawers, and returned with a card. It said, "Turtle Vectors. Graphics. Specializing in Adobe Illustrator, Photoshop, Painter, and Sketchup," the writing inside a logo of a snapping turtle, and there was a New York City address and telephone number.

"You can keep that; I have another one." She handed him the card, sat down, and crossed her legs.

The sight invigorated Howard and restored his memory.

"Thank you for the card," Howard said. "Dot, the reason I came to see you today is you know this town better than anyone. Who would have a motive to cut down the last great elm tree on the Trust lands?"

Mrs. McCurtin laughed. "Look, most people in this town support the Trust, because young Birch has opened it up, but at the same time you know that the Center Darby commuters, the river farmers and their ilk, and Darby Depot trailer park and shack people resent Upper Darby, the money, the snootiness. They all remember what a pompous ass the Squire was, how he took advantage of hard times to grab up hill farms and wood lots for his so-called conservancy. I predict that history will swamp any goodwill that Birch has built up. Half the folks in Darby would be happy to tweak the nose of Upper Darby."

"While the other half kisses their behinds. If I understand you correctly, Dot, you think cutting down my tree might have been a prank just to get Upper Darby's goat?"

What does that mean, getting somebody's goat?

"Maybe. It's just a tree, Constable. People love to mystify others."

"I named myself after that tree."

The more you say it the truer it sounds. Is the key to truth repetition . . . repetition . . . repetition?

"Constable? Are you talking to yourself?"

"Sorry, I was having a senior pimento. I think somebody was out to wound me to the soul by cutting down my tree."

Dot laughed again. "I'm sorry, Howard. I don't mean to laugh at your pain. I can't help it. The world is one big laugh-in." She paused and grew serious, or anyway played serious. "I didn't know that little fact about you naming yourself after that tree, and I know everything in Darby, so if the crime was done to spite you, the perpetrator would have to be somebody very close to you, somebody who knew the story."

Howard could feel the air drain from his lungs. The only people who knew the story were the ones in his own family. Motive, opportunity, and now he remembered the third thing — means. Of his family members only Birch had the means to hire people to cut down a tree and haul it off.

No, it couldn't be Birch. Please.

"What do you know about PLC and their plans for this town?" Howard asked.

"That's a toughie. My sources are nearly all local, and they don't know any more than what's been in the *Sentinel* about the town's master plan which, from all appearances, is to make a combination historical site, shopping center, and gambling casino to quote unquote save Darby from . . . what? Well, I couldn't say."

"You don't have an opinion?"

Mrs. McCurtin shook her magnificent head. "If I'm going to do my job, I have to stay objective, and that means training myself not to have opinions. I will say this: Center Darby, River Darby, and Darby Depot folks are more afraid that Upper Darby and the Trust will swallow up the town than they are of Keene or even of some outside interest like PLC. It'll all come out at town meeting in March. Meanwhile, best thing you can do to learn more about PLC is go to that planning board hearing set for the middle of January. I heard that the mysterious H.C. Wentworth, the CEO of PLC, is going to personally present the company's case. I couldn't get much with a Google search because it's a private company, and their website doesn't give you anything beyond their motto."

"Which is?"

"They want to connect tradition with technology."

"What do they mean?"

"I don't know. Sounds like double-talk to me. We'll know more after the planning board airs out the ideas."

"Dot, I got one more question for you: Whatever happened to Hadly Blue?"

"After Persephone died he moved permanent into their place in Tasmania. He's there still writing a memoir."

"How could you possibly know that?"

"No detective work required. He's a Facebook friend."

Over the next week Howard fell into a routine. He breakfasted on stew every morning with Cooty in the centenarian's cabin. Birch had spread the word to all Manse visitors to pick up any car-killed creatures they observed along the highways and bring them in—birds of different feathers, coyotes, deer, porcupines, woodchucks, squirrels, muskrats, beavers, raccoons (many raccoons), a bear cub, and even a fisher cat. No skunks, please. The prime cuts all ended up in the stew pot along with vegetables, an occasional noodle or grain, herbs, and salt (as Leo Lavoie used to say, not too much now). Luci had assigned herself the task of skinning and dressing the road meat and cutting it up for the stew pot. Her management resulted in a stew that was as tasty, nourishing, and unique as it had been in the days when Cooty was hale.

After breakfast Howard drove to sawmills, furniture makers, and firewood dealers in the region to see if they'd handled any green elm wood lately.

Think, Howie, think. Elm is hellacious to split for firewood.

No doubt God, if there was one, did not mean for elm wood to be split: famous Ollie Jordan saying. Birch says because of its tangled grain elm wood is used for chair seats, wagon wheel hubs, and turned bowls.

Really? Is there a market for wagon wheel hubs?

The Amish maybe. Like Amish and Andy?

Don't be a wise-ass, Howie.

In olden days elm was often used as piers, its wood resistant to rot submerged in water though not resistant to damp from wet ground. Indians covered their wigwams with elm bark. In starvation times one could eat elm seeds for food and boil the bark for a nutritious tea.

He had no luck finding anyone who had seen any elm logs lately, but he learned that elm had been favored by coffin makers, and that nugget of knowledge gave him an idea. When he tracked down his elm tree he would mill some of it for his own use. He'd always been handy with tools, and he decided it would be fun to make a casket. He told Cooty about this goal, and the centenarian had said, "You could nap in it, die in your sleep, and save everybody the trouble of burial prep."

Howard marveled at how busy Birch was. He met mornings and nights with business leaders, environmentalists, contractors, workmen, and politicians, all in service to his role as steward of the Salmon Trust lands, while at the same time he managed and oversaw the creation of Darby Doomsday by the minions of Geek Chorus Software. Despite his schedule, Birch always found time in the afternoon, usually when Howard took his nap, to go off by himself in the woods on his cross-country skis. He followed a trail that went into the old forest that was off limits to the snowmobilers. He'd be gone for an hour or two, sometimes more. On occasion, he would call in to the Manse on his cell phone to explain that he was going to spend the night in the woods. He always returned from his excursions fresh-faced and in a good mood. When Howard asked him what it was about the Trust that perked him up, Birch said, "I melt the snow. It's my energy drink." There was a bit of a horse's ass in his grandson. Howard swelled with pride.

After his nap Howard would dub around in the Manse, browsing in the library. He was tempted to sit in the Squire's leather chair, but he still couldn't bring himself to do it. He'd check his email from one of several public computers lying around for use by guests, or he chatted with the geeks, or accosted visitors who came and went with his opinions. At 5 PM sharp he'd have a beer or two or three and visit with Cooty until the centenarian went to bed around 7 PM, and then Howard would dine with the minions in the Manse, serving himself from the long table in the dining hall.

Howard told himself he was living the good life, but he was lonely as hell for the comfort of a woman, and he was discombobulated in Upper Darby. Sometimes the pain of the thought of his sold-off land in Center Darby was so bad it brought tears to his eyes. One night he actually woke up crying.

What was it Elenore had said? A man grows old he gets more like a woman. He could see how he must have hurt the feelings of his daughters back in his days of gore, because now he could feel what they must have felt.

♣ ♣ ♣

It snowed. Howard drove by Ike's Auction Barn almost hourly. For three days, not a sign of disturbance. On day four, Charley Kruger returned from the gun show out west and plowed out the driveway and parking lot. Howard questioned Kruger and learned that he hadn't seen Critter, but he had received a check in the mail for the plowing, and that Critter must be around because his truck had been moved. Sure enough, the Bedford was parked in a different locale. Howard went into the flea market. Nothing had changed. The body had not miraculously come to life; it still resided where Howard had left it, comfy under mover blankets. Howard checked with Dot McCurtin. No news.

🦗 🦗 🦗

For most of Darby's menfolk the Sunday afternoon before Christmas was set aside for watching National Football League playoff games, but at the Manse it was just another haircut day. The barber was Arnold Myzo, a legend in Cheshire County, a great pool player who had beat all the big-time TV pool players of his generation, but he didn't like the Vegas life and had returned to his family home in Darby with his Israel-born wife and their three children. Arnold still took on all comers in pool, but never for money. His game fell apart when he had to play for money. He played for pride and for the love of the felt. Arnold's family income came mainly from his wife's job as a guidance counselor at Keene High School and his trade as a barber working with Roy Carroll and Ernie Lake at their barber shop on Roxbury Street in Keene, but every other Sunday he moonlighted at the Salmon mansion. He got double the Keene haircut cost, so it was a pretty good gig.

Arnold wasn't one of those chatty barbers. He worked fast and with intensity. If you were sitting in his chair, you didn't want to disturb him with speech for fear of upsetting his brain, which would send an untoward signal to the hands that would screw up your haircut and sometimes draw blood. These errors of judgment, distractions, just plain old fuck-ups had happened to more than one customer. They happened on the felt, too, which was why Arnold, perhaps the most gifted pool player in America, made his living cutting hair.

Origen had his hair buzz-cut to the skin, followed by a depilatory. Suddenly Howard understood that the problem with the torment of baldness was not the baldness; it was the remaining hair that mocked the baldness. So it was that Howard Elman had Arnold Myzo give him his first total-head haircut. The depilatory left his head cool and sensitive to touch. It brought back some of the manhood he'd ceded to his feminine side. He was his defiant self again. Watch out world.

That afternoon, instead of retiring to his room for a nap, he went out with the loggers, Obadiah and Charley, to cut Christmas trees for the Manse and for Cooty's cabin. The loggers walked on the packed snow of a snowmobile trail, pulling a plastic sled. They walked slow so Howard could keep up. No reason to bring chain saws or the horses. Their only tool was a sixteen-inch bow saw. Finally, Howard said he was a little winded.

"Hop on, it ain't far," said Obadiah.

Howard sat on the sled, and the loggers took turns pulling him. He enjoyed the ride. It was like a hay ride in days of yore, which no doubt constituted the weekends of a workingman in the days of gore.

"When Birch goes out for his afternoon ski, where does he go?" Howard asked.

"Who knows? He don't tell us," said Obadiah.

"Probably he goes to the tree house in the primeval forest," Charley said.

"The prime evil forest," Howard said.

"Uh-huh."

"First thing Birch did when he took over the stewardship was to put that section off limits," Obadiah said.

"So what does he do, expands the tree house on the edge of it. Spent a fortune," Charley said.

"Remember we had to haul all that stuff with hosses because he wouldn't allow no machinery, and they taxied carpenters in a cart, so Birch could build his cabin in the trees without no road?" Obadiah laughed as if he'd made a huge joke, and Charley joined in. The two men were almost always together, and you really couldn't hold a conversation with them, because they would end up talking to each other as if no one else was around.

Big ignorant Obadiah Handy, little over-educated Charley Snow: what had brought these two bozos into connubial combobulation,

Howard could not imagine. Such marvels that a man past eighty could still be surprised by human behavior made getting up in the morning a continuing adventure.

The loggers must have shared, among other things, a great common eye, because they cut two trees—balsam firs, one tall, one short—without measurement or discussion. Howard climbed off the sled, and the loggers tied the trees down with cord on the sled and hauled them down the trail. Howard hobbled along with them. Thank God it was downhill. He didn't want to ask for help a second time. Twice they had to make way for snowmobiles barreling through. Howard watched scenes on the Trust with the same appreciation that he watched the Ken Burns Dayton Duncan TV specials. Beautiful. Elenore had made two words out of beautiful—beauty full: he loved the way she spoke them.

Upon return to the Manse Howard's age caught up with him, and he retired to his bed for the nap he had put off earlier. By the time he was up and around, the tall Christmas tree was standing proud in the main parlor of the Manse, it's star just touching the ceiling twelve feet from the floor. The loggers had retired to their room, while Birch and Missy and several of their geek colleagues decorated the tree.

Howard went to the Manse library to look at maps of the Trust. The latest showed the elaborate tree house Birch had built in the primeval forest.

Birch, you aren't satisfied with a mansion full of your friends? You need a cabin in the woods to be alone? You are just crammed jammed with busy-dizzys, aren't you?

It was now late afternoon dark, the beer hour, and Howard figured it was time to visit with Cooty, see the little Christmas tree in the little cabin. But first Howard decided to check his email on one of the guest computers. No messages from family. Instead there was an email from Delphina with an attachment. The message window said, "Here's that pic of Billy I told you about."

Howard opened the attachment. It showed Billy Jordan sitting on the saddle of a new snow machine on bare ground, but Howard hardly noticed the boy. His eye was drawn to an object at the edge of the bushes. Was it a sawed off elm tree burl? The picture must have been taken around the time his elm tree was cut.

The next day was grim. Warm, humid air from the south had infiltrated into the North Country. It raised a shifty, dense fog from the snowbanks that depressed the human spirit. It was as if God had made repulsive body odor visible. Howard sniffed the air. It did not stink.

What stinks, Howie, is how you think.

Rain was forecast, followed by Arctic cold. He printed the photo Delphina had sent him, then drove to Center Darby to a pretty two-acre lot shaped like a slice of pizza that included stone walls, a handmade house left over from the 70s counter culture, with swings in the yard, and a small gray-board barn. Over the door of the barn a sign said, "Donald A. Jordan. Wood Turned Objects To Admire."

Since Donald Jordan Sr. named all his sons Donald Again Jordan, each son went by a different name to avoid confusion. The Darby Donald A. was known as Turner. Donald Sr. had been Ike and Ollie's brother and the only Jordan of that generation who had never purposefully broken the laws of the land. Donald Sr. had his own brand of notoriety: inventive swear words. He had operated a junk yard in Keene, taken over eventually by another of Donald's sons, also named Donald Again, known as D.A. Jordan. Donald Sr. and wife number three or maybe four started new lives in Florida. Howard read his ohbitchyouworry in the *Sentinel* a couple years ago. Donald Sr. had passed away from natural causes, although the paper didn't specify which "natural cause" had done him in.

You people who laud "natural" this and "natural" that, what do you think about "natural" causes that put out the flame of life in creatures?

Turner Jordan married well, into a prominent Keene family. His wife operated a dress shop in the city. Turner was a lot bigger than most Jordans, taking after his Amazonian mother. He had long graying blond hair, a full beard, flint colored eyes, acorn colored skin, and the thick hands of a working man. He looked like the offspring of a lost Viking and perhaps a Connissadawaga Native American maiden. He was known around Darby as quiet and philosophical, but don't rile him. The word around town was when Turner's temper flared "watch out." It was never clear what "watch out" meant, because nobody in Darby could remember a time when Turner had displayed extreme anger. Turner's reputation as a hothead was the result of the kind of unsubstantiated gossip that Dot McCurtin despised, because it gave her vocation a bad name.

Turner was a well-respected woodworker. He had a reverence for wood, a magic touch on the grain, which was not gossip but fact, validated by the objects he made. His specialty was turning wooden bowls from local woods on a lathe. Howard had always thought that his shop was the neatest he'd ever seen in a woodworker's. The floor was always swept, a vacuum system kept the wood-dust down, tools were hung on peg board and as well-ordered as the table of contents in St. Peter's accounts book.

As he approached the shop, built into what had once been a barn holding goats, pigs, and horses, Howard found the door propped open.

Turner stood at his massive work bench, his massive hands sanding a massive spalted maple salad bowl. The lines in the wood looked like a map of Keene streets spidering off Central Square, which was not a square but a circle. Howard smiled. It was obvious that Turner had been tricked by the warm spell and had overloaded his woodstove.

"Geeze, it's hot in here," Howard teased.

"Damn thaw—I hate it," muttered Turner. He didn't look up from his work, but Howard knew that Turner had recognized the PT Cruiser through the window over his work bench. You couldn't see his lips when he talked, just wiggles of mustache and beard hairs.

"This warm weather is going to knock down most of the snow. No white Christmas this year," Howard said with deliberate false cheer designed to annoy Turner.

"Sure, rub it in," muttered Turner, sanding sanding sanding.

Howard's hearing aid acted up, so that the sanding sounded like the giant in Jack-in-the-Bean-Stock zipping his fly.

Howard walked forward until his presence distorted the wood worker's shadow, "Turner, I got some questions to ask you."

Turner finally looked up, but he kept sanding, sanding, sanding, and said, "Howie, you got a blue light on your old lady's car, and you're running around asking questions like you're a real cop. People at town meeting didn't elect you to actually do police work."

"Maybe you heard what goaded me into it."

"I guess I did. Somebody cut down an elm tree on the Trust, and

Howie Elman is taking it personal." Turner's laugh was a little bit too loud.

Howard could see now that Turner felt backed into a corner. Howard was cheered. He figured he could bluff Turner as easily as he had bluffed his cousin Critter.

"I know your kin brought you an elm burl," Howard said, droll.

Turner went pale behind his red-gray-dust-colored beard. "Listen, Howie, I don't care for myself, but if I get in trouble with the cops it's going to hit my wife and kids. You got to show a little heart."

"Turner, I have no intention of rubbing your face in the snow. You just have to tell me the truth."

"Promise?"

"Cross my heart and hope to die," Howard said, crossing his chest with his fingers, though he didn't actually hope to die, at least not in the next fifteen minutes or so.

"Listen, I always made a point to stay away from cousin Critter. I don't trust him, and he knows it. I tell my kids: don't get mixed up with my side of the family. So even though we live in the same town, I don't see Critter all that often." Turner resumed sanding sanding sanding the bowl.

"And?" Howard said, making a come-hither gesture with his hands.

"Okay, so I'm surprised when he shows up here with this beautiful elm burl. I didn't know he stole it, honest to God. He says make me a bowl. I says Critter you don't look like the type to appreciate wood grain, and he says a beautiful bowl will go a long way to win back his ex. I says I'll work it green, but then it's got to slow dry with a coat of wax of my own special formula."

"If it dries too fast it'll crack, right?" Howard said.

"Not exactly crack, more like Chubby Checker doing the twist. Wouldn't you know it, but he comes back next day and picks it up and tells me he'll pay when he's sure it don't Chubby Checker. I figure I'll never see any money from that chiseling little creep, I just wanted him out of my domain, and something else—you know this, Howie, you were friends with Uncle Ollie—the Kinship! The freaking Kinship. You never get away from it if you're a Jordan. You going to arrest him?"

Howard stood brooding over the question for a moment. Ollie and

Estelle had introduced Howard into the world of the Jordans. They had their own rules and ways of thinking and doing. The Kinship was an idea, a historical process, an outlaw band of blood relations, more important than family, town, state, and nation.

If you belong to the Kinship you're a member of an a cappella choir crying in the wilderness.

Who had said that? Was it Ollie?

No, it was your son, F. Latour, the poetizer.

Oh, yeah, I remember now.

"What was that, Howie?" Turner looked baffled.

"Nothing, I was keeping company with myself. Tell you what, I will definitely arrest him but leave you out of it. Do you know what he did with the elm logs?"

"I didn't even know he cut the tree down."

"Well, he didn't cut the tree down. Not personally, anyway. Who would Critter call for a job like that?"

Howard could see Turner's face working. He was the kind of guy who found it hard to lie. No wonder he and Critter didn't hit it off.

"I don't want to get anybody else in trouble, Constable," Turner said.

"I'll respect that and will not ask no more discombobulating questions," Howard said in as conciliatory a voice as he could muster. "Turner, how well do you know Tess Jordan?"

"Not too," Turner said.

Howard could tell by Turner's tone that he knew more, so he gave him one of his steely looks, and Turner said, "I know she's the apple of her father's eye."

"You been in touch with your cousin Turtle?"

"Yes, he's a LinkedIn compadre. He doesn't like Critter any more than I do. Turtle and me, we're trying to give us Jordans a better name. It's hard—you know, the Kinship."

"Yeah, I know—the Kinship. Turner, the Kinship is gone. It died with Ollie and Ike and when the Witch left the county."

Turner shook his head. "It don't feel dead. It feels like an east wind promising a storm."

"Yeah, sure. I heard that Turtle is legit, in the big city." Howard showed Turner the card that Dot had given him.

Turner smiled, "I've been there, quite a place."

"Does he come and visit you?"

"Never. It's not because he's unfriendly. It's because he can't leave his studio."

"Really?"

"Yeah, some kind of rent control bullshit. If he leaves, the landlord can take over, and he loses his place. Turtle is a prisoner in his own domicile."

Howard remembered seeing the picture of the meetinghouse in Tess Jordan's apartment. Did her father draw it? Maybe Tess and Critter were holed up Turtle's studio.

HI-TECH TREE HOUSE

IT WAS DAWN, Christmas Day, and no one but Howard Elman was awake in the Manse. Howard went downstairs to the kitchen with its walk-in refrigerator and two gas stoves. He made some instant and ate co-op store grain with one percent milk and maple syrup. Birch and his minions wouldn't touch white sugar, but they slugged down the maple syrup. He checked the weather online. Today was the last day of the thaw; the forecast called for snow and a hard cold. Howard figured he had a window of opportunity.

Window of opportunity? Like the crooked window Cooty built in his cabin?

I don't know. Why is so much lingo so uncombobulatable?

Howard emailed Charlene, Pegeen, and Freddy. Excuse me, Frederick or F. Latour, or just Latour. Merry Christmas all. This will be my last communication, for today I will die.

Don't mail that.

An ad popped up on the screen for a smart phone that featured an oleophobic coating.

How can a phone be "smart"? What is oleophobic — fear of margarine?

He put on his parka and boots and went outside with a second cup of coffee. Gray sky glowered down in disapproval. Rain had flattened the snow that lay in big goopy patches between expanses of bare ground that was matted and a little embarrassing to look at, as if Jack Frost had been caught with his pants down. Underneath, the soil was still frozen, providing good footing.

Even an old man can traverse this terrain.

If you take your time. If you don't have a stroke.

Why did they call it a stroke? In the old days they called it a shock, a better word to describe the condition.

You can make it, Howie. If a knee doesn't crumble, or a hip, or a vertebra, or an ankle. If.

He barged into Cooty's cabin. The centenarian was sitting barefoot but fully clothed in bed in some kind of trance. His nurses had trimmed his toenails. Howard sat at the tiny table and sipped his coffee.

"Where are you today?" Howard asked.

"Back in Lowell," Cooty said, staring with fascination at the wall.

"You were born and brought up in Lowell, Massachusetts, right?" Howard said.

"I was brought up in Lowell, but I was born in Scotland, or maybe Nova Scotia—can't remember the century or the country. I get the whens and wheres mixed up. My mum and dad brought me to Lowell. Was that dad, or the other one? Oh, look, there's a foot race. I'm winning." Cooty pointed to the wall as if the sticks he had hung up bore evidence of his veracity.

"You're remembering the old days."

"Yes, I can see some boys racing. Look at that Kerouac kid run. But I beat him."

"You act like you're actually seeing the past."

"That's the great thing about reaching one hundred years old, Howie. Everything is like a movie. All day long I sit here and watch my life. I can hear the projector sputtering, see patrons walking the aisle, hear the girls giggling."

"Everything but the popcorn."

"No, in the afternoon Luci and Wiqi bring me popcorn while the three of us watch the matinee."

"Cooty you're talking over my noggin again—I'm going up in the woods."

"I bet you're curious where Birch goes."

"Yeah, how did you know?"

"Because Birch figured you'd figure and he told me and I told Luci and she told the writers and pretty soon everybody will know and when everybody knows, why then . . ." Cooty abruptly stopped speaking.

127

He lost his thought. Maybe one of the bots in his head collided with a punctuation mark.

"Why then . . . what?" Howard asked.

"Why then we go on to the next hunch."

"Cooty, you know where Birch goes. Why don't you save me the trouble of berating the truth out of you and just tell me."

"That would ruin the fun, Howie. Here, take my cane." He handed Howard the latest version of his cane, a walking stick. Cooty had carried a number of "canes" over the years. They were just branches or saplings left over from firewood cutting. Cooty would whittle off the bark to reveal the sap wood. Eventually he'd grow tired of the cane and cut it up for the woodstove or notch it, tie a string around it, and hang it on his wall. Replacements were not hard to come by. Most of the canes were of maple, but this recent one was cherry. The wood had darkened to a deep reddish brown that Howard imagined the skin of a Connissadawaga sachem of old would acquire by standing day after day facing dawn light. Howard liked the feel of the cane in his hand. It made him think about touching Birch's artificial foot, the warmth.

Howard finished his coffee, left Cooty to his world of brain-cinema, and followed the trail that he had seen Birch take every day on cross-country skis. The walking was harder than he had thought it would be, and the walking stick came in handy for balance, leverage, and confidence. The land quickly steepened, and he discovered that, despite the thaw, there was still plenty of snow and ice under the trees. He limped on, taking his time, ignoring the ache in his bad leg.

You don't want to fall: that was the advice old folks got at the clinic. Trip, fall, break a hip, the old man's death warrant.

No, that's just inconvenience. The death warrant is when they take away your driver's license.

Did you bring matches in case you have to build a fire?

No.

Fool!

It was so warm that he removed his parka, and threw it over his shoulders, a cape.

Hey, I'm Superman.

Yeah, Superman after a dose of Kryptonite.

He got a rhythm after a while and stopped thinking about falling, his loss of manhood, his emerging female attitude and turned his thoughts to his detective work.

Howard was certain now that Critter Jordan had gone to much trouble and no doubt some expense to cut down the elm tree.

Means yes, opportunity yes. But what was the motive?

Did Billy getting himself killed have something to do with the downing of the tree?

All a man knows for sure is he don't know nothing for sure. Another of Ollie Jordan's sayings.

Ollie had been Howard's friend back in the glory days before the booze got to him and in his madness, had managed to freeze to death with his favorite son, Willow, the retard. Howard had found the bodies, delivered them to the Jordan Witch, Estelle. Now, a generation later, Critter Jordan, the son of Ollie's brother Ike (a rival in the Jordan clan) was on the lam after his son Billy had found a way to die before his time.

Family is all about same old same old.

Yet another of Ollie's sayings.

Howard was so preoccupied with his thoughts that he came upon the magnificent structure in the forest rather suddenly. The flight of a crow drew his eye upward, and there it was: an elaborate tree house. Howard knew that Birch and his friends, Missy and Bez had built a tree house when they were kids, but this structure, in Elenore's lingo, took the cake.

Takes the cake — what the hell does that mean, Howie?

The tree house was spread out on platforms held up by half a dozen red oak and a sugar maple trees. It had full-sized doors and windows, spacious decks. Smoke curled out of a metal chimney.

Hey, Elenore, look at the white smoke, they've chosen a new Pope.

How she hated it when you teased her about her religion. You should have laid off.

The house in the trees was beautiful, but somehow didn't seem real. It was like looking at a movie that had trued itself into material reality.

Is this how Cooty perceives the world? If so, is it so bad to grow beyond old and into a state of being where make-believe reigns?

Howard turned up his hearing aid, and now he could hear the rushing of a brook. It came down out of the hills and passed below the tree house, then descended to a pool. Here the fresh meltwater flowed over thick ice, then cascaded over a small man-made dam and continued on to Grace Pond.

What made the place so quaint was what was not in the scene: no road, no driveway, no wires, just a carpenter-made tree house in a muddle of nowhere. As Howard got closer he saw solar collectors high up in the trees, a rope and winch attached to a canvas sack, no doubt for pulling up supplies and firewood from below. A spiral staircase wound up around one of the trees to the main landing. It was a steep climb for an old man, but he had a railing to hold on to and he made it to the top. From this vantage point he could see Grace Pond several miles below with a cluster of new second homes. On the landing of the tree house was a depleted firewood stack under plastic and a snow shovel leaning against the wall of rough-cut boards. The front door was painted light blue. Howard didn't knock. He walked in and yelled, "Anybody home?"

Howie, you sound like a firecracker going off in a toilet.

Which is what Ollie Jordan used to say about my voice.

At first glance it was as if he had stepped into another century. Red oak logs burned brightly in the fireplace. On the wall over the hearth hung a Revolutionary era musket. On the hearth were a couple of jugs, dried gourds, a powder horn, and figurines of a pioneer farm family. A bear rug lay on the pine board floor in front of the bricked fireplace. On a wall was a computer painting that looked just like the tree house he was now standing in. Howard put on his reading glasses. In a corner of the painting was a stamp by the artist, a drawing of a snapping turtle, and in tiny handwriting the words "Turtle Vectors."

Howard walked through a passageway to the next room where furnishings included a four-poster bed, pillows laid out for two people.

Howard took a quick look-around at a compact contemporary kitchen, bathroom with shower and cat box, and returned to the main room. He knelt on the bear rug to gaze at the fire. Close up, the bear rug didn't look right. He sniffed the hairs on the hide. They smelled like a new car. He looked at the bear's glass eyes, the black spongy nose, the shiny plastic fangs. Mouth agape, the fake bear seemed to transmit the morality of the situation. You are an intruder here. You have no right. Howard quickly withdrew from the tree house, making sure not to disturb anything. He returned to the path, huffing and puffing, and was almost out of sight when he sensed movement.

He turned and stood watching as a figure emerged from the forest. It was Tess Jordan. She looked radiant, healthy, at home.

So, then, the tree house is where Birch goes every afternoon. He brings Tess Jordan food and supplies. No doubt Birch and Tess are carrying on, which would account for Birch's good mood upon his return to the Manse.

But what does it mean, Howie? How does it fit into the matters weighing on you, the downed elm, the death of Billy Jordan, Critter out there on the loose, probably conjuring up mayhem?

Best thing you can do for your peace of mind and for your family is to return to South Texas and beg Charlene to take you back.

I won't do that.

Why?

Because I'm a horse's ass.

No, that's not it. You are a horse's ass, but defying common sense is not part of your horse's assness.

Well, then, it must be just plain curiosity.

Okay, that's part of it. There's something else, isn't there, something bigger than you?

It's this town. The town is in danger.

Save Darby, Constable; it's your one chance for a grand farewell.

Howard felt a cold slap from the north wind, and he put his coat and hat on his spectacular bald head. Halfway back he almost fell, but the cane saved him. It started to snow, real light stuff. He was picturing Dot McCurtin, wondering if there was a big enough dose of Viagra to allow him to pleasure her, when he slipped on some ice, fell. The cane went flying, and he lay flat.

Ha-ha, you broke a hip. Serves you right.

I don't think so — I always did have good hips. Dot, do you prefer strong hips or fast-moving hips?

He struggled to his knees, crawled to the cane, shoved it hard in crusty snow, pulled himself to his feet, and stumbled down the path.

The ground was now completely covered with new snow. Winter had returned.

It began to snow harder, with a wind.

You will lose the path, wander like so many old folks who discover their oncoming dementia when they go in familiar woods and cannot find their way out. Perishing in the prime evil forest: your fate.

A moment later he was out of the woods. The view opened and he could see the Manse.

So what are you going to do, Howie?

Howard spoke aloud to the snow, "I'm going to give Cooty his cane back, go to my room, and sack out."

❦ ❦ ❦

After his nap, Howard discovered that it had stopped snowing and Birch had left a note on what looked like a shoe box wrapped in paper with a logo at the top of the Trust, a splash of green that resembled a pine tree. Howard put on his reading glasses, picked up the paper. His lips moved as he read, "Hi, Grandpa. I'm headed for West Leb to spend the day with Dad, Katharine, Sephy, Nigel, and a turkey. I hope you like your present. Merry Christmas! Love, Birch."

Howie, you forgot to buy presents for your loved ones. Just like last year. And the year before.

Howard tore off the paper and opened the shoe box. Inside were new slippers. They felt good on his feet; he tested them by strolling around the Manse.

The minions had cleared out to be with their families. Missy and Baby Grace were with her parents at their place on Grace Pond. Even the fairy loggers had cleared out to spend the day with Obadiah's people, retired hill farmers. Luci and Wiqi made a brief appearance to sedate Cooty (so that he was no fun) then left on cross-country skis with back packs. Howard figured they were bringing stuff to Tess Jordan. Howard was almost tempted to hike on back to the tree house and invite himself in to spend the holiday with Tess and the nurses.

His mind did a dipsydoodle, and now he was thinking about that creche he'd never set up, the wooden Jesus he had carved. Maybe this lonesome feeling was God's way of punishing him. He thought about drought in nether parts of the world killing thousands of babies, no doubt the Creator's retribution for high crimes and misdemeanors by . . . who? Their elders? All human kind? Original sin?

What's the point, Jesus?

He ended up alone in the Manse drinking beer, mind pleasantly blank for a while. For supper he made himself a sandwich of leftovers in the fridge and slugged down some leftover wine, in Leo Lavoie's words, belly wash. Then he took off his wonderful new slippers and, fully clothed, crawled under the covers of the bed. He kept the lights on, which alleviated his loneliness somewhat. He was bone weary. Used to be he could do a day's work, no problem. Then it was half a day. Today just two hours of walking in the woods had done him in. By 7 PM, he was asleep, waking only in the night to pee and shut the light off.

Next morning, though refreshed and ready to fight World War III, Constable Elman couldn't figure out what to do with his new knowledge. Confront Birch? Notify the state police of Billy's death and turn in Tess Jordan? Return to Dot McCurtin's place? Give it up and head south? He decided to wait for a sign. That was what his Catholic wife used to say, and he would scoff. Now he thought that she was right all along; it's not so bad sometimes to wait for a sign.

⚜ ⚜ ⚜

Sure enough, next day came a sign. What stimulated him was a short ohbitchyouworry in *The Keene Sentinel*. Estelle Jordan, the woman the Jordan clan referred to as the Witch, had died "after a short illness" at her home in Florida, where she was known as the Manatee Mom of Del Ray Beach for her work on behalf of the big sea-going mammals.

Now that she's dead, Howie, you're free to tell Ollie Jordan's story.

Who would listen? Who wants to hear the story of an uneducated alcoholic?

The only course of action that makes any sense is the pursuit of knowledge. Tell the story to Cooty, Cooty will tell it to Luci, and she will tell it to the writers of Darby Doomsday who will write it up for the game.

Maybe.

Oh, but, Howie, there is someone else who will want to know the fate of Ollie Jordan.

He dug out the business card that Dot McCurtin had given him. Punched in the telephone number on his FFone.

"Turtle, it's Howard Elman from Darby — you remember me?"

"Of course. You were my father's best friend."

Turtle spoke in a gravely voice, but not in a Jordan accent. He sounded like a businessman or politician.

"I heard you got your ears and your back fixed."

"More or less, yes — what can I do for you, Howard."

"I'm constable in Darby these days. I'm working on a case, and I want talk to you about your daughter, Tess."

"What could I possibly tell you?"

"I'm not sure. Have you talked to her recently?"

"Yes, she keeps in touch since her mother broke off contact. She texts me every day."

"You're divorced from Tess's mother?"

"Yes, she has returned to her family in French Canada. What do you want, Constable?"

"I'd like to talk to you in person, Turtle, about Tess."

"I don't think so, I think you should talk to her." Turtle was very smooth in the way he delivered his words. He'd outgrown his shack-people shyness.

"There's something else," Howard said. "I know how your father and your brother Willow died and where the bodies are buried. I've known all these years, but I promised Estelle Jordan I wouldn't say anything until she passed on."

"The Witch? The Witch is dead?"

"Yes. I'll tell you the whole story."

There was a long pause on the phone. Howard didn't have to explain to Turtle that they were making a deal to exchange information.

THE MASTER OF MESH

THEY CAROMED OFF one another in the library of the Salmon mansion, Salmon Conservancy Trust Steward Birch Latour scrutinizing law books, Constable Howard Elman making a nuisance of himself by pacing, noisy handling of periodicals, and muttering.

"This is Reggie's journal, right?" Howard waved the book.

"Part of it," Birch said. "Grandfather Raphael actually kept several journals. Some were account books, but in the green journals he wrote his most intimate thoughts."

"It's the paper you wrapped my present with."

"That's right. He left reams of it, more than I'll ever use."

"Because you don't keep a journal."

"I do keep a journal, but it's on note cards that an assistant inputs into the cloud."

"Birch?"

"Yes, Grandpa."

"Thanks for the slippers. I'm sorry I forgot to buy you something for Christmas. Back when your grandmother Elenore was alive, she took care of all that."

"I know, Grandpa, it's okay."

Howard, embarrassed at his outburst of affection, returned to the subject of the writing tablet. "The Squire's scrawl looks like a poke in the eye," Howard said.

"Nobody's cursive is perfect," Birch said.

"You'd think with all those pages he filled he'd a gotten the hang of it after a while. Now take someone like me, never had much schooling, I didn't get the practice . . ." Howard talked on, and later reported to Cooty that he had no idea what he said in the middle stages of the conversation. It wasn't until he realized he'd gotten on the nerves of his grandson that he snapped to. He put the journal back in its place on the shelf, and said, "I'm going to New Yawk."

"Really? What's in New York?"

"Turtle Jordan."

"He's one of Ollie's sons, if I remember correctly," Birch said, trying to sound like he wasn't too interested.

"Right, and Turtle is Tess Jordan's daddy. I figure he might have some information to help our case."

"Not likely."

"I'm going anyway, Birch." Howard was proud of himself, figuring he'd put a bug up his grandson's behind.

Maybe the irritation will lead to . . . what? The runs? Is it clarity you seek? Is that why you are wasting your golden years as Constable Elman?

Yes, that's it: clarity. A man ought to know the hours on his timecard before he stands before the paymaster for that last check.

Birch explained to Howard that the best way to travel to the big city was to take the Amtrak train from Brattleboro. After a relaxing ride to the city, it would be a short taxi drive to his destination on East 30th Street between Madison and Park.

"You're going to the Nottingham," Birch said.

"No kidding," Howard said.

"It's a Stanford White building."

"No kidding."

"Famous architect of desire, beauty, and danger."

"Sounds like my kind of guy," Howard said.

"Have a good trip, and remember that all can be saved." Birch gave Howard that sly-shy closed-mouth smile that maybe he had picked up from Elenore, turned, then walked out of the library. Howard watched him. With his new foot there was no trace of a limp.

Do you think he knows that you discovered Tess in that souped-up tree house?

Not sure. Does it matter?

Maybe not now, but eventually it will.

⚜ ⚜ ⚜

It was nowhere near as cold in New York as it had been in New Hampshire, but it felt colder because it was windier — a nasty, damp wind that came out of an alley, slapped your face, and disappeared unpredictably, like a thug hired by an enemy to stalk and harass you.

Howard was very good at reading maps, and with the sun shining he could always tell north from south, and with the streets laid out mainly by numbers, he had a pretty good idea how to get to his destination. The big city did not intimidate him. All these people walking briskly and brusquely did not intimidate him. He was a pretty brusque character himself. It was the yellow taxis that intimidated him. He told himself that he wanted to stretch his legs and that was why he decided to walk instead of taking a yellow taxi, but the fact was he didn't have a script in his head of how you behave in a yellow taxi. Eighty-something years old and he had never stepped foot in a yellow taxi. Too old to start now. He walked.

Howard Elman didn't gaze at the tall buildings, the pretty women, the people of color, the varied storefronts, the business folks going in and out of restaurants, the giant pretzels sold from sidewalk golf carts; he focused his attention on the tiny dark splotches on the dirty sidewalks.

What are they? Foot-squashed expelled wads of gum?

He imagined himself teasing Elenore. In New Yawk the street sweeper takes DNA samples of the gum on streets and sidewalks and uploads the information to St. Peter. When you die, St. Peter checks your DNA against the discarded gum. If he finds a match, you get more purgatory time for litterbugging.

Howard giggled to himself. He and Elenore had had such good times. Would he see her in the next world?

Howie, there is no next world, and if there was, why would Elenore want to reunite with you, you horse's ass?

He emerged from his thoughts when he saw Turtle Jordan's apartment building, the Nottingham. It was maybe ten stories high, tucked in between red brick buildings two and three times taller. Once it must have gleamed white, but a century or so of grit had left the stone facing the color of week-old city street snow. A torn awning projecting into the sidewalk sagged and seemed to want to collapse. Howard, following Turtle's instructions, pressed a button beside "Turtle Vectors" on a panel. There was a buzzing sound to unlock the door, and Howard entered the building. The inside smelled like an old sofa left out in the rain.

The elevator was cramped and grimy and, for Howard, creepy crawlie.

Suppose the electricity shuts off, you'll be trapped in here with the ghost of that horny architect.

I'd find a way out.

Your way out is the grave.

The elevator stopped at the ninth floor. From there it was up a flight of stairs to what might have been, in its heyday, a luxury penthouse. Turtle Jordan was waiting for him at the door. He was a small, dark gnome of a man with intelligent but suspicious eyes. As a youth he'd had a hunched back, which was why he was called Turtle, but apparently doctors were able to cure this infirmity and now he simply looked like a man without much of a neck, though his head tilted to one side about the same angle as Cooty's crooked window, which gave him the appearance of man in a constant state of perusal. Two hearing aids, bigger than Howard's, hooked over his ears. He was wearing blue jeans and a black long-sleeved T-shirt; on his feet were brand new slippers exactly like Howard's.

Howard pointed to the slippers. "Christmas present?"

"Great guess."

"Sentient," Howard tapped his temple.

"Come in — quick," Turtle gestured.

Howard entered, and Turtle shut the door behind him, latching it with several locks.

"You can never be too careful," Howard said, looking around. On one side were two closed doors, straight ahead a small kitchen and bath, and on the other side a great big studio, walls on two sides with many windows, the space dominated by eight or ten computer monitors, half of them not on, the others blinking and winking as if in conversation with one another. The desk chair was on rollers so that Turtle could propel himself effortlessly from one computer station to the next. The place was as rundown as Ike's Auction Barn. Paint chips hung from the ceiling. Cracks ran along the grimy walls like the broken brain network of an Alzheimer sufferer.

"What's that smell?" Howard asked.

"Dead rats. I leave poison out, and they expire in their domiciles in the walls. Have a seat." Turtle talked like he was gargling with sand.

Howard sat on the only seating provided for a guest, a couch that looked vaguely familiar. It sagged under Howard's wide ass. He took off his Darby Police hat off and put it on his lap.

"You get this couch from your cousin Critter?"

"Yeah, they delivered. How did you guess."

Howard tapped his head again.

"Sentient," Turtle said.

"Except when I get tired."

"You look pretty good for an old man," Turtle said. He sat on his office roller chair.

"Lucky to be alive and mobile," Howard said, rubbing his bald head. "This is quite a place. Why are you letting it go to hell?"

"That's what I like about you, Howard. My father had a lot of sayings that were pretty smart, but he never said anything directly. I had to reason out his every utterance. You, you never bothered with subtlety."

"That's true. I was never smart enough to see more than what I could see. Ollie wasn't educated, but he could conjure, at least by the lights of the Jordan Kinship."

"The Kinship," Turtle shook his head. "I couldn't get away fast enough from that shit. To answer your question of why my studio is so rundown, I'm feuding with the landlord. They want me out, but I signed on to rent control eons ago when I left art school. They don't fix anything and they don't send me bills, so I don't pay them."

"You don't pay your rent?"

"No, I've been advised by my attorney to put the rent money in an escrow account. I haven't paid rent in fifteen years."

"Middle of the world city and you got free shelter?"

"The down side is I can't leave my apartment. If I do, they'll change the locks and I won't be able to get in. I have not stepped outside my door in more than a decade. I had a choice, the studio or my marriage." Turtle lowered his gravelly voice to a whisper so that Howard had to crank up his hearing aid, a gesture that seemed to signal Turtle to crank up his.

Turtle showed Howard how he took jobs over the Internet and made drawings for ads in newspapers, magazines, and online. That is, until he went to work full time for Geek Chorus Software. He got carried away talking, it appeared, not to Howard but to some invisible figure that he needed to impress. Howard tried to sort out the true from the untrue parts of Turtle's rant.

"I use Photoshop and lots of 3D stuff—Sketchup, Strata, Maya— but at heart I'm an Adobe Illustrator vector guy," he said. "I'm the master of mesh, the gradient guru of Midtown."

Howard nodded wisely, the way people do when they have no idea what the speaker is talking about.

Turtle gave Howard a drink, some kind of superbooze from Iceland, while Turtle smoked marry-wanna.

"Whoopie-doo, what's in this stuff?" Howard asked with delight after he took a pull.

"Think of it as essence of glacier run through a volcanic still," said Turtle. He grabbed an iPad and used it to control one of the computers. On the big display flashed drawings that looked surprisingly familiar: Colonial-style tavern greatly resembling Dot McCurtin's place, a town common, an old-time one-room schoolhouse converted into a private home, and a New England meetinghouse.

"It's Center Darby, like out of a history book, but brand new too," Howard said.

"Yes, a virtual Darby, New Hampshire, but I don't think anybody who desires peace of mind would want to live there," Turtle chuckled, a sound like a laugh running through a leaf shredder.

"You're an architect of desire, beauty, and danger."

"Exactly. In my world the meetinghouse has been turned into an IED containing a nuclear device."

"Blow up Darby?"

"Ah, that depends on the skill, maliciousness, and luck of the player." More pictures flashed on the screen: a virtual Grace Pond with flamboyant homes on the shore, Cooty's cabin with the apple tree that held three apples, Howard's former property complete with junked cars and maple tree with swing, and — surprise! — the high-tech tree house that Howard had discovered on the Trust lands.

"Did you draw all those pictures?"

"Yes and no. Tess drew the shapes. I colored them, gave them dimension, shadow, and texture."

Tess? Howard, now's your chance.

I think I'll wait.

"They look so real, and I swear I've seen a few of 'em before," Howard said.

"At the Darby town hall, in the files for PLC, no?"

"Yeah, I remember now. What — did PLC steal your computer files?"

"Good question, all I know is they're going to build in real life what we've designed for our game."

"You're one of the geeks from the Geek Chorus, but you work from here?"

Turtle bowed to Howard. "I am proud to say that I am a significant part in the creation of Darby Doomsday."

The booze had a nice effect on Howard. He felt as if his body had gone virtual and he had become a character in his grandson's video game of desire, beauty, and danger. It was getting dark, and Howard could see lights through windows from the taller buildings.

Howie, ask him about Tess.

Not now. I'm enjoying myself.

"What are you going to do about your rectal rental problems?" Howard said.

"I'm going to wait them out." Turtle got up from his chair, walked over to the window, raised the shade, crossed his hands behind his back, and gazed at the towering brick buildings that surrounded his own.

"Because I never leave this space doesn't mean I'm out of touch. I follow the world in my own way." Turtle reached into a drawer below the window and produced a pair of binoculars. "Shut the lights off, please." He pointed.

Howard got up from the couch and flicked off the old-fashioned light switch. There was still illumination from the computer monitors and from the lights outside coming through cracks in the shades. "I bet it's never dark in this town," Howard said.

"It's one of the reasons I love New York." Turtle raised the binoculars to eye level. "Look at this."

Howard joined Turtle at the window. Turtle parted the shade and handed the binoculars to Howard. Turtle gave off a whiff of BO, the kind that comes from nerves. Howard looked through the binoculars.

"Lower, where the lights come through the green curtain."

Howard could see a youngish woman watching a giant wall TV. Her head was bowed. It took a sec before he realized she was sobbing. "She watching a soap opera, or what?"

"She's watching a video of herself and her soldier husband. He was blown to smithereen land in combat. Every night around this time she sits down and watches him on video and has a good cry."

"And you cry with her," Howard said.

"That's right. How could you know?"

"Old age has its benefits."

Don't you feel stupid voicing words you don't even believe?

Half-believe — is close enough good enough?

You need a wife for counsel.

Turtle snatched the binoculars from Howard, pulled down the shade and turned on the studio lights.

"Back in the day when I lived with dad and mom and Willow and the drop-in kin seeking succor, people called us a clan. We were more than a clan, more than a family. We were members of the Jordan Kinship."

"It was all about ascendency and succor," Howard said.

"That's right, old man. You sought ascendency but when you achieved it, you were required to provide succor to those in need. There were a lot of things about the Kinship that I hated, but without it a person can get awful bored. You miss the arguments, the intrigues, the constant tension between the craving for ascendency and need for succor."

"You found Kinship through the windows of your neighbors."

"I've seen birth, death, illness, love, marriage, divorce, triumph, one suicide, and two deflowerings."

Howard could see now that Turtle was seeking his applause. Howard humored him with a nod and an uh-huh.

"Willow was my father's favorite even though he was mentally deficient," Turtle said. "How I hated them, and how I loathed myself for that hatred."

"Turtle, I think I can help you," Howard said.

"Really?"

"Really. Sit down for a sec." Howard told the story of why Ollie was so close to his first son, how they died, and what happened to the bodies afterward, their connection to the Witch. "Get it?" Howard said. "Ollie and Willow were a little more than kin."

"Thanks, Howard, that means a lot to me. You lifted a great burden from my shoulders."

"Now you know why Willow was Ollie's favorite."

"Yeah, all I can feel now is . . . how sad." Turtle stared out the window again, and there was a long silence. Howard knew Turtle wasn't looking at his neighbors; he was looking into the tragedy of his own clan and family.

Okay, Howie, now is the time to make your move.

"Turtle, who gave you the slippers? It was Tess, wasn't it?"

"Yeah, they arrived day before Christmas, Federal Express. Tess, she's the only loved one I have left. In fact, she may be the only loved one I ever had."

"What about Helen?"

"My mother is in a nursing home. She doesn't know me anymore — if she ever did. And my ex is remarried in Canada."

Howard told Turtle about his suspicions that Critter had something to do with cutting the elm on the Trust lands and that Critter was hiding out somewhere. He left out the business about Billy getting shot dead. He reported Delphina's phony news that Critter and Billy were holed up in some monastery doing penance for their sins.

"I thought penance was a Catholic thing," Turtle said. "Born-agains, they don't do mortification of the flesh. They get by on faith alone, right?"

"I don't think either one of us is an expert on religion, Turtle," Howard said. "All's I know is I can't locate Critter to question him, but I think Tess might have some information that would help me find the dirty low-down scumbags who cut down the last great elm in Darby."

"You're probably right, it was probably Critter," Turtle said.

"I know, but why? Why?"

Turtle shook his head. "And you think Tess has a key to this knowledge, and furthermore that she will confide in you?"

"I do. You can tell me how to approach her. How do you get a straight answer out of somebody who is so crazy that they carry a fake cell phone to talk to voices in their head?"

Turtle chuckled.

Howard was suddenly angry. "What is so goddamn funny? For all we know your daughter may be in danger."

Turtle read distress on Howard Elman's face. "Okay, you did a lot for me today, so I'll tell you what I know. Tess can take care of herself. She is not mentally ill."

Howard gave Turtle his best "what the?" look.

"The fake cell phone. It's a prop. It gives her cover."

"Cover? For what?"

"Beats me. Maybe she works for a black ops unit. Truthfully, I don't know. You're in the town, what do you think?"

"PLC, Paradise Lots Covenant," Howard said, and as he spoke another thought dawned on him. "Your computer combobulation where the meetinghouse is rigged as a booby trap, you got the idea from Tess, didn't you?"

"Well, yeah, but who knows where she got it? She's like me, a visual artist, not the type to spin off some guy-plot out of her head."

"Just what did she tell you? And, Turtle, no black ops bat guano."

Turtle paused. "Okay," he said. "She told me that in the real world PLC wants to hold a presidential debate among the candidates in the meetinghouse to promote renewing Rust Belt America. The writers for Geek Chorus Software love the idea. The excitement, the possibility for theatrics and disaster, it's perfect for a video game."

"But what if there really is a plot to bollix the U.S. political system?"

"To tell you the truth, I don't care. I'm just a vector man trying to make a living. As far as I'm concerned, the only real world is the here and now, and that's you and me in this room. Everything else is rumor."

Turtle sent out for some kind of shrimp glutch that arrived half an hour later. By the time Howard had eaten he was pretty drunk from the Icelandic elixir. Turtle gave Howard a blanket, and he sacked out on the couch, half sleeping, half observing. Turtle worked during the night on his computers. Periodically he'd take a break, gazing out through his binoculars scanning the hundreds of windows on the surrounding buildings to see what the people of his virtual Kinship were up to.

Early the next morning Howard woke to find Turtle in a sleeping bag sacked out on the floor. Howard put on his Darby Police hat and limped off for Penn Station without a good-bye. His mind was whirling.

Probably Tess is crazy.

I don't think so, I think Turtle told the truth.

To be on the safe side, Howie, you really should bring the state police in on your investigation. You don't have to tell them where Tess is hiding out, but you have to reveal the body of Billy Jordan. If nothing else, it will provide closure for Delphina.

Closure—where did I get that word from?

Probably from Oprah.

I don't watch Oprah.

But Elenore did.

Why is it that I was the smoker and she got the cancer?

It doesn't seem right, does it? It's like you half killed her.

Howard was so preoccupied with his thoughts that he walked down 30th Street in the wrong direction to Park instead of Madison. Later, on the train traveling home, he called Charlene, chatted with her for a while about his visit in New York City, asked about the grandchildren and the great-grandchildren, didn't have the courage to confess that he couldn't remember any of their names.

"In New Yawk they have a street called Pahk Avenue but you can't pahk on Pahk Avenue," Howard said.

"Is that a joke, Daddy?"

THE BEST KIND OF RELATIONS

UPON HIS RETURN TO the Manse, Constable Elman napped. When he got up at 4:30 PM, he checked his email and was thrown for a loop by a message from Delphina. She wrote: "I don't know what you done but thank you thank you thank you. I got a check from Critter in the mail today." She went on to say that she was in a "chat" with Billy.

A check and a chat! Howard had no idea how to process this information, so he grabbed a beer and walked over to Cooty's cabin and was surprised to find the centenarian wearing a new outfit—some kind bathrobe and a plain round hat. Luci explained, "Birch thinks Cooty looks like the Bruegel the Elder's self-portrait, so we dressed him like Bruegel the Elder. At Cooty's insistence we made a modification to the hat so it resembles the cap of an acorn," Howard nodded as if he knew what she was talking about.

"I'll leave you gentleman to your private conversation," Luci said.

"Private? Cooty's going to tell you everything anyway—right?" Howard said.

Luci giggled and left the cabin, returned with two bowls of stew, and departed for good. Her last words were, "Cooty, show Howard your fan mail."

"Oh, yeah, I forgot there for minute. Look at this, Howie."

Cooty lifted a paper lying in a hand-carved wood tray on top of the footlocker. Howard put his reading glasses on and frowned at the paper, his lips moving. "Dear Mr. Patterson, the article about you in *The Keene Sentinel* made my Flipboard. Congratulations on turning one hundred years old. I would like to visit you, taste your stew, and listen to your advice." It was signed Tahoka Texas McCloud.

You heard that McCloud name before.

The TV program?

No, it was somebody you know, but not personally.

It'll come to me.

Doubt it, brother, doubt it.

"This McCloud character show up?" Howard asked.

"Not yet, but I'll be ready with the advice."

Cooty Patterson never actually gave advice, nor did he ever seem to know what was really going on in a conversation, but he had a knack for saying the right thing to stimulate the minds of his friends. Howard, Latour, and Birch—all visited Cooty when they were confused, depressed, or just needed to talk. Latour called him his muse; Birch his therapist; Howard his instigator.

Cooty's face was clean, and his teeth had been professionally whitened. His blue eyes seemed to glow.

"Are you wearing contact lenses?" Howard asked.

"Yeah, Luci got 'em for me."

"They work okay?"

"A little too good. Without the fuzz, everything is scary."

Howard sat down, and between slugs of beer and spooners of stew he told the old man most everything about his investigation thus far, except for the Billy part, ending with the message from Delphina.

"I know Critter," Howard said. "No way is he paying alimony. So, who is—I wonder."

"Wondering is the finest thing a person can do."

"Cooty, you like the questions, me I like the answers."

Cooty began to tremble. Howard knew something totally unexpected would come next. Cooty struggled to his feet, walked a couple steps to his crooked window, and said, "Snow."

"Just a flurry or two. Won't amount to much, I imagine."

"When I was a kid in Lowell, I used to stand outside in the snow and stick out my tongue to catch the snowflakes. I could never break the habit."

"Okay, I get it."

Howard got the centenarian's coat and cane, helped him on with his galoshes, and held onto his arm to keep him vertical as they shuffled out the door of the cabin. For a moment Howard forgot his troubles and took in the view. Just a dusting of snow. The old apple tree beside the stew pot still held three punky apples. Cooty stuck out his tongue. Eventually, a snowflake or two kissed it. They went back inside. Cooty was so fatigued now that Howard helped him to his bed.

"You want to take your acorn hat off?" Howard asked.

"No, it covers the holes they drilled."

Howard didn't know what to make of that information, so he nodded with an accompanying uh-huh, and changed the subject. "You like the taste of the snow, the feel?" Howard said.

"I like the religion."

"You lost me, Cooty."

Cooty shut his eyes, and his body began to slump. Howard eased him, still in his robe and acorn hat, down under the blankets. By the time the old man's head was on the pillow he was asleep, but he had worked his magic because Howard had an idea of what he should do next.

He walked to the Manse, ascended the magnificent staircase to Birch's office and announced to his grandson that he was moving out.

Birch looked up from his three-by-five table, perhaps a little surprised, perhaps unsure if he should display his delight that his grandpa was backing off.

"Going back to Port Mansfield?" he said, perhaps imitating Howard's droll demeanor or maybe just naturally droll, the start of an adulthood characteristic that he might be better off without.

"Not exactly. I want to thank you for putting me up, and Lord knows I do like it here with all these crazy young people, and that big bathtub — geeze! — but I don't like mooching off you like the rest of these freeloaders, and I want my own place now that I no longer own my own place."

Birch looked at Howard a little cockeyed, maybe unconsciously imitating Cooty gazing out his crooked window in his Bruegel outfit or maybe Turtle with his cocked head.

Get it, Howie? Head cocked to one side is a smart way to look at the world.

Well, I can play that game.

It was all Howard could do to keep a straight face as he spoke, "I'm moving into Ike's Auction Barn — I got a key." He waved the key

Delphina had sent him and walked out the door leaving his grandson with a dropped jaw.

How do you feel putting one over on your favorite human being — sick to your stomach?

Actually, I feel pretty good.

Howard packed the PT Cruiser with his few clothes and belongings and drove off. His first stop was at his old homestead on Center Darby Road. The place lay abandoned and forlorn. He parked on the roadside and walked to the mobile home house shell. With the first step his giddy mood vanished. He could feel a deep ache coming on. It wasn't physical, it was a grief, the kind of ache that does not go away. He had turned over the keys to the representative of the buyer, but of course he'd kept duplicates, and anyway the door was just the way he had left it, unlocked. Inside it was ice cold. Nothing had been disturbed. It seemed to him that it was a hundred degrees colder inside than outside. He wanted desperately to build a fire in the woodstove.

You don't have the right. It's not your place anymore. Take all that money they gave you and vacate to Vegas and meet that grandson you never met, whatshisface.

No.

The shivers drove him out of his former domicile. He did manage to gain some comfort from the sight of his junked cars — so pretty.

He trudged over to the barn and entered.

He jimmied open the secret compartment. The .357 magnum double action Ruger pistol lay where he'd put it besides the box of ammo. He liked a double action revolver because in an emergency it didn't require a safety to screw around with. You didn't even have to cock it. Just pull the trigger.

Howard didn't know where Critter was hiding out, but he believed that Critter would be tempted to return to the auction barn.

If I can't find him, I'll move into his place and he will find me.

He stuck the gun in his pants under his belt.

You're going to shoot your whang off.

So what? No loss to American women.

As he had done when he owned the property, Howard left all the doors unlocked and drove away to take up residence in the auction barn.

One week later Howard felt almost at home in Critter's apartment. He'd drunk all of Critter's beer, cleaned out the fridge, brought in his own supplies, and washed the bedsheets and the clothes in the hamper. He slept in Billy's room with its posters on the wall of motocross motorcycles and snow machines souped up for racing. He lost track of time so that he missed New Year's Eve. In the glory days he and Elenore would sit down in front of the TV and watch the ball drop in Times Square, then go to bed. This year he'd slept right through the celebration, waking New Year's Day to watch football games on Critter's TV, which was still tied in with the cable. Who was paying that bill?

Days went by, and he fiddled with the remote, going through a couple zillion channels, but there was nothing on. He rifled a file cabinet in Critter's den and discovered a list of bank account numbers and passwords that allowed him to log on to Critter's computer, where he found gigabytes of porn. No doubt Billy had known about the porn, too.

What is it like for a teenager to happen on all this stuff on the Internet, stuff you only heard about when you were in the Army, Howie? Can you know too much too fast too young?

I can't combobulate questions like that.

Howard quizzed Charlie Kruger, Critter's snowplow guy. Charley had the key to Critter's post office box. Following instructions given to him over email, Charlie picked up the mail every day and left it in Critter's truck. Howard staked out the truck for a couple days, but it was boring work, and though he never saw anyone show up, the mail magically disappeared. Ike had always bragged that he could come and go as he pleased whenever and wherever he wished; he must have taught his stealth secrets to Critter. Howard told Charlie Kruger a whopper, that Critter had hired him to manage the auction barn, and so he convinced Charlie to give him the key to Critter's post office box. Every morning Howard checked the box. Bills bills bills — Howard felt sorry for Critter, but he still wanted to face him down.

Critter might have some Jordan quirks, but he's no dummy. He's younger than you are, stronger, and he knows the territory. Doesn't the idea that your life is in danger trouble you?

Just the opposite. It gives me a boner.

Howie, be honest.

Okay, a half a boner. I'm living for the cheap thrills.

You're not living, Howie, you're preparing to die.

We're all preparing to die. Preparation is what love is about.

No, that's procreation. Family, friendship, yearnings, unfulfilled desires: they're all part of your preparations/procreations, Howie.

Hey, I'm beyond normal preparations; I've reached the Preparation-H stage of life. Preparation-H is all about letting go.

Get serious.

Okay. If Critter cut my tree why'd he do it? Bring him on — maybe he'll tell me before I shoot him.

Or he shoots you. And what about the bigger question, the threat to this town?

You mean to blow up the meetinghouse during a presidential debate? That's just the game.

Your grandson's video game, and his personal game shacking up with a Jordan woman.

And on and on his thoughts whirled, leaving only wreckage where notions once stood.

Howard imagined a knock on the door, a threatening email, a telephone call, the sudden appearance of Critter as he left the auction barn and walked to the PT Cruiser. Nothing like what he imagined happened. Instead, it snowed, and Charley Kruger's son showed up instead of Charley to plow.

"He's an old man," the son said, "he's got a condition."

Howard didn't ask for an explanation of the condition. He didn't want to know. He never liked Charley when they worked together at the cotton mill, but now that Charley, like himself, was an old man, he decided Charley wasn't such a bad egg. There was a brief thaw, and then it snowed again.

The son does not do as a good a plow-job as the father. Rack one up for the old guys.

Howard decided to visit Bev Boufford. He walked into her office and caught Bev actually standing up pouring herself a coffee. She might appear big and imposing sitting at her desk fondling the ball on her IBM

Selectric, but standing up she shrunk. She had a long broad trunk but very short legs; he towered over her.

"Hi, Bev."

"Hello, Constable, what can I do you for?" Bev returned to her power chair. He imagined she was the kind of woman who liked to rassle in bed.

"Pin me," he blurted out.

"What?"

"Never mind. No doubt you heard I'm managing the auction barn."

"So I did," Bev said. "I never would've guessed that Critter Jordan would turn over his daddy's business to a third party."

"He's a born-again."

Bev gave Howard a neck bite of a smile, and said, "I wish I was born again. I'd come back as one of those skinny-minnies and go to Hollywood, no winter."

Howard perked up. She was flirting with him, which is a kind of the luck old men sometimes have. Women think geezers are harmless, so they're unafraid.

"You know why all those movie stars get divorced and screw up their lives with drugs?" Howard asked.

"Oh, I don't know — ambition, what-do-call-it, hubris?" Bev said.

Hoo-breeze? Sounds like owl breath.

"No, they have to make the weight to look good on the screen, so they're always starving themselves. Hunger will dump cow patties on anybody's cheerfulness."

Bev had had enough. "Constable, you have something you want from this office?"

He was thinking, yeah, my hands on the hooks of that mahonchus bra. Instead, he said, "I want to look at any public records you have on the auction barn property."

Bev wrote something on her yellow legal notepad, ripped the paper off, and handed it to Howard. "Here you go. I trust you can find your way to the file room."

Howard took the paper from her. "Suppose the town hall burns or blows up from a terrorist mono bot, then what?" he asked.

"A what?" said Bev.

"A mono bot is like a no-see-um computer chip," Howard said. "I learn all this stuff from Birch and his gang of freeloaders."

"Really? The world moves too fast for me. As to your question . . ."

"Did I ask a question?"

"You wanted to know what would happen to the paperwork if the town hall blew up. No big deal. The originals are at the courthouse and in the computer cloud." Bev paused. "Something's fishy about you managing the auction barn."

There it was, Bev's challenge. He admired her. She was unafraid.

"Sometimes Bev I think you're a spy for Dot McCurtin."

"We all are, aren't we? If we didn't want people to know our business, we wouldn't live in Darby. If we didn't want Dot McCurtin spreading our manure around town, we would've burned her at the stake long ago."

"Ollie Jordan used to say, how come they crucify the men and burn the women," Howard said.

"I never trusted anything coming from Ollie Jordan," Bev said.

From the public records Howard confirmed what he already suspected, that Critter owed the town back taxes on his property.

⚜ ⚜ ⚜

Later that day, just before 5 PM beer time, Howard decided to check on Billy's body. The temperature always felt colder in the flea market than it did outside. Howard carefully removed some of the mover blankets so that Billy came into view without being disturbed.

"How are you today?" Howard said. He cupped his ear pretending to listen for a response.

Long silence.

"Should I tell your mother that you're dead? Or is it better that she thinks you're born again? Heck, maybe you are born again. Maybe you'll wake in a beaver lodge come spring. Spend a lifetime building nuisance dams. What do you say?"

No answer.

The days lengthened and winter's grip strengthened, as the local saying went, and Howard got into the habit of checking on the body of Billy in the late afternoon just before beer time. He could depend on it that Billy would always be there.

Billy is the only family you have these days.

I'm fond of him. He's the best kind of relation: doesn't interrupt, doesn't talk your ear off, no complaints, never disagrees with you, doesn't drink your beer, and you can rely on him to be home when you drop in.

THE HONCHO OF GREAT MEADOW VILLAGE CHILDCARE

AT FIRST HOWARD merely cruised Critter's hard drive, telling himself he was looking for clues but actually spending more time than necessary eyeballing the porn. The exercise began as exciting, grew tedious, then disturbing, and finally educational by telling him something of Critter's disposition. Critter didn't settle on any particular sexual activity. He filed away a little bit of everything, with emphasis on the illegal, near-illegal, and downright embarrassing stuff. The pictures were always accompanied by notes regarding the posters of the material along with mysterious codes such as "In 3g." It occurred to Howard that Critter was less interested in the collections than in the collectors. Howard remembered that it was Internet porn that had ruined Critter's porn shop and peep show emporium. For Critter porn was neither a hobby nor an obsession, it was a business.

But what kind of business? How does Critter Jordan make money from Internet porn?

Critter's metal desk included a station for his laptop beside a much bigger desk where he would write with thick-point Number 1 pencils on yellow legal notepads. By going through the file cabinets, Howard found manila folders that referenced the computer files. The "In" in "In 3g" was short for "incest"; "3g" meant the third last name starting with the letter G. In the manila envelopes Howard found websites, email addresses, telephone numbers, and notes. Critter was a regular in chat lines and had discovered the identities of some of the porn collectors. What was odd was he was selling them items from his flea market: "Roll top desk, primo condition." He was asking for and getting two or three times the going rate for the objects he was selling.

Makes no sense.

Yes, it does. Think about it.

Howard did think about it, but nothing in his mind fired off. Then, that night while he was in the bath tub, imagining what it would like to be unable to get out, his anxiety was relieved by an intrusive thought: Critter is indulging himself in low-grade blackmailing.

He's not after big money. Probably most of the perverts he tracks down are not all that rich. He allows his victims to keep some pride by selling them items they can use, even if the price is outrageous.

Howard lay there in the tub thinking thinking thinking. Howard recognized Jordan reasoning at work: Critter's system of blackmailing helped Critter justify himself in his own mind, that he was not felon but a successful business man.

Congrats, Howie. You're a real cop now—well, sort of.

No doubt some of Critter's victims were not amused. He must have scores of potential enemies who would want him dead.

Suppose one of his victims came after Critter but got Billy instead? Was poor Billy collateral damage?

Funny how that word "collateral" changed over time. For years I thought it was money or property you promised to fork over if you didn't pay off your loans and was preceded by the words "put up." You "put up" collateral. Somehow the word got changed around to mean the killing of innocents along with those targeted. Now "collateral" is associated with the word "damage," as in "collateral damage."

In the end, the porn connection only confused Howard's main line of inquiry, which was to discover who had cut down his elm tree and why. It was the why—the motivation—that nagged at him. Was he, Howard Elman, mere collateral damage from the felling of a tree?

No, Howie, you were the target. The tree was the collateral damage.

Constable Howard Elman successfully struggled out of the tub and went to bed wearing only his cockeyed thinking cap.

A couple of days before the planning board hearing, Howard got a lead while he was going through Critter's files. It was just a scrap note in a manila envelope marked "Lucre Out." The note said, "Tubby coming by this afternoon for his filthy lucre." The note was dated the day after the elm had been taken down. Tubby McCracken had been a high school friend of F. Latour back when he was Frederick-don't-call-me-Freddy. Elenore had referred to Tubby as "the bad influence." Tubby had left Darby, served time out west someplace, and now he was back; it was safe to assume he would be short of cash.

It used to be that the shame of Darby was in the shacks Ollie Jordan and his kin lived in underneath the old Basketville sign that could be seen from I-91 across the river in Vermont (the sign was in New Hampshire because Vermont banned billboards), but the Jordans never owned the land, and they were driven off and the sign was taken down. Today the shame of Darby was Great Meadow Village in Darby Depot, a trailer park built by a company owned by another company that was owned by another and so forth, business as a Russian nesting doll. Tubby had moved into the trailer park with his lady friend Gisele and a child whose parentage and other details Howard was uncertain of.

⚜ ⚜ ⚜

Howard drove off, headed for Great Meadow Village. As he entered the trailer park he turned on the blue light.

The mobile homes were close together, which didn't bother Howard as much as the fact that they were equidistant from one another. The place reminded him of the rows of wood barracks at Fort Bragg in North Carolina. He was a seventeen-year-old, already married and a father, when he enlisted.

Maybe you were only sixteen or all of eighteen?

Elenore and me discovered each another in a foster home. She was fourteen or fifteen, and I was . . . what?

You have no idea. When you finally met your birth mother decades later, she was old and forgetful and could not remember what year you had been born.

Now I'm old and forgetful.

But not forgetful enough to soothe the pain.

There was only enough room for a driveway to park two vehicles in the trailer lots. The yard was so small you could mow the lawn with toenail clippers. Howard had to park the PT Cruiser on the street hugging the snowbank to leave enough room for other drivers to get by. Just before he knocked on the door he cranked up his hearing aid, and now he heard a melee inside the trailer that sounded like the cries of mating foxes.

His knock was answered by Tubby himself. Tubby was built like a linebacker for a Division 2 high school football team, and Tubby was not tubby. Freddy had told Howard that Tubby got his nickname from a tactic he had used to seduce girls back in high school. He would give them baths. He was far from handsome, but he had long, dirty blond hair that he was very vain about, and he gave off starbursts of daring that must have attracted girls. He was wearing jeans and a faded T-shirt. Behind him in various states of locomotion and the source of the fox vocalizations were half a dozen preschool-aged children.

"Welcome to Great Meadow Village Childcare," Tubby said. "Oops, excuse me." He turned to a boy about age four on the floor and pulled something out of his mouth. The boy started to cry. Tubby whispered in the boy's ear, and the boy quieted.

"What did you say to him?" Howard asked, scanning the room for a place to sit down.

"I told him to shut the fuck up, or I'd hang him upside down by his Velcro jacket. When they screw up, we put the kids in Velcro jackets and hang them against the wall until their parents pick them up in the afternoon. Upside down is for really bad asses." He gave Howard a "don't I wish" look.

"You had me going for a minute there, Tubby." Howard waited for relative calm so he and Tubby could talk. Meanwhile Tubby told him that Gisele had started the day care center, but then she'd gotten full-time work at Walmart in Keene, so Tubby, who didn't have a job, was elected to be the "Childcare Honcho," as he liked to call himself.

"It's not that bad; it keeps me from drinking in the daytime." Tubby had a way of talking so that his every utterance came across like a sarcasm. Tubby was not indubitably anything — he was just a wise ass. Howard could relate.

"You like it here in the trailer park?" Howard asked.

"It sucks, but it don't matter — we're going to be out of here pretty quick. Lease ends and the park's closing because the new owners have other plans for it."

"Really? Let me guess: the new owners are PLC."

"They're buying out this town. I hear they're going to make it like Disneyland. Excuse me." Tubby hauled a little girl to the potty. When he returned, he was smoking a cigarette. "How's my old buddy, Freddy?"

"He changed his name from Frederick Elman to F. Latour, and he doesn't like to be called Freddy."

"I know, that's why I call him Freddy. What's with everybody being touchy about their name? Me, I could care less."

"I was a foster child, Tubby. Didn't even know my own name until a few years ago when Elenore traced back and found my kinfolk. Seems like my real name is Claude de Repentigny Latour, which made me grateful that my mother gave me away so I got to name myself Howard Elman. You get it, Tubby? I'm the elm man, Howard Elm Man, and that tree in the *Samiin* Trust that you, you piss-aunt, cut was the Elm Man's lo and behold elm tree." Howard's droll cut right through Tubby's wise assness. Howard watched him blanch.

Tubby jumped to duty. He expertly changed a diaper, played with a boy and his toy truck, put a glass eye back into a doll, and butted his cigarette on the sole of work boot — all of this activity to avoid a face-to-face with Constable Elman. Howard bided his time. Eventually, Tubby realized he'd have to talk to Howard.

"Look, I was incarcerated. It's hard for me to find a job. Gisele, she's the provider — right?"

"Tubby, I didn't come here to screw up your family or your parole. You answer my questions with no more bullshit like Velcro day center, and I will walk away from here and not file you in my report."

"Okay, deal," Tubby said.

Well, that was easy, thought Howard.

"I didn't know it was an illegal job when I took it, honest to freaking god," Tubby said. "All's I know is that me and this other guy who had a truck and a mini dozer and operated the cherry picker, we, like, cut down this big tree."

"I didn't know you did tree work," Howard said.

"I don't. I don't even own a freaking chain saw, but the other guy, he had the equipment and the know-how. I was just the helper."

"Where did you bring the tree?"

"To the sandbank on River Road."

"On the old Hillary farm?"

"I guess, I don't know. The other guy had a hole already dug, and we just dumped the logs in there and buried them. Except a burl. Critter told us to cut him a burl."

"Where on the sandbank? There's acres and acres of it."

"I couldn't tell you. I wasn't paying attention."

"Did Critter or this other guy tell you why they wanted the tree cut down?"

"It was Critter's idea of funning somebody. That's why I figured that it was nothing that would break my parole. You ain't going to turn me in, are you?"

Howard was thinking—means, opportunity, motive. Motive motive motive. What would be Critter's motive? "Funning somebody! You didn't question it?" Howard said.

"'Course not. I was a hired man. Not my place to ask any freaking questions."

"Tubby, you should watch your language in front of these kids."

"Look, if there's one thing I know about myself, it's that I have to express my feelings, okay? Gisele taught me that."

"This other guy, you get his name?"

"He didn't know who I was, and I didn't know who he was."

"That was the way Critter set it up, and that was okay because you didn't take responsibility, right?"

"I guess. Tell you the truth, I don't think that deeply."

"That's an understatement. This other guy, where'd he come from? Let me guess, PLC."

"How could you know that?"

Howard ignored the question. "How did you know he worked for PLC?"

"Critter told me."

"You seen Critter lately?"

"Sure, he was here in this living room most recently."

"When is most recently?"

"I don't know, I learned in the tank to ignore what day it is. He was here, okay?"

"Where's he staying?"

"The auction barn, where else?"

Howard shook his head. "No, he's not staying there. I know because I am." He could tell from Tubby's blank stare that he didn't know where Critter was living. No doubt with some kin. "What was his attitude like when he visited you?" Howard asked.

"You know he's a drinker, but he ain't no Bob Crawford kind of drinker; well that night he had tied one on. He was sad as hell. He didn't tell me why, but he said somebody was going to pay."

Howard knew that Critter was sad because his son was dead. "Pay for what? Who?" Howard pressed.

"I don't know, but he was pee-ohed, I can tell you that."

Howard was at the door and about to leave when Tubby said, "Howie, I mean Constable Elman, what brought me around was the love of a good woman. I'd appreciate it if you wouldn't mention our conversation to Gisele. It would upset her. Sometimes she gets a little . . . hormonal." Tubby tapped his right temple.

Howard pointed at Tubby's finger and said, "Watch out that thing doesn't go off." He knew what Tubby was really saying, which was that he didn't want his woman to know that he had two hundred extra dollars in his pocket.

How can you know what the man was thinking, Howie?

Because I know how a man lies to a woman.

Because you done it yourself.

Yes, and it's always about money.

What about the shameful Fralla Pratt episode? That wasn't about money.

That was a one-time deal for St. Peter to mull over.

On his way to the pt Cruiser Howard slipped on the ice and, luckily, fell in the snowbank.

Nice cushion, no broken hip, no harm done, but there's message here: your balance isn't what it used to be. One of these days you'll need a cane like Cooty Patterson. After that a wheelchair. Then a sick bed. Finally, a casket.

Well, I want a good one, so I'll build it myself. Traditional. Elm wood. I'd hate to spend eternity in an unindubitable coffin.

He brushed off the snow and looked around. So plc had sucked in this place, too. Golden Meadow Village was a goner. Was it all for the best that the town's only trailer park would be lost? He was thinking that PLC and Latour and even Birch and Geek Chorus Software and Dracut and Cod Prell had one thing in common: spite for people like Tubby.

The ordinary working people, the people without no education, the people who made mistakes in youth and paid for them over a lifetime, the people with no family values, the ones that built the pyramids, and the cathedrals, and that stupid wall in China, and sawed the Scrabble squares, and mined the coal, who built literally everything — they were all fucked. And fucked again. And fucked over. And fucked forever.

Howard drove directly to the sandbank. It was still a working operation, but the guys on the job were PLC people from out of town. After talking to them he realized that they had no knowledge of where his elm tree was buried.

On the drive to the auction barn Howard brooded over the information he had gathered. He'd proved to himself that Critter Jordan managed the cutting down of the lo and behold elm, but the why still eluded him as well as the felon himself. He didn't believe for one minute that cutting his tree and salvaging only a burl had been in service of a practical joke. There had to be another reason, but it was obvious that Tubby didn't know what it was. Constable Howard Elman had reached a dead end in his investigation.

Later, sitting at Critter's computer with a Natural Ice, Howard emailed a note to Charlene to wish her a Happy New Year. He wanted to do something for her by way of an apology.

For what? For not loving her enough? For being preoccupied with other matters when she was a baby?

He ended up telling her that the weather forecast was for an iffy storm — could be snow, rain, or something in between.

THE AWFUL ANSWER

LATER THAT DAY Howard decided to inspect the grounds outside the auction barn. Nothing back there but a tarp that he'd seen before.

Look under the tarp.

He pulled up a corner of the tarp. Ah-hah! The snow machine that Critter had promised his son. Been sitting here all along. Where did Critter get the money to buy it? Wonder if Billy had the pleasure of at least one ride before his demise.

Back in Critter's apartment in the auction barn, Howard rummaged around in search for the keys to the snowmobile, which he found in a sneaker in Billy's room. Now he had the means to visit Tess Jordan on the Trust land. Plus he could have some fun running the machine over the magnificent trails that the Darby snowmobile club kept groomed.

He went through Critter's file cabinet for the umpteenth time and found a receipt for the snowmobile. Critter had paid cash. Did he get that much dough blackmailing perverts? While he was screwing around in the files Howard happened upon a green paper with the Trust logo. The page had been ripped out of a book. Critter must have been burgling in the Salmon library and made off with this page. Howard peered through his reading glasses and puckered his lips. The words seemed to tremble as he read them one by one.

Raphael Salmon didn't say outright that he had shot and killed Ike Jordan, but that was the conclusion any reasonable person would come to. From the Squire's scrawl and limited info, Howard couldn't figure what exactly had gone on, but this much was clear: Ike had been blackmailing Raphael Salmon for a couple of reasons, one of which was the Squire had been carrying on an affair with Estelle Jordan, though there must have been another reason.

Do you get it, Howie?

Yeah, I do. If Ike were murdered, the Squire would be rid of a nuisance while at the same time he could blame Ike's death on the company that had wanted to build a shopping mall in Darby.

The Squire had believed that the death of a lowlife like Ike Jordan would be beneficial to the Trust, to the town, to the world. This new information supplies the awful answer to a question that you and others asked yourselves a long time ago.

Howard recalled the town meeting when the Squire had made a dramatic appearance on behalf of the Trust and against the company that wanted to build that shopping mall. He had invoked Ike's name, had told the town that he had information that Ike was murdered. The Squire had accused the company of taking Ike out for his opposition to the mall, and then the Squire had collapsed. The Squire's theatrics and later untimely timely death worked to defeat the mall. Constable Godfrey Perkins had pursued Ike's son, Critter, as a suspect in his father's death, instead of pursuing the mall company. What was crazy was that Critter acted as if he'd done the deed, but Perkins couldn't prove anything and eventually the case went into a deep freeze file.

With his discovery, Howard understood that Critter had a motive for a vendetta against Birch as the Squire's heir and against the Trust.

But what does he have against you, Howie? Hard to believe that Critter would go through the trouble of cutting down and hauling off a single tree on the Trust just to harass Birch, and he probably was not even aware of your tall tale about naming yourself after that tree.

Tall tale?

Never mind—what about Birch? Birch, if he knew the truth revealed in the Squire's Journal, would have wanted to protect the memory of his grandfather Raphael. Something happened and is still happening between Critter and Birch. The Squire was capable of murder, we know that. But . . .

No, not Birch. Not Birch. Not Birch.

All this thinking was wearing on Howard, so he reduced it to one conviction: he had to protect Birch. From that thought he concocted a plan to do One Great Thing before his inevitable farewell. If had continued to think, he would have realized that the idea, though spectacular, was not a good one. But instead of continuing to think, he did what he'd always done over his lifetime. He followed a course set by another of Ollie Jordan's sayings: when in doubt, do something, even if it's wrong.

He telephoned Bev Boufford and asked her to inform the board of selectmen that Constable Howard Elman would make an appearance that evening at 7 PM at the selectmen's weekly public meeting to report his findings on the vandalism and theft of the last great elm of Darby, New Hampshire. He also asked Bev to contact the state police, and he requested that a trooper be present at the meeting with an arrest warrant.

Howard then took a hot bath in Critter's bathtub, with razor and depilatory freshened his new totally bald look, and put on clean forest-green trousers and a matching shirt. He didn't want Dot McCurtin to spread the word that Constable Elman looked like a bum at the selectmen's meeting.

Around five o'clock Howard showed up at the Salmon estate with two cans of beer. He helped himself to a bowl of Cooty's stew and walked into Cooty's cabin. The centenarian was sticking a pushpin through a paper to fasten it to the pine board wall.

"Hi, Howie, I been expecting you, get a load of this," Cooty said.

Howard looked at the paper on the wall, a hand-written poem.

"Did you write that poem?" Howard asked.

"I doubt it."

"Well, where did it come from?"

"In the mail from Tahoka Texas McCloud. You know, Howie, after you turn a hundred you start remembering things that didn't necessarily happen to you. Everybody you know and everything they did goes into your own personal stew pot." Cooty tapped himself in the temple.

"Sounds like a lot burdensome mind clutter to me."

"Oh, no, it's like you pay your admission to the movies, get the popcorn, and walk right into the screen: technicolor, 3D, and dooby-dooby-doo sound."

"I think it's Dolby sound, you're trying to say, but dooby-dooby-doo is close enough. Cooty, you seem crazier than ever, but smarter too."

"I think it's the therapy from Luci and Wiqi. See?" He rolled his eyes upward as if trying to see into his own head.

Howard put on his reading glasses, removed the acorn hat from

Cooty's head, and inspected the old man's skull, running his fingers through the wispy white hair. There was a small shaved section with a bandaid over it that looked harmless enough. "Your head smells like a freshly powered baby's bottom," Howard said. "What did they do to you?"

"They drilled a hole and put in some magnets."

"I don't think so. It was probably some of those bot computer chips."

"Whatever it is, it's done wonders for me. Things are less foggy and more misty."

Howard wondered if it was possible that Cooty was being outfitted with a brain prosthesis. The idea was more than he could deal with, so he pushed it aside.

They took seats at the tiny table. Howard sipped his beer and slowly ate the stew, all the while telling Cooty everything he could think of that had transpired. By then Cooty had lost energy and his mouth had gone slack, revealing recently whitened teeth. He was too tired to comment, so he did not speak.

Keeping your mouth shut is always a good tactic for picking up information, Howie. You ought to try it sometime.

Howard helped the old man undress to his long underwear, brought him to the curtain, and put him on the potty. He no longer peed standing up because of the spray. Afterward Howard put Cooty to bed and tucked him in. There was a curious satisfaction in the work. He wondered if Tubby McCracken, that honcho of Great Meadow Village Childcare, had the same feeling when he took care of the kids.

Howard shut off the lights and left the cabin. He was tempted to pay a quick visit to the Manse, but the Bronco was gone, which meant that Birch wasn't home, which maybe was all for the best, because Howard was afraid he'd spill his "one great thing" idea, and Birch would talk him out of his plan, and anyway it was getting on toward 7 PM, and Howard didn't want to be late for the selectmen's meeting.

The town hall held the usual crowd, meaning hardly any crowd at all. Everybody knew that the selectmen did their important business in private, and that nothing eventful ever happened at the public gathering, unless they called a hearing for some item that required discussion by local people. The important meeting was two nights away when the

Darby planning board would hold its hearing to air its master plan and listen to the public response. That hearing would draw a crowd.

Those in attendance at the selectmen's meeting included the three selectmen — Lawrence Dracut, Frances Peet, and Harvey Colebrook — along with Trooper Durling and Bev Boufford. The only members of the public were Cod Prell, planning board chair, and Dot McCurtin, who got the word that Howard was giving his report and that he'd requested that a member of the state police be on hand. No doubt she smelled a story in the offing. Howard admired her at the same time that he would have liked to drag her behind a boat in Grace Pond.

Dracut opened the meeting with some discussion about preparing the warrant for the town meeting in early March. Then he turned the meeting over to Cod Prell, who said that PLC, which had been working closely with the planning board, would explain at the public hearing its plan to "reenergize" Darby. He also mentioned that Birch Latour, the steward of the Salmon conservancy, was working with the board on the master plan for Darby.

"I do have a surprise for you," Cod said. "I have confirmation that the case will be presented in person by PLC's CEO, H.C. Wentworth."

Dot made a note on her skinny news reporter's pad.

"Thank you, Mr. Prell," Dracut said. "And now Constable Elman has graced us with his presence and will make his report."

When Howard joined the army, he had told himself that if he was captured, he would torment his captors by acting cheerful. He never did get captured, but now he believed he was on the cusp of something like that experience. He felt rather privileged; the cheerfulness came naturally. He was going to save his grandson by sacrificing himself. Howard hopped to, as if he were about to receive a trophy.

He started by making a production of removing his reading glasses from their case in his pocket and putting them on. "I'm good looking but I don't look good," he said, which was his standard Leo Lavoie line at town meeting.

"Constable, have you been drinking again?" Dracut interrupted.

"Of course I've been a drinking."

"A man your age ought to have accumulated some will power," Dracut said.

"I have will power, I just don't have any won't power," Howard parroted another Leo Lavoie line.

Howard pulled out papers from another pocket. The papers were somewhat crumpled, but it didn't matter, since they didn't contain any writing. Howard pretended to read them over to himself, and then he began to speak, detailing certain aspects of his investigation of the downed elm in the prime evil forest of the Salmon Trust lands, leaving out those references that might implicate Birch Latour. He ended his talk with his shocker.

"I was trying to arrest Critter for cutting down the last great elm of Darby, but the dirty little coward pulled a gun on me. There was a shoot-out, and I killed his son Billy. Critter got away."

The confession left his audience wondering if what they had heard was what they had heard. Dracut said, "You dispatched Billy Jordan, and Critter is at large?"

"Dispatched—I like that word."

Dracut turned to the Trooper Durling, "Officer, didn't you tell me that Mr. Carleton Jordan has been in contact with the office of the state police?"

"Yes, sir, by email only this morning and then with a follow-up phone call," Trooper Durling said.

"And what was the nature of the communication?" Dracut asked.

"Mr. Jordan was filing a complaint that Constable Elman had invaded his home without a warrant and indeed had taken up residence in same while Mr. Jordan was away on business."

Howard was surprised but not dismayed. "No doubt something fishy is going on," he said. "I can clear the air by producing the dead body."

"Constable, are you all right?" Trooper Durling asked.

"I'm fine, Al," Howard said. "You still got that tracker bloodhound?"

"Oh, yeah, he's a good boy."

The meeting broke up, and Howard, Trooper Durling, and Selectman Dracut drove to the auction barn. Howard led the men into the flea market.

Something was wrong. The mover blankets had been disturbed. Howard pulled them off to reveal the chair, but Billy Jordan was not in it. The body was gone. Dread rolled over Howard.

"Well, well, what do we don't have here?" said Selectman Dracut.

"Howie—Constable Elman—I'm afraid you'll have to come with me," Trooper Durling said.

So, just as he expected, Howard was taken to a holding cell in the new county jail, and he was charged, but not for the crime that he had confessed to. He was charged with breaking and entering, burglary, and filing a false report. He did not ask for a lawyer, and even declined to make a phone call. He was a little disoriented, but not wrought up, nor even in want of anything. He felt rather secure, or safe, some goddamn temporary mood that was not justified by his situation, but there it was anyway. It was like in war where you can see that the enemy's artillery barrage does not have your range—yet.

He asked himself if he had imagined the body of Billy Jordan.

See, Howie, Tess Jordan is not crazy, but you are.

No, I'm not; the world is crazy.

That's what all crazy people believe.

If you're crazy and know you're crazy, doesn't that mean you're not really crazy? Then if you believe you're crazy, it might mean that you really are not crazy. It doesn't matter what you think or feel, because you can't never know whether you're crazy or not.

There you go again: boxed into a corner of thought. Now what, Howie?

I don't know, I'm going to wait and see what happens next.

※ ※ ※

That night, 2 AM. Wide awake in his prison cell.

In the days before Birch was born, you believed your great crime was littering the Trust lands to spite Upper Darby and the Salmons, but that was no big deal. The big deal was what you did to your family. Ignoring your first three children—Shan, Charlene, Pegeen.

I was just a kid myself, so I didn't really want kids. I felt tricked into parenthood.

By Elenore.

No, not by Elenore. She was tricked, too. I don't know who the trickster was.

Some people blame God and some give him credit for the same miscombobulations.

Maybe people invented God for somebody to blame. Me, I don't believe in God, so I got nobody to blame but myself, and I was no good at that, especially when I was young.

Result: Shan ran away never to be heard from until you got news of her demise. Charlene and Pegeen turned out okay, but they resented you, kept their distance from you, and you from them. They were hard to love, because you were hard to love. Now, it's too late. You will never really be able to love them or love their children and their children's children, and they will never love you. The only great thing you can do for the unloved loved ones is to die.

I improved over time — sorta. When Freddy came along, the only boy, I was ready to be a parent.

Ready but not willing.

I was working long hours in the mill — worn down, grouchy, in the clutch of a grief. Where did it come from? Why did I feel a loved one had died?

You died, Howie. Your grief was a response to the death of your potential.

Shop work kills potential in a man, I understand that now. I made do by loving my land, my stone walls, my guns, my junk cars.

But not your home.

Elenore claimed the house. You can't have two claimers without push coming to shove, so I backed off.

Yeah, and you backed off on your parenting duties, too.

True, I didn't pay the boy the attention he needed and deserved. I could never talk to him, because . . . well, I don't know. It was a word thing. A lack of word thing.

You bombed every bridge he tried to build to you. He was sensitive and, like you, pig-headed, and he seemed to go out of his way to piss you off. If you went this-a-way, he went that-a-way. You were dirt and he was star dust. You were fart gas and he was fresh air. You berated him, and he scoffed you.

And then the great surprise.

Yes, with the birth of Heather you had grown so that you were able to feel love for a child. Indeed, the love came involuntarily. She took your heart without either one of you even trying.

Howard stopped ruminating for a moment to listen to a memory of Heather singing. He had bought her a guitar, and she used to sing country songs, even songs she made up about her cat Music, about yearnings that a man such as he could never know.

Teeth, straight teeth! The thought seeped out of his depths like leakage in a colostomy bag.

Howie, you never noticed that Elenore had buck teeth, that Charlene, Pegeen, and Heather had buck teeth, but they noticed, and the world noticed. Teeth, straight teeth! Remember when you lost your job, and Elenore was laid up in the hospital, and you thought you would lose your land? Remember after that shop accident where you lost your finger, and then the job itself because there was the big lay off?

Yes, Mrs. Zoe Cutter offered to pay to straighten Heather's teeth.

That was the beginning of the end, and you knew it. You knew it! You knew you were making a deal with the devil. Eventually, Heather moved in with her and away from you. Remember signing the papers, the sick feeling when Mrs. Cutter adopted Heather?

Mrs. Cutter took Heather from us.

She didn't "take" Heather. You included Heather in a deal to keep a portion of your property. For all practical purposes, Howie, you sold your daughter, the only one of your children you really loved, in exchange for a little piece of Darby, New Hampshire. This is the great sin you must atone for before you can depart in peace.

When he woke in his cell in the morning his thoughts of sin and atonement were still with him; he was thinking that turning himself in had been a mistake, his life was a mistake.

I did this to protect Birch.

From what?

From truth.

Birch can take care of himself.

And where is Billy Jordan's body? Did Critter claim it?

Constable Howard Elman lay flat on his back, eyes wide open, brain frying.

After a gray dawn and a breakfast of chalky scrambled eggs, toast, and passable coffee, Howard was brought to an office. A very tall young woman (in Howard's thinking "young" was forty-five) asked him a lot of questions, all of them obviously designed to prove he was demented. Howard went out of his way to bollix the interview.

"I would like you to copy a sentence," Tall Woman said.

"Copy? Don't you want an original thought?"

At the end, Howard said, "How'd I do?"

Tall Woman laughed out loud and answered, "Great—just great!" Two hours later Howard was released from his cell and brought to a different office. Behind a desk sat a man in a white shirt, a Limbaugh era wide tie, and a past-its-prime sports jacket.

"You're free to go, Elman. The charges against you have been dropped." The man spoke the words with soft reluctance.

"Somebody must have pulled some strings. My grandson, Birch La-tour—right?" Howard said.

The man seemed about to say something, broke off eye contact, and gave Howard his car keys. "It's parked right outside—they left it for you," the man said. "Excuse me, I have work to do."

All of his stuff, including the .357 Ruger revolver, was now neatly packed in the car. It struck him that his idea to sacrifice himself was a combination of stupidity and disguised self-aggrandizement.

What was it Bev Boufford had called it?

Hoo-breeze: the expelled breath of a windbag.

Howard headed for Upper Darby to talk to Birch.

TALKIN' TAHOKA

AFTER HIS CONVERSATION WITH Birch, Howard left the Manse, helped himself to a bowl of stew, and visited Cooty in his cabin. The centenarian was dressed and alert in his Bruegel robe and acorn cap. They sat down to eat, Cooty's hands on the tiny table folded as if in prayer. He was clean, his teeth gleamed, his eyes with their new contact lenses glowed; only his thin white hair refused management, flying up the sides of the cap like continually flapping angel wings. Howard ate slowly, as he always did with Cooty's stew, and recited the story of his foolish idea to turn himself in for killing Billy Jordan only to discover that the body was missing, how Critter managed to get him incarcerated—"admirable, I have to admit"—about his release from jail and his subsequent meeting with Birch at the Manse.

"So, I says to Birch this tall lady shows up and asks me all these questions. She says, 'I understand you're a widower.' I says, 'No I'm divorced.' She says, 'There's nothing in your record of a divorce.' I says. 'I promised to love, honor, and so forth until death do we part. My wife dies, we part, it's in the Bible—death is a divorce—not that I actually read the Bible.' She says, 'I believe the phrase until death do you part does not come from the Bible but from the Anglican Book of Common Prayer.' I says to her, I says, 'Angle-kin? I got no angle-kin that I know about.' She says, 'It's my understanding that you believe in reincarnation.' I says, 'I believe in re in car nation, yes.' She says, 'If you could come back in a future life as an animal, what would it be?' I thought about that for fifty seconds, and I says, 'A cow.' She says, 'You mean like a big strong bull?' I says, 'No, a farmer-in-the-dell cow. Moo.' She says, 'Now why would anyone want to be reincarnated as a dairy cow?' I says, 'Because your life is mainly mealtime, eat all day, and when you rest, you cough up your cud and get to eat your meals all over again, plus you get the bonus of having your tits played with twice a day.'"

"Sounds reasonable to me," Cooty said.

"I says to Birch, 'You sent that tall lady to prove I got old timers disease to get me out of the hoosegow, right?' He laughs and says, 'Yeah, Grandpa.' I says, 'So, am I demented?' He says the results were 'inconclusive,' but he got me out anyway, because Critter Jordan wouldn't file a complaint, no doubt because he wanted to keep a low profile."

"Inconclusive — that means they're not sure if you're demented or not," Cooty said.

"Indubitably," Howard said with an expression of exaggerated gravity, then added, "Inconclusive being the very conclusivity I combobulated myself."

"Conclusive about being inconclusive — that kinda scares me, Howie."

"Cooty, I would have sworn a month ago that you had crossed over into the land of woodchucks and angels — or maybe angle-kins — but all of sudden you seem younger, smarter, almost normal, and I'm the one with the holes in his head."

"Oh, I wouldn't want to be normal. That's the scariest mentality of all. Ever since Luci and Wiqi drilled those holes and put in the magnets, it's like I can figure better. You come to say good-bye, Howie?"

"How'd you know that?"

"Birch talks to me, like you and Freddy talk to me, and then I tell it to Luci, which makes me remember it better," Cooty said.

"I already know that," Howard said, echoing one of his grandson's favorite sayings. "It's some kind of plan, but I don't know whose." Howard took a last bite of stew. "Usually Birch and I talk alone in his office, but this time he wanted to talk in front of a fire downstairs, burning big green logs so they snap, crackle, and pop like Rice Krispies. I says to him, I says, 'You knew all along that Critter Jordan cut down my elm tree, right?' He says 'Not really, but I strongly suspected, though there was something peculiar about the very idea. Seemed too elaborate for Critter.' I agreed with him on that one. No doubt Birch had had trouble with Critter before, but he didn't want to talk about that. I says, 'Why do you think Critter hates you so?' He shakes his head."

Howard was tempted now to tell Cooty about the awful answer, the Squire as killer of Ike Jordan, but he refrained. There were some things he didn't want Cooty spilling to Luci.

"Critter was causing all kinds of problems for Birch," Cooty said. "He set that brushfire on the Trust last year. It didn't amount to much, but if we ever have a real drought Critter is going to be ready with the gas can on the Trust lands. And he spread rumors that Birch and Missy were carrying on behind Bez's back and that Baby Grace is Birch's, all kinds of nasty stuff. Birch thought if he could find out why Critter hated him, he could, you know, make it right somehow, so Critter would stop."

"Cooty, that's the longest most combobulative speech I've heard you talk in decades," Howard said.

"I'm getting smarter, must be something that happens after you turn a hundred and . . ." He stopped talking in mid thought and pointed to his head.

"Does it hurt when they drill?"

"No, they numb it. It kinda tickles."

"Birch believes that everyone has a good heart like him," Howard said. "You know how he used to get embarrassed when he was a little kid when he told a lie. Funny how 'embarrass' sounds like 'him bare ass.' You don't suppose long ago in merry old England some knight got caught with his pants down, and next thing you know we had a new word?"

"Could be."

"You know what worries me, Cooty? Birch thinks he can negotiate with Critter. That's what he said: 'negotiate.' I don't think you can negotiate with a Jordan, certainly not with Critter. And what are they negotiating for, I wonder?"

Howard looked at Cooty for more information. Cooty blinked something in Morse code that Howard couldn't read, then said, "Stick around long enough and it'll be in the video game, I imagine. Then what happened, Howie?"

"Birch says to me, 'Grandpa, there's lot of things I can't tell you right now, but I have to say . . .' And of course he couldn't say it. Which was that, no doubt he wants me on Mars or some such place far from

Darby. So I says, I says, 'I think I'll hit the road. See if I can't make up with your Aunt Charlene.' He kinda got all bashful, but I knew he was relieved that I'm leaving town. So I'm headed out right now. Gotta beat that storm coming in tomorrow."

"You won't be around for the planning board hearing?" Cooty said.

"No, I wish I was, though—I hate having my curiosity frustrated." Howard paused, looked around at the cabin—the rough-cut pine board walls, the mysterious footlocker, the woodstove, the tiny table. "I don't knows what I'm going to miss more, old man, you or your stew."

"You can take some with you, if you want."

"Naw, too drippy—see you later," Howard said, and walked out the door. He hated good-byes, especially good-byes accompanied by frippery language and embraces.

Embrace embarrass: note a connection in the way the words are spelled. There's an "ace" in embrace, and a "race" and a "brace," and a "bar" and an "ass" in embarrass.

So what?

So don't expect to be understood.

Howard had shut the door to the cabin and had started walking away when he heard Cooty calling. Howard turned and saw the centenarian blocking the doorway.

"Don't go, Howie. Love it, don't leave it."

"Nobody needs me here, old man," Howard answered, but Cooty had shut the door and Howard was talking to the hoo-breeze coming down cold from Abare's Folly.

He headed for the town hall to officially submit his resignation as Darby Constable, but he could hear Cooty's words echoing in his head, "Love it, don't leave it," and he kept on driving. He thought: I'm going to be constable until I get voted out at town meeting or die, whichever comes first.

Die? Suppose you did die!

Leave me alone.

Wouldn't your timely demise be the best thing for all concerned? They don't want you here, but they don't want you in South Texas either.

How to do it?

Think about a tree. Couple feet across off the edge of the road on a slight down slope. No ditch between. A ditch would cushion the impact. You don't want to cushion the impact.

⚛ ⚛ ⚛

Howard pulled over, disconnected the air bag, turned on his blue light, and barreled down the road again in search of a tree to crash into.

He saw some kids just out of school standing by the roadside dealing dope (or so he liked to think), and he turned on the siren to give them a little thrill. He speeded over the roads of Darby, New Hampshire; back and forth he went: PLC's construction site on River Road, old Hillary farm and the sandbank where his elm lay buried, new residences, Golden Meadow Village and its crowded together mobile homes, Ancharsky's Store, the little brick library, the (shut down) Grange Hall, the concrete block elementary school, sugar bushes awaiting their networks of plastic tubing for that first run of sap, the grand manses of Upper Darby, slick new houses surrounding Grace Pond, and everywhere in the back drop, the forested hills of the Trust topped by Abare's Folly, where red people went to worship long before people of other colors arrived.

It's just a New Hampshire town, nothing special, but it's your town, Howie. Love it, don't leave it. Every person is called to a certain place. The word for it is home. Most people reside here and there, and eventually they cave in and mix up their loved ones with the idea of home. But home is not a person, nor a group, nor an idea. Home is a place. It's the soil, the rocks, the boiling lava under your feet, and that little piece of sky above. It's that elm tree that was taken from you, it's a tree, home is a tree, is a tree, a tree, tree, eeeee!

He drove over narrow paved and narrow dirt roads, all of them bumpy with frost heaves at this time year. In another month or so the melting would begin, bringing on the sap run, then mud season would start another round of frustration, followed by black fly season, and finally four or five days of glorious spring.

You are going to miss it all, Howie.

It came back to him now, as he sped down the road that led to what had once been his property, that the person who mattered most in the death of Billy Jordan was the boy's mother, Delphina Rayno Jordan.

Elenore is gone, my children no longer need me, and neither does Birch, but maybe I can do something for that poor woman who has lost a son. She needs me, and I promised her, promised her, promised her.

He was ashamed of his selfishness and he took his foot off the exhilarator. He must keep his promise. Howard slowed as he came up over the rise to the former Zoe Cutter house.

What's this, a new sign? "Paradise Lots Covenant / Connecting Tradition and Technology to / You." PLC had moved into the Zoe Cutter house. Down the hill was his former property. He could see his house, his barn, the maple tree with the swing, the washing machine full of bullet holes, the bathtub Mary, the junk cars of Re In Car Nation, those monuments from the age of petroleum. He aimed the PT Cruiser for home.

The driveway had been plowed, and he could see a few stakes in the snow. Apparently, the new owners were planning some activity here soon.

What are they going to do with my land?

Probably connect it with the Cutter place. Do you get it now?

Yeah, it was PLC that bought my property.

He was surprised again to see smoke coming out of the chimney. Somebody had built a fire in his woodstove. What the hell! He had a sudden eureka moment. Maybe Critter Jordan was on his couch at this very moment. Never mind negotiations. Never mind constant brooding. He would confront Critter. He reached in the glove compartment for the Ruger and put it in his coat pocket.

He shut off the blue light and engine of the PT Cruiser, got out, advanced like Clint Eastwood in a Dirty Harry movie or maybe John Wayne in *The Searchers*, but actually more likely Gabby Hays or Francis the talking mule as he slipped and fell. He lay there for a moment, then fought himself to reach his feet and finally succeeded. No broken hip.

Third time this has happened, Howie. How much more luck do you think you have?

It doesn't matter; probably Critter is in my home and will shoot me dead.

No, you'll shoot him.

I doubt it; I don't really want to shoot him; let him shoot me.

Howie, you need some Viagra for your Ruger.

In this mixed up mood, Howard Elman arrived at the front door of what had once been his shell house encompassing his mobile home. Thought he heard something. Paused to crank up the hearing aid. Guitar. Singing. For a split second he was thrown back in time, and he was listening to Heather making sweet music. He had not deserved to be so moved. Howard pulled his pistol, and barged in.

She was sitting on the floor cross-legged, a teenage girl, holding the guitar as one might hold an elongated baby. She had long honey-blond hair, skin that wanted to be gold, shocking blue eyes full of wonder and hurt. Howard put the gun on the end table and said, "You play good."

"Not good enough for the grand ole opry. I need practice," the girl said, unfazed by the sight of an armed octogenarian.

"If you want to get to the grand ole opry, you gotta strum your heart out," Howard said.

"Sometimes I think effort's all I got for talent."

He would have remembered if had seen this girl before, and he had never heard an accent like that, southern but the words spoken very fast, and yet the voice sounded familiar and he involuntarily warmed to it.

I don't know this kid, but I'd give my life for her.

Of course you know her.

"Nice and warm in here. You built a fire," Howard said.

The girl stood, leaned her guitar against the wall, and said, "I love wood fires, and I brought some food. You want something to eat?"

"No, I've eaten." Howard sat in his favorite chair. "My name's Howard Elman."

"Yes, I recognized you."

"From what? I never seen you before."

"When you came in the door, I knew it was you, and I knew you'd come."

"And who are you?"

"My full name is Tahoka Texas McCloud, but everybody calls me Tahoka."

"You're the one that wrote a letter to Cooty Patterson." Howard was thinking — McCloud, McCloud, where did I hear that name?

"Yes, Cooty told me how to get to this place."

"I like your name. How'd you come by it?"

"My father had a horse named Tahoka that was named after the town he was born in and where I was born, too, Tahoka, Texas. I'm named after a horse named after a town."

"Well, I'm a horse's ass, so maybe we're related. Where's your daddy now?"

"Re-hab, I think. I'm not sure exactly."

"I'm sorry," Howard said.

"Me, too."

"You often break into people's houses?"

"No, this is my first time. Anyway, I didn't break in. The door was unlocked. Like I knew it would be."

"Like you knew it would be?"

"Uh-huh, can I ask you a question?"

Howard paused before answering. He was enjoying the conversation, the presence of this girl. She seemed to be holding back tremendous energy and at the same time a great sadness. It was the sadness of youth. So different from the sadness of old age. He'd seen the sadness in his children, remembered experiencing it himself oh so many years ago, a feeling that there was so much to see, so much to do, so much to grab for, and you didn't know what it was, but you wanted it all—but not alone, you wanted it all with that special person that lived only in your imagination. All of it. Knowledge. Love. Adventure. The admiration of elders. The respect of peers. Thrills. Many thrills. All of it. And the sad part was that all of it appeared to be out of reach.

"Go ahead and ask me a question." Howard said.

"That beautiful quilt, where'd that come from?"

"Why, my beautiful wife, Elenore, made that quilt."

"What happened to your finger?"

"Which one?" Howard played dumb.

Tahoka said nothing, but the look on her face was disappointment.

"It got caught in a gear in a factory a long time ago. I forgot it was gone until you just reminded me. That's what it's like getting old."

"Oh, I'm sorry. Tell me where you came from, your heritage. Where are the Elmans from—maybe, Wales?"

"You're just asking to be polite," Howard said.

"No, I'm not polite. Rudeness is one of my many flaws — ask my mother, she'll tell you. I really want to know things about you . . . for my own selfish purposes. Selfishness is another one of my flaws."

"I don't believe you have flaws, Tahoka. It's the world that's flawed. I haven't seen you around town. You one of the new people?"

"I'm new today."

Something dawned on Howard. "You're a runaway, right?" he said.

"I never ran away from anything or anybody in my life. I'm always running toward my destiny."

"I'll sign on to that."

"I don't know what to call you."

"Call me Howard or Howie, anything you want, but don't call me late for supper."

"I don't feel comfortable calling you by your first name, and Mr. Elman doesn't sound right. Can I call you Grandpa?"

"Sure. That's what my grandson Birch Latour calls me."

"Birch Latour is my hero."

"How do you know Birch?"

"When he was on TV, and he talked about saving the forests for ours and future generations. And then I read about him and his grandfather Raphael Salmon in Wikipedia and how Birch's father F. Latour is a poet and a craftsman of wooden spoons who brought him up in the woods. How come they have a different last name than you?"

So Howard told her the lie of how he was brought up a foundling without a name until he had seen this elm tree in the woods. Tahoka Texas McCloud, call me Tahoka, was very attentive, and then he asked her how she happened to seek her destiny in Darby, New Hampshire.

"I have this guardian angel, actually she's more like a guardian gargoyle. She's part rodeo queen and part goth girl, probably not the kind of figure that you would find exemplary, Grandpa, but I like her. I channel her through these." Tahoka opened her mouth and gave Howard a wide and foolish grin that displayed glittery silvery braces on her teeth. "I could have had plastic ones that wouldn't show, but I wouldn't get any reception on them, and anyway I like the bright metal ones, the way they vibrate and reflect light."

"You get signals from this rodeo queen through metal in your mouth?" Howard said.

"Yes, signals from the big bang of creation in my misshapen teeth. You think I'm crazy?"

"Indubitably," Howard said.

They both laughed.

"I'm wondering, where did you run away from?" Howard asked.

"They'll say I ran away from my private—and, I might add, very expensive—boarding school, but I was not running away, I was running to get someplace. I wanted to get to here, this little property, in Darby, New Hampshire, that I always wanted to see with my own Tahoka eyes, and now that I'm here, I want to stay until it disappears from boredom. Pooffffff!" Tahoka paused.

Tahoka's words gushed out in her speed-talking southern lingo faster than an unintended consequence with its bloomers on fire, so fast that Howard couldn't catch up with her meaning.

Disappear? What does she know that you don't, Howie?

Tahoka continued, in a droll voice now that reminded Howard of his own, "You aren't going to turn me in, are you?"

"I don't know, Tahoka." He liked voicing her name.

"Grandpa, I am seventeen years old—I will be eighteen in less than a month, and then it'll be legal for me to run to anywhere I please, so just give me those three weeks. I need them to find . . ." She paused again before speaking. "I need that time to find truth and deep meaning."

"That's why you came here—truth and deep meaning?"

"Yes, Grandpa."

"Then what?"

"Then I will go to Nashville, to the grand old opry to learn to become a country singer so I can save the world and fulfill my destiny."

"Since you only got three weeks, why not just go back to your school and wait it out?"

"Because my mother has a plan to frustrate me. She's going to put me on a plane to Switzerland to another private school until I'm twenty-one. I'm not strong enough in my heart to last another three years. She'll break my spirit, and I'll live a long long life unfulfilled and bare of meaning and meaningful relationships."

No doubt the girl was either misinformed or an outright liar, but it didn't matter to Howard, for he had been taken with an idea.

"Tahoka, minutes ago I was thinking, not seriously mind you, but close — close — about ending it all by crashing my car, actually my dearly departed wife's car. All's I know for sure is I mislaid whatever purity of spirit was in me. You have brought it back. I won't squeal on you."

"Thank you, Grandpa. All can be saved."

"You got that from the TV."

"Yes, that's Birch Latour's motto. Now what?"

"Now I take a nap and you do as you please."

۴ ۴ ۴

That night Tahoka sang sad songs and wrote in her secret diary, an app on her phone. Howard took apart his FFone because he was curious to see how it worked. A disappointing experience. The good stuff of the gadget was hidden, inaccessible in little bitty closed containers. He decided that you could not trust electronics. A mechanical device presented itself to the human eye. You could bear witness to it: gears turned, belts whirred, springs sprung, screws screwed; the effects of weight, motion, and wear were apparent. But an electronic device was simply a collection of packets that housed other packets, and the functions of the innards remained invisible to the eye and unresponsive to touch. Human senses could tell you nothing of how a cell phone worked. People today lived, loved, and died without ever experiencing the entirety of their existence.

I feel cheated.

Cheated by who, Howie?

God. There I said it. Maybe I'm starting to believe.

You sure it's not the Devil you believe in?

When he got the phone back together he ran across a texted note that said, "set up jesus."

What the hell did that mean?

You can't remember, can you Howie?

Tahoka stopped singing. "What was that, Grandpa?"

"It's nothing. I talk to myself sometimes. Tahoka, are you religious?"

183

"Oh, yes. I believe in Jesus and angels."

"Because you have an angel that hangs around to advise you, the rodeo queen goth girl."

"Yes, that's right."

"Does she appear so you can actually see her, or is she just a voice — or what?"

"I feel her presence, and sometimes I get glimpses," Tahoka said.

That night Tahoka made hot buttered popped corn and she and Howard discussed the meaning of life. The effort made Howard tired, and he lay down on the couch, falling asleep to the sounds of Tahoka's soulful singing.

The next morning when Howard woke, it was still dark. The door to the bedroom was closed, and Tahoka and her guitar were missing. He built up the fire. Tahoka had bought some kind of blueberry pop tarts, and Howard ate one with a cup of instant. He listened to the radio. The weather man was calling for a "wintery mix."

Speak your piece, Mister Weatherman, or shut up, no yah-buts, no maybes, no wintery mixes. Snow or rain, sun or cloud, hail or hell fire!

It was another hour before Tahoka emerged from the bedroom. She walked sleep-eyed to the bathroom. When she came out, she was radiant.

"Now what?" Howard said.

"You could give me a tour of your property."

"It's not mine anymore."

"In my heart it will always be yours, Grandpa, and I want to see it in its current incarnation before it vanishes."

"It was an in car nation, now it's a re in car nation," Howard chuckled. "Let me put my boots on, and we'll go outside, and I'll show you the sign."

"Great! I want to know everything about this little place."

"Really — I mean, you really want to see this old man's indubitable endeavor?" Howard said, but he was touched. This girl made him feel bashful. He was in awe of her. "Everything in the mobile home is pretty much Elenore's — that was my wife."

"Of course, Grandma Elenore." Tahoka whipped out the iPhone, thumbed it. "Are you taking notes?" Howard asked.

"Yes, please continue," Tahoka said.

"Elenore kept finding ways to improve this or that, in other words spend money. They say my wife was old school, meaning she never worked a job. Not true. She raised the kids, and she did housecleaning to tide us over, and then there was that coupon business with our two middling, I mean middle, daughters that I never did understand, but it brought in money."

"You had two daughters?"

Howard held up four fingers. "Charlene and Pegeen, the two middle daughters. The first, Sherry Ann—we called her Shan—grew up too quick. She met some guy when she was in high school and ran off with him and . . ." Howard paused, took a deep breath, and said, "Died. It wounded me to the soul and almost killed her mother."

"I'm sorry. I like the way you said 'died'—'doid' to make it rhyme with droid. What about the youngest daughter?"

"Heather—oh, she was a surprise. In every way. Arrived unexpectedly. One day I came home from work. Saw this stork, or maybe it was an egret, which is a southern bird named after a regret. Regrets, egrets—I've had a few but too few to mention. That's a joke that my son Latour came up with. Regrets—egrets. He's got a streak of sarcasm that makes me look like a piker. Piker? Did I say piker? What the hell is a piker. . . . What was I talking about, Tahoka? Train of thought got derailed."

"Your daughter Heather coming into the world." Tahoka pointed upward to a possible distant star.

"Right, the stork, the egret, whatever the hell it was, was carrying something plump. Fat baby, it turned out. Actually, sixteen hours of labor Elenore endured. Some will say that child was born wailing; I say it was singing. Heather had a knack for singing, just like you. In fact, when I hear your voice, it brings me back."

"Did she look like me?"

"Not really. You're blonder and much prettier. In fact, Tahoka, if you'll pardon an old man's saying so, you are about the prettiest girl I have ever seen."

"Thank you, Grandpa. You think I'm prettier than your youngest daughter, really?"

"Really. What's the matter? Are you crying?"

"Yes, Grandpa, I am crying. The least little thing can make me weep, but when the big things happen—like your parents get divorced, or your daddy goes into rehab, or your mother announces she's going to ship you to a school where you don't have any friends or access to your phone and your Internet is filtered, and she is aided and abetted by her snobby second husband—why those big things just make me angry and vengeful."

"Vengeful, no kidding."

"Yes, I take after my mother that way."

Howard reached for his socks. "Put your coat on and let's go outside. This mobile home was Elenore's domain. The outside, that's Howie Elman's world. I want you to behold it."

"How come this trailer is built inside a house which, near as I can tell, isn't really a house."

And so the stocky old man with a bent back and a limp, in his forest-green work duds and his cap that said Darby Police, tried to explain it all to the beautiful blond girl with a wild west look as they went outside. Tahoka left her guitar on the couch, but she thumbed notes on her iPhone as Howard talked.

"Underneath this ice and snow is hard-packed gravel," Howard said. "A man knows he's getting old when he takes pride in his driveway. Over there is the garden. That's the one thing Elenore and I do—done—together. She grew the flowers and tomatoes, and I grew everything else—the hot dogs, the pizzas, the m&m's, and the Schafer cans, the one beer to have when you're having more than Juan. You know Juan, he's quite the drinker. But I can't find Schafer at Ancharsky's Store anymore, so I make do with Natural Ice, or maybe I just make doo doo."

"Grandpa, what are you talking about?"

"Just wanted to see if you were paying attention."

Tahoka pointed, "And that kinda tilted appliance with the bullet holes, what is that?"

"That's a washing machine. Hard to tell with the snow cover on it. See, decades ago I salvaged a ringer machine from the old burning dump in Keene, and when it stopped working I set it up by those trees for target practice. It was quite attractive full of bullet holes. This particular washer is a replacement, not nearly so attractive — I couldn't find one with a ringer — but it's the best I could do as a stand-in."

Tahoka walked through the snow to the washing machine and inspected it. "I'd like to pour some lead in this thing, reminds of a certain somebody," she said.

"You shoot?"

"Yes, my daddy taught me, but my mother and her stuck up husband are against firearms of any kind." She started back through the snow to the plowed driveway where Howard stood.

"Hold the fort, I'll be right back," Howard said. He went into the house and returned with the Rugar.

"Aren't you afraid somebody will call the cops?" Tahoka said.

"I am the cops," Howard said. "Hang on, I'll get some ammo from the barn."

Howard and Tahoka took turns shooting at the washing machine. Even at his advanced age, Howard was a pretty good shot, but Tahoka was better. "Say, you can outshoot Missy Mendelson," Howard said.

They followed their footsteps back to the washing machine for a closer view of their work. "I like it full of holes," Howard said.

"Yes, it has character," Tahoka said. She handed the gun to Howard, and thumbed some notes on her phone. Howard knew it was time to continue the tour.

For the next forty-five or so minutes, while Tahoka took notes, Howard gave her an exhaustive description of his junked cars, where he had acquired them, and what use he made of the parts from time to time.

"I like the way steel ages, the fading of the finish, the varying of the original colors, the rust, but mainly the . . ." Howard searched for a word, and swished his fingers in the cold air.

"The stories," Tahoka said.

"That's it, the stories. The longer the car stays out in the weather the more story it acquires." Howard paused for moment, his brain deep in absurdity. "You ever ask yourself why 'a choir' is a singing group and 'acquire' is taking possession?"

"All the time, Grandpa."

"In the summer I like watching tall grasses and wildflowers grow around the fenders and bumpers, and, by the way, if you want to burn brush in the rain, an easy way to get a fire going is with a little bit of kerosene and an old tire." He pointed to the iPhone. "It makes dark inky smoke."

"Great for diary entries, I suppose."

"Kinda smells bad, though," Howard said.

Tahoka pinched her nose, thumbed furiously, then sang the song that she had made up on the spot, "You built a far under me / and burnt a hole in my heart. / My love is up in smoke. / Ah kin see the writing in the sky, / Pee-you, pee-you, pee-you to you. / Your love was just joke. / My heart is up in inky smoke / Your sky writing was just a lie" She walked over to the giant maple tree and tugged on the rope of the swing.

"I used to push Heather for hours on that swing," Howard said. "When she could do it herself, she pumped and pumped and leaped from the seat. She used to measure her jumps."

"My turn," Tahoka said. She broke through the crust of snow on the seat, brushed it off, and hopped on.

Howard put his hands on the small of her back and pushed. Once he started her, Tahoka pumped, and Howard got out of the way and watched. Tahoka pumped until she was high up and then she leaped, arms and legs out stretched. Then splat. She rolled around in the snow, laughing, and eventually crying again. When she had composed herself, she asked, "Which one of us jumped farthest?"

"Heather, but she had more practice than you."

After that he took her through the barn, showed her the pit that he and F. Latour had dug to work on the undersides of cars. He talked to her about his tools, where he had acquired them, how they had served, and how now they belonged to PLC, and he wondered again just what was going to happen to this property. "You saw the stakes," he said.

"They're going to destroy it, Grandpa," Tahoka said with a certainty that took his breath away.

"How could you know that?"

"I don't know for sure, I don't know anything for sure, but why would they buy it if they didn't want it for their own reasons, and those reasons surely would not be yours?" she said.

"You got wisdom, Tahoka; that's why life pains you so. Let's go back outside," Howard said. He felt light, airy, youthful.

I wish I could bottle this mood, sell it on eBay, bring peace to the world.

That would be a great thing, Howie.

They left the barn and walked through the snow along the stone wall. Howard pointed up slope to the Cutter place that PLC had taken over, and he told her the story of his struggle with Zoe Cutter to keep his property, how in the end, he had won — sort of — but lost a daughter, and how it was the one sin he could not atone for. "What do you think of all this, Tahoka?"

"I'm just overwhelmed with gratitude and love for you, Grandpa."

Neither spoke for a long minute until Howard said, in as kindly a voice as he could manage, "Tahoka, I think it's time for you to go back to your school."

"Do I have to?"

"Yes, you have to."

"It was cold on that rickety bus."

"I got something to take care of that problem. Let's go in the house."

Howard gave Tahoka the "Darby Old Home Day" quilt that Elenore made, then drove her to the bus station in Keene. They waited. Tahoka wrote her email on Howard's arm with a runny pen. He wrote his email address on her arm. The bus arrived. Tahoka put her arms around Howard, and they hugged, and she said, "I love you, Grandpa."

It wasn't until later, back at his place, sucking on a Natural Ice, thinking about Tahoka Texas McCloud, the wire braces on her teeth that picked up signals from distant worlds, her questions about family, the tears, and the ride on the swing, that the obvious dawned on Howard Elman. Tahoka was Heather's daughter by her first husband — that bum McCloud. And then Howard Elman surrendered to his sorrows and wept, involuntarily and inconsolably, in the grip of that awful sin so many years ago, the loss that followed it, the love of this granddaughter that he did not deserve and likely would never see again.

FOUND ELM

HOWARD REMAINED AT his old homestead, waiting to be evicted. Tahoka Texas McCloud was on his mind. What could he do for this granddaughter? Call her mother? He didn't know how to find Heather. He had googled her under Heather Elman and Heather Cutter and Heather McCloud, but nothing turned up.

Ask Latour, he'll know.

I couldn't do that.

You can't ask anybody for anything. You're a hopeless case, Howie.

He took the bullets out of the Ruger and put it in the glove compartment of his car. When they came to evict him, he would go peacefully. He didn't want Birch and Tahoka to hear that their grandpa had died in disgrace.

The "wintery mix" ended up as a very nasty ice storm. The weather honchos were right. The sky really did produce a mix — snow, rain, hail, and the pay balls of a pool table at Cliff Knox's place in the basement of the Latchis Theatre in Keene oh so many years ago. The power in most of Darby was out for a week. Because of the ice storm and maybe because of politics within the planning board and PLC, the planning board postponed its public hearing until one week before town meeting.

Howard liked living without electricity. The woodstove kept the house warm and the gas still flowed to the kitchen stove, though the burner had to be lit with a match. The well pump was out, so Howard melted snow on a big pot on the woodstove to get water to flush the toilet. Thank the creator of the universe who made shit float downhill. He liked burning candles. He liked sitting in the dark. "I'm a pioneer," he said aloud, as if to Elenore.

Meanwhile, the word spread around town that Howard Elman had Alzheimer's. He was no longer a horse's ass, no longer an intimidating presence, he was an object of pity. The selectmen met in a special meeting with the town attorney to decide what to do about Howard's status as town constable. The attorney advised them that it would take some time, not to mention expense, to prepare a case to bring before a judge to remove Howard, because technically he was an elected official. He could not be fired; he had to be impeached. The selectmen decided that since town meeting was only weeks away, it was best to wait, and the town no doubt would not re-elect Howard Elman as its constable.

The ice storm caused considerable damage in Great Meadow Village, where roofs of the flimsy mobile homes collapsed from the weight of ice on the snow already there. "God's wrath, know what I mean," opined Buzz Dorne. *The Keene Sentinel* reported that several children were injured in one of the roof collapses in an unregistered daycare center in the trailer park, and the director of the operation, one Gerald McCracken, was in serious condition at Cheshire Hospital. According to the paper, he had interposed his body between a couple of kids and falling debris. Tubby McCracken had become the hero that Howard Elman had always wanted to be. When the lights came back on, Howard felt happy for Tubby and sad for himself.

🌾 🌾 🌾

One morning at dawn Howard was finishing up his coffee when he saw a pickup truck pull into his yard. On the door of the truck was a logo of a meetinghouse steeple and the words "Paradise Lots Covenant / Connecting Tradition and Technology to / You." Howard watched through a window while a man in his forties dressed in blue jeans and a blaze-orange vest over his parka got out of the truck. He was husky with a swagger in his body carriage, but his face didn't convey any meanness.

Howard went out to meet him.

"Something I can do you for?" Howard said.

The man smiled, not exactly a sarcastic smile. No doubt he was amused by the sight of the old geezer that he had heard had Alzheimer's.

"My name's Bernard LeClair, but everybody calls me Bugsy. I represent Paradise Lots Covenant, who I believe are the owners of this property."

"So they sent you to kick me out."

"No, sir, I'm not in that business. I'm a heavy equipment operator and contractor in charge of site prep on this lot."

A little alarm bell went off in Howard's head. He was visualizing a small bulldozer. "I have a lot of respect for a guy that can operate machines."

"Thank you, and you would be the former owner of this property, Howard Elman."

"Constable Elman to you. The company got plans for my lot?"

"Yes, but I haven't seen them yet. I'm waiting on orders from the CEO, H.C. Wentworth."

"I'm glad the head guy is taking an interest in this little piece of heaven."

"H.C. Wentworth ain't a guy. Look, Elman, I know it must be hard for you to leave your property, but you really should get out before you get served papers, because I'm going to have to report your presence on the premises."

"I know you're just doing your job, Bugsy, which is all a working man can do. Go ahead and write up your report. Meanwhile, I'm going to stay right here and play pocket pool."

"Thank you, you'll excuse me while I look around." Bugsy tipped an imaginary cap and started walking the land with a tape measure. Howard watched while Bugsy took notes, planted a few stakes, moved some of the old ones, then drove off.

⚜ ⚜ ⚜

There was a thaw that included a warm rain, which led to runoff and some flooding behind ice dams in low-lying areas; much of the snow disappeared. Howard didn't do much, but he remained on his former property brooding. He almost wished they would evict him. So many unanswered questions, most of which circled around Birch and Tess Jordan.

What in the world did Birch see in a crazy woman and a member of the Jordan Kinship? And if, like her father insisted, she wasn't crazy, why did she act crazy and why did Birch go along?

No doubt she or Birch or both of them are implicated in the murder of Billy Jordan. No wonder Birch wants you out of sight, out of mind.

What should I tell Delphina about her son?

Howard had no answers except the awful answer from Critter's files that only discombobulated the questions. He talked out the questions with Cooty and, inspired by the centenarian, decided to forget the big questions for the time being and make do by resuming his investigation of the downing the last great elm tree. He decided, too, to remain on the Re In Car Nation property until he was served papers to leave.

March first came around, with cold nights and warmish days, and the maple sap flowed from the trees through the plastic tubes into tanks. Early mud season coincided with the sap run and logging operations were suspended until the ground dried out. Obadiah, Charley, and even Birch's mouthy, free-loading geek chorus minions were involved in the Trust conservancy maple syrup operations. When the wind was right, Howard could smell the sugar thrown off by the boil of the evaporators. Howard often visited Cooty in his cabin, but he stayed away from the Manse, which seemed to suit Birch. Grandfather and grandson didn't know what to say to one another.

One afternoon after a bowl of stew at the cabin, Howard said: "Cooty, I got a hunch."

"It's always a thrill for me when you get a hunch, Howie."

"How come hunches always come to me when I'm talking to you?"

"Because I collect hunches," Cooty said. He pointed to the sticks hanging on the wall of the cabin, and said, "Those are all hunches, but they don't mean much until you put hunches in bunches."

Howard told Cooty: "I think Critter hired one of the PLC working men to steal my tree, and I got a hunch I know the guy. If it was a local yokel, the word would've got around."

Howard drove to Ancharsky's Store and after making some inquiries he learned that PLC was putting up Bugsy LeClair at a motel in Keene, one of the new ones on the edge of the city. That night Howard turned on the blue light on the PT Cruiser, but not the siren, drove to the motel, and used his authority as Darby Constable to acquire Bugsy's room number from the clerk. Howard resisted the impulse to turn the knob; he banged on the door.

Bugsy answered right away. "Well, ain't this a surprise?" Bugsy said.

From the smell of booze and the look of Bugsy's glassy eyes and good-humored smile, Howard surmised that Bugsy was drunk but not yet pie-eyed.

"You going to offer me a drink, or what?" Howard said, and pushed past him.

"I suppose," Bugsy backed up, a little off balance.

Howard sat at an easy chair by the gas heater and watched while Bugsy sat at the desk in front of a laptop computer. Beside the computer was a bottle of Jim Beam, just a corner of liquor left in it. The desk was made of composite wood fiber and glue, covered with a slick of plastic so that unless you looked closely the desk wood resembled maple boards stained and finished.

It's the way of the world, Howie. Nothing is real any more.

Maybe it's all for the best.

Doubt it, bro, doubt it.

Bro? Where did that come from?

Birch's minions.

"I've been playing online poker with this guy for the last week," Bugsy said, never taking his eyes off the computer screen. "We broke about even, but today I hit him good, made a couple hundred pound sterling. You know how much a pound is? Never mind, I know you don't. So I'm playing with this guy, and I notice he spells favor with a u, so I type are 'you a Brit, me I'm from the states', so he starts bad-mouthing America, so I type, 'You write very good English. If it wasn't for America you would be writing very good German.'" Bugsy laughed and laughed at his own cleverness.

Howard laughed with him. In Bugsy LeClair, Howard saw a younger version of himself in the primo of horse's assness.

Finally, Bugsy turned away from his screen, took a slug of Jim Beam, and handed the bottle to Howard.

"I don't want to drink the last of your consolation," Howard said.

"That's okay, I got more stashed away."

"Kinda hitting it pretty hard for middle of the work week," Howard said.

"I'm taking a sick day tomorrow. They owe me."

"Bugsy, I was thinking about your small bulldozer. Couple planks, drive it up on the bed of a logging truck." Howard tipped Jim Beam to his lips and frenched the last two ounces.

"You think I care?" Bugsy said. "Like the old South Boston whores, I don't give a fuck for nothing."

"You're lying to yourself, Bugsy. Of course you give a fuck or else you wouldn't of let me in and offered me a drink."

"I tend to err when I'm drinking," Bugsy said.

"Tell me about it, err today gonzo tomorrow. No, don't tell me about it. Tell me why a guy with an honorable position with PLC would take a rinky dink job from a sleaze bag like Critter Jordan."

That got Bugsy's attention. He paused to give Howard a long look.

"They were wrong — you're not demented."

"No, they were right — demented is what makes me dangerous."

"I'm sworn to secrecy," Bugsy said, and went to the bathroom. He returned with another bottle of Jim Beam that he opened as he sat down at the desk.

"Tell me about the elm tree," Howard said.

Bugsy shook his head.

"It's the money, isn't it?"

Bugsy took another pull on his darling new bottle before he spoke. "Yeah, it was the money. Would there be another reason? See I kinda fell behind, and I don't actually work for PLC. I work for myself — independent contractor."

"Let me guess your problem, gambling debts."

"Yeah, I'm a haunted man, Constable. Are you going to arrest me? I almost wish you would, though I'd hate having to explain to my old lady."

"You're not a bad guy, Bugsy, and I'm not like a real cop, so I am not going to turn you in, but I am going to tell you a story." Howard told Bugsy how he acquired his name and how the elm tree was really like the long lost dick of his young manhood. "Critter Jordan hired you to cut that tree down. Tell me if I'm wrong."

"You're not wrong — sue me," Bugsy said.

"Bugsy, I got nothing against you. I want the story. Give me the story, and I'll leave you alone. Stonewall me, and I'll bring the state police in and the boulders will collapse around you." Howard stood, grabbed the bottle from the desk top, took another drink, and handed the bottle to Bugsy.

Bugsy tipped the bottle, and a few drips found their way down the corners of his mouth. "What I don't know is how Jordan knew me," he said. "My name, my experience, my position as an independent contractor, even my cell phone number. Kinda freaked me out. He told me he had a job for me."

"Bottom line. You buried my elm at the old sandbank that PLC bought."

"I knew we had an excavator parked there for some work that was coming up. I could do the job alone, but I could do it faster with a little help."

"And fast is better than slow when it's on the south side of legal."

Bugsy nodded. "I really didn't want to implicate one of the other guys on my crew. So I cut the tree and then me and that trailer trash punk, what's-his-face . . ."

"Tubby McCracken," Howard said. "He's a hero."

"Yeah, that's the guy. He did time he was telling me, reformed . . . yeah, right. He's a hero?"

"Yes, but never mind. Stay with me."

"Okay, so we cut the tree, that is, I cut the tree, because Tubby was chicken shit, and he helped with positioning and chaining while I worked the loader. We brought the tree to the sandbank and buried it."

"Except for the burl," Howard said.

"Yeah, the Jordan guy wanted a burl to make a bowl to charm his ex-wife."

"He wanted to resume relations?"

"That was my guess. I don't know for sure."

"Where at the sandbank is my tree?"

"I couldn't tell you — in the sand. That was the idea, easy digging, no rocks. Glacial moraine."

"You can't tell me where in the sand, but you could show me."

"I suppose I could but not at night."

"Bugsy, I'll come back in the morning, and you and me will take a ride to the sandbank."

"Okay, Constable."

Howard was about ready to leave when he got the idea to spring a big question. "Bugsy, what's the story behind Paradise Lots? They pay good but . . . clue me in."

"They're weird, lots of secrets," Bugsy said. "They'll hire somebody for a job, and then hire somebody else to do the same work. They'll show you drawings for a job, but never all of the drawings."

"They don't want any one crew to know the whole picture — know what I mean?" Howard said.

"Don't start in on 'know what I mean' with me. I've been through it with that idiot Jesus trucker."

"Dorne, his name is Buzz Dorne," Howard said. "You got his name from Critter, right?"

Bugsy nodded.

"Gimme a for example of PLC business practices, the weirdest for example you can think of."

"That's easy. My crew was hired to excavate the basement of the new meetinghouse. This guy from Mexico, Maine, shows up — or maybe it was Egypt, Maine, I don't know. His people are going to put in the foundation, but his specs don't match up with mine. He's got a floor drawing with weird passages in the walls. Then the PLC suit, gentleman with an accent, he impounds both specs, tells us we ain't suppose to be talking to each other."

"What kind of accent?"

"Beats me. Not American — what else do you need to know?"

"Different sets of drawings for the same building, so what?"

"So it's not like PLC don't know what they want. They are very particular and organized. They are just weird."

"Weird passages in the walls, like you could hide a body in there? What do you mean, what size?"

"Nothing the size of a man, maybe a baby or a spaniel. Me and the old lady, we have a spaniel. You have to be careful you don't overfeed them. They are the original chow hounds." Bugsy talked on, Howard stopped paying attention.

He remembered now the message on his phone, "set up Jesus." The baby Jesus he had carved for Elenore's nativity, which he had failed to set up for the Christmas season.

"Bugsy, suppose you wanted to blow up a building so that everybody in it was . . ." Howard paused to search for a phrase, remembered something Tess Jordan said at Cooty's birthday party and that was later repeated by her father. "A building relegated to smithereen land, and you knew this place would get more than a once over by the Secret Service. Where do you put the charges?"

"What are you trying to say?"

"I'm saying I'd build my bomb into the foundation during construction."

"Weird, so many weirdos in New Hampshire." He took another pull from the bottle.

"Yeah, well, next time you think about our state, look at the number plates on our vehicles. Live free or die, Bugsy, live free or die!"

By the time Howard was getting up to leave the motel room, Bugsy LeClair had entered his own private smithereen land. He was talking about going into the snow to piss out his territory like a wolf. He even howled like a wolf. He had left the world of drunk and entered the world of pie-eyed. "If I can't live free, I'd sooner die," Bugsy said.

"Have another drink, and I'll see you in the morning." Howard eased toward the door. He figured Bugsy wouldn't remember too much of their conversation, which was all for the best. Howard, too, wished he could forget it, forget "set up jesus," forget everything.

Forgetfulness is the ultimate blessing for the demented and the dead. Unless you are religious, in which case you are confronted at the pearly gates by St. Peter or some other asshole holding a ledger of your sins, who will remind you there are places to go after death besides oblivion. "I'm just gathering the evidence," St. Peter will say, "God is the judge."

Why should God give a flaming fuck what my sins are? Doesn't he have enough to do without bothering with a doofus like Howie Elman?

Howard let himself out of the motel room. The wind had turned from the north and it was very cold.

Hey, how about a little of that global warming.

He was in the PT Cruiser just pulling out of the parking lot when he saw the door to Bugsy's room open and the man himself step into the night. Apparently he was going to make good on his promise to piss out a territory like a wolf. Howard rolled down the window and shouted, "Live free or die," but the wind was hard and hungry and swallowed the words.

Howard arrived back at Re In Car Nation tired but wired. He noted that the temperature had dropped twenty degrees. He knew he wouldn't sleep until the effects of the booze wore off. He decided to check his email. Charlene included pictures of the great-grandchildren.

Howard was not very good at writing. He had taught himself to understand the written word, and sometimes he talked a blue streak (was it blue streaks that turned people blue in that movie?), but he had trouble spelling, and he could only type rudimentary thoughts with his fat fingers. He should tell Charlene that he had met Heather's daughter, Tahoka McCloud, after all these years, but he didn't want to start another family avalanche. What he wanted to tell Charlene was that he had discovered that Critter Jordan had paid men to cut down his elm tree but for reasons unknown. He wanted to tell her that there was a dark secret in the town: the Squire had murdered Ike Jordan. He wanted to tell her that Bugsy LeClair was going to show him where he had buried the elm tree, that he planned to build his coffin with boards from the logs.

Don't tell her your selfish desires, apologize to her for being a bad father.

Howard typed, "Cold, wind from the north. See you later." His note got him to thinking.

Why is "see" spelled two different ways?

Actually, Howie, three if you count the letter "c." "See," "sea," "C"?

Why would a word for look and a word for ocean sound the same?

He clicked "send" and off his email went.

He wondered if St. Peter, that cranky gatekeeper of Catholic heaven, lurked on the Internet to keep track of people's sins. And it was that thought that told him he'd had too much to drink.

He was about to log out when a new message came across his machine. It was from Delphina. "can't sleep. too many mixed feelings, critter sent me mucho $. this is not the critter I know. he must be a changed man. he never mentioned billy and I haven't heard from billy. what's going on?"

No doubt Tess and probably Birch had something to do with the death of Billy, but who was on the Internet pretending to be Critter and Billy Jordan in emails to Delphina?

Do you really want to know the details?

Yes. I want to know everything—for peace of mind.

Everything and peace of mind can't exist together: Ollie Jordan saying.

Howard emailed Delphina. "sit tite I am on the case."

The next morning was very cold but with bright sunshine. Howard was eager to fetch Bugsy. On the drive to the motel Howard was thinking about the Devil, which of course he did not believe in, at least not strictly—guy with horns sticking out of his head and a tail.

Why would the Devil have a tail?

Balance?

If there is a Devil he will not look like the Devil. The Devil would be a smoothie; he would look like Lawrence Dracut.

Howard suddenly realized that Dracut resembled that boring band leader Elenore had a crush on.

Lawrence Welk!

You may or may not have to face the Devil, but you do have to face death. Think about the possibilities. In bed sleeping. Car crash. Slo-mo and incapacitated in a nursing home. A fall. Lost in the woods. Lost in dementia. Icepick in the ear. Gun fight, like John Wayne in The Shootist. Squashed rasslin' with Bev Boufford in a giant bowl of Jell-O.

And the afterlife?

Forced to listen to the Lawrence Welk band for all eternity.

He arrived at the motel as the last cop car was leaving. It was Trooper Durling. Howard flagged him down and got the story. Apparently, Bugsy had wandered off in his drunken state and couldn't find his way back. Froze to death in the fens behind the motel. Howard remembered bird hunting in the area decades ago.

Bugsy would not have drunk so much if he'd been alone. You and live free or die sent him to smitherland land, Howie.

Wonder if they have revenge in the afterlife. Is Bugsy LeClair lying in wait for me on the other side?

It was this last thought that allowed Howard to slide out from the twentieth century stockade of guilt into the loony toon arcade of the twenty-first century.

Howie, there is no point in guilt, no point in shame, no point in ambition: it's all a show. Cooty's got it right. You grab the popcorn and walk into the movie screen.

⚓ ⚓ ⚓

He drove to the sandbank. He knew it well; it was quite extensive, half a hillside. Much of the moraine had been hauled away. The remaining half resembled a giant somewhat munched upside down pineapple cake.

Actually, Howie, you only have the vaguest mental picture of an upside down pineapple cake, so why conjure a comparison?

There it was: another loony toon.

The thing about a sandbank is that it's always visibly changing. What you see today is not what you get tomorrow. It is like watching the evolution of a celestial body speeded up. Aging is like that, too. When you're a kid time goes by very slowly, but the older you get the faster time appears to move. Conclusion?

No such a thing as time.

That's correct. What we think of as time is our perceptions of change. The town of Darby was compatible with the human perception of change—until PLC *showed up. Their plan will obloberate your sense of time.*

Horror rolled over him like a fog. He had created Darby-time in his mind, an anchor holding him in the harbor of his identity.

The destruction of your personal Darby is speeding up. It began with the tree, then your property; it will end with the complete recombobulation of the community itself.

He parked and limped around, avoiding patches of ice as best he could. He never expected to find his elm tree. One of these days while, say, a cellar was being excavated for a house on top of the sandbank, the elm might turn up. More likely it would remain buried for zillions of years, eventually transmorgifying into peat, then petrifying (peat-tree-frying?) into a monument. Some future civilization would unearth it, put the stone logs in a museum to be gazed upon and admired. He imagined himself buried with the tree, petrifying with the tree, tree to stone, man to stone, monument to an era. Era today gone tomorrow.

He was gnawing these thoughts like an old dog his bone when his foot caught, and he tripped and almost fell. His first thought was—oh-oh hip—but he regained his balance, and there it was: the corner of a log sticking out of the ground. He had found his tree. His eyes brimmed with tears.

Are you weeping out of happiness, Howie? Or is it the great sadness of The End? Maybe some guilt thrown in for your culpability in the demise of Bugsy LeClair? Just an old man's female hormones? Or did you get yourself in a mood with your thoughts?

Probably all those things. So now what?

The answer is obvious: bring the logs to a saw mill, make boards, erect that casket, lie in it during that long sleep that nobody wakes from.

⚓ ⚓ ⚓

A couple of days later, Birch Latour on behalf of the Salmon Trust arranged through the Boston office of Paradise Lots Covenant to retrieve the elm tree that had been stolen from the primeval forest. The elm logs were excavated and sold to the Cersosimo Mill. Birch worked out a deal with the mill for access to the mill's markets for the log. F. Latour, as one of the writers for Darby Doomsday, would "follow the trail of the tree"; all the commercial uses of the tree would be cataloged, not just as lists but as stories that would find their way into Darby Doomsday. Birch negotiated with the Smithsonian Institute and Spofford Films Inc. to create a TV documentary on the future of the forest centering around the elm tree. That move led to a book contract for F. Latour. At Howard's request, some of the lumber was returned in varying sizes to the grounds of the Manse, and stacked for drying behind a screen of trees. Howard Elman would build his casket, but "Not right away—in due time. I gotta find Critter first," he told Cooty, who told Luci, who turned over the transcription to Geek Chorus Software.

Howard went, as usual, to fetch Critter's mail, but he learned Critter had closed his post office box and left no forwarding address. Howard lay on his couch bed and tried to figure out what to do next. In that borderland between sleep and wakefulness he heard Elenore's voice, "Wait for a sign, Howie."

Three AM piss call. Snowing hard. Snow would do for a sign. Hop on Billy's snowmobile and visit Tess Jordan in her tree house.

VECTOR WOMAN

DAWN. HOWARD WAS AWAKENED by vibrations. He cranked up his hearing aid, and now he could hear a truck in his driveway. He went outside. It was still cloudy, but the snow had stopped. About six inches had fallen. Nice little storm. Junior Kruger was just finishing up plowing out the driveway. Howard walked over to the truck. Junior rolled down the window.

"How much do I owe you?" Howard asked.

"Nothing. Keeping this place plowed out is in Dad's new contract with PLC."

"How is your dad?"

"He bought the farm yesterday," Junior said, just as calmly as one talking about the weather.

Bought the farm? How did that come to mean kicking the bucket?

Kicking the bucket and buying the farm mean the same thing?

Kicking a bucket and buying a farm at the same time would kill anybody.

"I'm sorry to hear that, Junior."

Actually, you're not sorry. In fact the news gave you a jolt of vigor: well, I outlived that bastard.

"It was so sudden it hasn't sunk in yet," Junior said. He held the steering wheel in a kind of caress. Howard figured Junior's only emotion at the moment was glee at the thought of inheriting an almost new truck. The grief would come later.

Howard didn't have any idea just how he was going to approach Tess Jordan, so he did what he always did when he was stumped. He visited Cooty, figuring that at least he could grab some breakfast from the stew pot. Probably what Howard liked best about visiting Cooty was the loony toons mentality. It relaxed him. He didn't have to think about his own loony toons: confusion in the face of old age, grief, and bodily decombobulation.

He arrived as Luci and Wiqi were finishing up a treatment for Cooty. The centenarian looked quite rakish in his robe, medieval acorn cap, with his whippy hair blown outward like dandelion parachutes lifted by the wind. They all sat around the tiny table, Howard and Cooty eating stew, Luci and Wiqi sipping some kind of herb tea concoction.

Who put the "h" in erb tea?

"How did you people happen to wind up here?" Howard asked Wiqi, who was flipping virtual pages on his handheld.

"Luci and I met online in a role-playing game," Wiqi said. "Which led to my Uncle Web writing this book about us, but he never found a publisher."

Luci laughed. "In the book Wiqi and I are robots."

"Sometimes I think the two of you are robots," Howard said.

"What makes you think we aren't?" Luci said.

"Does it matter?" Cooty asked.

"Not to me it don't," Howard said.

"Hic, hec, hoc," Wiqi said, as if speaking to his handheld.

"What are you studying?" Cooty asked.

"The Latin language."

"When I was an altar boy, we used to speak Latin in church," Cooty said.

"So, you could teach me Latin," Wiqi said.

"I don't know that much; they didn't tell us what the words meant. Do you care what the words mean?"

"I'm dyslexic, and I think maybe another language, especially one that has a lot of root words in English, will help me," Wiqi turned to Howard. "Constable Elman, Birch says you're dyslexic, too."

"That's what I was told. I always had lot of problems reading, still do."

"I'll give you a Latin lesson," Cooty said to Wiqi. "What do you know so far?"

"Not too much; I just started," Wiqi said, and mispronouncing the words on his handheld, "Hic, hec, hoc, huius, huius, huius."

"The correct pronunciation is "hick, hike, hock, whoweeus, whoweeus, whoweeus," said Luci. "I think huius is short for Julius, like Julius Caesar. He conquered much of the known world."

"He was probably compensating for having a sissy name," Howard said. He could see from her expression that Luci knew he was kidding, but Cooty and Wiqi didn't.

Cooty turned to Wiqi. "Me and Howie, we're hicks, so that's the hick part. Hike could be like when you're playing football and the quarterback says 'hike,' or maybe it's like take a hike, and hock is like you leave something at a pawn shop, but it also could be a hunk of spit."

"Put them together," Luci said, "hick, hike, hock could be translated as 'Country boy pawns his football.'" Luci looked at Howard with a little mischievous grin. He decided he liked this girl. Maybe she *was* a robot. If so, robots of her ilk were better than humans of his own ilk.

"Wouldn't that be hick, hock, hike?" Wiqi asked.

"By gosh, you're right," Cooty said.

Wiqi shook his head in confusion, and said, "I'd much rather deal with computer code, where an expression always means the same thing and where even variables vary within logical parameters."

After a pause, Howard said, "Cooty, you still don't make any sense to me, but you're talking more and you just seem . . . with it."

"He is more than with it," Luci said. "In fact, I think he's ready to be regressed."

"Regressed? What do you mean?" Howard said.

"They're going take me back to the place where I forgot," Cooty said.

"That might not be a combobulative idea," Howard said. He was talking to Cooty, but he was looking at Luci.

"We shall see," she said.

"Hick, hike, hock," said Wiqi to his handheld.

From his seat by the tiny table, Howard had a view through the crooked window of the estate grounds. Presently, he could see a trash collection truck coming up the long driveway that led to the Manse. The sight of it gave him an idea. He said his good-byes to Cooty and the nurses, went outside, and walked over to where the trash-collection truck had backed up to the dumpster. Howard greeted Pitchfork Parkinson and his helper, Long Neck MacDougal.

"Pitchfork, I need a ride to the auction barn," Howard shouted. "I don't want nobody to see my vehicle parked in Critter's lot, so I'm going to leave it here."

"Why sure," Pitchfork said.

Pitchfork Parkinson was one of the great unsung heroes of Darby, New Hampshire, and the U. S. of A. Howard credited Pitchfork's calm disposition to his bachelorhood and devotion to his Down syndrome sister.

Howard was happy to be back in a honeywagon. He liked the scenery from the height of the seat, and he liked the smell of trash, swill, and the mechanical friction of the honeywagon itself. It was the smell of money. Pitchfork as he approached retirement was a very careful driver, a little bit too cautious to please Howard. "How do you make a living on the honeywagon driving like an old lady?" Howard said.

Pitchfork, who had always been immune to Howard's horse's assness, just laughed. He dropped Howard at the auction barn. "You call me if you need a ride back, Howie," he said, and drove off.

⚜ ⚜ ⚜

Howard didn't think he'd need a ride. He had a plan.

He walked around the rear of the auction barn. Billy's brand-new snow machine with its cover lay undisturbed. Howard had the key. He hoped the battery hadn't run down too much. He whisked off the new snow and the gravelly old snow, hopped in the saddle, and turned the key. The engine made protesting sounds, started, farted, then smoothed out. The muffler was quite good, so the engine wasn't too loud. Howard, who had always been good with machines, quickly figured out how to operate the snowmobile. What surprised him was its power. He crunched the throttle and the machine did a wheelie and almost bucked him off.

It went bump, bump as it chewed through crunchy old snow, but the ride was better when he reached the packed-down path. The Darby Snowmobile Club was very good at maintaining its network of trails that connected to trails in other towns, so that it was possible to travel by snow machine all the way to Canada. There were even road signs at intersections. Billy's rig made it to the old forest in minutes. He parked off the trail a little bit. "Now comes the hard part," he said aloud to nobody.

He'd have to walk over a knoll, down a hill, and up another hill to reach the tree house on the edge of the prime evil forest. For a young person in the bloom of health it was a five-minute jaunt. For an old man with a limp left over from his broken leg decades earlier the effort was exhausting. Finally, Howard, huffing and puffing, his bad leg killing him, stood on the second knoll. He could feel the cold on the tip of his severed finger.

Christmastime you hiked in all the way from the Manse. Howie, you're on the downside.

This time he caught Tess Jordan home. She was waiting for him at the base of the steep, winding stairs of the tree house. No doubt she saw him approach.

"I have come to visit with you, Tess."

She reached for her fake cell phone, but Howard halted her, "I know you're not crazy, Tess. I talked to your father."

Tess took a moment to think. She looked like a champion something or other that you saw on the Olympics, one magnificent human specimen, or maybe speciwoman.

"You think you can make it up there?" Tess pointed to the steep stairway that led to the tree house.

"I'll give it a shot," Howard said. "Maybe you'll have some luck, and I'll have a heart attack."

"That would be convenient," she said with Estelle Jordan sarcasm.

Tess got behind him and pushed on his bottom, helping him up the stairs, until he finally made it into the main room of the tree house. It was nice being touched by a woman, and he was grateful. Flames from ash and hard maple logs rocked and rolled in the fireplace.

"It's like we're in a Darby farmhouse from eighteen hundred something or other," Howard said.

"That's half the idea," Tess said.

"The other half being solar power and all the other conveniences of today."

"That's not exactly accurate. This structure is all about yesterday and tomorrow, and forget about today."

Watching the flames was Dali, the cat with the smooshed face. Howard plopped down in a chair. The bear head on the bear rug seemed to stare at him critically.

Tess brought Howard a mug of hot chocolate.

"Thank you," Howard said. "You play a crazy girl pretty good."

"I know the drill; mental illness is rife in my family," Tess said. "Birch told me you've been busy playing constable."

"Must be a pain to watch an old man pretending he's a real cop, but here I am, running on fumes and curiosity."

"Just what are you trying to prove?" Tess said. She sat on the bear rug and lounged like a model posing for a photographer.

"It's varied. I started trying to find out who cut down a certain elm tree, and I pretty much know it was your Uncle Critter. Now I want to know why. And to tell you the truth I'm curious about you and Birch. He's your boyfriend, right?"

"More than that, he's my fiancé. Birch wants an heir for the Trust lands, and I plan to give it to him. I love him, Grandpa. Is it okay if I call you Grandpa? See I don't have anybody in my family I can call Grandpa."

"Sure, Tess, you can call me Grandpa. Seems like it's the thing to do."

"Birch loves you, you know that, don't you?" Tess said.

Howard, embarrassed by the word "love," gave an involuntary snarl. "Great, but that's not going to stop me from finding out the truth. You moved into the auction barn to spy on Critter, isn't that right?"

"Yes, it was my idea, but all of us in the Chorus talked about at it at length."

"Didn't it occur to any of you dodo heads that you'd be in harm's way?"

"No, not at all. I thought I knew Uncle Critter. I never believed he was violent. Then he started doing all these bad things. We thought if we could find out what was troubling him about the Trust, we could do something about it. What we hadn't counted on was that he changed after Aunt Delphina left him. He became unpredictable, unstable, and angry angry angry."

Howard wanted to brag that he knew the awful answer: Critter

Jordan had it in for Birch and the Trust because his grandfather Salmon had killed Critter's old man, but Howard held back.

"And he hit on you or maybe it was Billy who hit on you, and you ran away," Howard said.

"No, Critter was very courtly toward me, and Billy was shy and a little stupid, I'm afraid. I left because I couldn't stand my own hypocrisy. It's too bad — I should have stayed. If I had more courage, I might have found out what was nagging at Critter."

"Did you know that Critter was back in the family burglary business?"

Tess looked away from Howard. "Yes. What bothered me the most was Billy, poor Billy. Critter was teaching that boy the burglary trade, just the way Granduncle Ike taught him."

Howard figured from the way Tess was talking that she knew that Billy was dead. He decided it was best to keep that knowledge out of the way for the time being.

What's the matter, Howie, are you afraid to ask?

Maybe.

Right, because maybe Billy's death is a fig newton of your imagination.

A creepy feeling came over Howard. Was it possible that he had imagined a frozen cadaver in the auction barn?

It's okay, Howie. A life of make-believe is better than the real thing.

Howard realized he was not listening to Tess.

She talked on.

It must be pretty lonely out here. She seemed happy to have a visitor, even if it was a nosey old man.

"Critter reverting to criminal behavior and bringing down Billy with him, it wounded me, Grandpa," Tess said. "Birch and I talked so often about us breaking through the barriers between Upper Darby and Darby Depot, between the Salmons and the Jordans."

"You want to bring peace and love to the world," Howard said, droll.

"Exactly," she said, and her sincerity shamed him.

"Young love has its limits," Howard said. And he wondered, now where did I get that old line from? It was too ordinary and schmaltzy for an Ollie Jordan saying. Maybe Elenore picked it up from Oprah.

"We would do it with our baby," Tess said.

"Your baby?" Howard figured the look on his face must have been pretty comical, because Tess burst out laughing.

"That's right, Grandpa, I'm pregnant," she said, "which was another reason for me to get away from Critter and hide out. If he had learned Birch was the father, it would have made him even wilder and crazier."

"Where does Critter think you went?"

"To New York to work in my dad's graphics business."

"I guess that explains why you're not living at the Manse. Eventually Mrs. McCurtin would learn you were in Darby, and in twenty minutes the whole world would know. Turtle is stuck in the top of a building, and you're up a tree."

"What I told Critter is almost true, because I am working with my father in Turtle Vectors. I'm just not in New York. With the Internet, physical location is irrelevant, since we're always connected. I may be up a tree, but it's a tree with a satellite feed to the world wide web."

"How long do you think you can live out here — alone?"

"I see Birch most afternoons, and for the rest of the day I'm content with the company of Dali. Once in a while, Birch takes me to Keene or even the Upper Valley to see his dad and Katharine."

"You keep busy chucking wood in the fireplace."

"I have more to do than that, believe me. I'm drawing eight to twelve hours a day."

Howard looked around. "I don't see any pictures."

"Here, I'll show you." Tess grabbed a remote from a table. Click! A moment later half a wall was not a wall. To Howard it looked like a big flat TV screen. The illusion of the eighteenth and nineteenth centuries morphed into the illusion of the twenty-first century, skipping the twentieth century entirely.

Click! And now he was looking at a line drawing of a traditional New England meetinghouse.

Click! Drawings of characters who all looked vaguely familiar.

"These are basic black and white drawings that I do in Google Sketchup and Adobe Illustrator," Tess said. "I email them to dad. He colors them, gives them depth and shadowing using the mesh tool in Illustrator. By the time he's done, the images are as realistic as photographs, but more vivid and otherworldly."

"That stubby lady with the machine gun looks like Bev Boufford," Howard said.

"It's the best I could do drawing her, given our deadline for a Power-Point presentation that I'm putting together for our video game so Birch can schmooze potential investors."

Click!

"Geeze, look at that — the meetinghouse blowing up!"

"Yes, and with it the presidential candidates," Tess giggled a little bit.

Joke. Everything was a joke to these young people. "I can't say I like this game," Howard said.

"It'll grow on you, Grandpa. What you have to remember is that the player can always change it. The dystopia ending is just one of many options in Darby Doomsday."

"Is one of your investors PLC?"

"Good guess. The only thing Birch really cares about is the Trust. Getting involved in the worlds of show business and finance and even love are his means to that end. It's expensive to create a classy video game. Designers, like my dad, will refine my basic drawings, make them realistic. Meanwhile, our writers Josephine Abare, Web Clements, and Birch's dad are creating a movie script as well as scenarios for the game. And Trek, Jayu, and Solomon have to turn it all into code."

"What does my son write for this outfit?"

"Among other things he writes the scenes that feature a Howard Elman like character. Let me show you." Tess booted another file.

Howard watched fascinated as a character very much like himself investigated a crime very much like his investigation of the downed elm tree.

"Does he get shot in the end?" Howard said.

"Of course. But that's not the only ending. In one scenario he's run over by a bulldozer. In others he . . . you get the idea. F. Latour is still working on the endings."

"No doubt he gets a kick out of killing me off in different ways," Howard said, droll.

Tess showed him more "storyboards," as she called them.

"Hey, that's my yard, my junked cars, everything," Howard said. The drawing was more detailed than most of the others.

"Technically, Re In Car Nation belongs to PLC, so it has a lot of possibilities for conflicts, especially class conflicts."

"How do you know that PLC bought my land?"

"I know many things that you don't, Grandpa."

"What does Darby Doomsday have planned for my lot?" Howard asked, forcing droll, though he didn't feel droll.

"There are several scenarios in the game, but real life?" Tess paused, then added, "I can't say."

"I don't think I want to know what the scenarios are."

"Wise decision."

There was a pause. No talking. No points made in the PowerPoint presentation.

Howie, now is your chance. Ask her about Billy.

No, it's not the right moment.

You're afraid.

True.

As Ollie Jordan would say, do something even if it's wrong, because she's trying to figure a way to get you to leave.

"Your dad told me you worked for a black ops unit."

Tess laughed, a Jordan laugh. "Daddy is such a joker."

"Where'd you get the idea for the fake cell phone?" Howard asked. He sipped the hot chocolate. It warmed him.

"I wanted to appear peculiar and marginalized, like a Jordan woman of old. I didn't grow up a Jordan, but I wanted to experience that part of my heritage. My father told me about the days when the Jordans were itinerant charcoal burners, moving from one devastated woodlot to the next, and how they lived by a code of succor and ascendancy."

"I know the Jordan code," Howard said. "You sought succor from Critter Jordan."

"Yes, that's right. I wanted to see what the sensation of submission Jordan-style felt like."

"And?"

Tess laughed a little. "I can't say I was comfortable granting Critter ascendancy, but I learned a lot. I saw that the Jordan thing was still strong in Critter and Billy, and it's somewhere inside of me, too. I wonder if I'll pass it on to my baby. Grandpa, what I can't figure is you, your agenda."

"Find Critter and prosecute him for cutting down the lo and behold Elman elm." *Now, Howie — now! Spring the question.* "Also, there's the Billy problem." He made his hand into a gun, aimed it at the head of the bear rug, and said, "Bang, you're dead."

Tess stood mute. Howard could read her discomfort.

"See, I found Billy's body frozen solid and naked," Howard said, droll. "And, wouldn't you know it, but when my back was turned, somebody moved the body. Tess, did my grandson Birch kill Billy Jordan, and did he abscond with the body, and where is it now?"

Tess appeared on the verge of blurting out something, but she caught herself and held back. Finally, she said, "There's so much that I can't tell you, Grandpa. The best thing you can do for Birch, for the Trust and for Darby, is . . ." She invited Howard with a wiggle of her fingers to fill out the thought.

"Yeah, head south on I-91; everybody wants me out of the way, and normally I might fold. But there's another person involved in this mess, and she's the reason I'm staying. Delphina Rayno Jordan. She deserves to know the truth about her son. She needs . . ." Howard struggled to find that word.

"Closure," Tess said.

"Yeah, that's it."

"Delphina's peace of mind is very much in Birch's thoughts," Tess said in a harsh whisper and grabbed his arm.

"As Leo Lavoie used to say, if I had a grip like that, I'd be a bully," Howard said.

"Whatever you do, you can't tell her that Billy is dead. Understand?"

"No, I don't understand. I plan to tell her everything when I think the time is right. When I can produce a body to prove it. Delphina is living in high anxiety — I figure the truth will, as I keep hearing, set her free."

"I believe that truth is overrated, and freedom is an excuse people use to persecute others," Tess said. She let go of his arm.

"Probably you're right — you young people seem to be ahead of me in so many ways — but in my experience truth hurts, but not as much as the unknown that piles on with the little lies. Maybe we can start by you telling me about Birch, his involvement in Billy's murder."

Tess shook her head. "No, I can't do that, but if you promise me not to tell Delphina anything about Billy's death, I will give you a key to finding Critter."

Howard paused for a moment. In the end it wasn't the deal Tess offered that persuaded Howard to agree, it was her demeanor. There was a desire to do good in Tess Jordan. He had seen that same passion or yearning, whatever it was, in Birch, in Tahoka, in Trek, Jayu, Solomon, and in the other minions of Geek Chorus Software, though not in Origen.

Old man, you must succumb to youth, even if it goes against your better judgment.

"Okay, mum's the word," Howard said. "Your turn."

"I don't know exactly where Critter is, but Cooty Patterson does," Tess said. "That's the best I can do."

"Really? How does Cooty know?"

"You'll have to ask him."

Howard nodded. "Just what are those weird nurses doing to Cooty?"

Tess clicked her remote and a video appeared of Luci standing beside Cooty's stew pot, cabin in the background. "This will give you an idea," Tess said.

Howard squinted at the screen, listening while Luci read from her tablet.

"Report to Birch Latour from Luci Sanz. Besides the purely scientific study of Corey Patterson, besides the chip implants in his brain to retard the aging process, we've enlisted him in a psychological and sociological study. I wish we were advanced enough to tap directly into his thoughts. We tried, but the resulting data was like the equivalent of a poetry slam at a family dinner of comedians and their therapists. Instead, we're gaining access to his mind the old fashion way: interviews, transcriptions, and voice recordings."

"I like that Luci girl," Howard said. "She's going to rule the world some day."

THE CENTENARIAN'S TALE
OF WAR AND WOE

HALF AN HOUR LATER, having followed Birch's cross-country ski trail to the Manse, Howard parked the snowmobile and limped to Cooty's cabin. Of course he entered without knocking, and was surprised to find not just Cooty on hand but Luci, Wiqi, Birch, Missy, and F. Latour.

You should have figured that Tess called Birch—on her real mobile phone.

No, wait. They're not here because I'm here; they're here because . . . because?

You'll find out soon enough.

Howard faced his son, "Holy guacamole, Freddy, what are you doing here?"

"Hi, Pop, I happened to be the area," F. Latour said. He was built like Howard, thick, heavyset, but unlike Howard he kept a trimmed full beard, and the hair on his balding head was long and in a ponytail tied with a piece of rawhide. He dressed in blue jeans and a blue work shirt, his pockets bulging with pens and notecards. Howard thought he looked clean and healthy.

"How are the kids?" Howard asked. Wrong question. F. Latour launched an elaborate explanation of the activities of his young son and daughter.

Howard blinked with the sad awe that only a parent can feel on behalf of an adult child who talks too much. Even Birch appeared bored. Finally, Missy interrupted F. Latour and said to Howard, "We're trying an experiment with Cooty."

Howard, just now catching up with the scene, gaped at Cooty who lay supine on his narrow bed. His eyes were closed, but he didn't appear to be asleep because he was smiling. Wires attached to suction cups on his head traveled to a console on wheels, where Wiqi stood seemingly on the verge of pushing buttons.

"Geeze," said Howard.

"Do you want to stick around?" Missy asked.

"I guess. Can I have Cooty when you get done? I came here for a private conversation with him."

"I don't know," Missy said, and looked at Luci, "What do think?"

"He might have some temporary memory loss, but other than that he'll be cogent," Luci said.

Howard turned to Birch. Amazing how Birch in his looks took after Elenore's side of the family, the side nobody knew anything about. "What are you going to do to Cooty, electrocute him?" Howard asked.

"Sort of," Birch said with a smile that announced he enjoyed the alarm on his grandfather's face. "Luci and Wiqi have been working with Cooty, through talk therapy, medication, electroshocks, and, of course, infinitely tiny brain implants. The idea, Grandpa, is to regress Cooty to that moment in his past when he was traumatized. We want to get him through that gate to the other side."

"The other side of what?" Howard asked, unsure whether to be curious or furious.

"We don't know," Birch said. "Nobody has been there to report the scene."

Cooty opened his eyes. "It's okay, Howie. I want to do this."

"Cooty, these people might kill you," Howard said.

"That would be entertaining," Cooty said.

"Actually, if it works," Luci said, "the process may trick his DNA into halting cellular deterioration."

"In other words," Missy said, "Cooty might live another fifty or so years."

"Maybe forever," Luci added.

Howard noticed now that F. Latour was writing on a notecard. "What's his stake in this?" Howard said to Birch.

F. Latour winced, but he kept writing. Howard remembered now how much his son hated it when Howard talked about him as if he wasn't in the room. Howard wanted to apologize, but he didn't know how. He had the motive and the opportunity, but he lacked the means for such expression.

"Dad is the writer for this part of the script," Birch said.

Howard turned to his son, and snarled at him, "What the hell are they doing to Cooty?"

"These treatments have three purposes," F. Latour said. "The first is to make Cooty happier, more comfortable, and long-lived. The second is to add to the science of gerontology—that's the study of old age."

"I know what it means," Howard lied with a straight face. "What's the third?"

"The third is that everything that happens to Cooty will find its way into Darby Doomsday. As one of the writers, I wanted to be here to witness the event and record it as accurately I can."

"If you haven't figured it out yet, Grandpa, Cooty feeds us much raw data for our game," Missy said.

The wonder of it! All Howard could do was nod.

You feel stupid.

No, not stupid—just tired. What I feel is a nap coming on.

"It's okay, Howie," Cooty said. "It's all part of the hunches that come in bunches."

"I guess I'll have a seat and watch the show," Howard said, and sat down at the tiny table. Cooty remained on the bed, while the others stood around him.

Wiqi hooked up more wires to Cooty's veiny head. There was a map of the world on that head, but which world? Even with his hearing aid cranked up Howard couldn't understand what Luci and Wiqi were saying, then he realized they were not talking American. Cooty closed his eyes again. Birch clasped one of the centenarian's hands in his own, F. Latour took the other. Missy took a seat at the table with Howard.

Howard shoved his head in the direction of Luci and Wiqi. "What language are they talking?" Howard asked Missy in as quiet a voice as he was capable of.

"I don't know, some kind of science jargon," Missy whispered. "They communicate in their own special way because Wiqi can't deal with words that have multiple meanings."

Howard watched while Cooty jerked and writhed when Wiqi

administered the electrical jolts. Birch and Latour held him down, preventing him from rolling off the bed, and then his body relaxed; from all appearances he seemed to have expired.

"He'll wake in less than a minute," Luci said, and sure enough, seconds later Cooty sat up with open eyes and trembling lips. He seemed to want to speak.

"Remember what we covered yesterday?" Luci said.

"Yes, I remember. I couldn't talk about it then," Cooty said. "It made me cry."

"Can you talk about it now?"

"I think so."

"You'll feel better when it's over. Go back to that moment when everything changed. Tell us the date if you can, and where you are."

"It's toward the end of the war," Cooty said, his voice strong now. "Me and Howie, we're in North Africa in a tank we named Pasha, who was a friend of mine."

Cooty went on to relate in great detail how they came under attack, how only he and Howard got away, because they happened to be outside the tank looking for mines at the time that the .88 round hit, how their buddies in the tank were killed, how he, Cooty, broke down, panicked, fell apart, and how Howard saved Cooty's life but not his sanity. It was a heart-rending story that demeaned the centenarian and exalted Howard, and it left Birch, F. Latour, and Missy deeply moved.

Howard listened in silence. It passed through his mind that Cooty's story suggested that he, Howard, had done that great thing in his youth. Trouble was everything Cooty said was make-believe.

"You were a hero, Grandpa," Birch said.

Howard grimaced. "What should I say, Cooty?"

"Verify my story, Howie," Cooty said, then turned to Birch and F. Latour, who stood side by side. "Ever since, Howie's been taking care of me."

That part of the story was more or less true. It was the reasons that Cooty had omitted.

Howie, you're the only one who knows the source of Cooty's strange personality.

I think so, yeah.

Corey Francis Patterson was brought up on the streets of Lowell, Massachusetts, where the tenement houses provided shelter for the mill workers. From the very beginning Corey was a daredevil. He loved speed and risk, he lived for the feeling of exhilaration. He raced motorcycles and stock cars at the Big E in Springfield. Even his love life was full of risk. Corey fell for and pursued the girlfriends of known mobsters, though he insisted he never actually romanced these women. They were his friends, he would say. He did have a secret love, though he would not divulge the name.

When World War II came along, he immediately enlisted. When he met Howard a couple years later, Howard was a just a kid fresh out of basic training, having lied about his age to get into the military for patriotic reasons.

More likely to get away from fatherhood. Even now, in old age, you're not sure what your motivations were, are you?

Corey adopted Howard, taught him how to get along in the world, protected him, and never asked anything in return. Without Corey to look after him, Howard figured he never would have got through the war. It was Corey who had pulled him out of that tank at just the right moment, Corey who had saved his life, Corey who had got him through the trauma of losing the rest of the tank crew, Corey who had kept his cool during the horrors of war, Corey who had taught Howard Elman to be a man.

Corey's trauma came after the war. He was driving his sister and his parents and the secret loved one he would not talk about in his Hudson Hornet. As usual, he was driving much too fast. Corey knew no other way to live than on the edge. Corey had no memory of the actual crash. Whether he remembered that he was the sole survivor was unclear. Whether Corey's subsequent personality change into Cooty was the result of guilt or brain damage from the head injuries he suffered in the crash, or both, was also unclear.

Fifteen years after the war, Howard found Corey — now Cooty — a homeless man in Lowell. He got Cooty a job at the textile mill in Keene where Howard was a weaver and later a shop foreman. After the shop closed Howard started his trash collection business and Cooty joined him on the honeywagon. It was Cooty's choice to live in a cabin in the woods, Cooty's choice to sustain himself with road meat, dumpster leavings, and the stew pot that was never emptied.

Endless stew nourishes endlessly. Who said that, Ollie Jordan?

No, it was you, Howie.

Luci and Wiqi stayed with Cooty while everyone else grabbed bowls of stew and went inside the Manse to eat. They sat around the burning logs of the great fireplace. Trek, Jayu, and Solomon sang old Celtic songs. Howard wished he had taken up playing the harmonica, which he had learned from his birth mother that his natural father had played.

"Grandpa," Birch said, "Dad is going to read from his book of poems here at the Manse before the planning board hearing. Hope you can make it."

"Freddy's book, oh, yeah; it's got that funny word for the title," Howard said.

"Yes, *Interstices*," F. Latour said.

Later, at beer time, after F. Latour had left and headed north to his family in West Lebanon, Howard opened a can of Birch's Smutty Nose ale and visited Cooty. The centenarian was still in bed, but he was not wasting away; he was alert, sentient, also quite cheerful.

"Cooty, I visited Tess Jordan today. You know where she is, right?"

"Oh, sure, she's in the tree house. Birch tells me about the drawings she's making."

"Yeah, well, I asked her where Critter Jordan was hiding, and she said she didn't know, but you knew. How could you, stuck in this cabin, possibly know?"

"Because Critter comes to see me."

"You're kidding!"

"I wouldn't know how to kid anybody," Cooty said. "I never learned. Critter comes to the Manse quite a lot. But sneaky, so nobody knows but me."

"Why? To scope the place out?" Howard said.

"He wants to set fire to it, I imagine, but it's easier said than done. You have to disable the sprinkle system. You want to put some petroleum in all four corners. You want the fire department to believe there's ammo stored all over the place, so they keep their distance. They won't get too close if there's mucho ammo in the house."

"Cooty, how do you know that firemen fear a house full of ammo?"

"Because you told me, Howie."

"So I did," Howard said. "I remember now, but that was some years back and it was just a general supposition and not about the Manse. What did Critter tell you?"

"Same things. Commonsensical arson."

"Plus he actually told you where he was staying," Howard said.

"He did, yes he did."

"Well?"

"Well what?" Cooty blinked in Morse Code the word "maybe" or maybe not. Actually, Howard had forgotten Morse Code except for dot dot dot dash dash dash dot dot dot.

"Well, where the hell is he?" Howard snarled with such ferocity that Cooty recoiled, and Howard felt bad for the outburst. "Sorry, old man."

"I'm sorry, too, Howie, I forget where he's at. I thought you knew."

"Well, no, what makes you think I knew?"

"You said he was in the town of Large, New Hampshire."

"What?"

"You told me he was at large."

Howard gave Cooty one of his famous glowers and said, "You are pulling my chain."

"Maybe."

"Maybe?"

"Maybe it will come to me bye and bye," Cooty said with a little mischievous smile.

"Bye and bye" is another stupid thing that people say that nobody really knows what it actually means. Maybe Wiqi Durocher, who wouldn't broker with such language, was the only clear-thinking human being in Darby.

A MOTHER'S WILL

HOWARD RETURNED TO Re In Car Nation via Billy's snowmobile. He had claimed it in part because he thought he might piss off Critter enough to smoke him out and in part because driving it pleased him. The next day it snowed again, another six inches. Two just-right storms in a row. From Priscilla Landry Howard acquired a New Hampshire snowmobile map and discovered he could drive the snowmobile all the way to Goffstown, New Hampshire. He also learned from Priscilla that the family general Store had been sold to, guess who, PLC.

It was a three-hour snowmobile jaunt through the woods with numerous road crossings (routes 63, 12, 9, 123, 137, 202, 47, 136, and 13) to Delphina's place in Goffstown, and he was tired but happy when he arrived Sunday at noontime. Delphina rented an apartment from her eldest son Isaac, a successful businessman who lived in Massachusetts somewhere. The main feature of the neighborhood was the state women's prison down the road. He pulled in just as Delphina was getting back from church.

She was dressed in her Sunday best. Howard didn't like worship services very much, but he liked the way women looked when they went to church, all dressed up but no sexy stuff. It was the kind of look that gave him hope for the human species if not for the existence of a creator. Delphina used to have one of those va-va-voom profiles, but in recent years she'd lost some va and added a too much voom. Her face reminded him of an Irish setter's, kind of dumb but friendly, no meanness. She gave Howard a look that he was familiar with these days from people who hadn't seen him in quite a while. The look said, "My how Howard Elman has aged."

"Nice place," Howard said.

"My son Isaac found it for me. 'Course he does charge me rent, but it's reasonable."

"He did okay for himself in Fitchburg, or so I heard," Howard said.

"He does make a good living, little on the shady side, I hate to say, and he refuses to have anything to do with New Hampshire or his father."

"Protecting himself, I imagine," Howard said. "Whatever happened to your sister, Soapy?

Delphina laughed, "Mercy, don't call her Soapy. She'll have a conniption fit. She's Shelia these days. After Birch eased LaChance out as Trust steward, he and Shelia moved out West to work for some organic-this and organic-that outfit. She made me an auntie, twice over."

They went inside and, just as she had promised in her email, Delphina made him Sunday dinner. While Delphina futzed in the kitchen, Howard sniffed around in the parlor. The place was dominated by dolls. All kinds and they were everywhere. In frames on the walls. In arrangements on the floor. On shelves where other people put books and knickknacks. Sitting on chairs. And what's this? A turned bowl of elm wood in the early stages of warping that held junky stuff—stubby pencils, cheapo reading glasses, couple spools of thread, lottery tickets, receipt for an umbrella, prescription for antidepressant, small statuette of St. Anthony, patron saint of lost objects. Howard hollered into the kitchen, "Present from Critter?"

Delphina turned and looked through the door space between the two rooms at Howard holding the bowl. "Yes, how did you know?"

"Just a lucky guess. He's trying to get back into your good graces."

"Yes, kinda pathetic, in-nit?" Delphina said.

Howard put the bowl back on the table beside the easy chair.

Well, at least your elm tree has been put to good use.

Yeah, some consolation.

Why does "consolation" combobulate so indubitably with "constipation"?

Like Dot McCurtin says, life's surprises keep me bopping.

Howard took off his boots and lay down on his back on the couch, sharing it with two dolls. He put on his reading glasses and looked at the *Manchester Union Leader*, holding the newspaper in his hands outstretched, like you put in a storm window. A gun shop in Peterborough had been burglarized in the middle of the night. Police theorized that the thieves were professionals, because they had been able to disconnect the alarm system and took no money but only weapons, including a doozy-Uzi submachine gun. Looks like Critter Jordan's work, thought Howard, as he fell into a half sleep, the paper over his face.

It was one of those beautiful light naps where one is still in touch with the material world, and because Howard left on his hearing aid, he could hear Delphina humming, walking around, the door of the oven slamming shut. And he smelled the wonderful smell of the ham, then suddenly the even better the smell of a woman. Howard pulled the paper off his face and opened his eyes.

Delphina was standing over him, an apron around her broad waist. Was there ever a more beautiful sight for a man to behold? "Time to eat," she said.

"I don't need to be told twice," Howard tried to jump off the couch to impress Delphina, but his action lagged behind his desire, and he almost fell over. Not that it mattered. Delphina had already turned around and walked away, her back to his awkwardness.

The home cooking made Howard wistful. He wished Elenore was here. He wished he was sixty years old, hale, hearty, and erectile.

Howard ate slowly but he didn't say much. It was just pleasant enjoying the food and listening to Delphina talk about her life. The reason Delphina had moved here in the first place and the reason that her eldest son had bought the house was that one of her daughters was incarcerated next door in the women's prison for stabbing her boyfriend. The other daughter lived nearby; she worked two shifts, one as a waitress and one as a cook, in a "nouveau cuisine" restaurant. Delphina's new life was taking care of grandchildren, selling cosmetics over the Internet, partnering with another divorcée in an online flea market business, and brokering dolls for collectors. "Just too doggone busy," she said.

It wasn't until Howard was eating a dessert of ice cream and homemade apple pie with a mug of coffee that they began to talk seriously.

"I don't mean to pry, but I think it would help my investigation . . ." *Just what are you investigating—you're not sure any more.* ". . . if you could tell me why you and Critter, everybody thought you and him were pretty convivial together, suddenly busted up."

Delphina started to sniffle, a dignified, barely noticeable cry so that Howard was not upset by it but rather attracted to it—almost a turn-on. He wanted to protect this woman.

"I can remember the exact moment when he changed," Delphina said. "He came in late one night and he had a look in his eye—it scare't me. I said, 'Critter, what's the matter?' He told me to shut the eff up, none of my effing business. He had never talked to me before so rough. Even then I knew it was the beginning of our doom. For a long time I just tried to pretend that everything was normal, because for a long time—years—everything had been normal, which was why Isaac turned out so good, well, sorta. Critter was a good man, he treated me right, but even then something in me knew it was an act with him, that deep down . . ."

She stopped abruptly as if she was afraid to speak. Howard waited her out.

Finally, she continued. "Deep down he was a Jordan. They say that the stain of Cain is an old story, that it doesn't apply today. Don't you believe it. That stain is in the Jordan blood. I could see it in my husband, the love of my life," Delphina laughed, sad and rueful. "Heck, at first it was part of his attraction, the forbidden fruit and all that crapola."

"What about your own children, or your grandchildren, do you see the stain in them?" Howard asked. He was thinking of Tess Jordan and the baby she carried.

"I never saw it in Isaac, though because of the way he makes his living, I wonder. I saw it from the start in my incarcerated daughter. I knew from day one she was going to be trouble, and she didn't make a liar out of me. Luckily, I didn't see it in my other daughter, and the grandchildren are going to be all right. They're dolls, all of them."

"And Billy? You sent Billy back to live with Critter."

"He wasn't doing diddly-squat with me, getting in with a bad crowd; he needed a father."

Howard noted that Delphina's demeanor and tone shifted when she talked about Billy. She sounded to Howard as if she were back to lying to herself again. Howard pressed her.

"Just what was Billy's problem?"

"What was not his problem? Stealing, fighting, mouthing off, lots of mouthing off—but only to women. He wouldn't let his sisters or me advise him or mother him, anything like that."

"Do you think he had the Jordan stain on him?"

"No—no," Delphina said with some fury in her voice. "He's a beautiful boy. He's just full of hurt, and he's straightening himself out. I even see hope for Critter."

"Really. So what's the lastest news?"

"As of last night. Ever since he and Critter joined that church and on retreat, they've been born again. Billy shares his pictures, and he tells me that he's reading the Bible, people he's meeting, plans for the future, divinity school. I can't believe it, my boy a minster! He's a changeling or a changed dingaling, whatever. He's not the bad boy he used to be."

"I'll say," Howard said. "I'd like to see some of these pictures."

"Why, sure." Delphina scrolled her cell phone.

Howard put on his reading glasses, and he watched as the snapshots flashed by. A modest looking church. Out of focus men in suits, ladies in flower print dresses and big hats. Howard thought he recognized some of the Geek Chorus minions. Even a couple blurry pictures of Critter and Billy. How'd they do that, he wondered. Everything—objects, people, landscape—all looked vaguely familiar to Howard, which puzzled him until he realized he'd seen versions of these pictures on Turtle Jordan's many computer monitors in New York.

Are you going insane, Howie?

Going? I think I'm already there or if not me, the world. Might as well enjoy the roller coaster ride.

"Where were these pictures taken, Delphina?"

"I don't know. Billy says it's a secret. He hinted, and I'm guessing, New Zealand," Delphina said. Doubt crossed her face. "The only thing that bothers me is I'm afraid this church they joined is, like, a cult. I worry a little."

"That's why you want me to find Billy?"

"I'm not so sure right now what I want," Delphina said. "Billy seems happy. He's changelinged himself, and he's changelinged me. I'm going to church now. I'm busy and happy. Critter—well, I don't know where his head is at — but he sends me money, and the only thing better than money is a glass of Cupcake Chardonnay."

"Which you need money to buy."

"Correct. Oh, the mysteries — ain't it grand to be alive!"

⚜ ⚜ ⚜

Later, during the snowmobile ride back to Darby, Howard tried to think through his visit with Delphina. No doubt Birch and Latour and Missy and Tess and the Geek Chorus were working hard to convince Delphina that Billy Jordan was alive, that everything was all right.

Everything is not all right, Howie, but you are an ignorant old man, and you don't have the wherewithal to make wrong right.

What the hell is a wherewithal anyway, a wheelbarrow to carry burdensome ideas?

Howard tried to figure whether to give Birch the incriminating paper with the Trust logo. Did the boy who worshipped his grandfather Salmon really need to know that the Squire killed for his Trust?

Maybe Birch was willing to kill, too.

Howard drove the snowmobile to Re In Car Nation, built up the fire in the woodstove, and immediately went to sleep on the couch. His last thought was that he might be awakened by the PLC gestapo and be evicted, or perhaps arrested, or maybe even executed on the spot.

Bring 'em on. Who had said that?

The Tex prez.

Ike?

What do you prefer, Howie — lethal injection, hanging, firing squad, flattened by a steam roller?

There are no steam rollers any more; they all run on diesel.

Just a manure of speaking.

Yeah, well, everything is a manure of speaking. That's why geniuses like Wiqi Durocher have it so hard. You can't say something without it meaning something you don't want or don't even know you said.

Words corrupt everybody, Howie; it's all a big pile of manures of speaking.

What do you mean by "it's"? That adult learning program where they carried on about pro-nouns? They never said anything about amateur nouns.

227

INTERSTICES

CONFUSING DREAMS ON the couch. The women of his life once again seemed to pass in review — the mother he only met in her old age, who was dead before he really got to know her and couldn't even remember the year he was born; his daughters, who he could never keep up with; Zoe Cutter, his arch enemy who had reduced but not defeated him; the Squire's widow, Persephone Butterworth Salmon, who was more fisher cat than human; Katharine Ramchand, his son's wife and grandson's cousin, another admirable woman who had no use for Howard Elman; Tahoka, the granddaughter who he wished to know better; and Elenore, the love of his life, who divorced him by her death that no doubt he had caused with his second-hand smoke.

And what about Fralla Pratt, your only oops girl? Bev Boufford, Dot McCurtin, Tess Jordan, and even Missy Mendelson who was running for the New Hampshire state senate and who you taught to shoot? She'll probably be president some day.

And now in that half asleep, half awake state he could see Missy, candidate for prez, kicking butt in a nationally televised debate with her opponent in the other party.

Howie, can you hear that ticking?

Yes, it's the bomb. But that's only in the game.

Comes there a time when the difference between game and world disappears?

He could see the building exploding. Heather, gentle Heather, the daughter he had shunted off, in the shards of the explosion. He forced himself to wake up, and the images faded into mundane materiality, followed by the forgetfulness that dreams bring on. It was morning.

On the kitchen table were his car keys and a note in Birch's handwriting. Howard looked out the window. Sometime while he was in dreamland, Birch had returned the PT Cruiser to its usual place in the driveway, entered the domicile, and left a note, all the while his grandfather slept. Howard put on his reading glasses and whispered Birch's words from the paper. "Grandpa, you shouldn't leave your keys in the ignition, and you should lock your house doors at night. I have it on good authority there are some bad guys on this planet. Love, Birch."

Howard had hardly finished his coffee when his FFone buzzed in his pocket. It was Dot McCurtin. "Constable, you could do me a favor and take a look at the trailer park. Something's going on, and I need some verification from an official source before spreading the word."

"Okay, I'll take a run down there." He was about to hang up, when he found himself blurting out, "Dot, I'm not demented."

"I never thought you were."

"Then why did you spread it around town?"

"It wasn't me. It was Dracut and his ilk."

Are there more in an ilk than in a minion?

"I'm sorry, I didn't get that," Mrs. McCurtin said.

"My apologies, Dot. Just mumbling to myself."

"No, problem. Listen, Constable, Critter Jordan was seen last night at the auction barn."

"Really?"

"Really."

"Thanks, Dot. I got a question. Do you go out with men?"

"No. It's too much of a bother."

"I like your attitude, Dot."

"And I like your attitude, Howard. You and me, we love this town."

"That's true. I'm glad you said it. Dot, are you religious?"

"Well, I go to church."

"Because you believe in God?"

"I do believe in God, yes, but that's not why I go to church. I go to church because church is the original social network. Constable?"

"Yeah?"

"I'm eager to check out what's going on at the trailer park. Get moving, please."

Howard hurried as best he could into the PT Cruiser. He wanted to drive to the auction barn in hopes of catching Critter, but he owed

Dot, so he headed for Great Meadow Village. On the way he passed a "wide-load" yellow-light car followed by a flat-bed truck pulling a mobile home going in the opposite direction. And another. When he arrived at the "village" it was as if he were at the border crossing of another country. There was a "gate" of yellow police tape, and he was stopped by a somewhat cute uniformed security guard. "Private property, no entry, sir," she said.

Howard wanted to tell her that women didn't look right in cop uniforms, especially around the hips. Instead, he pointed to his cap, and said, "Excuse me, I'm Darby Constable Howard Elman."

After a pause she let him through.

He parked on the little knoll that overlooked the settlement, stepped out of the vehicle, and phoned Dot. "It's me, I'm here," he said.

"Okay, I'm going to broadcast you to all my subscribers."

"What the hell does that mean, Dot?"

"It means that I'm going to stream your report to my website. My fans and followers will catch you live. I'll also be recording. Later, when we get some improved video of the scene, I'll dub you in."

"I always was a dubber."

"Okay, no more jokes. You're on NOW!"

Howard reported, "This is Darby Constable Howard Elman. I'm looking at Great Meadow Village, or what's left of it. PLC has got quite the crew down here hauling away the mobile homes, one by one, on flatbed trucks. Meanwhile, excavators and bulldozers are rearranging the landscape. I don't know what they have in mind, but I figure in a week or two Great Meadow Village mobile home park will be no more."

Howard talked on, describing the activity, sending crude video snapped on his FFone. He drove down into the village. All the residents had cleared out. Howard transmitted until the battery on his cell phone phtted out. He signed off, got back into the PT Cruiser, turned on the blue light and siren, and sped over the frost-heaved roads of Darby to Ike's Auction Barn.

He parked in plain view. If Critter was here, Howard wanted him to know he had a visitor.

Maybe he'll jump out of a dark corner and kill you.

That would solve a lot of problems, wouldn't it?

Howard went through the flea market first, returning to the disturbed mover blankets, hoping somehow that the body of Billy Jordan would have reappeared. The idea brought him a weird comfort, but there was no Billy Jordan. He rummaged through the tool section of the flea market until he found a crowbar.

Crowbar? Didn't Ike Jordan own a hound named Crowbar that Critter inherited.

Yeah, dog was killed chasing cars.

The crowbar was rusted, but he liked its heft in his hand. Was Ike's dog a rust-colored hound? Howard couldn't remember.

He went into Critter's lodgings. He didn't find any sign that Critter had been around until he opened the fridge door. Inside was a note. "Help yourself, Howie, but leave a beer for me." Howard was startled. Critter was toying with him. There were three cans left from a twelve-pack of Natural Ice. Howard put the crowbar down, grabbed a can, flipped off the top, and took a long swallow.

Why does beer always taste better when somebody else has paid for it?

Because you're cheap, Howie.

Crowbar in one hand, beer in the other, Howard moved to Critter's office. He was about to pry open the file cabinet drawer when he discovered that it was unlocked. He went through the papers. None had the Trust logo. Apparently, Critter had taken the incriminating journal entry from Raphael Salmon out of the file cabinet along with some plain paper for his own notes. He'd blackmailed the porn collectors and their ilk. Maybe he was blackmailing Birch with the dirt on Raphael Salmon. The idea made sense, but Howard didn't believe it. Something else was going on. He had an inkling what it was, too.

How many inklings does it take to make a fact, Howie? Are ilks and inklings related? How many smatters to make a smattering?

Howard's last stop at the auction barn was the shed. He saw that the gas can for the snowmobile was missing.

Now what, Howie?

Let's see what Birch has to say.

☙ ☙ ☙

When Howard arrived at the Manse just before dark, he was surprised to see extra cars in the driveway, including his son's station wagon with its SPOONWD vanity plate. Howard walked in as F. Latour was reading from his book of poems.

Howie, you forgot your only son's poetry reading.

Howard was surprised to see that Tess Jordan had come out of her tree house for the event. She sat with Birch on pillows on the floor in front of the fire. Every once in a while their hands would brush together. Howard turned to Latour, and took a long look at him.

Unlike Birch, who was clean-shaven, slight, and handsome, Latour was bearded and, Howard thought, like himself, kind of ugly. He was built like a fifty-something in-shape Santa Claus. He had a touch of Howard's droll, though it came out softer, less as sarcastic commentary than as a sorrow brought on by too much knowledge of the human condition. He spoke in a soft voice, very tender.

Don't you wish you could talk like that?

I do.

"These last two poems are from notes I took when I was raising Birch in the woods after his mother died giving birth to him," Latour said. "I was a confused young man full of anger. For too long I solved my problems with Old Crow. I took Birch into the woods to get away from booze and to confront myself." He paused, then added, "Today I have a new love, a new family. They have given me the strength and the inspiration to face the old life through these poems."

TESTIMONY

We bend to our knees,
scoop up the water and drink it.
We remember the cold on our skin,
the taste on our tongue,
the tactile feel
as the water goes down our throats.
Later, when we stand before our friends,
or perhaps the jury, we say,
"I held the river in my hands."

"This last poem is called 'Interstices' and it's the title poem in my collection," he said with restrained intensity to those gathered. "It's distilled from a memory of taking Birch on a boat ride on Grace Pond when he was an infant. We saw a great blue heron catch a yellow perch." Latour turned to Birch. "Do you remember?"

Birch answered, speaking to the audience. "Of course. I remember everything but not in poetry, dad. My memories are more like filed away documents."

Memory is a burden Birch carries. He remembers everything. Even his birth.

Yes, he told Cooty that, who no doubt told it to Luci.

Every human cry and gurgle, they are all part of the game, Howie.

Howard turned his thoughts back to F. Latour. His son had been so much more successful as a parent than he had been. It was obvious there was a connection between Latour and Birch that did not exist between himself and Latour. Howard felt proud, if left out. He wanted to wave a flag or something. Instead, he stood in a shadow in the doorway, and turned up his hearing aid as Latour read the poem in a dreamy, restrained manner, so unlike the bluster of his father.

INTERSTICES BETWEEN DARK MATTER AND US

I put my son in the front pack baby carrier,
for a walk in the woods headed for Grace Pond.
What do you see, boy?
I can read his answer in the thought he sends me.
Spider webs in ferns, in trees, in the interstices
between the comet dust that makes up
the rings of Saturn
and the loved one who left us too early.
Give me water, father, give me water.
I tip a moose wood leaf toward my son's mouth,
and droplets of dew quench his thirst.

When we reach Grace Pond I place the baby carrier
on the stern seat of the John boat and tie it down.
I row out into the pond to the cove

full of lily pads and the grey skeletons
of dead pine trees rising out of the shallows
like big ideas that just don't work.
We've come to see the heron.
She walks on her stilt legs
until she finds a station.
She stands motionless waiting for the judgment.
I hold the oars so they don't part the waters.
My son sends me a thought.
I answer with my own thought:
I'm thinking of your mother, too.
The heron darts her beak into the water
and comes up with a yellow perch.
Fish crossways in her mouth she begins
a laborious takeoff,
tucking her stilt legs behind her,
huge wings slapping water as she strains for a height,
finally rising on an air current,
circling back into the nest at the top of a dead pine.
I look through the binoculars
and see a chick's open mouth.
I let out a celebratory whoop.
My son throws up his hands and imitates my whoop,
his first word.

There was some applause, murmurs, and little bit of laughter, and then Latour was surrounded by well-wishers, but Howard Elman remained in the shadows.

How to say how moved you are by F. Latour's poem, how to tell him he deserved better than you for a father, how to say it? Howie, you couldn't even tell Elenore that you loved her without embarrassment. What is it with you? What is it?

Minutes later Howard pulled himself together and pretended he was just coming in. He exchanged a few polite words with Birch and F. Latour; people started to leave. It was only then that Howard remembered it was the night of the planning board hearing.

234

Howard went out with the rest of the crowd and headed for the town hall. Soon the only person remaining on the premises was Cooty Patterson in his cabin. Luci and Wiqi had determined that the centenarian was in good enough condition these days to do without his nurses for a couple hours, though they monitored him electronically. They led the caravan on their bicycle built for two that they rode through rain, snow, solar flares, volcanic ash, and bulletins of dark matter broadcast from the Big Bang.

Birch drove the Bronco, Tess riding shotgun. In the back seat sat Missy and her baby, strapped into one of those carriers that resembled the space capsule that brought Kal-el to Smallville. Howard in the PT Cruiser followed the loggers in their Dodge Ram and the Geeks in their foreign cars, down the long scribble of road that linked Upper Darby with Center Darby.

Howard's thoughts turned to his life, coming at him in the contrarian voice that had marked his old age.

Never made big money.

But earned what I had.

Only formed two worthwhile friendships, Ollie Jordan and Cooty Patterson.

Had good times with both. Served my country best I could.

Worked, worked, worked to build the country best I could.

And failed.

Hunted the white tail deer, gave up hunting, returned to hunting, kinda, think maybe hunting is an inherited thing, like a serious overbite.

Smoked the Camel.

And with great pleasure. Gave up the Camel.

Not soon enough to save the wife.

Married too young, but stayed together through the hard times.

Never really got to know her.

Produced healthy children.

Except too many.

That last surprise a doozy with a singing voice startling and sweet as boiling maple sap spilled on fresh snow.

With the ache of her loss resides a guilt. A feeling you resist.

I don't respect guilt-riders, because such people use their guilt as a minor self-punishment to allow them to commit crimes that deserve greater punishment.

But there it is, Howie, a guilt.

The past hangs over me, preventing me from hiking that last trail into the gloom of dark matter.

Forget it, Howie. A man can look neither to the past nor to the future, because there is no such thing as time. The only legitimate questions are found in the pauses between changes. The calls for immediate action. The "now whats." Your son got it right with that word you can't pronounce, the "interstices."

Oh, shut up!

Will not. Listen to me, do not dwell on conditions that presume a flow of time, such as hope, yearning, nostalgia, regret.

The voice in his head quieted, but the guilt remained, an alien gnawing on the walls of his intestines.

The contingent from Upper Darby arrived early at the town hall, which was a good move, because the place soon filled up until all the folding chairs, laid out for seating by the Darby Snowmobile Club and Center Darby Quilters, were taken and people stood in the back. Four box woodstoves, set up by the Darby Volunteer Fire Company, threw off heat like embraces. You could get a little seasick walking on the undulating pine board floors. Here and there were piles of sawdust left by the relentless carpenter ants. Occasionally a disoriented bat flew out of the ceiling. A long crack on a plaster wall that resembled a lightning strike was evidence enough that the building was collapsing in slow motion. The Geek Chorus took a chunk of seats near the front. Birch and Tess separated as they entered. Tess stayed in the rear and resumed her career as the schizophrenic girl, fake cell phone hanging from the cord around her neck, wild don't-tread-on-me eyes. Howard wondered where she kept her real cell phone.

He sat on an end chair, Missy beside him with her baby in her arms. Birch surprised Howard by joining the planning board members at the front of the hall, sitting on one side of a long table facing the citizenry. The board members looked like early losers on *Jeopardy*. Birch fiddled and shuffled through notecards. At five minutes past the hour, Cod Prell rose, approached the podium, and addressed the gathered.

"Quite a crowd. Usually, our meetings only attract lawyers and the what's-in-it-for-me brands," he said with a sly smile that provoked mild titters from the audience. "In case you don't know, my name is C. Odysseus Prell, and I am the chair of the Darby planning board. We have been creating a master plan for the future of the town to be presented for voter action at the town meeting on Tuesday of next week. Mark your calendars.

"The purpose of this hearing is to present our vision to the public and to answer your questions. This is not a routine master plan. It recommends sweeping changes in how we in Darby see ourselves and the future of our town. I will now turn the meeting over to Birch Latour, steward of the Salmon Trust lands and the prime force for change in Darby, New Hampshire."

Birch received a tepid round of applause from the crowd. Howard turned to Missy and whispered far too loudly into a cupped hand, "What's the matter with these people — they should be on their feet?"

Missy smiled at Howard, made her hand into a pistol, pointed it at him, and whispered, "Bang, bang, you're dead."

"You always did shoot low, Missy."

"Maybe I should get new glasses, because I always aim high."

Howard thought Birch spoke well and persuasively if too long. He gave a history of Darby from its beginnings as a frontier settlement decades before the American Revolution, right up to the present. And then he made his main point.

"Communities are always changing, but when we look at the history of a place we identify two important time periods — the idealized time period, what I call the Magic Moment, and the End Time, when change has so degraded the place that its Magic Moment identity is lost forever. Think of those communities in the southeastern part of our state. Darby is on the verge of its End Time. If we don't do something in the next few years, the Darby we know will cease to exist. What the planning board is proposing in its master plan will save this town and serve as a model for our state, our nation, our world.

"Darby's Magic Moment occurred in the decades following the American Revolution. Farmers grew crops, raised cattle, sheep, pigs, chickens, and turkeys. Local industry thrived: blacksmiths, tinsmiths, candlemakers, glass blowers, sawyers, and timber framers. Every neighborhood had its own one-room schoolhouse, twelve in all. Every child could walk to school, because school was right around the corner. When the demographics changed, the townspeople moved the school with their oxen. There were three different Christian churches. Citizens met at town meeting to govern themselves. Darby town was pretty much self-sufficient.

"By the Civil War, Darby's Magic Moment had gone by, and the town has been in decline ever since. We've lost almost all of our farms. We no longer manufacture the goods we need, but buy them elsewhere in the global economy. In another generation River Darby, Center Darby, Upper Darby, and Darby Depot risk merging into one amorphous suburban blob, with its citizens commuting to jobs in Keene, Brattleboro, or Bellows Falls, and infested by an outsider element of desperate working poor and criminals: druggies, burglars, bullies, poachers, arsonists, mothers with children but no fathers to help out. Meanwhile, property taxes continue to rise, state and federal laws cut into our autonomy. Our children are schooled elsewhere in large, expensive, unnecessary warehouses of education. This very building that serves as our town hall and meetinghouse is expected to be too dangerous for use within the next five years. The timbers that hold it up are too degraded to be repaired. Soon Darby will only be a name for another taxing station."

Birch paused to let his words sink in, and then he said, "It doesn't have be this way. We can do more than postpone the End Time; we can recreate the Magic Moment of Darby in a new and creative way. This master plan is the starting point. We will bring back the Magic Moment at the same time that we lower your property taxes."

Someone in the audience yelled, "What's the catch?"

Birch talked on as if he had not heard. "The master plan will create incentives for an economy based on tourism, technology, and sustainability. Darby will again be vibrant, unique, a model for other communities to emulate. The plan divides the town in zones that call for:

"One: River Walk, which features shopping at the site of the former county jail on the bluff in River Darby that will include a fully functioning meetinghouse for community activities. The monetary anchor of this development will be a riverboat in the Connecticut River, the center for CNAC, SeeNack, the Connissadawaga Native American Casino. New Hampshire and Vermont will be linked by a ferry in the summer, a cable car in the winter until ice out. Tax revenues from the casino will lower your property taxes.

"Two: Poocham, a reconstructed colonial village but using high-tech materials and engineering on the site of Great Meadow Village trailer park in Darby Depot.

"Three: Pockets throughout the town zoned for commerce combined with incentives to bring in new clean industries, such as software developers like the company that my business partners Missy Mendelson and Bez Woodward and I created. Darby will be self-sustaining once again.

"Four: the Salmon Trust Conservancy, a nonprofit entity open to the public for hiking, hunting, and fishing with the exception of the old growth forest, which will remain in its primeval state.

"Eventually, tourism dollars will give us not only a strong economy but a broad and stable tax base so that homeowners will see a fifty percent drop in their property taxes.

"I'd like to finish with a few words about education. Originally, consolidated schools might have provided resources, a variety of curricula, skilled teaching professionals not available to town schools, and opportunities for youth to get away from the small town. But all that is now available on the Internet. There is good reason to bring back the one-room schoolhouse, which, connected wirelessly to the world, will give all the advantages of the consolidated school with none of the expenses. Instead of sending our children to schools in Keene, they can remain in Darby in neighborhood schools in private homes, connected to the Internet. For instructors, we will depend on the expertise and volunteer spirit of our own people. Home-schooling and community-schooling will converge. This move will result in a closer-knit town and drastically lower taxes." Birch paused again to let his words sink in.

Howard surveyed his fellows townspeople. They had funny looks on their faces, like sleepwalkers coming into half-wakefulness as they stroll toward a cliff edge.

Birch smiled, and challenged the gathered. "Questions?"

"Who's going to pay for the development costs," shouted someone in the audience.

"Yes, that is the big question," Birch said. "To get started, we will need a huge infusion of cash, which will come from a private real estate development company, Paradise Lots Covenant. If you've been reading Google News, you'll know that PLC recently acquired Magnus Corp. I'm sure that name will ring a bell with some of you old-timers. PLC has already purchased properties in key sectors of the town. To explain PLC's role in the master plan, I would like to introduce PLC's Chief Executive Officer, H.C. Wentworth."

But before the CEO of PLC came forward, a voice shouted from the rear of the hall, "No, let me speak." From the doorway appeared a rangy man with a potbelly, a scraggly beard, long hair dyed Reagan red sticking out of a John Deere cap, wearing greasy jeans and a sleeveless blaze-orange parka. It was Critter Jordan.

"Critter, you'll get your chance to have your say after the formal presentation," said Cod Prell in his role as moderator.

"I have to leave, I got serious business, let me speak," Critter said with the urgency of a man who has got to go to the bathroom.

"I'm sorry, you'll have to wait," said Cod Prell.

Murmurs from the audience and shouts of "let him speak" persuaded Cod Prell to change his mind. "Go ahead, Critter."

Howard glanced at Birch, who looked ashen. "Oh-oh," said Missy to no one.

Critter might have been a Jordan, but he was also a well-known local businessman, and he knew how to address his fellow citizens at a town function. He spoke slowly, over-emphasizing his words so that he sounded like a preacher of old. It struck Howard that Critter was as sincere as he was capable of being.

"Cod, I'd like to begin by apologizing to the chair for speaking out of turn, but I have a very important personal errand to perform, so I must leave this hearing early. I'm going to do something for my departed father. You all remember Isaac O. Jordan, how he was shot dead, no doubt by somebody in this town. I'll tell you all right now secrets don't die. They sit in the dirt like seeds and await the flood. After I've run my errand, I'll be back here to finish my work. We will make the papers to-morrow, and not just *The Keene Sentinel*. The TV people will be here in droves. Mark . . . my . . . words.

"I oppose this so-called master plan for Darby on the basis that it's prejudiced against you, my friends — you. You approve this plan, and Upper Darby will squeeze you out. You will end up living in tenements in Keene and trailers in the poorer high-taxed towns in this county, be-cause there won't be no place for you in Darby.

"You approve this plan, and there will be a stampede on I-91 from downcountry that will ride you out of town. You'll call Center Darby Road your own personal trail of tears. They will rip down your houses and barns and build mansions fit for Malibu and Myrtle Beach; they'll turn your sugar bushes and apple orchards into parking lots; they'll point up your stonewalls; they'll pave your driveways; they'll ban brush burning, gun racks, and deer hunting; they'll shame your kids for the way they talk; they'll bring in people who don't speak our lingo to take your jobs. Your children will spite you for your stupidity and leave you forlorn. In the end you will spite yourselves.

"I know you people think us Jordans are a bunch of hicks who go our own way and never mind what other people do and think. Well, you're right! Isn't that what America and this town is all about? Our right to be . . . how shall I say? Peculiar. Our right to be peculiar with-out condemnation. Our right to live in a shack, in a three-bedroom house, in a trailer, in a rat's nest. It won't matter about your rights once this plan is in effect, because you'll already be squeezed out. I say this so-called master plan is going to spill the guts of this town like a car-killed skunk, and the smell will linger in your pores and tear ducts until doomsday. Vote it down at town meeting. Vote . . . it . . . down."

A few people stamped their feet, then more, until half the crowd was cheering and stamping their feet.

Critter stopped speaking and just took in the applause until it qui-eted. Then he handed the mic to Cod, said, "See you later," leaped off the stage, marched down the aisle, and out the door. There were some laughs and what-the's. Hard to measure the mood of the gathered, hard to tell whether they were merely entertained by one of their more no-torious townsmen or whether he had planted an idea of insurrection

241

in their heads. Critter's speech had done something to them — but what? Perhaps they did not know themselves what they felt or thought that day. It all happened so fast that just about everybody in the hall was unable to catch up to the real meaning. Everybody but Constable Howard Elman. Critter's performance had opened his mind. Jordan mayhem was about to burst upon the world.

Howard was so wrought up that he wasn't listening while H.C. Wentworth was introduced, but he turned his attention to her when she stepped forward holding the microphone.

The CEO of Paradise Lots Covenant was thickly built, but not overweight. She might have been a retired tennis pro. She was probably pretty at one time, but her face had acquired some lines and a hardness that gave her the authoritarian aspect of a garden maven who has taken in too much sun; her expression was guarded, and there was a tightness that served to mask any vulnerabilities that might have remained from her youth. It was the face of a woman in politics or enterprise: intelligent, assertive, attractive without sensuality, a forced warmth that comes from one who needs to be admired, and something else that is hidden and leaves the observer wondering — who is this, what is inside?

She has perfect teeth.

Howie, if you had been born female, H.C. Wentworth is what you would have looked like in middle age. Remember the words.

Daddy, I want to swing, push me.

You start her off, release her, watch her. She's on her own now. Pumping the swing, pumping, pumping, leaping from the greatest height possible into the great big chasm of her destiny.

"Does anyone here recognize me?" Her voice was still rich and musical, but it had cultivated a sense of command. She waited a moment. "No?" H.C. Wentworth looked directly at Priscilla Landry. "Priscilla?"

"Heather? Is it you?" asked Priscilla.

"Yes, it is." H.C. Wentworth's smile revealed just a trace of regret. As if embarrassed, she broke eye contact with Priscilla, her childhood friend, and addressed the gathered in formal tones. "My name is Heather Cutter Wentworth, but my handle at Paradise Lots Covenant is H.C., and some of you long-time residents in this town knew me as Heather Elman."

Howard's breath caught the mocking echo from the distant past: teeth, straight teeth. And then he was knocked sideways by an intrusive thought from the recent past — the missing gas can.

What was it Cooty had said? "He wants to set fire to it."

Critter Jordan is going to burn down the Manse.

Howard Elman rose from his chair and limped out of the town hall as quickly as his bad leg would allow.

No doubt H.C. Wentworth took note that her father was walking out on her talk. If she felt any disappointment or resentment, she didn't let it show as she laid out her company's plans for Darby with a PowerPoint presentation on a screen set up beside the planning board's table. She expanded on captions of drawings of buildings; she explained graphs and, as Dot McCurtin noted later, narrated in a voice that gave you confidence it could sing the "Star Spangled Banner" without a strained note.

"We at PLC are dedicated to the idea that with technology, investment, commitment, faith, and hard work we can bring back Darby's magic moment, make it real." H.C. Wentworth flashed the PLC slogan on the screen, and read it aloud: "Paradise Lots Covenant / Connecting Tradition / and Technology to / You.

"We take our motto seriously. Like my brother F. Latour and my nephew Birch Latour and the Darby planning board, we at PLC believe in bypassing the twentieth century. Our vision is to recast Darby into an eighteenth- and nineteenth-century community with twenty-first-century know-how and technology. Our goal is to recapture Darby's Magic Moment and put off Darby's End Time until doomsday."

H.C. Wentworth ended her remarks by telling the gathered that whether the voters approved the master plan or turned it down, PLC would still "gift" Darby a new meetinghouse. The company and selectman had been working with the political parties on a plan to host one of the presidential debates in the next election in this new structure, which would represent rule by the people.

"Paradise Lots Covenant will put Darby at the center of the national map. Let me add that to show my own faith in this community, I plan to build a house on Center Darby Road for my own family on property once owned by my birth family."

Afterward, H.C. Wentworth, Birch, Cod Prell, and Missy, in her role as state senate candidate, took questions from the audience. Quite a sight to see a political candidate kissing her own baby. Local people were suspicious of the proposed radical changes to their town, but they thrilled to the promise of lower taxes on their properties. The idea that what was at stake was Darby's identity hadn't sunk in.

STORYBOARD

WHILE HIS DAUGHTER WAS addressing the people of Darby, Constable Elman limp-jogged to the PT Cruiser, slid behind the driver's seat, and opened the glove compartment. He grabbed the pistol, enjoying its heft in his hand; he slipped in the bullets, rolled the cylinder, put the pistol on the seat beside him, and drove off.

When Howard arrived at the Manse, he spotted an open window where no doubt Critter had let himself in. This struck Howard as funny, since the front door was unlocked, a fact that Critter must have known. *He just likes to sneak around.* The insight warmed Howard to Critter. In the end, he was just a guy with yearnings and faults like any other guy.

Your enemy is like your brother, Howie.

I don't have a brother.

Gun drawn, Howard entered.

Birch and the minions talked often about "sustainable" living, water conservation, climate change, energy crisis, dependence on foreign oil, solar collectors, windmills, clean coal, nuclear (did a nuclear freeze bring on a nuclear winter?), and, yes, conservation, but in their daily lives they left the lights on.

Howard was wondering just what he was going to do when he found Critter when, entering the library through the wide entry from the hall, gun in hand, he found Critter sitting in Raphael Salmon's special leather chair, peering through his reading glasses at one of the Squire's green journals. Beside him on the floor was the gas can. Howard smelled it before he saw it.

Critter didn't even look up from his reading material when he spoke. "You're not very stealthy, Constable," Critter said. "You wouldn't pass a class in burglar school — you make too much noise."

"How'd you know it was me? The limp?" Howard was impressed.

Critter gently closed the journal and put it down on the end table as he spoke, but he still avoided looking at Howard. "Yeah, the limp, plus I heard you drive up in your retro shitbox."

"I keep meaning to get a new muffler, but it's only a pin hole, and I can barely hear it even with my hearing aid."

"Old age has degraded you, Constable," Critter chuckled, though he didn't sound happy. "I've watched your every move since you started to hassle me."

"Let me inform you that I am armed."

"Yes, you're a walking argument for gun control laws, Howie." Critter still hadn't turned around and could not have known for sure that Howard had a gun pointed at him. "I don't believe that old men and little children should be allowed to carry firearms. They're dangers to themselves and to the public."

"You're mighty calm for a fugitive at large and a burglar caught in the act," Howard said.

"I don't feel calm; I feel justified, I feel ready for the great event of my life." Critter suddenly rose to his feet and wheeled in Howard's direction. The movement—so quick—sent a wave of fear through Howard.

Shoot him, Howie, shoot him.

I can't.

You got too many of those female hormones.

Critter advanced toward Howard as he talked, then did an about-face when he came too close. With his back to Howard, Critter spoke, "Your son and grandson have been playing with my mind, and they are going to be the first ones I get." He turned slowly around to face Howard. Critter had a far away look in his eye.

"Freddy and Birch never did anything to you. Freddy doesn't even live in Darby anymore."

"What a laugh, you don't even know what they're up to, do you?" Critter sounded maniacal now. "They think they can negotiate with me. I played along, but I was just biding my time." Critter advanced, stopped not three feet from Howard, leaned forward, and rotated his head and shoulders like a cobra mesmerizing his prey before striking.

Howie, you better shoot him now, because he's going to take advantage of your advanced age — you're 87 years old.

No, I'm only 86.

Well, actually you might be 88. Or a mere 85.

Doesn't matter. I'm going to be a hero.

Yes, now, do it. Shoot him. Shoot him dead.

Hero and zero sound like a connection — it's not. Why does "it's not" sound like "it snot"?

Howard felt Critter slap his hand and send the gun flying.

"Sit down, old man." Critter walked Howard toward the Squire's chair and pushed him into it. Then he picked up Howard's gun, sat cross-legged on the floor, and stared up in glee at Howard.

If only you were sixty, you could of taken care of this creep.

"Shoot me and get it over with," Howard said, but he didn't mean it, and Critter knew he didn't mean it. He just wanted to talk himself into believing he wasn't scared.

Look on the bright side, Elenore used to say.

Well, I'm in the Squire's chair and it's comfortable. Is that bright enough?

"I don't want to shoot anybody, Howie. I'm going to have to, though. It's the only way to make my point. This is America. It's how we get attention. Isn't it better for you this way than decaying in a sick bed in a nursing home?"

"You got a point, Critter," Howard said, and he meant it, and Critter knew he meant it. "I knew when you stalked out of that meeting that you were coming out here to torch the mansion. Right?"

The truth knocked Critter off his pins. He got suddenly emotional, jumped to his feet, and said, "You think of Birch Latour as your precious grandson. Well, I'll tell you, old man, he's more a Salmon than an Elman, and the Salmons drove me to this state of mind. They killed my father, they killed my son, they tormented me with their logic, their sanctimonious speeches about saving the damn trees," Critter paused, apparently unsure what to say next, then he started again. "The long war of Upper Darby against us native-borns is about to enter another phase."

"Ain't no such war," Howard said.

"There's a long war all right," Critter said, going off on a mad rant. What horrified Howard was that it was a version of his own rant. "I'd like to take credit for declaring the war, but it was going on before you and me were born. You think it was the knights of old that built the castles? You think it was the tycoons that laid the rail tracks, put down the asphalt for the highways, stoked the foundry fires, built the rockets, and packed the computer chips? It was dirty-faced men like me and you, Constable. You were a working man. You ran the looms in the cotton mill, you hauled the trash. Without you there would be no civilization.

"But your offspring have betrayed you, Constable. Now they're ashamed of you. What we have in common, old man, is your son and grandson want us to get out of the way, and if we don't, they're going to kill us with their robots. It was them declared the war. Them the pursuers, them the whip hands, them the judges pronouncing the sentences while the working man built his own gallows.

"When I fought back they tried an amnesty trick with me. Freddy, he and me met. 'Call me Latour,' he says. Denying his roots, denying even his name—it must have hurt you, Constable. And what about Birch? It must have hurt you to see your grandson kissing the behind of his Salmon grandfather. But you took it from your kin, because deep down, deep fucking down you have no self-respect, no self-belief. You're a clown, Howard Elman, a buffoon, a fuck bump. Freddy, he thought he could make it all good by tricking me, thought I was stupid. We're not stupid, we who built America, we who burnt the hardwoods to make the charcoal to run the steamboats, we who drove the nails and poured the concrete, we who hauled the trash and emptied the bed pans. We were just biding our time . . ."

Howard interrupted, "You're wrong, Critter—see, I'm not the jealous type. And, what do you mean 'we'? You ducked honest work all your life, and so did Ike. You don't deserve to speak for the working man, because you avoided real work. You're a common crook."

"I may be common, but I'm not menial. You, Constable, you and the rest of your kind, like Pitchfork Parkinson and Long Neck MacDougal and all the diner waitresses and convalescent home nurses under God's creation, the working people, you can't or won't speak for yourselves;

248

you'll go to war only when the general gives the order; you're as menial as your labors and your attitude. I have to do your manly work for you. I have to speak for you, because you can't or won't speak for yourself. I'm not alone either. There's others like me out there. They gave me succor while I laid my plans."

As Critter rambled on, Howard pieced together Critter's disjointed tale. Critter and Billy had sneaked into the Manse numerous times. It was part of Billy's training as a burglar and part of Critter's war against the Trust and the Salmons that he had embarked upon after he had found the damning page from Raphael Salmon's journal. One night Critter and Billy were caught in the act in the library. Billy had a gun and he pulled it, but he dropped his weapon when he was shot in the thigh by Missy Mendelson. Critter was allowed to flee with Billy. But the bullet had severed a main artery, and by the time the Jordans arrived at the auction barn Billy had bled out.

"When I realized he was gone, you know what I did?" Critter said. "Nothing. I hallucinated—it was like I was on acid or abducted by aliens and they were probing my brain for reactions. I didn't feel what I was supposed to feel, no grief, no anger, just a nowhere-man feeling and the brights of my brain waves. It's still with me, Howie. That feeling is what's going to happen to regular people if the Trust and PLC get their way."

When Birch had called him on his cell phone wanting to know how Billy was, Critter, still in that zone between the hell of real life and the hell of imagined life, had told Birch the truth—Billy was dead.

Minutes later, some of the geeks showed up and took Billy's body away. Critter's phone rang. It was Latour. Apparently Birch had phoned his dad, and they'd worked out some kind of plan. Latour had told Critter that Birch wouldn't report the burglary if Critter wouldn't report Billy's death.

A week went by, and slowly Critter came out of his traumatic state. He made inquiries and learned from his kin, Abenaki Jordan, who had moved to Wilder, Vermont, near Dartmouth College, that Birch had visited his former brain science professor, Mordecai Taliman. That night Critter broke into Professor Taliman's laboratory and was again thrown into a traumatic state when he discovered Billy's body laid out

249

naked on a slab. He had quickly covered the body in a sheet, carried it out to his truck, and driven it back to the auction barn. He couldn't bear to look at Billy, so he brought the body to the flea market section, set it in a chair, and covered it in mover blankets.

After that, he and F. Latour had been in constant communication. "Negotiating," Critter said, spitting out the word so that it sounded like the worst of swears.

"Why did you move out of the auction barn?" Howard asked.

"I couldn't bear to be there knowing that Billy, my poor Billy, was next door frozen solid, dead. These Upper Darby people are crazy and evil."

"Let me guess. You had places to stay all over the county, because you sought succor from your Jordan kin."

Critter gave Howard a bare nod.

"What did you do with Billy's body when you pulled it out of the flea market?" Howard asked.

"It wasn't me that done that, it was Birch and his people. They brought the body back to Professor Taliman's lab at Dartmouth College."

"How could you know that?"

"Because I read Birch's emails on his computer right here in the Manse. I know his password: all can be saved. I wanted to go back to the professor's lab and pull the body out and give it a proper burial."

"But you couldn't muster the courage."

"You got me there, Constable."

"Ok, I get your war against the Trust and Birch and even Upper Darby, but why did you cut down my elm tree? What do you have against me?"

"I got nothing against you, Constable. I did it for the money. I promised Billy a snowmobile, but my credit cards were maxed out."

"The money? Somebody hired you? Who was it?"

"I don't know, who cares? The money was there. They trusted me to do the job. What else can a man ask for besides cash on the barrelhead?"

"Cash on the barrelhead? What's a barrelhead, and why do you put cash on it?" Howard blurted out his thought. It was the first time the Voice had actually spoken loud and clear from Howard's mouth.

"Because the old-time general stores used a barrelhead to take money from their customers."

"You're guessing."

"No, my dad told me," Critter said. "Ike was a scholar in his own way. He knew antiques. He knew what a barrelhead was, and he taught me."

Critter is telling the truth, or anyway his truth. He doesn't know who is behind the cutting of your lo and behold elm.

I'm going to my grave without discovering who cut my elm tree and why.

A wave of dread and darkness washed over Howard Elman. The mocking voice inside said, *Howie, your life has been a waste.*

I can't die now. I have to do something.

You can't do anything. You're too old and decrepit.

Well, I'm crepit enough to talk.

"Critter, why don't you just hop into your Bedford truck and drive off into the sunset," Howard said. "Birch and the geeks won't go after you. They have other plans."

"Like what?"

"Like they didn't report you, and they're covering up Billy's shooting because they're protecting Missy," Howard said. "She's going to be their state government connection when she gets elected. And another thing, they're going to make you and Billy famous."

"Famous? What does that mean?"

"I mean everything you've done so far is finding its way into their video game."

Critter shook his head in exasperation, laughed, just a little snicker, then he stood up and began to pace, moving the pistol from hand to hand.

Howard lay back in the big easy chair, looking for an opportunity to rise up and wrestle the gun from Critter.

Oh, to be sixty for only a moment.

"I've already planned for my future fame," Critter said, "and it has nothing to do with no video game. I'm going to burn this building to the ground, Constable. I've already disconnected the sprinkler system. Then I'm going to mail this paper to *The Keene Sentinel*, make it all public: Squire Salmon murdered my father. Then I'm going to drive back to that planning board hearing and shoot the place up. Start by shooting Freddy, Birch, and that witch who killed my son. Then I'm going to retrieve Billy's body."

"Then what?" Howard said.

"I don't know, I don't have a clue—I never did." Critter made noises, half self-mocking laughter, half sobs.

Howard tried to think of something to say to divert Critter from his plan.

In a weird way you admire Critter for his lonely war against the forces of change.

Yes, I do.

Critter pulled himself together and pointed the pistol at Howard. "They'll find your body where you're sitting, Constable. Don't worry. You won't burn to death. I wouldn't do that to a good working man. I'm going to put you out of your misery with a bullet to the brain."

"So be it," Howard said.

He shut his eyes, and he saw himself as a teenager with that beautiful girl he met in the foster home. It was summer and he and Elenore lay on a blanket under an apple tree remaking the world. And now he was seeing the distressed apple tree in front of Cooty's cabin. Last time he looked all three remaining apples from the last growing season were still hanging on.

You know, Howie, when the apple tree falls over, it grows out of its own remains. It's quite a tree. All trees are quite . . .

And then he heard a noise, but it wasn't a gun shot, it was the voice of Cooty Patterson: "Hey, Critter, you left your spit fire in the car."

Howard opened his eyes. The centenarian stood in his sandals, Bruegel robe, and acorn hat, holding an Uzi machine gun.

Critter was startled. "Be careful with that thing, it might go off," Critter said.

"I hope not. It would scare the heck out of me."

Critter advanced toward Cooty. "Come on now, give me the weapon. I'll take the bullets out." He held out his hand.

Cooty smiled at Critter, raised the Uzi, pointed it away from Critter, and pulled the trigger. Bullets jabbered into the library shelves. Book pages flew out of their bindings. Words separated from their sentences.

Forgotten authors rose from the dead. The Uzi jumped out of Cooty's hands and fell to the floor; for a moment all was quiet.

Before the startled Critter could respond, two wraiths appeared as if out of the air — Luci and Wiqi moving with robot-like speed. In seconds they disarmed Critter, pulled his hands behind his back, tied them with his own belt, and marched him out of the room along with his gas can.

Howard and Cooty were alone.

"The noise scared me, Howie," Cooty said. "What's that smell?"

"Gun powder," Howard said.

"I'm pooped," Cooty said.

The two old men sat, exhausted, just catching their breath, when Birch, Tess, Latour, Missy and her baby, the loggers, and the entire Geek Chorus, even Origen, seemed to appear as one before them. Luci and Wiqi were right behind.

"What happened to Critter?" Howard asked.

"We gave him a sedative," Luci said. "He'll be in dreamland for the next couple hours." She turned to Wiqi. "Let's clean up this mess."

"No, don't touch anything — it's evidence," Howard said. "Birch, call the state police. Critter has got to be locked up."

"Grandpa, we'd rather not," Birch said, looking at his father.

"Birch is right," Latour said. "We can find a place for Critter in our company."

"Using cajole-therapy, we can make him a productive employee," Tess said. "Uncle Critter has vitality."

"We'll have to break him from playing with matches," Birch said in that sweet way of his.

Everybody laughed. Howard couldn't tell just how serious the suggestions were. "I'm too tired to argue," he said. "I'd like a Smutty Nose beer. How did you people happened to come in at just the right time?"

"When Cooty left the cabin, he set off an alarm that Luci and Wiqi monitored," Birch said. "The hearing had ended anyway. We just put a little hurry-hurry into our exit."

"You and Freddy — excuse me son, F. Latour — were in cahoots with Heather and PLC all along, weren't you?" Howard said.

"Of course — we're family," F. Latour said.

"All can be saved," Origen said.

253

Later that night there was a dinner party at the Salmon mansion that included Birch and his minions, along with Cod Prell, Frances Peet, and members of the planning board. The only geek missing was Origen, who was on his way to Hanover to meet with Professor Taliman for reasons not made clear to Howard. Luci and Wiqi had put Cooty to bed, and carried off Critter to parts unknown for his re-education. Howard had to look at the smashed book shelves and the bullet holes in the walls to remind himself that there had been some shooting. He was weary, but he hung around anyway and more or less kept his drinking under control.

There was a lot of talk by the geeks about the planning board's master plan. Even with his hearing aid cranked up, Howard had a hard time following the quick swings in conversation.

TREK: You can't have a free country without having a free country. Either you have freedom or you don't.

JAYU: Freedom is overrated as a quality of life module.

SOLOMON: Freedom does not actually exist. It's another one of those excuses to persecute people you don't agree with.

JAYU: No, freedom is real, and it is real important.

TREK: And you only know what it is when you no longer have it.

SOLOMON: The fine points don't matter; what matters is that freedom is a fundamental value of the American — and, I might add, Haitian — way of life.

Another voice joined in. "Individual freedom is a value that the Europeans who settled here absorbed via cultural osmosis from our families and our clans," said Josephine Abare.

Howard noted that Birch and Tess gradually withdrew from the conversation and spoke often to each other but rarely to the table, until Birch announced, "Tess and I are leaving. We're going to do some storyboarding."

Before dessert was served, the lovers took off under a big moon on cross-country skis. No doubt they were on the path to the high-tech nineteenth-century tree house in the woods.

Minutes later Josephine left the mansion.

Howard tried with only partial success to pay attention to the table chitchat, which got going strong after Birch and Tess had gone.

TREK: The weakness in the master plan is the damn Indian casino —riverboat gambling, give me a break. Especially their rep. Nobody likes Josephine Abare.

JAYU: She is a Native American.

TREK: She better stay out of the woods, because if a mosquito bites her it might suck out that little bit of native blood.

SOLOMON: Since CNAC is the anchor for the whole operation, generating the most revenue, there's the possibility that the Connissadawaga Tribe will gain too much power.

TREK: No way. PLC and us geeks, we'll be running this town, not the Injuns.

SOLOMON: Better not talk that way in front of Birch, or you'll be writing code to run washing machine cycles.

TREK: I don't get it—what do you mean?

JAYU: Apparently, you haven't heard. Birch has been working with a genealogy team and has discovered that his grandmother on his father's side was born to a Connissadawaga woman. The proof's in the DNA.

TREK: So Birch Latour is another one with a mosquito prick of Native American blood—that's pretty funny.

SOLOMON: I predict eventually Birch will be elected the freaking chief and will move the whole tribe onto the Trust lands.

Howard could bear it no longer. He drove back to Re In Car Nation, and lay on the couch exhausted.

DARBY DOOMSDAY

THE NEXT DAY Howard met with Birch, F. Latour, Tess, and Missy in Cooty's cabin.

F. Latour and Howard separated from the group and stood together in a corner of the cabin. F. Latour showed Howard the papers that Birch had dug up. Elenore was Irish, English, French, and Native American. Father and son talked in whispers.

"Too bad we didn't do this research when mom was alive," F. Latour said.

"Yeah, it made her sad that she didn't know who her people were," Howard said.

"She found some solace in religion," F. Latour said.

Howard shook his head, then struggled to speak to his son, but no words came out.

Go ahead, say it.

I can't.

Then just drop dead right here.

Okay, I'll give it a shot.

"I never treated you the way I should have—I'm sorry, Freddy. I mean Latour."

"It's okay, Pop."

For a moment it might have appeared to an observer that father and son would embrace, but they didn't. They left the corner and joined the group.

The treatments Luci and Wiqi were giving Cooty had worked wonders. He might not be able to operate a machine gun, but he could take care of himself. Cooty was fully dressed in his robe and acorn hat sitting at his table with folded hands. He looked fifteen years younger, an elderly gentleman, not a slack-jawed centenarian. The company gathered around the table eating stew with wooden spoons made by F. Latour. They conversed as they ate. Light chatter.

Howard stood, took Cooty's cane off the footlocker, gestured with it as if he were Moses parting the Red Sea, and shouted, "Okay, now what?" And he put the cane back on the footlocker and sat down at the table.

Birch, sitting cross-legged on the floor, glanced at his father beside him. F. Latour got that funny looking-at-the-sky face that used to infuriate Howard when F. Latour was Freddy and a young kid trying to distance himself from a domineering dad. F. Latour seemed about to speak, but halted and just shook his head.

"Grandpa Howard should know the truth," Tess said.

"Good idea," Howard said.

Birch was not so sure. "Grandpa, why do you have to know our business here?" he said softly. "Couldn't you just . . ." He couldn't bear to speak the words.

"Just retire, turn in my badge as town constable."

"You don't have a badge, Pop," F. Latour said softly.

"He don't have no stinking badge," said Missy. She was the only one at the table who had never allowed herself to be intimidated by Howard Elman.

"Something's bothering me," Howard's voice thundered. "It's the forgotten woman, Delphina Jordan. The woman lost a son and a husband. If I don't deserve the truth, she does. And I plan to tell her everything I know. Her boy is dead and in cold storage at Dartmouth College, and her ex has been kidnapped. Who can say what his end will be?"

Birch put his palms against his forehead, looked at his father. "Dad?"

"Okay, I'll explain it," F. Latour said. "Pop, I want you to listen, and don't interrupt, okay?"

"Okie-dokie," Howard said as if he meant it.

"For Birch and me, everything is about the Trust lands, the conservancy," F. Latour said. "Squire Salmon had a vision, but he was a little short on legal niceties and cash flow. Our goal is to build an ironclad land trust for the future. To accomplish that purpose we can't allow the town of Darby to morph into a burb, or worse into a trailer park community. The best way to do that is to partner with the Connissadawaga tribe and PLC, which we've done, and to create zoning laws to exclude the people we don't want and include the people we do want, while at the same time generating income. Bottom line: we need a grip on this town.

"Missy, when she's elected state senator, will look out for our interests in the state house. If the public learns that Missy shot a sixteen-year-old boy, even if it was justified, Missy won't be elected and, worse, the publicity will cast a pall over the Trust lands, our video game company, and the Salmon name.

"Then there's that other element that has the dollar signs in front of it. The Trust doesn't quite pay its way. It needs a subsidy. That's where Geek Chorus Software comes in. If Darby Doomsday is successful — and early indications are it will be — we save the Trust and we save Darby. We have a percentage of the profits from the gambling casino as a backup.

"Myself and the other two writers, Web Clements and Josephine Abare, along with our religion and philosophy consultant, Origen, have included Billy and Critter into a subplot of Darby Doomsday. In our version Billy goes to Tibet to study Eastern philosophy. Critter joins an evangelical church. Lots of possibilities for father-son conflict over religion. Eventually, Critter goes to the Middle East to spread his gospel. Maybe he's killed. He becomes a martyr. But maybe not. It all depends on how the real Critter takes to de-programming and re-programming. You following me, Pop?"

"What does all this do for Delphina?" Howard asked, droll.

F. Latour looked at this son, "Your turn."

"Her truth will be that Billy is still alive," Birch said. "We have his email and his social media passwords — we have his identity. Delphina and Billy email every day. He tells her all about his life. She tells him the news from back home. They have a beautiful relationship not only individually but as intimates in social media that they share with others in circles."

"You can't keep the truth from her forever."

"Yes, we can, Pop," F. Latour said. "That's the beauty of a circle, it goes round and round forever. We're creating a database of information, a growing, maturing identity for Billy Jordan that includes virtual

258

reality photographs of Billy in various environments, all created with computer software. In another ten or twelve years, Luci and Wiqi expect to construct a fully functioning Billy Jordan. He'll be reunited with his mother as a successful man. He'll support her financially in her old age. He'll make a grandmother out of her. She will be overwhelmed with good feeling."

"Good feeling is our ultimate goal," Tess said.

"That's just crazy," Howard said.

"No, it's a calculated risk," Birch said, and turned to his father, "Tell him, Dad."

"Okay, Pop, the truth is that Billy Jordan is not dead, not exactly anyway."

"He's only sort of dead," said Missy with a little snicker.

"Sort of dead?" Howard said to nobody.

"You see, Pop, when we retrieved Billy's body, we were able to get him on life support. Get some blood into him. We even found activity in the brain, though not consciousness. Billy is in a vegetative state in Professor Taliman's laboratory."

"But I saw the body frozen in the auction barn. Critter stole it."

Latour shook his head. "The body that Critter took was a reproduction of Billy created by a 3D printer. You see, Billy's body and organs are too far gone. The goal is to replace the entire biological body with synthetics, but we want the body to look like Billy. The 3D printer gives us exact measurements of the shapes. We're going to transfer Billy's identity, his very self, into an artificial reproduction. It will, however, take many years before the technology improves sufficiently to affect the transfer. And, really, it may not work. I mean the part where Billy wakes up."

"Then what will you tell Delphina?" Howard said.

"If Billy does come back from the dead—we'll deal with that problem when it arises. If Billy dies for real, we'll hire a human actor to impersonate him," said Tess. She turned to Howard. "Isn't a virtual Billy better for Delphina than the never-ending grief for a son who died too young?"

"And it's all going to be in the game—Billy the Buddhist, Critter the born-again?" Howard said, fascinated now because he was in over his head, and there was nothing to be done but appreciate the power of inundation.

"Yes, it will all end up in Darby Doomsday," Latour said.

"Grandpa, the human mind makes a game of reality anyway, why not embrace the idea and run with it, partner with the illusion the mind creates?" Birch said.

"What about the meetinghouse business, the bomb?" Howard said.

Latour chuckled, and in that little sarcastic laugh Howard heard himself. He experienced a flash of paternal pride. "We're still working on that plot, Pop, how to integrate realpolitik with virtualpolitik — it's a challenge. PLC is very close to an agreement with the political parties to hold a presidential debate in Darby's new meetinghouse. If that happens, PLC's experiment in recreating Darby's Magic Moment will be a success no matter what the voters do at town meeting. Tourists will flock to this place."

"Yes, Grandpa, if nobody gets killed, it's kind of lame for the game," Tess said.

"So you have to blow up the meetinghouse."

"Not just the meetinghouse. The explosive device is a nuke; the entire town is destroyed," Missy said.

"The bomb will kill not only the candidates but everybody?" Howard said.

"In several versions of the game, that's correct — Darby Doomsday earns its name," Birch said. He made an explosion sound, which seemed to amuse everyone at the table.

Howard turned to Cooty. "You knew all about this?"

"That's right. I'm the only one who knows everything." Cooty tapped his temple.

"You see, Grandpa," Tess said. "You, Birch, Latour, and even Critter confide in Cooty, and he inspires you. He's the only one with a database of all your thoughts, because you don't confide in each other. Thanks to the treatments by Luci and Wiqi, Cooty has been able to convey his memories for transcription."

"For the game, right?" Howard said. He was thinking that Cooty had lied to Luci about his role in World War II. What else had he lied to her about?

"Yes, for the game, and perhaps in the future real world, for transfer of thoughts in brain matter to computer chips," Birch said.

"Who came up with the big idea for this game?" Howard asked, but he already suspected the answer.

"The game was my idea, and transforming Darby into a history village was Heather's," Birch said. "I don't know where Heather got her idea from, but I'm guessing it's from the same source that I got mine. The big idea is from you, Grandpa. What you did with your property after Grandma Elenore passed away. When Dad named it Re In Car Nation everything fell into place. You brought back your own Magic Moment, Grandpa, and lived it—and by all appearances quite comfortably. You brought virtual reality to this small town, Grandpa. Darby Doomsday started with you."

Howard nodded, pretended a little bow, and said, "I'm flattened," though he meant to say "flattered." His comment produced a shared superior laugh from the gathered.

Soon the cabin emptied, and Howard and Cooty were left alone.

Cooty smiled at Howard in a way he never had before. It was a smile that was full of mirth, mischief, and perhaps some cunning. He reached into a pocket in his robe and produced a key. "I remembered where I put it, Howie."

"The key to the footlocker," Howard said.

"Yes, I put it under a rock for safekeeping," Cooty said.

Howard was puzzled. For the first time in decades, perhaps for the first time ever, Cooty seemed sane, with the world. A gain for him, but perhaps a loss for his friends.

"So are you going to open the footlocker?" Howard asked.

"Yes, right now," Cooty said. "I wanted you to be the first one to see."

"You know what's in there?"

"Yes, I remembered the minute I touched the key." Cooty carefully removed the objects from the top of the footlocker—the acorns, the hatchet, the bow saw, the cane. He handed the cane to Howard and said, "Here, you need this more than I do."

Howard took the cane and leaned on it. "I shoulda got one of these long ago."

Cooty wasn't listening to Howard. He was on one knee in front of the footlocker. He put the key in the lock, turned it. Pulled. The lock unclacked. Not a sound that Howard's hearing aid picked up, but he could hear it in his memory.

Cooty set the lock down and lifted the top of the footlocker, reached inside, and pulled out a dress, the kind a woman might wear to a ball, then another dress, and another.

Howard understood now. The dresses were Cooty's wardrobe. He looked at Cooty and said, "Now what?"

"Now I fulfill my destiny."

"Ain't you smaht," Howard said, and for once there was no sarcasm in his voice.

On his way out Howard noticed that one of the apples that clung to the apple tree had fallen off.

HOWARD ELMAN'S FAREWELL

HOWARD SPENT THAT NIGHT on his couch at Re In Car Nation. He tried to contemplate his next move, but he was so tired he just fell asleep. The next morning when he went outside and stood in the driveway, something about the property didn't feel right, though he couldn't figure out what it was.

Maybe it's the presence of Cooty's cane in my hand.

No, that's not it. Something is missing.

He turned around and saw wood smoke in the former Cutter house up the hill.

On impulse, he got in the PT Cruiser and drove the short ways to the Zoe Cutter house, recently reopened by PLC. A Lexus SUV with Massachusetts plates lay broadside in the plowed lot. Howard frowned. Motorists that took up two spaces with their vehicles annoyed him.

From this prospect on the ridge of the knoll, the view below of Re In Car Nation stoppered his lungs from taking air for few seconds: the expanse of field, the stone wall, the gray barn, the house shell with the purple asphalt shingles, the maple tree, the junked cars. It all looked both superreal and unreal from this vantage point. He stood gazing at it for a long time.

If it was an ice cream cone, you would lick it, wouldn't you, Howie?

I'd lick it if it was a cow pattie.

Because you created it.

Right.

And then he had that same feeling that he had earlier standing in his driveway. Something was wrong with the scene below. What was it?

A loss.

Yes, but a loss of what?

A loss that even St. Anthony could not fathom.

He shook the thoughts away.

Howard did not plan on knocking. He was going to barge in and make a grand appearance. However, Heather must have heard him pull into her drive because she opened the door before he reached the entry.

"This is a surprise. Come in," she said in a cordial voice, though her jaw was set like a rusted-stuck vice, and she avoided looking him in the eye.

She pointed at his feet. It took a second before Howard understood; he removed his boots. In all the time he was married, he had never taken his shoes off upon entering his house. Often he hadn't even bothered to wipe his feet.

I suppose I was inconsiderate. Sorry, Elenore.

He didn't voice his thought, but his lips moved.

He looked Heather over while she looked him over. Heather wore dark slacks and an off-white blouse that hung loosely over her hips, designed, he imagined, to play down her somewhat wide middle. Around her neck was a rawhide cord holding a carved piece of cherry wood in which was inlaid a silver pendant shaped like a feather with matching earrings, the Connissadawaga tribal totem. Was she going to claim tribal membership? Her chestnut brown hair was medium length with just a twist in it. She must have some gray, but he couldn't see any in the roots. She wore makeup, but not too much and not too lurid. Her lipstick was subdued. Nails medium long and polished but not colored. Complexion clear. He wanted to tell her that he liked the way she looked, but he didn't know how to formulate words for a compliment that didn't have counteracting sarcasm in it, so he didn't say anything.

"You're a big man, Daddy, but nowhere as big as I remembered you."

"You reach a certain age, and you start to shrink," Howard said. "Eventually you just disappear."

"What was it Elenore used to say, 'That's nature's way'?"

Howard frowned. He didn't like Heather referring to her mother by her first name.

Heather offered him a cup of coffee, and he accepted. The house had been converted into an office where PLC employees could work in cubicles in what had been the spacious parlor of the Cutter house. Heather led him to a smaller room converted into a conference room, where a propane-gas fire blazed in a phony fireplace. On the walls were bookshelves and a painting of contra dancers. Howard thought the room looked both Colonial and modernistic at the same time. They sat around a table too big for two and stared at the fire so they wouldn't have to gaze at each other.

"I don't remember this house looking like this," he said.

"It's been remodeled by our architect friend Cod Prell into an office building. Quite ugly, I'm afraid. I should have paid closer attention to the plans."

"You said you were going to move in here."

"Not exactly," Heather said, droll. "I said I was going to build a house in this location. Once PLC has finished acquiring properties in Darby I'm going to close this office, tear down this structure, and start over."

"Where will you live in the meantime?"

"I already have other houses in other parts of the country and a flat near our London office."

A flat? What is a flat?

Let it go, Howie.

Howard noted that she was not specific on just where her American abodes were; he figured she didn't want him to visit her.

"I guess a house is not a home if you got more than one," Howard said.

"Daddy, you've always tied the idea of home to a place. For me, home is people. My husband, my family, my friends, my colleagues at PLC — they are my home. A house is a house is a house."

"I imagine you're right, but for me home is . . ." He pointed out the window in the direction of his property.

Howie, it's not yours anymore.

As long I can wake up in the morning on my couch, it's mine.

"Before this was PLC and the Cutter place, it was the Swett house, one of the oldest in Darby. Seems a shame to tear it down," Howard said.

She looked at him hard without speaking.

He realized he'd wounded her. He tried to find a way to apologize, but could not. Finally, he said, "I'm sorry your mother couldn't be here to see what a big shot you've become."

265

"Excuse me, but Elenore Elman was not my mother."

"She brought you into the world."

"She gave birth to me, yes, but my mother was Zoe Cutter," Heather said.

Some of the old anger roiled inside of Howard. "It wouldn't have been too much of a bother to pay your mother, your birth mother, a visit during her last days," he said, and he immediately regretted that he had thrown that old hurt into Heather's face.

"Even if I had wanted to reconcile with you and Elenore, what would have been the point? We had nothing in common. After all, it was you that pushed me out the door. You, Daddy. Do you have any remorse for what you did?"

"I knew you'd be better off with Mrs. Cutter. She'd fix your teeth, educate you, teach you the finer things."

"That's not what I asked you. I asked you if you felt remorse."

Howard stopped and thought for a moment, then he said, "To tell you truth, I don't really know that remorse has any good use."

"You never did have a range of feelings, did you?"

"I guess not," Howard said. "I got droll, super droll, and no droll, and that's about it."

"You got rid of me. Why? I was just a kid who wanted nothing more than to play with her cat and sing."

See the hurt in her, the rage. It's spite that fuels her engine.

This is the crucial moment to say the right thing to bring you closer to your daughter. Howie, tell her that that bitch Zoe Cutter seduced Freddy, then worked it so you had no choice but to give up your daughter and burn your own house down. Tell Heather the truth.

No, the truth is not always a good idea. She derives her strength as H.C. Wentworth from her belief that her birth parents voluntarily gave her up, not that her adoptive mother forced the issue. It's too late to tell her the truth.

What, then? What do you want from her?

I want her to think well of me.

That might be the best thing for you, but what is the best thing for her? What, Howie, is the right thing to do?

After a few more seconds of thought Howard believed he understood what he had to do to preserve his daughter's confidence in herself and her values. He had to hurt her again. He had to keep her wounds open.

"It was my idea to sell you off to keep a little piece of my land," he paused, then added, droll, "I don't regret it."

"The land came first."

"Yes, the land always came first."

Howard could see his daughter struggle to control her emotions. Finally, she said, "Well, at least you're honest. That's something to put in the bank." She turned her back on him, and looked out the window.

"Heather, do you love this town?" Howard asked.

"Not really. I love what it can be, I love its potential." She spoke with her back still turned to him, so that he had to fiddle with his hearing aid to understand her words.

"You and Birch and Freddy, you want to change the world," Howard spoke loudly, which was his way when he was uncertain.

"Daddy, the world is on a course for doomsday. Birch, Latour, and I are doing our best to put off the end time."

The sound of a country song jarred Howard until he realized that Heather's cell phone was ringing. He watched her while she answered it and knew right away from the look on her face that something was wrong.

"Excuse me," she said to Howard and went into another room and closed the door.

When she returned, Heather looked rained on. "What's the matter?" Howard said. He wanted desperately to put his arms around her, protect her from the world, but he remained seated, detached, full of self-loathing.

For a moment Heather almost broke down, but she pulled herself together. "I have a daughter, Daddy. She doesn't like my second husband, Mister Wentworth. She turned eighteen and ran away from her school."

"Where is she?"

"I don't know. I'm very worried," she added, but then something in her changed, a belief, no doubt, that she'd revealed too much. "I wish you'd go now, please."

Without another word or even a glance at his daughter, Howard stood and limped off. Heather did not follow him. He put his boots on, grabbed his cane from where it was leaning against the wall, and walked out the door without lacing the boots. He was about to get into the PT Cruiser when he stopped to look down the hill at Re In Car Nation. He could see right away now what was missing. Why hadn't he noticed before? On a hunch, he turned to the Cutter house and walked over to the wood shed between the house and barn, and there he found the swing and the seat that had spent so many years hanging from the maple tree on his property. Apparently, Heather had it removed from the tree. Why? A souvenir?

It was later in the day when he was at the Manse, waiting for something to happen, that something happened, and he understood why Heather had taken the swing. Mrs. McCurtin called him on his cell. "You told me to be on the lookout, well I hate to tell you this, Constable, but it has begun . . ."

Howard drove the PT Cruiser to Re In Car Nation and parked on the side of the road. An army of workman had showed up with heavy equipment. He watched as the men labored all day and all night and into the next day. They dragged off his junked cars. They tore down his barn and the shell house he had built over his mobile home. All his tools, furniture, everything, went into dumpsters that were taken away as soon as they were full. They cut down the maple tree and pulled the stump out of the ground and took it away with everything else. They even knocked down the ancient stone wall that had been a property line. They smoothed over the rough spots. Their excavators and bulldozers rearranged the landscape so that it blended perfectly with the Swett/Cutter/PLC field. They brought in loam and seeded it. He shut his eyes and pictured it months hence, with grass and wildflowers. On day three, when they had barely finished their work, a surprise snowstorm covered everything, and it was impossible to tell what had been there before.

☙ ☙ ☙

Darby voters at the annual town meeting narrowly defeated its planning board's recommendations to rezone the town, but accepted a gift of a new town hall from Paradise Lots Covenant; voters tabled the proposal for a riverboat gambling casino on the Connecticut River. Company CEO H.C. Wentworth said PLC, working with the Darby planning board, would return with a revised proposal at town meeting the next year. In other action, Lawrence Dracut was defeated in his campaign for reelection, but Howard Elman—even though he was not present at the meeting—was reelected as town constable when his grandson, Birch Latour, read the constable's annual report, expenses identical to previous years, $0.00.

That summer the Swett/Cutter/PLC house was torn down, and construction began on what would be the grandest house in Center Darby, a structure to surpass the mansions of Upper Darby.

In November Missy Mendelson was elected to the New Hampshire State Senate as an Independent. Her husband, Captain Bez Woodward, returned from the war and joined Geek Chorus Software.

Billy Jordan's body remained at Dartmouth College in the hands of Professor Taliman.

Carleton "Critter" Jordan entered a monastery in a virtual Tibet built in the White Mountains of New Hampshire. Days later, Critter left the monastery, his whereabouts unknown. Birch Latour married Tess Jordan, and their child was born, a boy named Raphael Jordan Latour. Even as an infant he was called R.J.

Meanwhile, the writers for Darby Doomsday pieced together what they knew of Howard's end and wrote two versions for the new hit video game, Darby Doomsday.

VERSION 1: State police found Howard's PT Cruiser parked on the side of the road. His cell phone had been left behind. There was only one message—"set up jesus." The investigators surmised that Howard had been so upset by the destruction of his former property that he had walked into the woods in the storm and been lost. However, a body was never recovered.

VERSION 2: this version was derived from a report by Luci Sanz. "Cooty is quite mobile these days and indeed can be seen walking on the roadside looking for car-killed animals for his stew pot. During the day he wears his bruegel robe and acorn cap. After dark he puts on a dress, and after that who knows? We no longer monitor him from 8 PM to 8 AM. Cooty told me that Howard Elman had visited him, though he wouldn't say just when. Below is my summary of Cooty's rather long and perhaps deliberately disjointed tale.

"When Howard saw what had been done to his home, he immediately understood that his daughter Heather, through a PLC intermediary, had made the original deal with Critter Jordan to cut down Howard's 'elm man' tree for her own need for retribution against the father who she believed had wronged her. Howard was now bereft not only of his life partner, not only of his property, but of the very identity of himself that he had constructed. What he experienced from this realization surprised him. He had swelled with involuntary joy. 'All can be saved,' he had told Cooty.

"Howard had abandoned his PT Cruiser and driven Billy Jordan's snowmobile to the Amtrak station in Brattleboro, Vermont, and taken the next train south.

"In Nashville he found his granddaughter, Tahoka Texas McCloud, living on the street, impoverished, confused, and despondent. She had realized that she was not ready for a career as a singer, but she was too proud to return home. Howard had stayed with her for a month, caring for her, supporting her, telling her family stories, listening to her songs, until she made the decision to return to her mother's comfort. Howard had driven Tahoka in his new vehicle, a used S-10 Chevy pickup truck, to H.C. Wentworth's town house in Boston, dropped her off, watched as Heather greeted her at the door, and sped away. Howard's last words to Cooty were, 'I never done a great thing in my life, Cooty, but I done what I could.'

"Tahoka, contacted at the Julliard School in New York, would neither confirm nor deny Cooty's story, but she did email us lyrics of a song."

THE ONLY FRIEND I GOT
by Tahoka Texas McCloud

Since you departed, darlin',
he's all I got for company,
that confused old man in the bathroom mirror.
They say the day I won't remember him
Is the day I won't remember you,

so I treasure him
— he's the only friend I got.

They say he moves his lips
when he walks down the street.
They say he repeats himself,
They say he repeats himself,
And he misses when he shaves
And that's okay.
I say all he misses is you
— he's the only friend I got.

Remember when you did all the talking, darlin'
handled all the family trouble?
Remember those days, darlin',
when I checked the oil
and you wrote the checks?
I saw him this morning in that mirror
— the only friend I got.

He says better put on your reading glasses,
— if you can find them.
He looks at me, kinda puzzled,
kinda tired.
He says, we loved her, doncha know.
I nod and he nods.
I says to him I says,
you're the only friend I got,
all the rest are dead and gone.

They say he moves his lips
when he walks down the street.
They say he repeats himself,
They say he repeats himself,
They say he misses when he shaves
And that's okay.
I say he's the only friend I got
and all he misses is you

and all he misses is you
and all he misses is you.

Back at the Salmon mansion grounds, behind some trees, there still sits a small stack of elm wood boards that an eccentric old man might use to build, say, a coffin. The boards are seasoning, which Cooty Patterson told Wiqi Durocher meant "to spice up." As F. Latour wrote in notes for his new book, the *The Trees of Darby, New Hampshire*, "The rule for air drying hardwood is an inch a year. Plain, rift, quartersawn boards—there's poetry in the language of wood."

AUTHOR NOTES

First a thank you to friends who read various drafts of this novel and offered helpful suggestions: Dayton Duncan, Terry Pindell and members of my writing group, the Fubarians, Dawn Andonellis, David Akins, David Chase, Jack Coey, Stacy Greer, John T. Hitchner, Norm Klein, Sean McElhiney, and Ken Schalhoub, with a special nod to Kathy Medvidofsky who introduced me to a writing world in Keene, NH.

I also would like to thank Chip Fleischer, who got this project started with a suggestion he made, and singer and songwriter Ian Fitzgerald, who vetted Tahoka's song, *The Only Friend I Got*.

BOOKS IN THE DARBY CHRONICLES

The Dogs of March features Howard Elman's feud with Zoe Cutter (who later adopted Heather).

A Little More Than Kin is the tragedy of Ollie Jordan and his brain-impaired son Willow. We are introduced to Estelle Jordan.

Whisper My Name is a tale of personal and town identity, and a love story between an aphasic girl, Sheila "Soapy" Rayno and a news reporter, Roland LaChance.

The Passion of Estelle Jordan is a hard story of love and redemption. Besides Estelle, the story features Trans Am, who later appears as Origen in *Howard Elman's Farewell*.

Live Free or Die is the tragic love story of Frederick Elman (later F. Latour) and Lilith Salmon that ends with the birth of Birch Latour.

Spoonwood covers Birch Latour's peculiar upbringing and Frederick Elman's maturation as F. Latour, poet and shaper of wooden spoons.

Howard Elman's Farewell references three other books I have written that are *not* in the Darby series. Web Clements, one of the writers in Darby Doomsday is, as an adolescent, the protagonist and narrator of *Mad Boys* and, as an adult, the narrator of *I Love U*, which features co-protagonists Willard "Wiqi" Durocher and Luci Sanz. The Connissadawaga Native American tribe first appears in my historical novel, *The Old American*.

The time period is the near future in the small town of Darby, New Hampshire.

Two major political parties—the Biophilians and the Transfers—have replaced Democrats and Republicans, which have been rejected by the voters. A third group, The Edge, is a terrorist organization that has grown in power in recent years.

Philosophies of the Competing Political Parties

Biophilians represent a coalition of traditional liberal and conservative thinking. They are existentialists, environmentalists, constitutionalists, and just plain folks. They believe in human beings as biological creatures who are basically good. They believe that, in working through science and traditional culture models, human beings have a fifty-fifty chance to save the world's forests, oceans, grasslands, and deserts, necessary to carry on the human epoch here on Earth. Some Biophilians believe in God, some don't. The religious people among the Biophilians believe that human beings are evolving to a plateau where they will find God. The Biophilian motto is: "All Can Be Saved."

Transfers, the minority party, believe that changes in Earth's climate will make the planet uninhabitable to human beings, because human evolution is too slow to keep up. Their solution is that human beings have to change themselves in order to adapt. They must abandon biologically based bodies. Transfers are working toward a technology to "transfer" human identity into computer chips. People will still enjoy the pleasures of food, drink, sex, exercise, and work; they will see, they will hear, they will experience touch, they will smell the roses; but their sensations will be virtual. Some individuals will choose to inhabit fabricated bodies, replacing parts as they wear out; others will exist only in cyberspace as "spirits." Since parts are replaceable, a "transferred" human being for all practical purposes will be immortal.

Members of one branch of the Transfer party see themselves as colonists of other worlds in artificial bodies designed to thrive in unearthlike environments. That group plans a rocket to Mars as a starting point. Most Transfers are atheists or casual agnostics. They are heavily funded by wealthy old people who don't want to die. The motto of the Transfers is: "LiveOn."

A third group, outside of the mainstream, call themselves The Edge. They are on a mission to prepare the way where only a chosen few will remain to restore Earth. They believe that the idea of human-caused global climate change is a hoax perpetuated by the major parties, Biophilians and Transfers. The Edge want to destabilize the world through any means, gain power, and restart the human epoch at ground zero. The Edge are often at a war with each other. Besides fanatics of different religions, The Edge includes opportunists who only want power, technophobes, thrill seekers, racists, ethnic cleansers, and disestablishmentarianists.

Factions within the parties bring complexity and variety to the game to accommodate gamers who think out of the box.

Premise

Changes in Earth's environment and climate threaten the future of the human species. In particular, the world's forests are rapidly degrading. However, scientists think they have found a cure to the blight in properties found in an ancient forest in the Salmon Trust lands of Darby, New Hampshire.

How the Game Is Played

The game revolves around a town-meeting style presidential debate in the new town hall in Darby, New Hampshire. The winner, or perhaps one should say, survivor, of that debate is sure to be elected president and will lead the nation and the world toward its destiny.

Game players can be "Townies" (residents of Darby), "Flatlanders" (residents outside of Darby), or "Aboriginals," members of the Connissadawaga Native American tribe. Players can join a political party, terrorist group, or play as lobbyists, journalists, mercenaries, or independents (Indies). Players can join with other players of the same party to nominate their candidates and impede the opposing party.

Players belonging to the major parties gain maximum points when they end up being the party's nominee, win the debate, and discredit their opponents. Terrorist players gain maximum points when they disrupt the debate, destabilize the country, seize control, and establish a reform government, the politics of which is determined by the player.

Darby Doomsday is a game with great flexibility. Gamers can play alone or create alliances to gain more control and influence. Players can even choose to live and love as ordinary citizens in the town of Darby and not compete but merely watch the machinations of other players. Non-competing players are known as lurkers. They are important because they can influence the game by voting at town meeting. They can purchase building lots in Darby and nearby towns, make bank deposits, go to the dump, join clubs, take jobs, landscape their homes, and attend church services. Players can change their party affiliation at any time, or they can attempt to change the beliefs within their own party in order to implement their own ideas.

Players advance in the game by scoring argumentative points on a range of issues. Game judges (actually a computer algorithm) award points, as do the players themselves, who can rate each other's arguments. Each player is allowed one vote per issue, though more votes can be acquired through bribery.

The creators of *Darby Doomsday*, the minions of Geek Chorus Software, believe their game is more than just entertainment. It's a tool to provide information to researchers about human behavior to help world leaders make decisions. All the data from the game are fed into mainframe computers and analyzed.

Quirks of the Game

Play is continuous, with neither final winners nor final losers. There is only change. It's the same basic story over and over again, but with multiple endings that all lead to restarts. The writers, artists, and coders of *Darby Doomsday* are constantly adding new scenarios. The developers have included tools so that players can construct their own characters and plots. Players should understand that their contributions to the game are permanent, that is, that their scenarios go into a database that can be used by other players and by the developers.

Detailed information about The Darby Chronicles — maps, essays, images, everything anybody wants to know about that is not in the books — is available through my blog at erniehebert.com. Visitors are encouraged to comment and/or to add their own ideas, fictions, history, and character portraits to expand the world of Darby.